Sex, Sin
&
Brooklyn

Crystal Lacey Winslow

http://www.melodramapublishing.com

Sex, Sin & Brooklyn

For information address:
Melodrama Publishing
P. O. Box 522
Bellport, New York 11713-0522

Web address: www.melodramapublishing.com
e-mail: melodramapub@aol.com
author's email address: **melodramaticbrat@aol.com**
Library of Congress Control Number: 2005936569
ISBN 0-9717021-6-0
First Edition

This novel is a work of fiction. Any resemblances to actual events, real people, living or dead, organizations, establishments, locales are products of the author's imagination. Other names, characters, places, and incidents are used fictitiously.

10 9 8 7 6 5 4 3 2 1
First Paperback Edition

Sex, Sin
&
Brooklyn

Dedication

SEX
Stay protected

SIN
We all have one

BROOKLYN
The thoroughest borough

Dear Readers:

I usually open all my novels with an introduction. For this book, I wanted to open with a poem written from the main character's perspective. I hope you enjoy.

Lacey

I told him I was from Brooklyn
He said he could flow
He mentioned he was from the boogie down
That we should get up and keep it on the low

I was newly out of a three-year reclusion
Hesitant to make him an inclusion
Plus he said he had a wife
Who was no longer sharing in his life

Naively, I fell for his game
He had that religious thing going on
Truthfully, he wasn't exactly my type
But I wanted someone who'd treat me right

I was tired of dating bad boys
Who drove around in expensive toys
The type of men who were quick to "wife" me
Lace my neck and keep my fingers icy

I should have listened when he would allude
That he was just a *regular* dude
Instead, I propped him up on a pedestal
And ended up with someone calculating and cruel

He lived his life vicariously through rappers lyrics
Not in touch with reality
He wasn't man enough to keep it real
He moved cowardly

From day one he started off with a lie
He made more than a song cry
He always had to win
Cold and distant—I named him Iceberg Slim

When he'd criticize my actions
I thought he was just egotistic
When he started to harshly judge me
I finally realized he was misogynistic

He said he never wanted to hurt me
But that's exactly what he did
I never told him, but in love
Without warning I slowly slid

Stupidly, with him, I wanted to grow old
Contemplated wearing his ring
Even considered having his kids
Although, I was totally against those things

When I got close, he pulled away
Said we were moving too fast
But it took us four months to fuck
That lame excuse could never pass

I reflect and realize
His arrogance masked insecurity
In reality he needed to grow up
His age lacked maturity

Like the hit TV show
I guess I got punk'd
But through my hurt and pain
I was able to see he was a punk

I realize time is too precious to be wasting
I had to wise up and get smart
A *nothing* nigga I was chasing
Who treated me ungratefully from the start

I think I've been cursed since birth
My success with men is as slim as his penis
Don't get it twisted, I know my worth
But somehow I end up with men who are the meanest

The lesson of the day
Is you've gotta beware of the frauds
They're lurking everywhere
In sheep's clothing—nothing but dogs.

BOOK ONE
Spring, 2005

Prologue

COLD CASE FILE TAKEN FROM THE DESK OF THE 88TH PRECINCT IN BROOKLYN REPORTED TO THE *DAILY NEWS*:

"Four years ago, an 18-year-old white female was found bludgeoned to death with a baseball bat and left naked in the Brooklyn Navy Yard. It took weeks for her body to be discovered in a used suitcase. There were defensive wounds on her upper and lower arms. No forensic or trace evidence was found at the scene or on her persons. The body remained at the morgue unidentified until finally being carted off to Potters Field. When three more bodies were found, all fitting the same modus operandi, authorities began to suspect we had a serial killer on our hands targeting Brooklyn. Each victim, ranging from late teens to early twenties had a lot of similarities. They all were dark-haired women wearing their hair parted down the middle and were all bludgeoned with a hard object. Detective Darren Wilkens noticed another similarity, something that's the most telling clue. The murders are carried out in the same manner in which a 1974 serial killer executed his victims. Once dubbed The Poster Boy of Serial

Killers, Theodore Bundy terrorized the nation until he was executed on January 24, 1989. If Ted Bundy hasn't killed these victims, the question is, who? We have copycat murderer in our midst...."

1

Jinx

I always did as I was told. It was easier that way. Most times I stayed out of people's way because I felt as if I were a burden. My life has been one big, plump tear since the death of both my parents. I had been living with my grandmother ever since the 1986 American Airlines plane crash. I was on the plane, too. Only I didn't die. There were 119 people on the plane when it went down. An elderly man held on for fifty-two days before he succumbed to his injuries. Miraculously, I came out unscathed. I was born with a veil or caul which is a shimmery coating over your head and face and is easily removed by the doctor. My grandmother contributes this to my surviving the horrific accident. Many believe that being born with a veil is a sign of a great destiny and psychic abilities, or good luck. My grandmother said God speared me because he must have something great for me to do with my life. At this point, I can't really agree with my grandmother, but I don't tell her that. I know I should be grateful that I lived but God took *both* my parents. I've had to go through life feeling remorseful, empty and alone. It's rumored that the only reason we were all on the plane is because my mother wanted a better life for me and decided to leave the south and move back to Brooklyn, New York.

Today makes exactly three years since I broke up with my boyfriend, Jason. He was my high school sweetheart, and we dated off and on for ten years. He was my first and *only* love. During the relationship, he changed. In a rush to be grown, when I turned seventeen we moved in with each other, which was a mistake. We were too immature. When I was younger, I thought his little bouts of jealousy were cute. I thought it showed how much he loved me. He would control me verbally, telling me what I could and couldn't do. That soon escalated to being controlled physically. The first time he slapped me he apologized by holding me all night. The first time he hit me with a closed fist he apologized by making love to me. The first time he gave me a black eye he apologized with gold hoop earrings. Needless to say I stayed for six more years enduring his infidelities, physical and mental abuse. I can't give myself credit for finally finding the strength to leave because he put me in a situation where I just couldn't stay. Two weeks before my twenty-fourth birthday I found out that I was pregnant. I had been trying to get pregnant since I turned eighteen. I was elated. Having my family ripped from me, I always longed to be a mother and a wife. When I told him he lashed out and admitted that he had fathered three children in the past two years by three different women. I thought this was a cruel joke, that he was trying to scare me. But then he went up into the closet—*our* closet—and pulled out photos of kids that he'd hidden over the years. I stared at three little souls that looked just like him. My him…I was numb. For the following weeks he wouldn't speak to me. He gave me the silent treatment while walking around our apartment with an attitude, throwing and kicking things. I was the one who should have been walking around with an attitude, but somehow he manipulated the situation and made himself the victim, and I was his worst enemy. At that point I decided to have an abortion. Not to keep him but to rid myself of him. Now I look back retrospectively and wish I had kept my baby.

When I got up the courage to walk away, Jason said I could leave with only what I came with. Meaning he'd keep all the gifts, clothing and even the Yorkshire Terrier he'd bought for me. Talk about kicking someone when they're down. I got away from him and moved back in with my grandmother, Nana. She owns a small, decrepit house on Vermont Avenue in East New York, Brooklyn, that has seen better days. Nana has been in this house for over forty years. She had gotten the down payment when my grandfather died and left her a ten-thousand-dollar life insurance policy. Back in those days she was well off. She took the money and made a deposit on this house. Then she met her second husband and had her last child, a son. Her second husband and his family used Nana for everything she had. She was a hardworking woman who supported her whole family on only her income. When she got arthritis in her hands and couldn't work he stayed around, unemployed, and lived off of her disability checks. He would still be here mooching off Nana had he not found himself in the wrong place at the wrong time. He was shot and killed in a botched robbery attempt of the liquor store on Linden Boulevard, next to the Times Square Store.

Through Nana's guidance, I was fortunate enough to get a city job when I graduated from high school. Nana had me apply for every exam that came out in the *Chief,* a local paper that lists all open-competitive city jobs. I took about four exams—from conductor for the New York City Transit Authority to clerk for the Unified Court Systems. I scored high on each exam but the New York City Law Department called first. I've been working there for three years as a paralegal, and I get paid close to forty thousand dollars annually, which is really great for someone without any kids and living with virtually no overhead. But I dream for more.

I've been fortunate enough to save close to nine thousand dollars in my bank account and plan on investing that into a business very soon. I've always had an eye for fashion, and I'm an excellent seamstress thanks to Nana. She taught me to sew when I was no older than seven. I can sketch, cut patterns and stitch very well, and I've never technically studied fashion design. Nana taught me everything. I plan on opening up my own boutique, Spoiled, in the very near future. I've already gotten the name registered and trademarked with a hot logo. I want Nana to help me run it but I know she's too sick. She's more excited than me. It's all we talk about once I come home from work.

I got home from work around 6:30 P.M. and raced inside to cook for Nana. She can't get around like she used to. First, I went into my room to strip off my stuffy business clothes. I stripped down naked then stopped momentarily to admire myself in my mirror. I stared at my figure: curvy hips, small waist, full breasts. I had French vanilla–colored skin with a small, straight nose, high cheekbones and full pink lips. When I had my natural hair color, which was jet-black, everyone would mistake me for

Alicia Keys. When I'd get my hair braided, I had to actually convince people I wasn't her, the resemblance was so strong. Now that I've cut my hair into a Mohawk and bleached it blond, people say I resemble Eva Pigford from *America's Next Top Model*. An edgier Eva.

I turned around in the mirror to see my tattoo collection sprawled creatively on my back. I had a bowtie above my ass and butterfly tattoos flying around my back, over my arms and circling my right breast. I remember going to Washington, D.C., to a party in club Dream now known as Love and this guy told me that there was a dancer in the Maryland area that had the same tattoos as I did. I think he said her name was Wild Cherry. I told him that he must be mistaken but he was adamant about it. I'm thinking what the probability would be for that to be true....

After I threw on a white tee and a pair of sweats, I went in the back to Nana's room. I opened her door knowing she'd be watching *The Jerry Springer Show*.

"Nana?" I called as I approached her room. She always kept her door closed.

"Yes, pumpkin," she responded as I pushed open her door. It was freezing in her room. She always kept the window cracked no matter how cold it was outside to try and mask the fact that she was smoking cigarettes despite that fact that her doctor already warned her to quit.

"What are you doing, old lady?" I joked and jumped on her bed, and without hesitating, I snatched the cigarette from out of her mouth. She smiled a toothless grin because she didn't have her dentures in. She looked so adorable smiling at me with all gums.

"You caught me, huh?"

"Damn right," I said and rolled my eyes as if I were angry.

"Nana needs something to calm her nerves. You know they shot Noah today and Adrienne finally admitted that Jake isn't the father of her baby."

She was talking about her soap operas that she's been watching for close to thirty years. I just shook my head, planted a wet kiss on her leathery cheek and told her I'd go and make dinner.

While I was making smothered pork chops, mashed potatoes and broccoli there was a knock at the door.

"Who?" I called from the kitchen. But instead of someone answering they just knocked louder. I turned my pots down to a low simmer and went to the door. I looked through the peephole and there stood my aunt, Kim. I needed Nana to handle this one.

"Wait a minute," I yelled and ran to get Nana. "Nana, Kim's here."

"What she want?" Nana said, trying to get up from the bed. Her heavy weight made her struggle.

"Nana, what she always want? Money. I'm not giving her any money, Nana. I need you to help watch her. She's too quick. She'll steal something so quickly I won't realize it's gone until weeks later."

"Don't worry. I got somethin' for her ass," Nana said as she finally got to her feet. Nana was a large woman bordering on the line of obesity. Her legs were swollen and weak, which caused her to walk with a cane. She also had type B diabetes and had to check her urine every morning to test her sugar levels.

Meanwhile, Kim was banging the door down.

Nana and I walked to the front door together. As I opened the door to address Kim, a rank odor permeated our front foyer. Nana stood at the front door entrance with her hands firmly on her hips, and I positioned myself next to Nana's side.

"Whatchu want, chile?" Nana asked Kim. I looked at Kim whose eyes looked glassy, and her body looked emaciated. Her mouth was dry and white around the edges. Her clothes were worn, and she smelled awful. Her once long and silky hair had matted up and broken off in various places. Then I looked at Nana and saw the hurt in her eyes. Kim was her firstborn, and she'd lost her to the streets. Kim started getting high off weed when she was thirteen years old and graduated to any drug she could get her hands on. I couldn't say she was a crack head because someone might catch her sniffing dope. Just when I was about to call her a dope fiend, she'd be back to sucking the pipe. Now, I've heard she's tried the drug of choice for suburban housewives, methamphetamine, also known as crystal meth.

Nana had three children. Kim; my mother Gina, who was killed in the plane crash; and Corey, the youngest of them all. He's even younger than me at nineteen years old. I'm twenty-seven. He doesn't work and never wants to. All he does is live off women. He lived off Nana's disability checks before she kicked him out to go live with one of his baby mommas in Brownsville, Brooklyn. He comes around every first of the month to beg for a few dollars from Nana, and she gives it to him. No matter how hard she tries to shut her no-good children out of her life, she can't.

"Oh, I can't come in?" Kim said as she glared at me. "I'm your only child, and this is the way you treat me?"

"Kim, we go through these shenanigans all the time. You're not my only chile. God blessed me wit' three children."

"Well I'm your only *girl* child that's livin'. You can't replace me with Jinx. That's exactly what she is, a Jinx. My sister put Jinx 'bad-luck ass' on a plane, and the whole fuckin' plane blew up."

"Stop talkin' foolishness, chile. You workin' my nerves," Nana chastised her while holding her heart as if she couldn't breathe.

"How she the only thing that lived?" Kim pursued. "The whole fuckin' plane turned into kibbles and bits. Nothin' was left except the one seat she was sittin' in. You tell me how that happened?"

"Chile, why don't you go and mind your own business and leave this here girl alone. She's been through enough."

"MY SISTER IS DEAD BECAUSE OF YOU, BITCH," Kim screamed with her melodramatic antics and slapped my face so hard my ear started ringing. My head snapped back, and I nearly lost my balance.

Instinctively, I returned her slap with a swift kick dead in her pussy. She crouched over in agony and screamed out in pain. Nana jumped between us to stop us from fighting. I hated that on almost every occasion I had to defend myself from Kim. Sometimes when she has those drugs up in her no matter how hard I fight, she remains unfazed. Her whole body is numb. That's why she likes to pick fights with me. Not to mention Nana would give her a few dollars just to leave me alone.

"Chile, you dun fell off the coo coo truck. Git your crazy ass out of my house before I call five-0," Nana yelled and pushed Kim out. Before she left, Nana shoved a twenty-dollar bill in her hand then slammed the door. As she left, I could hear Kim threatening to beat me up when she caught me leaving for work. I ignored her because my mind had gone back to that fateful day when I awoke out of my sleep to hundreds of people screaming at the top of their lungs. I remembered how queasy my stomach felt and the fear in my parents' eyes. Every time I think about that day I get goose bumps. The memory gives me a headache.

Why didn't I die? Maybe Kim was correct. Maybe I was a Jinx.

2

Breezy

I'm Brooklyn born and raised, so it wasn't a stretch when my mother thought the name would be fitting for her only child. As I grew into a toddler, my parents began to call me Breezy. They said that I could run and get into mischief so quickly, that I was like the wind. I can hardly remember my mother—just sporadic, dark images of a beautiful woman with a fiery temper. Throughout the years I've heard so many stories about her. Some good…most bad. My father says that she "spit me out," because I look so much like her. I do. I stare long and hard at someone who looks like my twin. I have a picture of her taken in 1986 right before she died. She was twenty years old. She was wearing a pair of blue jeans with a red tank top and a pair of red Gucci logo boots with the pocketbook to match. Two sets of bamboo earrings adorned her ears, and the obligatory fat, gold rope chain swallowed her neck. My mother grew up in the era of hip-hop. My father talks fondly about this era. He reminisces about when young teenagers spoke pig latin as some sort of code, when the crack epidemic had gotten so out of control that the police started a Narcotics Unit called the A-Team, where they'd jump out of unmarked vans, pepper spray you in the face and tote you off to jail, and a lot of young black men lost their lives because they had saved enough money to buy a gold rope chain or sheepskin coat and didn't want to give it up. That era still resonates today and is often imitated in fashion or paid homage to in movies.

In the picture, my mother is standing on Forty-Second Street in front of a mural of New Edition that read Candy Girl. Her hands are placed seductively on her hips and her head is cocked grandiosely to the side. Even in the picture you can feel she had a presence. That image was everlasting. Lisa, my father's wife, swears that my mother died on her way to break up their marriage. Every time she speaks of my mother, she has this look of disgust on her face as if she'd just taken a bite of a sour fruit. Inwardly, I laugh. My mother still haunts Lisa even in death….

After my mother's untimely death, my father moved back to Brooklyn and bought us a four-story brownstone in the heart of Bedford Stuyvesant. I live on the top floor, my father and his wife Lisa have a duplex on the second and third floor, and we use the first floor as a boarding house to room runaways and recovering drug addicts.

It was the first day of spring, and I welcomed the warmth. We had a long, frigid winter, and I was more than ready for the summer. Tonight was clear with a light wind. I had just walked out of the shower, completely naked as small droplets of water cascaded down my baby-soft skin. I took a quick glance in the mirror to admire my curvy shape. I stood five-two with size 32A breasts, a twenty-two-inch waist and thirty-six-inch hips. My apple-bottom ass and thick thighs made up for my small breasts. I had my long, jet-black hair cut into layers, which gave me even more character. As if I needed help in the personality department. I had a habit of swinging my head from side to side when I spoke. I loved the way my hair bounced from left to right. It made me feel like I was grandstanding on people. That coupled with the fact that I spoke with my hands gave me a chic yet down-ass-bitch persona that made people take notice. When I walked into any room, I demanded respect. I also had a high IQ and spoke five languages fluently, which made me more than your average around-the-way girl.

As I began to massage Johnson's baby oil gel into my dark chocolate skin, I heard footsteps making a loud clapping sound as they came up the stairs. Soon my door opened and it was two of my girlfriends, Joy and Kesha. They smiled brightly as they entered into my plush apartment. We were all going to club Reign. They'd been announcing the party all week over the radio and I had a V.I.P. connection, which meant every-thing was free—which was the way it should be.

"Wassup, playa, playaaa?" Joy asked.

I smiled because Joy is just as animated as me.

"Nothing. I'm good."

"If you're good then I'm great," Joy stated and pulled off her Burberry trench coat to reveal a pearl-colored beaded top that exposed her flesh. She was wearing a Rock & Republic jean micro-mini-skirt and stiletto heels.

Joy was a cute girl. She had light skin, brown hair that was cut blunt at her shoulder blade with a Chinese-cut bang. She has big brown eyes, a sexy mouth, bow legs and a fat ass. Truthfully, I couldn't stand light-skinned bitches, but Joy is the exception. They all assume that they have an advantage over darker skinned sisters and that they have first choice of the men. What I hate most is when they say, "She's cute for a dark-skinned girl." As if pretty darker skinned women are as rare as a snow-storm in the desert. Joy went out of her way to get into my circle. We're around the same age. I'm twenty-three years old and Joy is twenty-two, but don't let the age fool you. She's seen more than the average twenty-two-year-old and is street smart beyond her years. That's what I like about her. She and I are from the same neighborhood, which is Bedford Stuyvesant in Brooklyn. We've crossed paths several times but never had any real contact.

Rumor has it that she had a major falling out with her best friend, Nicoli, and now she's looking for a new hang-out partner. No one in the neighborhood knows this, but Nicoli is my first cousin, and I hate her. There's no diplomatic way to say it. We don't speak and *never* will. She's one of those light-skinned sisters who used to think that she was better than me. We both have type A personalities, we're both only chil-dren, and we both had a parent that doted upon us. We are too much alike to have gotten along, so she and I fought on several occasions when we were younger, and as we got older we learned how to avoid each other. Our childhood riffs separated our parents, and they don't keep in touch either. Recently, after she'd gotten her pretty face sliced open by a jilted lover, she wanted to make amends with me. She came to my front door with her new Edward Scissor Hands face all apologetic. I slammed the door so hard in her face the glass could have broken. That was the last time I'd seen her trifling ass.

Now Kesha on the other hand is opposite of both of us. She's Joy's cousin. She's thirty years old, has three kids and is married. Her husband is a straight square from nowhere and allows her to run the streets. Looking at Kesha in her skin-tight jeans, sexy halter top, flat stomach with her boobs oozing out, you'd hardly ever guess that she's a sergeant in the 88th Precinct on Tompkins Avenue in Brooklyn. She's been on the force for a decade and keeps moving up in rank every few years.

Kesha has hazelnut-colored skin, sleepy eyes, full lips and she's sporting a new short haircut that fits her round face. Not every girl can get away with a short haircut. That cut on the wrong female can make them look masculine.

Kesha glanced at her watch and started complaining when her cell phone began ringing incessantly. "I knew your tired ass wasn't gonna be ready. And can you put some clothes on your naked ass. I'm tired of looking at your wild jungle pussy."

"Men love my shit," I commented about my wild bush.

"That shit looks nasty," Kesha replied in annoyance, as if my hairy pussy had offended her.

Ignoring her last remark I said, "I just got home a few minutes ago." I inhaled just to pull on my size 32 jeans. "I had a few mid-terms but as you can see I'm almost ready."

I was wearing True Religion jeans with the orange stitching but what was going to knock everyone off their feet was my top. I had Jinx go with me to buy mink fabric, and she made me a mink shirt. I had one arm with a bishop sleeve and one arm sleeveless. I had on a rhinestone beaded bustier and my flat stomach was exposed, showing off my tattoo that read: *What Nourishes Me Destroys Me.* I copied off Angelina Jolie who has the words written in Latin on her lower abdomen.

"I like those jeans," Joy remarked as she walked to my closet and started rummaging through my clothes and shoes. "Your jean game is tight."

Kesha joined her in my walk-in closet and began admiring my shoe collection. "Girl, you got every high-end shoe a woman could ever want. Jimmy, Manolo, Gucci, Ferragamo, Prada, Giuseppe. You got it going on."

"I was wearing Manolo *before* they made the Tim's," I bragged. "What? What happened?"

"Girl, there's at least a hundred thousand dollars worth of merchandise in this closet," Joy assessed.

"Those garments cost me a small fortune," I replied after thinking how a single pair of jeans could run you up to a thousand dollars nowadays. And let's not talk about the cost of a decent pair of shoes and pocketbook. It was just ridiculous.

"You mean they cost your daddy a small fortune, you spoiled brat," Kesha stated.   "You mean sneaky, spoiled brat," Joy instigated.

"And bitches better fear me," I joked.

"You better have niggas buying us bottles of champagne all night," Joy said, giggling.

"What's your pleasure?" I asked, playing into Joy's joke. "Dom P. or Clicquot? Because you know we don't drink Cristal after the company stated that they didn't want rappers drinking their champagne. They'll see in their net profits just how powerful the Black dollar can be."

We chatted a little more as I put the finishing touches on my makeup and then remembered that I was supposed to give Susan some old clothes that I wanted to get rid of. Quickly, I dialed her number.

"Susan, hey this is Breezy. You can come up and get the bag before I leave." She agreed and walked upstairs within minutes. Hesitantly, she tapped on the door before pushing it open.

"Hello, everyone," she said meekly with her eyes glued to the floor. She was extremely shy. Her androgynous appearance coupled with her being so timid gave my friends the creeps. In addition she didn't weigh any more than ninety pounds and stood four foot eleven. Her strawberry-blond hair was pulled back into a tight ponytail, drawing attention to her pale, gaunt face. The T-shirt she was wearing displayed tell-tale signs of her former addiction. Susan is a runaway we'd taken off the street over a year ago. She's from Mississippi and was prostituting her young body for some pimp over on the lower east side. He'd gotten her strung out on heroine before we rescued her. She's now clean, enrolled in school and helps around the house to offset her room and board. She lives on the first floor and needed some business outfits to go on job interviews.

I grabbed a large bag and handed it to her.

"It's heavy," I warned.

"I can manage," she said as she walked toward the door. "Breezy?"

"Yes."

"Why do you think Mary-Ann ran away from here in the middle of the night four months ago? I thought she'd come back."

Mary-Ann was another girl we had staying here.

"Same reason Jennifer left. She was ungrateful for everything my father did for her," I replied.

"I don't think that's it. She was very grateful. In fact, we all were. That's all we ever talked about. She was happy that she'd just gotten accepted into college and was looking forward to her new job."

I shook my head. "Susan, I can only speculate why she left. Maybe all of that was too much for her."

"Yeah…maybe…" she replied and closed the door behind her.

"She's a weirdo," Joy whispered after she left.

"More than you?" Kesha joked and Joy threw a lipstick at her.

"Children, children, let's not bicker. We have a party to attend. All the ballers are expecting me," I teased.

"Girl, please. You know I do shows when I walk up in the place," Joy said jokingly, trying to undo the tension Susan had built.

"Kesha, what's going on with your new sponsor?" I inquired while putting the finishing touches on my makeup. We called all the guys we dated sponsors because they needed to sponsor our shopping sprees, dinner dates and trips to the hair salon.

"I'm getting ready to drag him. I ain't answering his call for a week," she said, talking about one of many men she was having an affair with.

As I was deciding which pocketbook and shoes to wear, my dad quickly rapped lightly on the door.

"Come in," I said.

He pushed the door open and peeked his head in. His salt-and-pepper hair, goatee and broad shoulders had all my friends wanting to fuck him. Ever since I was a little girl my friends admired me because of my dad. He has this swagger in his walk that tells them he's packing a big dick. That coupled with his good looks gets their pussies moist every time he says hello.

"Breezy, you going out tonight?" he said, his baritone voice resonating.

"Yes, Papa," I said. I called him Papa Bear from the fable he'd read to me when I was little.

"Okay, be careful," he warned. "Hi, ladies."

"Hello, Mr. Whitaker," they both chimed, grinning like Cheshire cats.

Before we left we all took one last look in the mirror, and we all looked good. We were a unique trifecta ready to conquer the Brooklyn club scene one night at a time.

When we got to Club Reign the line was around the corner. The police were out there regulating and taking control of the crowd. For a moment they weren't letting anyone drive through the block. Kesha jumped out the backseat of my black Range Rover, badged her way through the crowd and spoke with a couple of police officers. When she got back in the jeep she said that they'd both heard great things about her. Kesha worked the narcotics unit and put more than a few criminals behind bars. The criminals are doing what we call "football numbers" for their crimes. That's when you get sentenced to a double-digit number, as in ten or more years.

Once she was back in the car they moved the barricade, and I was allowed to drive down the block. Before I drove under the train trestle to park, I slowed down directly in front of the club to see if we recognized anyone on the line. Before the car could come to a complete stop, Joy and Kesha jumped out and ran across the street when they saw a few familiar faces. I hated that they did that shit, which meant that I had to go and park alone. As I walked toward the club, I scanned the line. There were several V.I.P.-looking dudes waiting to get in, telling the bouncers to go inside and get certain dudes to come out and vouch for them. Others were using the money approach to pay extra to get in while some were recognizable and didn't have to play any games. I hopped on my cellular phone and called my friend, Terrence. It took him a few minutes before he finally made it to the front door. He tapped a bouncer on the shoulder then whispered in his ear. You could see the bouncer looking out at the crowd before finally settling on me. He waved for me to come through, and I grabbed Joy by her hand. We all pushed our way to the front of the line, and without incident we were in. Club Reign had a nice, classy décor with china white silk curtains, a small lit-up bar on the first floor and cushioned longue chairs. The second floor had another lit-up bar, a dance floor and a V.I.P. area toward the back.

The deejay was bumping "Shut Up Bitch" by Lil' Kim. We followed

Terrence to the V.I.P. section where he had a table with a few dudes I already knew—some I previously fucked, some wanted to fuck. All I saw were canary yellow and black bottles of champagne. I walked straight over to an unopened bottle, lifted it out of the bucket and said to anyone who was listening, "This me, right?"

"Who you?" one nondescript man said, trying to protect the pricey liquid. I looked him up and down and could tell he didn't have a penny in the dollars that purchased the Clicquot. I also knew he wasn't from my neighborhood because *everyone* in Brooklyn knew Breezy or knew of Breezy.

Before I could respond, Terrence intervened. "Let her and her friends live. Go ahead, ma, that's you."

I smiled graciously and popped the bottle. That's when the party started. I surveyed the room and saw everyone huddled with their cliques. I saw the East New York crew sipping on Hennessey and Dom P. There was Wonderful, El, Tee-Tee, Brazil, Trizzel and Phil who was technically from Bed-Stuy. Let's not forgot the East New York girls. There was Donnie, Cheray, Kisha, Meka, Renee, Claudia, Cookie, Boo and Kim. Next, there was the Brownsville niggas—the grimiest 'hood dudes in the place— Jack, Jock, Merciful, Black and Taj. The most familiar faces were from Bed-Stuy. There was 150, Eighty, Squirrel, Scarface and Henchmen. Last we had Flatbush. They were only girls—no niggas. I saw M&M, Rena, Jackie, Tisha, Crissy and Kashana who was technically from Crown Heights. When I tell you everybody and their mothers, fathers and brothers were in this party, I ain't never tell a lie.

I stood in place grinding my hips seductively to the music for a while until I felt a penetrating stare coming from across the room. There was another group of guys doing it just as big as Terrence's crew. When the stranger and my eyes connected he didn't break his stare. Neither did I. Instead, he nodded his head.

I nodded back.

Now, all he had to do was make the first move and I'd do the rest.

3

Kesha

Another year older—none the wiser. That's the most prophetic shit someone could have ever said. I woke up around eight o'clock in the morning to sausage and eggs with French toast. My husband had cooked and already had the kids off to school. Our youngest daughter was still asleep. That's because she doesn't go to sleep at night until 1:00 A.M. My husband said she stays awake trying to wait until I get home. When I got pregnant with our third child we both decided we didn't trust anyone to raise our baby. When I was a rookie cop, I'd arrested a lot of crazy nannies for abusing and even murdering defenseless kids so I was nervous about the prospect. Since I had just gotten my promotion and was making more money than my husband who was a chef at a local restaurant, he decided to stay at home and raise the kids. To help ends meet, sometimes he does catering jobs for small functions. So far, it's a beautiful thing.

"Good morning, darling," my husband sang as he brought me breakfast in bed. I sat up, trying to fully wake up while enjoying the aroma of the pork sausages. He kissed me on my forehead and began to pull out my clothes. Within seconds he was ironing my shirt.

"Daniel, what are you doing? I can iron my own shirt. I'm still your wife," I said while stuffing scrambled eggs in my mouth. We go through this every morning. I only pretend to want to iron my own clothes. Truthfully, I've already gotten spoiled.

"I enjoy ironing your clothes and seeing you off to work," he lamented.

I stared at Daniel. He is the sweetest man a girl could ever know. He is what you'd call pretty-boy cute. He has fine jet-black curly hair. No facial hair. Straight nose and high cheekbones. French vanilla–colored skin and a slender body frame. When I was younger, all I dated were pretty boys. As prejudicial and immature as this may sound, I always wanted to have children with light skin and good hair. I now have three beautiful kids, but I'm no longer attracted to the pretty boy. In fact, I haven't been sexually attracted to Daniel in years. I can't remember the last time we made love or when I even wanted to. I look at Daniel as a good friend, my children's father, and then as my husband. I don't know if the lack of attraction comes from watching him wear an apron and whip up three-course meals or from the fact that I'm sleeping with every rough-walking, tough-talking man I can get my hands on—the types of men who slap me hard on my ass while they're fucking me and calling me all types of bitches and whores.

I blushed at the thoughts.

I lay around in bed for another hour until I stiffly climbed out. My agile body was in need of a full-body massage. I hopped on my treadmill that we have in the corner of our room and did thirty minutes of cardio. I started with ten minutes of brisk walking and jogged the last twenty minutes, which amplified my adrenaline. After my quick workout, I showered, dressed and went in to work. Most people hate their jobs but not me. I think protecting and serving the community is definitely my calling. There's something about the feeling I get from putting on my gun holster that makes me feel complete.

"Hi, captain. Bosco in yet?" I asked, referring to my partner of six-years.

"Surprisingly he is. He's upstairs in your unit. It must be going to snow today," Captain Rooke joked.

I ran upstairs to my unit where a few officers were there talking shit about the recent string of unsolved murders being committed in our communities while other detectives were questioning perps who were either in our holding cell or handcuffed to a chair. They'd already ordered pizza and doughnuts, and it was barely eleven o'clock in the morning.

"Bosco, what's up? Wifey kicked you out again?"

"How'd you know?" he asked in amazement.

"That's the only way your tired ass will come to work on time," I said, laughing.

Bosco stood five-six with a muscular body frame. He was Jewish but looked Italian with his dark hair and features. He was somewhat attractive, and I heard he was a monster in bed. That's what was leading to all his marital problems. He couldn't keep his dick in his pants. I tell him all the time it's not that you cheat it's the way you cheat. Bosco is too sloppy with his infidelities. One day I mentioned to him that either his wife is going to get fed up and file for divorce or go out and get her a new piece of dick. He spent a full hour trying to convince me that he wife would never cheat. How much of a good woman she was. *Yeah, okay,* I thought. She's probably engaging in emotional affairs already with the postman, gardener and UPS driver. It was only a matter of time. Everybody has a breaking point....

"She's crazy," he exclaimed.

"Ain't we all? Ain't that the description of every woman who doesn't take a man's bullshit? She gotta be crazy," I said not to anyone in particular.

"No, she's really crazy," he protested. "Last night she accused me of seeing the Italian girl at the bakery."

"You *are* seeing the Italian girl at the bakery," I accused.

"I know but she can't prove it. So that makes her crazy," he reasoned.

"It's called female intuition. Our gut gives us proof."

"I can't listen to any more of this female hokey pokey. You sound like my wife. You ready?"

"I was born ready," I stated. "Why? What's going down?"

"We got the search warrant for Jefferson Avenue. We're kicking in the door waving the 4-4," he said, rhyming to one of the Notorious B.I.G songs.

"The Gotti Gang?"

"Yeah, those wannabe punks."

"I went to school with a lot of those wannabe punks."

"Do you want to sit this one out?" Bosco asked.

"Never that. This is the price you pay when you step onto the other side of the law. I've locked up people I've known in the past, and I'll continue to lock their asses up in the future."

"What did Beretta say? *'Don't do the crime if you can't do the time,'*" Bosco said, and everyone burst out into laughter except the perps.

This bust meant a lot to every detective who was assigned to this case. I'm sure if we successfully execute the arrest without incident we're sure to make the eleven o'clock news. This bust is definitely newsworthy. There are nine members of the Gotti Gang. Some are former Blood and Crips. The gang's leader is Henchmen. He's a dangerous guy and is known to get young boys to do assassinations for him by using manipulation. His motto is "while other guys are in the gym exercising their biceps, my face is buried in a book exercising my mind." It's alleged that he reads books such as *The Art of War* and *The 48 Laws of Power*. He's had a long run out here, and I hope today we put an end to his reign.

We got to the brownstone on Jefferson Avenue where he lived. A snitch confirmed that he also stored his money, guns and drugs there as well. I loved a stupid criminal. Four detectives went around back to cover the windows and back door while me, Bosco, our sergeant and two other detectives with reflective vests stormed the front door with a battering ram. Everyone had on their bulletproof vests, semi-automatic guns and was ready for action. My adrenaline was pumping, heart racing and hands were sweating. Our sergeant, Ronald Devlin, gave the order to Detective Snashall and Detective Williams to bust the door open. On the first hit the door flung off its worn and rusty hinges. I heard movement inside.

"Police! Don't no fucking body move," Bosco yelled as we all descended into the property. There was movement everywhere. Guys were trying to jump out the windows before being wrestled to the ground by my fellow officers. Others gave up without incident. I chased a guy with long dreds into a back room. He'd made it to the closet and tried to reach up and grab a shoebox where he had a gun. I grabbed him by the collar and tossed him up against the wall. He pushed back, and we both fell onto a bed. His heavy weight fell on top of me. I used my right arm and wrapped it around his throat in a choke hold. As we tussled my charm bracelet that my husband had bought me flew off and landed on the floor. I grunted and gritted my teeth, trying to summon more strength to restrain the perpetrator. It was alarmingly clear that he wasn't going out without incident. Exasperated, we both struggled as he tried desperately to free himself from my grip. To get away he unrepentantly head butted me, and I felt my head immediately lump up. I squeezed his neck tighter. When he head butted me again I felt my eye open up and blood dripped down the side of my face. I screamed out in agony but didn't loosen my grasp. Bosco came running in with his gun drawn. "Don't move, motherfucker."

Finally, the perp stopped squirming, and I was able to push him off me. Huffing and puffing I managed to handcuff him. Once handcuffed, I turned him around while Bosco held him in front of me and I hit him with a two-piece—a blow to his left jaw and lower abdomen. He doubled over in pain. I then kneed him in his balls, and he cried out in anguish.

"Fuck you, Kesha," he yelled.

"We tried that once, Henchmen, and your dick was weak. Get this piece of shit outta my face," I yelled while holding my head, which was throbbing with pain.

Detective Snashall came and dragged Henchmen outside to an awaiting squad car.

"You need to go get that checked out. It looks like you may need a couple of stitches," Bosco said, peering into my face.

"Oh fuck no," I said. "The one thing that scares me is a needle."

"Go ahead to the hospital, and I'll be there shortly to hold your hand. If you don't get that closed up, your beautiful face will be scarred for life," Bosco warned.

After we had arrested six of the nine individuals we had warrants for, we secured the crime scene with police line tape and traffic cones. We had to take inventory of everything in the house and collect it as evidence. I went out and brought in the plastic evidence bags, a pry bar and bolt cutters for a steel locked closet inside the house. The sergeant decided that the majority of the detectives would go back to the precinct to start the interrogations while two would remain. Bosco choose to stay behind with Detective Snashall while I wanted to go back to the station to interrogate one of the perps. I was known for getting confessions out of the toughest criminal because I spoke their language and grew up in their neighborhood. They were more inclined to slip up and say something they may not have wanted to because I made them feel comfortable and relaxed. Instead, I decided Bosco was right. I did need to go to the hospital and get my cut closed up.

We all headed out to our squad cars when I remembered I had forgotten my charm bracelet.

"Shit," I said under my breath. "Officer Wallace, watch this perp. I need to run back inside."

I ran back up to the crime scene. Detective Snashall was guarding the front. I raced in quickly with plans to head toward the back room and retrieve my bracelet when I startled Bosco. When he felt my presence he quickly tried to hide what he was doing but it was already too late. I'd seen him stashing drug money into his pockets and socks.

When his eyes adjusted on me he said, "Oh, it's only you," and exhaled.

"What the fuck are you doing?" My voice was stern and unwavering as I asked the ominous question.

"What does it look like?" he said matter-of-factly.

"It looks like you're committing a crime and I'm about to bust your ass in here," I yelled.

"Keep it down. Do you want Snashall to come in here and ask what the commotion is?"

I looked at the table with drug paraphernalia, guns and at least forty thousand dollars lying on it. "Look, Bosco, put the money back and I'll forget this ever happened," I pleaded.

"I'm not doing any such thing. Listen, Kesha, what's a few dollars taken from a drug dealer? We both have families that need taking care of."

"My family is doing very well," I said and rolled my eyes.

"Well take care of yourself. Didn't you say your friend is driving around in a new Range Rover? This isn't enough to buy you one but it's enough to upgrade your Camry to something flashier," he said, dropping down to his knees, lifting up my pants leg and stuffing a roll of hundred-dollar bills inside my socks. I said nothing. I did nothing.

He continued, "If we don't do it, someone else will. What do you think happens with the billions of dollars of drug money that's collected each year? Do you think they give it to charity? Hell no. They grease their law-enforcing pocket, that's what. Just look at it as a pay increase."

I didn't calculate the money until I had gotten home that night. My hands trembled as I counted each hundred-dollar bill. In total, I had stolen $5,500. What had I gotten myself into?

4

BROOKLYN BUTCHER STRIKES AGAIN, the caption of the *Daily News* read as I walked by the newsstand on my way to work. I reached into my pocket and dropped two quarters on the counter and tucked the paper underneath my arm and headed for the A-train toward Manhattan. Once seated, I began to peruse the article.

> *Yesterday, an unidentified homeless girl was found brutally stabbed and dumped on the side of the road in the rural area of Flatlands and Stanley Avenue. Her butchered body appears to be the work of an elusive killer the police have dubbed The Brooklyn Butcher. Police have linked this killer's modus operandi to four other slayings in the Brooklyn area. The body is being sent to the forensic lab to be combed for DNA and trace evidence.*

"No need for that," I said out loud. "There won't be any evidence." I laughed heartily as the bystanders on the train looked at me in annoyance. They probably thought I was losing my mind, but I wasn't. I was probably more sane than most of these parasites. This was the first time I'd made the front page of the newspapers, and I was elated. The past few murders had landed in the latter parts of the papers, but I still couldn't help but want my name mentioned in the articles. But I knew that the day my name made the papers would be the day the gig was up.

5

Breezy

I like to play my cards close to the chest and only gamble when the odds are in my favor. As much as I wanted to go home with the guy from the social milieu, I knew too much was at stake with this one. As soon as I saw him, my interest was piqued because I knew exactly who he was. His name is Black King, and he's the cream of the crop. He's a multimillionaire and also the father of my cousin Nicoli's son. I discretely gave him my cell phone number, and I left it at that. I knew he'd call. I also knew what *not* to do from Nicoli's mistakes. The whole neighborhood knew her business about how she lost her man. Sure he'd moved her and his son to a decent two-bedroom apartment that he purchased in Battery Park City. But with the amount of money he's worth that was hardly compensation for giving birth to your first born, which happens to be a son. This was so unlike Nicoli. I thought she'd go after more. Rumor has it she's found God and left her gold-digging ways behind. What a shame. As a black female we're stereotyped as gold diggers if we set out to marry a stable man with money when white women do it all the time and don't get the bad reputation. In fact, in some cultures where marriages are arranged, the first concern is that the man be able to provide for his family. Black women have so many stereotypical images on our shoulders put there by society and perpetuated by our own black men that I'm amazed at how strong we really are.

All I know is that if I get with him I'm staying with him. I tell all my friends all the time that any chick can get with a man. It's keeping him that separates the women from the girls.

I pulled up in front of St. John's University and beeped my horn so my friend Chris could see me. He played on their basketball team, and it's rumored that he's going pro. We fucked a few times in the past. It was all right, but not enough to keep a bitch in limbo while the NBA decided his future. I can't invest my time on a guy who *might* go pro. He used to try to play me like he was the shit but quickly he snapped out of that mode once he saw what I was working with. My father takes care of me very well and has made it so I never have to fuck for a pair of shoes. If I fuck it's because I want to. Not everyone realizes that it could go either way for a women, and I'm fortunate enough not to have to play the game.

"What's up?" I asked as he climbed in my jeep.

"Shit. Listen, did you do your homework for math class?" he asked as his bad breath lit up the car. Instinctively, I rolled down the windows and handed him my pack of Dentyne Ice. I watched as he popped two in his mouth and wondered if he knew or even cared how his breath was intolerable.

"What you think?" I responded as I looked away. I now smelled a peppermint-flavored stench.

"Hell yeah."

"You know it," I confirmed while I let my head rock back and forth to the radio that was softly playing.

This was my third year, and I was majoring in psychology. I wanted to learn how to pick a person's brain as a career. Excelling in school had always come naturally for me. I never had to study or bust my brain open when taking an exam.

"Let me copy it real quick."

"Boy, I'm tired of you playing into the stereotype of a young black dumb athlete. Get your shit together just in case this ball shit doesn't work out for you. Your broke ass will need a plan B," I said shaking my head from side to side and talking with my hands.

"Easy for you to say. You have a rich daddy footing all your bills, including your twenty-thousand-dollar a year tuition bill," he sarcastically replied.

"Stay out my business," I said as I pointed my finger in his face, noticing the palpable tension that was building in the air.

"Just give me the homework, Breezy. I ain't got time for your shit right now," he complained.

"Oh, you think shit is sweet? Get your illiterate ass out my fucking jeep and take time to understand how you speak to a person who's doing you a favor," I yelled.

"I'm sorry—"

"Out, motherfucker. Out," I snapped.

When he got out my jeep he slammed my door so hard my car shook. I rolled down my passenger's side window and yelled, "Hater's never win."

I drove around to campus parking to leave my Range Rover when my cell phone rang. The number was private.

"Hello," I said.

"Hello. May I speak to Breezy?"

"This is she. May I ask who this is?"

"This is Black. We met the other night."

"I know who you are. I was wondering why it was taking you so long to call."

"How did you know I'd call at all?" he asked without even trying to disguise his sarcasm.

Refraining from responding with a snide remark, I said, "I knew you would. How could you resist…"

I heard a soft chuckle over the phone before he said, "What are you doing right now?"

"I'm on my way to class."

"You're in college?"

Thinking quickly, I decided to distinguish myself from Nicoli. She was young and immature and I heard that drove him crazy. I retorted, "I teach college. I'm a professor at St. John's University."

"What?" he admonished.

"What part of what I just said are you questioning," I challenged. As I said the words my head bobbed back and forth and I made several gestures with my hands. I had on my mature business voice, which was assertive and cocky.

"I thought you were no more than twenty years old."

"I see you like them younger. Well I'm twenty-nine years old, and I've been teaching for seven years. I started as a paraprofessional, and now I'm certified with the state." I continued to embellish my lie as my story unfolded.

"Really? I'm a little surprised yet impressed. I must admit not much impresses me nowadays," he explained.

"Then you must be looking at the world through the eyes of a cynical man."

"I've seen and been through a lot," he said. "I'm at a point where I don't think I can take many more surprises." His voice had dropped an octave, and he seemed ready to pull out the violins.

I wasn't ready to partake in his pity party so I replied, "Trials and tribulations are a part of life. We all go through things, and the way we handle them will define who we are and build character."

"You're right…you're right…I don't know how we even got on that topic. I called to ask if you're free to go out for drinks tonight," he said.

I knew I needed to play this to the hilt.

"Tonight's no good. I have to give my students a mid-term first thing tomorrow morning, and I need to be sharp. I don't tolerate cheating. Maybe later in the week we could go out for dinner," I said and quickly changed the emphasis from drinks to dinner. There would not be any one-night stands going down.

"Sure, sure, that sounds fine. Listen, take down my telephone number and give me a call when you're free."

I took down his number and made plans to meet later in the week. With quick thinking I'd made an impression. I planned on keeping it that way.

6

Jinx

They say seek and you shall find. That's never been true for me. Anytime I've ever sought anything in life it's always just out of my reach. I didn't know it at the time, but I had foolishly thought that I was secure in who I was and that I would never allow myself to be abused or manipulated by another man. How wrong was I?

Today started off just like any other, only that feeling that Nana told me was my sixth sense was bugging the hell out of me. Something just didn't seem right, and I couldn't quit put my finger on it. This feeling lasted all day until I got home from work and had to rush Nana to the emergency room. She'd cut a deep, open flesh wound in her hand while cleaning chicken for dinner. I grabbed her sweater, called a cab, and we rushed to Brookdale Hospital on Linden Boulevard. Immediately they took Nana into triage so that they could stitch up her hand. She wanted me there but my stomach was too squeamish to watch. I sat back and closed my eyes to try and drown out the noise of a few kids crying when I heard a deep, baritone voice say, "Is this seat taken?"

I popped open my eyes and saw a tall, lean man before me. Dryly, I remarked, "Is anyone sitting there?" *Stupid,* I thought.

I was so annoyed that he'd disturbed me for the obvious. He plopped down and my chair jiggled from his weight, which only aggravated me more. I made it a point to open my eyes, glare at him then roll my eyes. And for emphasis I decided to suck my teeth, something I hadn't done since junior high school.

As if all of those gestures weren't telltale signs of an aggravated woman, he had the audacity to say, "Whew. I've really had a long day and now I'm here. What about you…long day?"

When I ignored him, he nudged my shoulder as if to say, "Wake up, bitch. You ain't sleep."

"Excuse you," I barked. I was ready to whip ass.

When he saw me lose it he gave the biggest smile I'd seen in years from anyone. I could tell that I'd played into his hands and he was thoroughly amused.

"Now that I got your attention I wouldn't want to lose it again. My name's Shawn," he said and extended his hand. He had on an outdated stainless-steel Movado watch and neatly manicured bony fingers. He was albino white with dark brown patches of skin with sandy brown hair, white eyelashes and freckles all over his face and neck. But there was something endearing about him that I couldn't quite put my finger on. Maybe it was his smile…Maybe.

"Didn't your mother teach you better manners?" I scolded.

He chuckled then got serious, "I never knew my mother. She gave me up for adoption when I was six months old. Never knew my father either. I was shuffled around from foster parent until I was old enough to take care of myself. Now I'm here meeting you," he said, oversimplifying his situation.

"Oh gosh, I'm sorry. I didn't know."

"Of course you didn't. And there's nothing to be sorry about. It's life. It happens."

I didn't even know this stranger, and in three seconds he had me feeling sorry for him and had my total attention.

"My name's Jinx," I said and extended my hand.

"Well, isn't that original," he replied, leaned down and kissed my hand, flipped it over and then kissed the inside of my palm. This sent light chills down my spine.

Was he flirting?

"Believe me, that name comes with a lot of baggage."

He studied my face for a long moment then replied, "I'd carry each and every bag on my shoulders if you'd just smile for me once."

Involuntarily I burst into a large grin. He seemed so sincere as I looked into his large, round, expressive eyes—eyes that looked as if they couldn't ever conceal a lie.

"Today, you promise to fix all my problems. Tomorrow you *are* my problem."

Now it was his turn to crack a smile.

"I've never been accused of that…causing anyone problems. But I'm just a regular dude, so anything's possible," he said, shrugging. "On a brighter note, guess what?"

"What?"

"You'll never guess," he baited.

"Guess what," I retorted playing into his hands.

"That I want your number."

I shook my head and laughed. "Really? I would have never guessed that."

"Well?" he said.

I tilted my head to the side and studied him again. He truly wasn't my type and a little hard on the eyes, but he seemed pleasant enough. The only thing is that I was celibate at the moment by choice—hadn't had a man or sexual partner in three years. Was I ready to step back out there and leave my heart open to get crushed again? On the flip side, I wasn't getting any younger. I'm twenty-seven years old, and my biological clock is ticking, but would I really consider having kids by this unusual-looking creature? I had to scold myself for my narcissistic thinking. I was jumping ahead of myself. All he asked for was my number. Quickly, I glanced at his fingers. They were average length and skinny, but did that mean anything? Next, I glanced at his shoe size. He had to be over six feet tall, and he looked as if he wore a size nine sneaker, but what did that mean? God knows that I haven't had any dick in years.

"Jinx?" he said, jolting me out of my perverted thoughts.

"I'm sorry but I'm not dating anyone at the moment."

"Then we won't date. We won't make it official until you say the word. Just let me call you to get to know you a little better," he pressed.

He was making it a little too hard to keep saying no. I hate being in situations like these with men. The more you try to dissuade them, the harder they pressed, which meant I usually folded.

"Maybe—"

"Chile, Nana had to turn them doctors out in there," Nana said. "Don't go givin' me them welfare recipient stitches. I worked for thirty-five years, and I paid my taxes. I want the good shit. You better go up in there and have a plastic surgeon stitch me up. I know my rights," she said.

"Nana, let me see how it looks." I jumped up and studied her hand. There were about eight small, reasonably neat stitches in her hand.

"It look good, don't it, pumpkin?" she gloated. "Nana don't play."

She was such a strong, feisty lady, and I loved her so much.

Nana grabbed hold of my arm and placed her weight on me so that she could walk better. We started walking out when Shawn came trotting behind me. I had forgotten about him that quickly.

"Jinx," he called, and Nana and I both stopped.

"Oh, Shawn, I almost forgot. I don't think that we should exchange numbers," I said dismissively.

Nana looked him over quickly. "Stop talking foolishness, chile. This here a good-looking man. Her number is 718-555-5859. You better had caught that 'cause Nana don't got time to be repeatin' herself. I'm seventy-seven years old, and I'm sick of looking in your face e'vry night," she said, startling and embarrassing me.

I couldn't do anything but blush.

"Jinx, enjoy your evening. I'll give you a call tomorrow. Miss Nana, it was a pleasure to have met you," he said and walked back into the emergency room. I pinched Nana on her old, fat cheeks, and she chuckled. She'd amused and entertained herself for the evening. She was satisfied.

7

Breezy

My new friend Black called and arranged for us to have dinner at Chi on Lexington Avenue. This was an upscale sushi restaurant in Lower Manhattan. As bad as I wanted to throw on a pair of Joe jeans and stilettos, I decided to tone it down from the first night he'd seen me. I needed to look the part. I wanted to be intriguing—as in a girl that could mix it up. Dress sexy when she's out on the town with her girlfriends. Dress sexy yet conservative when she's out on a date. That night I wore a tight-fitted lime green pencil line dress and lime-green-and-white Jimmy Choo heels. A large studded-and-rhinestone snakeskin belt hung loosely around my waist. I loved mixing up my outfits with a splash of color. I pulled out a garish red pocketbook to offset the lime green and white. It worked to my advantage. I had my hair in soft curls dangling provocatively around my face and a matte red lipstick.

I pulled up to Lexington and 23rd Street in front of the restaurant at 8:00 P.M. sharp and just as he said, Black was standing outside. I rolled down my window and beeped the horn so he would recognize me. I decided to not tell him what I was driving, and I could see the surprise in his eyes. A 2005 Range Rover was hardly the jeep a college professor would be driving. He walked over and hopped in the front seat.

"Hello, gorgeous," he said, leaned over and pecked me on my cheek.

I inhaled his cologne. Issey Miyake. Nice.

"Hi," I said and smiled. He was wearing a royal-blue Lacoste shirt, dark blue Seven jeans and a pair of cartoon blue-and-white exclusive Air Force Ones by Nike.

"Pull over there into the parking lot," he instructed. I did as I was told and pulled into a fenced-in outdoor lot.

"How long you stay?" the Mexican attendant asked as we exited the vehicle.

"A couple of hours. We won't be long. We're just having dinner," Black said.

"Thirty dollars," the attendant replied.

I began to reach inside my red Hermes Burkin bag to pay when Black quickly pulled out two twenty-dollar bills and handed it to the parking attendant. Inwardly I smiled because sometimes you never know. You could date someone who has money but feels he will only pay for the big things and let you pay for small things. Those types of brothers got on my last nerve and never last long in my bed. Then there are some brothers who want you to go half on everything. Last, there are men like Black who know how to treat a lady. As we walked back to the restaurant, he grabbed my hand and escorted me across the street. I couldn't help but find his gesture charming.

This one is going to be easy, I thought.

At dinner Black didn't talk much. He just really stared and relied on me to make all the conversation. He was purposely being emotionally unavailable, and if he didn't have the status he had I would have been turned off. But I flowed. I had to.

"So what do you do?" I asked.

"A little here and there. Nothing too heavy," he lied. I was a little insulted. Why was he being evasive? Did he make it this complicated for my cousin Nicoli to get to know him?

"Oh…okay. What do you do for fun? What are your hobbies?"

"Don't have any," he said and swallowed a large gulp of his Louis XVIII Remy Martin. I studied him for a moment and sensed that he was bitter. Luckily, I knew about his embarrassing situation with Nicoli and her lesbian lover. That was enough to make any man bitter toward women. I concluded that he was probably looking for something casual—a quick dinner, drinks then a long fuck. That was the run of the gamut. I was from Brooklyn. I wasn't going for that. I was determined to get something tangible out of this relationship. I looked into his distant, flat eyes and wondered if he was willing or ready to foster a relationship.

"I don't have many hobbies, but I do like racquetball and horseback riding. I also play a little chess," I lied.

"Really? You play chess?" he said, and I noticed his interest piqued.

"Yes," I said, laughing. "Why? Are you ready to get beat by a girl?"

"I've never been beaten in chess in my life," he boasted now suddenly vibrant and full of life. "In fact, I'm the best chess player this side of town."

Was Mr. King a bit of a braggart?

Mental note: *First thing in the morning I'll have my father show me how to play chess. He, too, is unbeaten.*

"Well there's a first time for everything," I said and started being co-quettish with Black. I let my hand linger on his for a long moment and licked my lips seductively. I could tell I had aroused him.

"What do you say we go back to my place and play a game of chess? I want to see what you got."

"I would love to—"

"Great," he interrupted me.

"But I can't. I need to get back home. It's getting late."

Black looked at his watch in the most peculiar fashion. He couldn't believe I was ending our date at ten o'clock on a Friday.

"Do you have any children?" he probed, thinking this could answer it for him.

"No," I said, leaving him to wonder. I decided not to ask him whether he had children because I knew the answer. He had a son with my trifling cousin, Nicoli. I'd use that piece of information to my advantage some-how at a later date. Whether Black knew it or not, the chess game had already begun…tonight.

8

Nicoli

My life began on a busy Brooklyn intersection when I was dragged out of my luxury vehicle and thrown on the graffiti-laden, dirty pavement to be pummeled by four strangers. September 9, 2003, is the day that will be forever etched in my memory as fists of fury pounded into my back, battering and bruising my helpless body at the behest of a jilted lover. Even though there isn't any proof, I think my best friend at the time, Joy, also took part in the crime. Her motive is unfathomable. All I know is that I had a way of making Joy feel diminutive and stupid in my presence. Sometimes there was flagrant tension in the air that was unmistakable. This tension only fueled my ego, and I was a tyrannical ruler. Since she hasn't been charged with the crime, I think to be politically correct I'm supposed to say she *allegedly* partook in getting my face ripped open, but I know better.

One girl pulled a razor out from her back pocket and began to slice my face as a butcher slices deli meat. My face burst open like fireworks on the Fourth of July. The sharp metal blade separated my face into parts like a math equation. Blood dripped in my eyes, ran down my cheeks and dripped into my ears. The lyrics of 50 Cent's song kept going through my head: *"Many men wish death upon me...Blood in my eye, dawg, and I can't see..."*

Before that awful occurrence I used to think that my beauty was beguiling. I thought I had the gift of beauty to bring any man to his knees, bowing at my feet in a submissive gesture. Then, I'd take my perfect size five feet and walk all over his heart. That was my makeup. I was a shallow, immature young woman who always put herself first. Second and third place was for losers.

I had just undergone my third reconstructive plastic surgery for my facial scars, and my doctor promised that this would be the last one. I know it's only been two years but it seems that these scars have been on my face for decades. Every day was a day too many.

Right now I'm laying in my recovery suite at one of the most posh plastic surgeons in Beverly Hills. My doctor is Raymond Corelione—a world-renowned plastic surgeon. This is all compliments of my baby daddy. His name is Black King, but he's more than the father of my son, Black King, Jr. He's also the love of my life. Two years ago he was just a millionaire with a big dick. It took the assault to bring me to my knees before I was finally able to be still and let God in. Once I was in that space, I was able to decipher what was important. I was able to understand love. I was able to give and receive love. But it was all a day too late. I had already hurt Black too much for him to ever forgive me for my indiscretions. It didn't matter to him that I was carrying his child or that I'd confessed my undying love to him. He was a man with his heart broken.

In that time I was able to realize that men and women love differently. We as women are so nurturing and forgiving whereas all men have is their pride. Black's pride wouldn't allow him to forgive me and move on. Cheating in his eyes was the ultimate betrayal, even though he cheated on me constantly. And I forgive him constantly. I'd still forgive him…but that's just me.

One week later, the bandages came off. I held my breath and expected an improvement but that's about it. I looked in Doctor Ray's eyes, and he was smiling. He was always smiling.

"Well?" I said impatiently.

"There's still a little swelling and discoloration, but I think I've done a fine job if I must toot my own horn," he bragged.

"Let me be the judge," I snapped and snatched the mirror. What I saw made my jaw drop. No longer did I have a road map carved into my face. Each jagged line was smooth and virtually invisible. "You did it."

"In a couple of weeks you won't be able to see a trace of your disfigurement. You'll be back to your beautiful self."

"This looks at least ninety percent healed."

"Yes. Of course there's no way to erase the entire evidence of what happened, but I think I've succeeded in restoring your face to its natural beauty."

"I cannot thank you enough," I squealed. "You don't know what this means."

"I'm just glad you're satisfied," he humbly retorted.

Now, I may have a shot at getting back the man that I love, I thought.

9

Jinx

"Don't fight it, Jinx. It'll only make it worst for you," a strong male voice demanded. I couldn't breathe. It felt as if someone was cutting off my oxygen supply, and I kicked out in a last-ditch effort to save my life.

Was someone choking me?

I felt myself gasping for air. I saw images but I couldn't make them out. It's too dark. I kept straining my eyes to get a clearer picture but everything was out of focus. I feel hot tears streaming down my cheeks, and this overwhelming feeling of betrayal.

"I'm pregnant..." I managed to spit out. "Don't do this...I'm having our baby."

I woke up as I've done on many occasions for the past twenty years in a pool of sweat. I was drenched and trembling at the same time from this recurring dream. In my dream someone is killing me, and I can't make out the faces or voices. At first, I thought it was just a nightmare. As the dreams kept happening, I started to think it was some sort of omen, some sort of prophecy. But who would want to kill me? Each time I have this dream, another clue is revealed but still I can't put the pieces of the puzzle together. It's so eerie that I've managed to stop trying to figure out what it means. When I started having the dreams, I was seven years old. And for years I'd just dream the very beginning. I knew that I was an adult and that I was fighting someone. I tried to explain the dream to Nana, and she started playing numbers at the local gambling spot. By the time I was ten years old Nana had me doing all types of crazy stuff. She'd have me knocking on wood, spinning around in circles and sleeping with tea leaves under my pillow to keep the bad demons away. As I got older, the dreams progressed and they really started to terrify me because I realized that I actually turned out to look just like that woman in my dream.

I glanced at the clock and it was eight o'clock on Saturday morning. Quickly, I jumped in a cold shower, got dressed and made breakfast for me, which was brunch for Nana. Nana was up every morning at 4:30.

After we ate, Nana and I started playing cards. I liked spending Saturday mornings with Nana because I worked so much during the week, and I always hung out with Breezy on the weekends. And I know Nana gets lonely.

"So, did the handsome stranger call you?" Nana asked just as she dropped down a jack of spade.

"Not yet," I replied and dropped a queen of spade.

Just as I was about to whip on Nana's ass my cell rang, and the number was private. I picked up. "Talk to me."

"Jinx?" the unfamiliar voice asked.

"Is that your final answer?"

He chuckled. "Good morning. This is Shawn."

"Speak of the devil."

"Nah, I'm not that bad," he replied. "What are you doing?"

For some reason I was eager to talk to him. His voice was milk-chocolate smooth, and he had a slight accent when he spoke certain words.

"Nothing," I lied and slowly got up from the table and put my finger in front of my lips to signal Nana to be quiet. She just grinned her trademark toothless smile. I immediately walked to my bedroom and flopped on the bed, and we began our discussion. I felt as if I were in high school because I had this fluttery feeling in the pit of my stomach that was a mixture of excitement and hesitation.

"So is your real name Jinx?"

"Yes. Don't ask me why…just because I guess."

"I like it. It fits you. It's a different name for an exquisite beauty," he commented, and I felt myself blush.

"How old are you?" I asked.

"Thirty-one. And you?"

"I'm twenty-seven. What do you do?"

"I'm a journalist for *Celeb* magazine."

"That sounds interesting. You must be very smart, huh?"

"I wouldn't go that far," he retorted and then said, "but I do have a few degrees."

"Do you get to meet interesting people?"

"Yup. Met someone very interesting just last night."

Again, he was piling on the compliments as thick as possible, but somehow I accepted them graciously. I hadn't talked with the opposite sex in an intimate setting in years. This felt good. Before I knew it we'd been on the phone for six hours and we both didn't show any signs of hanging up.

"So you go to church every Sunday?" I asked, amazed at meeting a religious man.

"Yes. Don't you?"

"Haven't been inside a church since my parents were killed."

"Well maybe you'll go with me sometimes."

"Are you inviting me on a date?"

"A date…well yes and no. I would have preferred our first date to be in a more intimate setting, but I'll take what I can get." He laughed quietly.

"Shawn, my life is uncomplicated and serene. I don't want to get on another roller-coaster ride that I'm sure a relationship would bring."

"I see someone had a bad breakup."

"Bad is an understatement."

"Do you mind me asking what happened?"

I thought about whether I should tell him the truth or lie. Should I really divulge all the intimate details about the kids, the women, the abuse and my stupidity? Then I realized that one lie leads to another, so I decided to give him the shorter version.

"What happens in most relationships? Infidelity. He had a few kids while we were together with a few different women. I swear that was the worst time in my life. I will never date another man with kids. It's the worst."

There was an uncomfortable silence and then said, "Don't let that bad experience stop you from living your life to the fullest. You only have one shot at life. Don't let it pass you by because of that idiot."

We continued to talk, which was an absolute record for me. We stayed on the phone for nine hours. Breezy kept clicking in, and I'd ignore her calls and sent her straight to voicemail. He even let his people go to his voicemail as well. I can actually admit that I liked talking to Shawn. We decided to meet for church the next morning and have our first official non-date that night. When I hung up the phone I called Breezy and was just in time to catch her and Joy. We all decided to go to Lindenwood Diner on Linden Boulevard to have a few drinks. I wondered if I'd tell them about Shawn.

As usual the diner was packed. Mercedes S430 and BMW 745s all littered the parking lot. Breezy had picked up Joy, and then they both came to get me since I was the closet to the diner. Joy was cool. She was a little loud and ghetto but sometimes she made me laugh. She's been coming around for the past two years, and her and Breezy are getting closer. At first I was a little jealous because I didn't want to share my friendship with Breezy, but Breezy always makes it clear that I'm her best friend and that makes me secure in our friendship.

We walked in and were greeted warmly by the manager Miguel who knew everyone by their first name, which only helped create a million little monsters. Everyone walked around that diner as if they owned it. Seriously, everyone thought that they actually put the money up to build that bitch. A lot of people have been coming to that diner longer than I've been alive. And a lot of them felt as if they owed that diner a lot of loyalty. Rumor has it that in the early nineties the feds set up a sting operation to knock off a few major drug dealers. They tapped all the phones in hopes to get wire taps on the major players. Only, the diner's loyalty was to its paying customers. How they made their money was their business. At the end of the day all money is green, so they tipped off their customers, and let's just say the most the feds probably heard on that phone was a church lady calling for a cab after Sunday brunch.

After we ordered our apple martinis and I felt a little buzz, I decided to confide in my friends.

"So last night I took Nana to the hospital because she cut herself, and I met someone that I'm thinking about going out with," I said.

"Do we know him?" Joy asked.

"No. He works." That was my response. Most of the guys we knew of were either celebrity or drug hustlers who thought they were celebrities. We rarely knew or associated with regular working guys.

"What's his name and what does he do?" Breezy asked but her attention wasn't really on me. She was scanning the room, looking for someone of interest who'd ultimately pay our tab at the end of the night.

"His name's Shawn, and he's a journalist."

"Oh, he's broke," Joy said and took a sip of her Martini. "Better you than me."

We laughed.

"He doesn't seem broke. He works for *Celeb* magazine."

Suddenly, everyone's interest picked up.

"He may be able to get us into the industry parties on a V.I.P. list. Jinx, don't fuck this one up," Breezy scolded as if it's that simple to maintain a relationship. No one plans on fucking it up. It just happens. And for the record I didn't fuck up my last relationship. He did.

"Well, the thing about Shawn is that he's not my type, but I like his conversation," I said.

"What do you mean not your type? Is he my type?" Breezy quizzed.

I shook my head. "He isn't any of our types, but I like his conversation," I repeated.

"You ain't seriously thinking about fucking a dude for his conversation?" Joy retorted.

"Who said anything about fucking? I'm just going to church with him in the morning."

"Church? What kinda corny lame shit you got going on? You on some bullshit," Joy chastised.

"Different strokes for different folks," I said defensively and shrugged.

"Jinx, I'm glad that he's pulled you out of that rut you were in, but you don't fuck him for that. At the end of the day you're settling, and you'll regret it later. Mark my words…" Breezy said.

"I hear you, but I think you're wrong. What I like about him is that he seems totally opposite of Jason. When Jason and I were together, I was sleeping with the enemy."

"The first thing you're doing wrong is comparing Shawn and Jason," Breezy scolded.

"I can't help it."

She shrugged and said, "You have to learn the rules. My father taught me well. He taught me how to think like a man in a man's world and to destroy your enemy from within. My father said that everyone, including him, is a potential enemy. All it takes is the circumstance. You think that Shawn isn't the enemy, and I'm saying he just hasn't revealed himself to you."

When Breezy spoke like this, it was always alarming. For some reason I felt as if she wasn't revealing her true self either. I decided to change the subject.

"You guys are getting way ahead of yourself. We're only going to church, and besides, he's not like that. He's different. I can tell…" I remarked, but their attention was already taken.

10

Breezy

I told my dad about my encounter with Black King. He knew of him and felt that this could be a big payday for me—if I played my cards right. My daddy had all faith that I'd be able to carry it out, but he was a man who moved on strategy. I had to be strategic to catch this one in my web.

I ran down to my daddy's apartment first thing the next morning and he instructed me on what to do. I knew I'd have to miss classes just for that day because he wanted to teach me chess. He almost wanted to kick himself for not showing me sooner. When I was younger I pleaded for him to show me but he refused. He felt chess was a man's game and didn't want his princess getting caught up.

I walked into my father's living room and sat down on his massive, chocolate brown leather sofa. A sturdy, antique coffee table sat on a Persian rug in the center of the room. On the outer wall he had a custom built, ten-foot bookshelf with thousands of books he'd read throughout the years. Heavy drapes covered the windows giving the apartment a dark, surly look. My father rarely allowed sunlight in. His chess set was perched in the corner almost overshadowed by the bulky furniture.

"What do you know about this guy?" my father asked.

"I know a few things that's enabled me to already start playing my cards right."

"Like what?"

"Like he has a baby with Nicoli."

"My sister's daughter?"

"Yes," I said and rolled my eyes.

"Interesting. What else?"

"They're not together anymore. She's had his baby but the relationship ended almost two years ago. He found out that she was having an affair with a lesbian."

"Is that the mess she'd gotten herself into and gotten her face slashed?"

"Yes, Papa. Rumor has it that he felt she was immature—always wanting to run to a club and take advice from her friends."

"So, what's your position? How did you get at him?"

"I lied about my age and occupation. He thinks I'm a twenty-nine-year-old college professor."

"That's a dim-witted plan and I'm disappointed with myself. I thought I'd taught you better."

"What? Papa, why?" I asked perplexedly at my father's outburst. "I thought you'd be proud."

"What were you thinking?" he spat. "How long do you think it'll take for him to find out your real age and occupation? He has a child with Nicoli."

"But they're estranged. By the time she gets wind of anything it'll be too late," I said, pleading for my father to accept my strategic logic. "Why are you this upset?"

"Don't you realize that how you handle situations is indicative of how I raised you?"

"Papa, I got this. Trust me…I'll make you proud."

"From here on out I want in on every detail…" my father stated and rubbed his beard. "Did you sleep with him?"

"Papa. No," I said and blushed. As close as I am to my father certain subjects still make me uncomfortable.

"I'm going to ask you one more time, did you sleep with him?"

"I said no. You didn't raise a fool."

"Good. Because a man in his position can sleep with any woman anytime he wants to. Make him wait, but make him believe that you make all men wait, not just him. If he thinks you're only making him wait he'll feel it's a game you're playing, so he'll play the game, and once he sleeps with you he'll leave. I know. I've done it on too many occasions."

"Yes, Papa," I agreed.

"Now if Nicoli could get this fool to plant a seed in her and dish out seven figures on a ring, you can get him to the altar. I've schooled you all your life for this challenge. Are you up for it?"

"More than you'll ever know. I'm ready."

"Good," he said, and we walked over to his most prized possession: his marble chess set. He'd spent fifteen thousand dollars on it years back when he went to Japan. "Sit down. Let's get started."

I exhaled and sat down to what I knew would be an intense night.

"Chess is a man's game. It's a strategic game that not many women conquer. Over the next several weeks I'll teach you the skills to put you in the loop. There are several introductory strategies in chess, which depend on how you approach your line of attack. Open or closed are two opening tactics. This is the pawn." He picked up the smallest set of pieces on the board and put one in my hand. "This can only take one step at a time unless…"

My father began explaining each piece and the movements on the chess board.

"Is Black a risk taker?" my father asked.

"Ummm, I would have to put that in the no column. He seems like the type who puts thought in all of his decisions."

"I thought so. Then I'm going to teach you a closed opening strategy. It's defensive. If he were a risk taker I'd teach you an open strategy. With that one you and your opponent begin to trade pieces quickly. The closed opening strategy requires more thought. Experienced players always opt to play this way because it's stimulating. An experienced player using a skillful defense will lull the inexperienced player right into a trap."

"What does this one do again?" I asked, picking up one of the pieces. We had been at it for two hours.

"It's the knight. He moves in an L shape."

Three hours later we were still at it, and I was becoming annoyed. It felt like I was in boot camp.

"Guard your queen," he yelled when I moved my bishop and left her exposed. I jumped and tried to move the piece back when he knocked down all the pieces, which meant we had to start the game all over.

Ten hours later we were still practicing. My eyes were tired, my fingers were cramped and my stomach was growling, but I knew better than to tell my father I wanted to quit and finish the next day. He hated quitters. Whatever you aspired to do you had to do it to the fullest capacity that you could.

After fourteen hours he finally let me go upstairs to get some sleep.

"When do you plan on seeing him again?" he asked.

"I don't know yet. I want to be fully prepared."

"Tomorrow, go see Nicoli and make up. See what her take on her relationship with Black is. See if she'll open up and tell you his likes and dislikes and why he ultimately won't come back. Meet me back here by 5:00 P.M. so we can start all over again. You'll need at least three weeks to play at an advanced rate and eight weeks to play at pro level. I'll teach you all my strategies, but your job will be to commit it to memory. I want you to eat, drink and sleep chess strategies and moves. Do you understand?"

"Yes, Papa."

"Breezy , I'm serious. He could very well be our meal ticket. You see it's getting more and more difficult to continue doing what we're doing. It's only a matter of time before someone comes around and starts asking questions. We gotta get out of the game before the game swallows us up."

"Yes, Papa. I'll make you proud. I promise," I said and ran upstairs to get some much-needed rest.

11

Nicoli

Some say hope is for fools. My heart tells me to hold on while my gut says that I have to let Black go. He was coming to pick up our son for the weekend, and this would be the first time he would see me after my third surgery, which was successful. I had been back in New York from Beverly Hills, California, for about two weeks. I was in California for six weeks recuperating while Black had our son. Even though I have full custody, Black has visitation rights. He's far too busy to have full or joint custody of a toddler. As much as I love him, if he ever tried to take away my baby I'd fight him with every ounce of conviction my small five-foot frame could muster.

I walked around my modest two-bedroom condominium and knew that everything was in place. Black allowed me to hire a housekeeper, Gretchen, who came by three times a week. She cleaned and organized the place and also went food shopping. I lived in an unpretentious high rise in Battery Park City, overlooking the water. This wasn't a celebrity-studded building with paparazzi lurking around downstairs. Corporate businessmen and women lived there, making low six-figure incomes. This place was far different from the plush, palatial apartment that Black owned or any of his estates. My apartment didn't have granite countertops or marble floors. Nor did it have the obligatory amenities that are present in any celebrity or celebrity's ex-wives' life. Although, I'm not a celebrity wife, nevertheless, I am his child's mother.

Two years ago, after I had gotten slashed, I appreciated this apartment. Now, as I look in the mirror and get a glimpse of the old Nicoli, I can't help but fight off my sense of entitlement. One strong part of me is back, but I can't let her win. I don't want to be that selfish person anymore.

Black came by shortly after two o'clock. I had washed my naturally red hair and blow dried it straight, and it hung a little past my shoulders. It really wasn't in a style. I hadn't had it cut or clipped in a long while. It was really boring. I contemplated whether I should apply a sheer powder blue eye shadow to accentuate my naturally blue eyes but then decided against it. I didn't want to look as if I were getting dressed up. I wanted to give the look that I was just lounging around the house, yet looked stunning. I ran into my bedroom and began to pace frantically. I threw several outfits onto the bed and began trying on different ones until I had broken out in a sweat.

"This is too sluttish," I said out loud as I tossed a low-cut dress onto the floor. Then I peeled on a pair of hip-hugging Rockin' Republic jeans and decided against those as well. Eight outfits later and I still wasn't dressed. My soft hair had begun to puff out, and beads of sweat rolled down the side of my face. Gretchen came in and noticed I was on the brink of a breakdown.

"Ms. Jones, what have you done to your room?" she inquired as she quickly scanned the room she'd just cleaned.

"Oh, Gretchen, I can't find anything to wear."

"Where are you going? I may be able to help," she said and walked over and started hanging up the garments back on the hangers. Embarrassed, I didn't know what to say. I just stared off into space. When I collapsed on the bed and began to whimper softly she came over to comfort me.

"Don't cry, Ms. Jones," she soothed and put both of my hands in hers. Gretchen was an elderly Russian woman with a petite body and strong hands. She had naturally golden hair and piercing blue eyes. I liked her immediately. She's been working with me for over a year.

I shook my head and almost gave up. When she said, "Sometimes simple is best. Go back and shower. Pull your hair into a neat ponytail and put on this." She went to the closet and pulled out an old powder blue J-Lo velour sweat suit. Her smile was warm and inviting. I knew I could trust her.

"Go and shower. I'll clean up this mess. Mr. King will be here shortly."

I raced inside the bathroom and showered again. I wet my hair and instantly it curled up. I got out the shower and brushed it back in a tight ponytail so Black could see my whole face. I didn't apply any makeup except a pale pink lip gloss. I put on the sweat suit and came out the bedroom barefoot. I had a perfect French manicure and pedicure. When I walked into the living room, I was startled that Black was already gathering up Black Jr. and was on his way out the door.

"Black," I said.

He turned slowly and said, "I'll bring him back Sunday night."

I was speechless. He still avoided eye contact with me and barely acknowledged my presence. I wanted him to see my face, that my scars were gone, but I didn't have a chance. He was gone in sixty seconds....

12

Jinx

Shawn arrived promptly as he said he would and picked me up in a white Toyota Corolla for church. We were going to the Christian Cultural Center on Flatlands in East New York, Brooklyn. I had heard so much about that church but was never interested enough to go. So many celebrities had sung and spoken to the congregation. I came outside in a two-piece orange Christine Renee skirt set. The skirt was about a half inch above my knees but that was the most conservative outfit I had in my closet. My blond Mohawk was silky, and I had large gold hoop earrings adorning my ears. When I got in the car I noticed that Shawn was wearing a pair of light blue jeans, penny loafers and a Ralph Lauren button-up shirt. He almost looked as if he were going to a club. He noticed me looking.

"You know nowadays you don't have to be so conservative going to church. The pastors and the congregations are younger," he said. "Nice outfit."

"Thank you," I said and looked away, putting on my shy girl act.

"So has it really been three years since you've been in a relationship?"

"Embarrassingly, yes."

"But you've had friends, correct? In those three years."

"What do you mean? Male friends?"

"Yeah. Someone to take you out to dinner…things like that."

"No. I've been hanging out with my girlfriends but I didn't date…anyone. It didn't start off like that. I mean, I didn't know that three years later I'd still be celibate. It just happened. I woke up and three years passed. You're the first guy that I've been in a one-on-one environment with."

He smiled. "That's really unbelievable but for some reason I believe you. I mean, when I look at you I don't see someone who'd not have about ten boyfriends. But when I speak with you, I see the sincerity in your eyes, and I know you're not lying."

"There really isn't a reason for me to lie," I said honestly. "I've only had one relationship in my life, and I'm not really trying to rush into another one."

"Well most women feel there's a reason to lie about the amount of men they've slept with. Some women only count the relationships that worked and leave out all the one-night stands and things of that nature. That's why I don't ask that question. I don't think I could take an honest answer."

Inwardly I had to concur with his point of view because he was right. Women do lie because society has given us the "whore" stigma that most women want to avoid. So if they've slept with ten men and only three resulted in long-term relationships, guess which number will roll off their tongues? And if I wanted to be totally honest with myself, if I had a lot of dicks on my jacket, I'd probably erase them from my head *and* résumé. "Lying is so selfish and something I don't do. Either you take me for who I am or beat it."

He chuckled and said, "I feel the same way."

We left church early afternoon, and I must admit that I had a good time. The choir was amazing, and the pastor preached so well. It was as if he was talking directly to me. He stuck a chord when he spoke about not settling for less in a relationship. He said that we as women are too precious to go for anything—abusive relationships, men with bad credit and men with several women. At one point I got teary eyed and tried to hide the fact that tears were streaming down my cheeks. I kept dabbing the corner of my eyes. Soon Shawn grabbed my hand and squeezed it. I turned to face him, and we stared in each other's eyes for a long moment, and I felt this indescribable transference of energy. I knew at that moment that he was right for me.

After church Shawn dropped me off and promised to return to pick me up for dinner. I couldn't wait. I couldn't understand how excited I was. You would think that I was an ugly girl who couldn't get a date rather than a sexy girl who had refused to date. It was only two hours since he'd dropped me off when I dialed him to see what he was doing. When I went to voicemail, I felt slighted, as if not answering my call was a calculated decision. I was acting desperate and needed to put on the brakes. I decided to fall back and take a nap until it was time for me to get ready.

"Don't fight it, Jinx. It'll only make it worst for you," a strong male voice demanded. I couldn't breathe. It felt as if someone was cutting off my oxygen supply, and I kicked out in a last-ditch effort to save my life.

Was someone choking me?

I felt myself gasping for air. I saw images but I couldn't make them out. It's too dark. I kept straining my eyes to get a clearer picture but everything was out of focus. I feel hot tears streaming down my cheeks, and this overwhelming feeling of betrayal.

"I'm pregnant..." I managed to spit out. "Don't do this...I'm having our baby."

When I woke up, dripping in sweat, I saw that I had missed a call from Breezy. I decided to call her before I hopped in the shower.

"Hey, gorgeous," I said.

"Hey, bitch," she said jokingly. We did this emulating Paris Hilton and Nicole Ritchie.

Then I went back into my regular voice and asked her what she was going to do for night.

"I'm learning how to play chess. My father is teaching me."

"Oh, sounds so uninteresting. Well, since you asked I'm going out tonight with Shawn."

"I'm so happy for you. And I'm happy that you didn't let Joy discourage you from hooking up with him."

"Please. Joy is the last person I'd take man advice from."

"I know. How dare she talk about broke men when she stay hooking up with broke dudes. The nerve of some people," Breezy stated.

"Well, that's your friend," I reminded her of the obvious.

"I keep telling you it's not that type of party with Joy and me. She's just convenient when you're not around. A fill-in. You're my best friend. She's just an associate."

When Breezy and I hung up, I jumped in the shower and began getting dressed. Shawn called and told me he'd be there in thirty minutes. I was doing good on time. I had already applied my makeup, nothing heavy. I applied a light MAC foundation with pink blush and pink eye shadow, black eyeliner, mascara and a sheer pink lip gloss. I washed and blew my Mohawk dry and added Sebastian hair gel to sculpt it. I accessorized with large gold hoop earrings and several gold chains on my neck and gold bangles on my wrist. I pulled out a pair of white snakeskin knee-high Gucci boots, circa 1998 and white Seven Capri jeans and a baby-doll shirt that hung off my shoulders and gave a sneak peek of my tattoos. I made that shirt, and it was part of my Spoiled collection. I grabbed my white, oversized leather Marc Jacobs bag and was ready to go.

Shawn arrived on time, and although I invited him inside to see Nana, he declined. He drove me to Green Acres Mall's Red Lobster, and I was a little turned off. I absolutely *hate* Red Lobster. There seafood is too salty. The wait is too long. And the place is always too noisy. There's no intimacy there. But instead of complaining, I smiled graciously and went with the flow. When Jason and I were together we never went to franchises. He always took me to the high-end restaurants. We did Chin-Chin, Mr. Chow, Cipriani, Chi and a host of other spots where the settings were intimate and inviting. But as Breezy said, Shawn's not Jason.

Our first date was pleasant enough. At dinner he surprised me when he broke out into prayer over his food. That was a first for me. He was the perfect gentleman, and I was his lady. When he dropped me off that night I must admit that I was more eager for him to call so that we could talk than I was on our date. In person he was a little different...reserved.

Shawn and I had been dating for two weeks, and we couldn't get enough of talking on the phone. As we chatted into the wee hours of the morning, I crept to the kitchen to get a swig of juice. I squinted through the darkness and finally focused my eyes on the refrigerator. I took a large gulp of juice when our flirty conversation turned nasty.

"What are you wearing," he breathed.

I took a look down at my boxers and wife beater T-shirt and replied, "Nothing."

"Really?"

"Uh-huh. Why? You wish you were here…"

"Do I," he exclaimed. "Are you in bed?"

I tiptoed back to my room and leaped into bed.

"Yeah," I replied, coyly. My voice was barely a whisper. "You wish you were in between my thick thighs…sucking my ripe nipples…"

"I want you to play with your pussy."

"Like this…" I sighed.

"Ummm, hmmmm, just like that," he moaned. "Go deeper."

"Ohhhhh, Shawn…you feel so good."

"How you like it," he asked, excitedly. "How you like your dick."

"Big."

"How big," he asked.

"Very big," I purred. "I *love* a big dick."

"So you love a big dick, huh?" he asked, cynically.

Noticing the shift in his tone, I immediately snapped out of the zone I was in and came back to reality. With my eyes stretched wide, I asked, "Are you upset with me?"

"I just asked you a question. Do you love a big dick?"

"Are we still role playing because you seem tense."

"Jinx it's a simple question."

"Well no, I don't *love* a big dick."

"Then you *love* a small dick."

"Well, I…ah…well no. I don't love a small dick either."

"Okay, so you don't love a big dick nor a small dick. Let me guess, you only fuck medium dicks. Is that it?"

"Don't patronize me."

"No, don't fucking patronize me!" he exploded, as accusations began to ring out. He started accusing me of being shallow, materialistic and a gold-digger. I was stumped. I didn't have a clue as to what brought on this outburst.

"Why are you looking for reasons to hate me?" I said, emphatically.

"Look, it ain't even that serious," he replied, calmly. "I just wanted to know."

"Know what? Shawn size doesn't matter."

"This isn't about my dick. I ain't trigger shy," he replied, cockily.

"I never said you were!"

"Jinx, do you like me? I need to know the truth."

"Shawn, I like you more than I've liked anyone in a long time."

"There's something I need to tell you that I'm not sure you can handle, but it's time."

My stomach dropped. What could he possibly want to say?

"What is it?" I said reluctantly.

"I'm married."

"What?" I yelled and felt my eyes well up with tears. I can't date a married man. How could he have kept this a secret for so long? How could we hang out and talk for so many hours without his wife finding out?

"I'm married but I'm getting a divorce," he explained.

"Yeah, right. You think I'm stupid. That's what all married men say. You're nothing but a liar."

"Jinx, I never lied to you," he said, speaking in a calm monotone. "You never asked if I was seeing someone, if I was in a relationship or if I was married for that matter. You can be disappointed that I've taken longer than I should have to tell you but please don't call me a liar. I just wanted to be sure that there was actually something between us before I divulged my personal business. That's just a defense mechanism for me."

"How long have you been married?"

"Two years. I need to add one more thing. I have a son. That's why I was at the hospital last month. He was ill."

When I heard that not only was he married but had a son I lost it and I was at a loss for words. I thought he was different. I decided that I didn't want to hear anymore and without saying a word I hung up on him and shut off my cell phone. Men...they will never cease to amaze me.

I decided to push Shawn out of my mind and out of my life. To stay strong and fight the urge to call him, I spent a couple of nights at Breezy's house. Hanging around Breezy and Mr. and Mrs. Whitaker took my mind off my own problems.

One morning I left for work as usual. It had been close to three weeks since Shawn and I had that conversation. To my surprise he was parked in front of Nana's house. He jumped out immediately and began walking toward me. His car was sparkling clean, he was clean shaven, and he appeared to have on new clothes. He was trying to make an impression. I tried to dodge him but he was too quick. He grabbed me by my arm and stopped me.

"Get off me," I said sternly while pulling away.

"Jinx, please listen," he begged. "Just give me five minutes, and I'll explain everything. If you listen to my reasoning and still don't want to have anything to do with me then I'll understand."

"There's nothing for me to understand, and there's nothing for you to explain. I'm done. It's a wrap."

"Just like that?"

"Just like that."

"I can't give up so easily. I need you to understand that I didn't want to tell you I was married and had a son because I knew how fragile you were, and I didn't want to scare you away. And I didn't even know if you and I were going to continue to see each other. You hadn't dated in so long that I didn't want to push it. As I saw we were getting closer I decided to tell you something that I should have initially done."

"I don't date married men. That's rule number one in the *Don't Get Your Heart Broken* book. Did you read that book?"

"Jinx you have every right to be mad, but it's not as if I'm living as a married man. We're done. The house is up for sale, and the divorce papers are in."

"How long...how long has it been?"

"Truthfully?"

"No, please lie to me again" I snapped.

"Okay, I deserve that. It's been four months officially—"

"Four months," I screamed.

"But, we've been separated for over a year. I just didn't move out for the sake of finances. Jinx, please, I know you're mad at me, but if you give me another chance I promise I'll never hurt you again. I'm a good dude, Jinx. Please give me the opportunity to show you."

"Kiss my ass," I said and pulled away. As I stormed down the block

I couldn't believe my ears. Married…a kid…a house….

For the entire weekend once again, I shut off my cell phone. I didn't want to hear any more lies. I kept thinking about how stupid and gullible I am. Why do I keep dating the same guy over and over? I mean I leave one lying asshole for another.

When I finally turned my phone on, my inbox was full. I had fifty messages. *Could any of them be from Shawn?* I wondered. Eagerly, I entered my security code, and I sat back and listened as Shawn poured out his heart.

"Jinx, I'm sorry for not telling you sooner. That's a mistake I'll always regret. But if you just call me so we could talk about this I promise you'll see I didn't think I had a choice."

That was the first message.

"Baby, please call me and tell me how you feel. I need to know you don't hate me."

Midway through his messages, I got a sense of strength. His begging and pleading was actually what I needed to continue to ignore him. I didn't realize that my last dysfunctional relationship had set the stage for my next dysfunctional one to seep through.

13

Kesha

For the next couple of days after Bosco and I had stolen the drug money, our situation had become tense. Neither one of us mentioned what had happened. Instead all we did was snap on each other every opportunity we got. Either that or we'd give each other the silent treatment. Finally, I couldn't take it much longer.

"Was that your first time?" I asked as we cruised around Bed-Stuy looking for a few perps we had warrants for. We drove down the brownstone-littered streets: Jefferson Avenue, Halsey, Nostrand and Hancock.

"Would you believe me if I said yes?"

"No, honestly I wouldn't."

"Then why the fuck did you ask? I don't have time for your bullshit, Brown. You've been acting more like a girl and less like a cop these past few days," he exploded.

"No, I've been acting more like a thief with regrets than a cop with morals these past few days," I spat back.

Immediately he pulled over. I thought he'd spotted one of our perps but he didn't.

"Listen, I'm not going to let you take me on this guilt trip. I've already spent the fucking money by upgrading my wife's wedding band. It's gone. I can't give it back, and I never planned on that. My wife's a happy woman. What's done is done. Now either you're with me or you're against me, but I refuse to have you sit in this car day in day out and act as if you didn't walk out that door with your socks stuffed with drug money on your own accord. You could have easily stood your ground and said no. I didn't force you to do shit. I may have used a little persuasion but once I mentioned your girlfriend's Range Rover that was all that needed to be said."

"Fuck you, Bosco," I yelled.

"Never that. You've fucked the whole squad. Now you want a piece of this good dick," he said and burst into laughter. I couldn't help but laugh as well. His cursing me out really broke the ice.

"What did you buy with your money?" he continued.

"I ain't bought shit," I said.

"You still got that money?" he said in almost a whisper as if we could be heard.

"Yeah. I hid it in one of my shoeboxes. No one will ever find it there," I reasoned.

"Are you crazy? Go get that money and get rid of it. I don't care what you do or what you buy but get rid of it today," he warned.

"Bosco, I'm scared. What if Snashall suspects something and runs to I.A.D.?"

"That would never happen. I don't give a fuck what the paper says about the blue wall of silence being knocked down after the Abner Louima scandal. We don't have any Frank Serpicos in our precinct."

Frank Serpico was a hard-nosed police officer in the 1970s who testified at the Knapp Commission about corruption within police precincts and the blue wall of silence. Al Pacino did a superb job portraying him on the big screen.

"Bosco, you and I are both first-grade detectives. We both just took the civil service exam for sergeant. I have a nagging gut feeling that we both could have sealed our fate for some drug money," I said introspectively then continued, "I have a husband and three kids to support. I wish I could give it back."

"Kesha, don't make me have to put a bullet in your head and blame it on a perp. I have a family, too, and you're making my trigger finger anxious with your constant turmoil over this situation. If you feel that bad about it then you can give it to me. I know just where I can spend it."

"I ain't giving you shit, bitch," I joked. "I'll get rid of that money today."

Bosco's comment about taking me out had unnerved me for a minute. He said it lightly but I wondered just how far he'd go to protect his family and their livelihood. Bosco and I may have a great relationship but like any savage animal backed into a corner, you turn your back on them and it's a wrap.

My shift ended early, and I raced home and grabbed the money from outside my shoebox. Quickly, I locked my bedroom door and counted it again. I had $5,500 and I knew exactly what I wanted to do with it. I kissed my husband and my kids on their cheeks and raced out. I still had time to make it to the diamond district to purchase me the watch I had wanted for at least ten years. I walked into Jenny the Jeweler's spot with my mind dead set on a watch. In the display glass sat a beautiful array of dainty presidential gold Rolexes. My eyes were drawn to the ruby-and-gold watch with the diamond bezel. I knew the exact price because I'd window shopped on several occasions. The last time I was there I came with Breezy when she came to cop a pink Chopard watch with the loose diamond dangling in the face. That was a sixteen-thousand-dollar watch compliments of her father for acing her finals.

"I would like to see that watch please," I said to the co-owner, pointing.

"Oh, this is a beauty," she said as she pulled it from the display case. "You have good taste."

I said nothing. I just put the watch on my small wrist and lost my breath. For a long time I didn't say anything, I just stared.

"That watch is on sale for fifty-four hundred dollars. It's worth triple that amount," she coerced. "If you pay cash I won't charge you any tax."

I knew the watch was used that's why it was so reasonable but you couldn't tell. It looked brand new. The gold shone and the diamonds sparkled. I had to have it. I looked around before I slowly pulled the money from out my pocketbook. I didn't need to count it. I had counted it over a hundred times since it had been in my possession. All I did was peel a hundred-dollar bill from the stack before I handed the rest to her. The co-owner smiled to see all the cash.

Soon she put the watch in a Rolex box and handed it to me with my paperwork. Just like the thief I had become, I walked briskly out of there with my merchandise. Once in my car I ripped it out of the box and put it on my wrist. Suddenly the guilt disappeared. In my head I started making all type of excuses to why I deserved this watch, how all drug dealers are bad and cops are the good guys. How I risk my life every day to help keep the streets of Brooklyn safe. And I have kids to think about. This was nothing more than compensation for the good work I'd done on the case. You name it, I used it as an excuse. For some strange reason this watch brought joy to my life. I mean, I thought I was happy. But this feeling was different. I felt *really* happy and couldn't wait to show it off in front of my girls.

On my way home I called my house to check on my girls.

"Hey babe," I said after my husband picked up. "How's everything going?"

"Everything is going well. Where are you?"

"I'm just leaving Manhattan. I had a few errands to run. I should be home shortly. Do you need me to bring home anything?"

"No. I went grocery shopping early this afternoon. I'm about to make dinner. I've already helped Laura and Kimberly with their homework. They're in the living room watching television."

"Well give them a kiss for me, and I'll see you guys shortly."

"Okay, sweetheart. Be safe," he said, and we hung up.

While we were talking Darren was beeping on my other line. I had let him go to voice mail so I dialed him back.

"Hey you," I breathed into the phone.

"What's up, sexy?" he asked.

"Not a damn thing."

"Pebbles will be out the house for a few hours over at her mother's house helping them paint the new den their father had put in. If you come over quickly we have time for me to fuck you really well. Can you make it?"

"I'm on my way," I breathed.

Darren and I have been fucking around for two months. He works the homicide unit in my precinct. I don't think anyone suspects that we're having an affair but sometimes the danger of the situation and the possibility of getting caught is an aphrodisiac.

Darren lived in Star Right City, a housing development in East New York Brooklyn. I parked my car across the street from his house and walked up the steps. He lived on the third floor. Slowly, I opened the staircase, which was centered directly in front of his apartment door. He already had it open waiting for me to dash in. I ran past him with lightning speed straight to the bedroom. I ripped off my clothing and jumped in the shower without so much as a hello.

Darren was particular about taking showers *before* we made love. There was never an impromptu, sweaty lovemaking session. Everything had to be scrubbed, disinfected and oiled.

I came out of his shower naked except that I was wearing my watch. He was lying on his back, naked as well on top of the comforter. He had his hands propped behind his head and a large grin on his face.

"Hey, Brown," he said.

"Hi, daddy," I purred and seductively walked toward him. Slowly I climbed on top of him. I began kissing from the base of his ankles, his calves, behind his knees and once I reached his pelvis his dick was standing at attention. I smiled, opened my mouth and engulfed his large, black penis. Even though he had dark skin, his dick was pitch black and I loved it. I played around with the tip, nibbling at first. Then I began to deep throat his massive penis. My mouth went up and down while my saliva left traces that I'd been there. At first I used to gag when sucking a big dick. Now, I've mastered the technique, and I must admit not too many bitches can do it. They choke at least once. But not me. I take the entire dick in my mouth and give the best blowjobs ever known to man. The trick is to concentrate on the tip. The small indentation where the vein is located is what gives men the most pleasure. I sucked his dick until his vein bulged, and he dug his hands into my short hair and pulled as his ass pumped in out and at a rapid speed. In between licks, I breathed, "It feel good, daddy?"

"You bitch. You fuck me so good," he crooned.

"Better than your wife?" I asked while vigorously jerking his dick with my hands and sucking the tip.

"Ohhhh, so good."

I continued to give Darren head and would occasionally peek up at him and see the look of pleasure plastered on his face.

"I'm about to cum…" he moaned, "I'm about to cummm."

Darren exploded inside my mouth, and as the hot juices entered my throat, I swallowed every bit of it until he was done. Immediately, he flipped me over, spread my legs wide and began to taste my pussy juices. He sucked on my clit until he heard me moan in pleasure, then he began to gently nibble and bit down on my clitoris just how he knew I liked it. I began to grind my hips in slow motion getting lost in the moment. When it started getting really good, I took his head and smashed his face in my pussy and grinded harder.

"Your pussy tastes sweeter than candy," he breathed.

"Eat it all up, daddy."

"Hold up," he said just as I was about to cum.

I flipped my eyes open in bewilderment, but I remained silent. I watched Darren go to a secret hiding place and come back smiling, holding a bag.

"Look what I got inside the goodie bag."

As I reached for the bag he pulled it back. "Close your eyes and relax. I got something that I bought just for you, and I don't want to hear you asking if I'm using it on my wife."

I closed my eyes and did as I was told. The silence coupled with the element of surprise was driving me crazy. Soon, Darren parted my legs and rubbed a cool cream on my clitoris. Next, I heard the noise from the vibrator before I felt it. I openly smiled but continued to keep my eyes closed. The heat from the vibrator coupled with the female response cream drove a bitch out of her mind. I bit my bottom lip softly and murmured words of love. I wanted to play it cool but the feeling was too overwhelming. As my legs began to tremble and I realized I didn't have any control over my body movements, I tried to get up but Darren wouldn't let me. He pushed me back down and made me handle it. Strong waves came cascading down through my body, and I screamed out in pleasure, "Fuck me! Fuck me, Daddy…" I crooned. "I'm about to cum…Oh Jesus…it's soooo good."

I came hard, and Darren didn't miss a beat. He mounted me and entered me rapidly. His dick was harder than a row of quarters, and I could tell he was in a nasty mood. He was talking dirty in my ear.

"Do I fuck you good, you nasty bitch?" he crooned.

"Yes, daddy."

"Call me Mandingo," he commanded as he slammed his dick deeper inside my cave. My pussy was so wet it was making its own melody.

"Mandingo…I love the way you fuck me," I whispered.

"You want me to go hard?" he asked, and I knew that if he did I wouldn't be able to walk straight for days. Still I encouraged him, "Go hard, baby…go hard."

"Like that?" he asked as he tore my insides up with his huge dick. It wasn't hard for him to hit the right spot. I loved the way he twirled his ass around, hit it to the left, then right. Then he'd slow it up and go deep…

We had sex in six different positions before the alarm he'd set went off and we knew we had to end it or get busted. He always set his alarm clock because there was a good chance we'd lose track of time if it was getting too good.

I made it home just in time for dinner. My husband made a delicious meal and set a lovely table. As we ate, he said, "You have tomorrow off, correct?"

"Yes. Why? What's up?"

"I have a few errands that I need to take care of. Could you watch the baby?"

"Sure. Not a problem. She's my child too."

"So act like it," he snapped.

After dinner that night I realized that every Wednesday my husband had something to do. Could he possibly be having an affair? We hadn't made love in months…

When he got in bed, I reached for him, and he pushed my hand away.

"Not tonight, sweetheart. I have a slight headache," he said and turned over.

As much as I tried to believe that my husband couldn't possibly be having an affair, I just couldn't get myself to think that he had the guts to jeopardize the marriage. I turned over and believed that he really had a headache. What else could it be?

14

Jinx

After work I came home sulking. As usual Nana was cooped up in her room watching *What's Happening?* reruns on TVLand. I could hear her laughing heartily as I made my way toward her room. I was almost tempted not to disturb her but I needed the guidance that only Nana could give. I dragged my body into her room with my usually bright eyes looking low and gloomy. Nana turned to face me with a huge grin, which quickly evaporated.

"What's wrong with Nana's pumpkin?" she crooned.

I began shaking my head as I said, "Nana, it didn't work out with me and Shawn. He turned out to be everything I'm not looking for."

As Nana reached out for me to come sit on her bed my cell phone rang, and it was Shawn. Just when I thought there wasn't a cure for how down I was feeling—that call took all my fears away. I can't explain how relieved I was. It felt like all stress that had weighed heavily upon my shoulders had instantly lifted. But why?

"Is that him?" Nana asked.

"Yes."

"Chile, don't answer until you tell Nana what he did to my baby."

I let Shawn go to voicemail but he didn't leave a message. I kicked off my shoes and climbed into bed with Nana, and she gave me her full attention.

"Nana, I just found out that Shawn is a liar. He has a wife and son that he didn't tell me about."

"What? He must be out of his cotton-pickin' mind lying to my grandbaby. How did you find out?"

"He told me a couple of weeks ago."

"Well if he told you then how did he lie?"

"Well he lied by taking too long to tell me."

Nana shook her head. "Pumpkin that doesn't make him a liar. It does challenge his integrity waitin' so long, but I'm sure he had his reasons."

"But Nana!" I objected, and she shushed me away. Her attention had gotten taken when Roger had to go and get the belt for a beating. Nana laughed so loud that I couldn't help but join in. We both watched intently for the remaining ten minutes of the show then Nana redevoted her attention to me.

"Chile, what is it that you're angry about? Tell Nana the truth."

"Nana, I'm mad because he already has a wife and son. I vowed to never go out with someone who has kids, and a wife is out of the question."

"What did he say is the situation with him and that hussy?"

"Nana, she's not a hussy. We don't even know her."

"Be quiet. If she ain't one of my grandbabies then she's a hussy. Now what's the deal?"

"He said that they're getting a divorce."

"Did you give him any?" she probed.

"Any what?"

"Don't work my nerves, chile. Any puddin'?"

"Nana," I said in shock, and we both broke into laughter. "No, Nana. It's too soon. I'm not ready."

"Have you gone to his house?"

"No."

"Okay, listen carefully. Take the fella's call. If he's truly getting a divorce he'll live alone and you'll know his whereabouts. If not then you have your answer."

"Nana, it's not that simple."

"Stop trying to make a mountain out of a mole hill. You have to face reality. You're not getting any younger so the men you'll meet will be a tidbit older than you. They're bound to have had a previous life before they met Jinx. I hate to tell you, but you're not the end all be all. You're twenty-seven, and you're going to run into men with children. You're no longer eighteen. My only concern is making sure that he's not with his wife. I'm sure it'll be easy enough to find out. Give him a chance. I hate to see you locked away in here for another year. You'll regret it in the long run. Live. Go out and live a little."

After Nana's words of wisdom, I told myself that if Shawn called again, this time I'd pickup. I hated to admit it but I wanted him to call.

15

Kesha

When you turn thirty, it's supposed to be a turning point. If you're not married, then it would be a good time to think about getting married. If you don't have any kids then most couples discuss this option. If you got fucked-up credit, most people start dialing 1-800-FIXMYSHIT. Getting married and having kids at such a young age, turning thirty to me meant that it was now time to live life as I should have in my twenties. I had already done the important things—all the responsible things that's expected of adults—so any chance I got to have a good time, I grabbed it, and today wouldn't be any different. Sure, credit card bills were reaching their limits. And, okay, my husband and I didn't make love like we used to. And the kids could use a trip to Disney Land. But overall, I had everything covered. We were all complacent, and that's better than most families.

My husband and I woke up around six in the morning. I wanted to go jogging in Fort Greene Park and he wanted to go fishing with his buddies on Long Island. Of course I couldn't tell him no but I sure wanted to. He gave me a stern look, challenging me to challenge him, but I wasn't falling for it. I was in no mood to hear him bitching.

"I had no idea you wanted to go fishing today," I casually replied as I stripped naked to jump into a cold shower. He didn't even glance at my nakedness, which bothered me.

"Yeah, well, you know now," he said, being short with me as he began pulling out a pair of army fatigue pants and old Timberland boots. I watched as his slim fingers rummaged through our closet. His light skin contrasted nicely against his shiny black hair.

I stood at the bedroom door and watched him for a moment. His sarcastic remarks weren't new. That was part of his personality. But still something didn't seem right about his demeanor. He must have felt me watching him and turned around to face me.

"Are you getting in the shower now? If not, let me jump in before you."

"If you're in a rush, by all means you can go first," I said, still trying to read him. When he smiled, I exhaled, but decided to probe further just to be sure. As he walked past me to go in the bathroom, I said, "Is there a problem? Are you mad at me for any reason?"

Violently shaking his head he said, "Why would I be mad with you?"

"I don't know that's why I'm asking. You seem strange lately. Things seem different."

His eyes popped open, and he put his hands effeminately on his hips—I hated when he did that—and kissed me on my forehead.

"Honey, I've been a little stressed lately with the kids. Between that and worrying about you in these streets, I guess I've been a little tense. That's why I need to go fishing with the guys to relive some of this stress. I'm sorry if I worried you."

Relived, I put on a robe and went downstairs to make coffee. There was no way I was staying indoors with the kids on a beautiful Saturday. Before Daniel came out of the shower I had already called my father and asked if he could watch the kids for the day. I had lied and said I was called into duty. He obliged and remarked how I only called when I needed a babysitter, which was true. I still resented my father for my mother's freak accident, which ripped our family apart nor would I ever forgive him for fathering another child. My mother was in her grave for seven short months before his new wife gave birth to a son. My father was elated. You wouldn't have ever guessed that he'd just lost his first wife and had a daughter. I couldn't stand to be under the same roof as him and his ready-made family. I went to live with my aunt Anita, Joy's mom and left after I graduated from high school at eighteen.

After I dropped off the kids, I took that jog in Fort Greene Park after all. It was still early, shortly after nine in the morning. As I was driving down Nostrand Avenue, I turned on Jefferson and saw my old beat coming out of Stacy's building. I knew that's where he was coming from but I didn't care. I pulled over. As soon as he saw me his face lit up.

"What's up, sexy slim like a bicycle rim?" he bellowed.

"You," I said, smiling.

"You on duty?"

"I'm free as a bird."

"Follow me," he said, getting into his white Tahoe.

I followed Rick to his apartment on State Street, downtown Brooklyn. Rick and I had met in grade school. By the time we reached junior high, we were a couple. I willingly gave him my virginity, and everyone thought we'd be together forever, but I had different plans. I broke his young heart when I called it off as soon as I got into high school, which was a different world to me. There were so many different flavors to choose from, and at that time, I'd just gotten into French vanilla ice cream and Rick was chocolate chip. By the time I had come to my senses and realized what I really wanted in a man, Rick was no longer that sad little puppy running behind me. When I had gotten pregnant with my first child, Rick went out of town to make a few dollars. Everyone knew he was hustling, and I feared for his safety. After I had my second child we hooked back up and began having unconventional, exhilarating sex. Rick was the first man to slap my ass hard and call me a whorish bitch. The arsenal of insults came as he pounded into my pussy sparing me no mercy. His broken heart poured into each stroke, and I realized that I loved rough sex. It turned me on, and fucking Rick became addictive.

I knew about the other women he fucked and he knew about my husband. We weren't together, and there weren't any ties between us but there was a bond. When the department started to take a closer look at him because of a criminal informant, I tipped him off. The C.I. turned up missing and although Rick's never admitted he had a hand in that situation, I knew he did.

Immediately, he left for a while, only breezing in and out of town on occasion. He bought a house in Maryland and moved out of his apartment in Bed-Stuy and rented an apartment on State Street. Years later his illegal money has washed itself and now is a little cleaner. As we walked into his apartment, I peeped the AK-47 assault rifle propped up against his wall by the door and on the table in his living room was a nine-millimeter. He didn't bother to conceal these weapons from me because we spoke the same language. I was from Brooklyn and knew how it could go down at any given moment, and you had to be prepared.

I kicked off my shoes and laid my own .357 Smith and Wesson revolver on the table next to his gun and made myself comfortable on his sofa.

"You hungry?" he asked.

After a long, sweaty jog I was starving. "Famished."

"Then get up and make ya ass something to eat," he joked. All my dudes new I didn't know how to cook.

"I was hoping you'd do it for me," I whined in a babylike voice.

"What I'm gettin' outta that?" he replied, already walking into his kitchen.

"Ummm, a PBA card," I called.

"Got one already. Try again."

"How 'bout a nice foot massage," I suggested.

"Just had that."

"Okay, you're forcing me to play dirty. What about the most memorable, mind-blowing BJ?"

He sucked his teeth. "I just had that too."

"Not by me you didn't. And I know Stacy can't fuck it up like I can," I protested. He walked out of the kitchen a few minutes later holding a plate with a vegetable omelet and a tall glass of orange juice and handed it to me.

"Here. I think I've spoiled you."

Greedily, I took the plate and began digging in. As I ate the omelet he sat on the sofa next to me and held his head for a while as if he was in deep thought.

"What's up? What's on your mind?" I asked.

"Nothing I can't handle," he replied.

"Bitch problems?"

"The only bitch that's a problem in my life is you. When you gonna leave your husband and marry me?"

That wasn't an option. But I was stunned that he'd said that. As kids we always said that we'd get married but I thought I killed those plans years ago. I didn't think that he still thought about it. Noticing that I was at a loss for words he said, "Remember you said that no matter who you're with or who I'm with that on December 31, 2000, we'd meet at Juniors Restaurant and run off and get married?"

"Yeah, we were so silly when we were kids."

"I thought we were in love."

"I mean, yeah, puppy love."

"Did you ever love me Kesha?" he probed and looked directly in my eyes. His eyes were so sad and despondent.

"Don't tell me that you went…on December 31?"

"I sat outside for hours in my car drinking a bottle of Hennessey. Every time I'd see a figure about your height and weight, I'd get all happy only to be let down moments later."

As Rick spoke, I realized how handsome he was. He had buttery soft, dark-chocolate skin. Full, jet-black hair cut low with thick waves. Sexy pink lips, Colgate-white teeth and a chiseled body that resembled a Greek sculpture. And not to mention he was the best sex I'd ever had.

"Rick, I had no idea that ten years after we'd made that pact that you'd honor it."

"I love you, Kesha. When you gonna see that? You think I keep coming through B.K. because I have to? I want to with hopes of seeing you. I already have a life in Maryland. I don't give a fuck about Stacy, Mary, Jane—none of them. My only high is when I see you. When we're together. I was hoping that you'd see that. I was hoping that you'd feel that when we're together. You should have never left me. I would have made you happier than your husband. And I know you ain't happy because of the way you come in here and make love to me."

All this talk about sex made me horny. I moved in closer and began to kiss him softly. We tenderly kissed until I felt him get aroused. I climbed over and straddled him. His dick was pushing into my throbbing pussy through his jeans as I grinded my hips in his lap. As I was about to take off my shirt, he stopped me.

"Kesha, I don't want to fuck. I just fucked Stacy. I want to talk seriously about us. I don't want to keep doing this. It's not about ass for me. There's something missing in my life, and I know that something is you."

"Rick, I can't leave my husband, my family. I just can't."

"Why? People do it every day," he snapped.

"Well not me. I said for better or worst, and I'm keeping my vows," I protested.

"Because of what happened between your parents?" he said in almost a low whisper. He was one of the few people who I had confided in about my mother's death.

"Yes, baby. I know you can't understand, but I can't be like him. I can't break up my family."

Rick nodded as if he understood and decided to quickly change the subject.

"I think I'm going to head out of here today and go home. I hate coming into Brooklyn. It's just not the same for me."

"When will you be back?" I said thinking about the dose of dick I would be looking forward to.

"I don't know. Not for a few months. If I stay around here I may catch a murder charge," he said seriously and I knew that something had jumped off.

"You got a beef?"

"A little something with this kid from the Bronx over some nonsense. I ran into him last night at Juniors, and we exchanged a few words. He's lucky I'm not the old Rick or else I would have rocked him to sleep."

"Fuck these niggas. Head back down the way and holler at me when you come through," I said and began to gather my things to leave. Rick seemed in a somber mood, and I wanted to run out and enjoy my day off.

By mid-afternoon I had hooked up with Breezy. We drove up to Harlem and had southern cuisine at Amy Ruth's on 116th Street. After that we went to 125th Street to buy this DVD called *Crackheads Gone Wild*. We heard that it had Jinx's aunt Kim on it wildin' out. I couldn't wait to see it.

"Look at this dude," Breezy said as she pulled over her jeep. She was referring to Anthony from Tompkins projects. He was standing on the corner trying to move bootleg CDs and DVDs. "Watch when he see me he won't even mention my money that he owe me."

"How much money he owe you?" I asked.

"He borrowed thirty dollars one night to get a bottle of Hennessey. I haven't heard from him since. He used to hit me on the phone every day. It's all good though."

Giving Anthony a brief nod, Breezy walked over to talk to this kid she said she knew from Harlem who was driving a CLS 500.

I took the liberty to walk over to Anthony.

"CDs, DVDs, White Ts…two dollars…five dollars…ten dollars…" he shouted repeatedly.

"What's up, Ant?" I asked.

"Ain't nothing. I'm out here on my grind," he announced.

"I see that. Why you ain't give my girl her money that you owe her?"

"What money?"

"The thirty dollars you borrowed from Breezy."

His face twisted up in anger. "Yo, Breeze," he shouted. Breezy stopped talking and walked over to us.

"What's good?" she asked.

"I'm supposed to owe you some paper?"

Breezy looked over at me in aggravation. "Nah, we straight."

"Then why your girl carrying me like I'm some bum-ass nigga. You looked out one night and blessed me with a bottle. I thought we were cool like that. I didn't know you were on some payback type shit. If you need your little thirty dollars, I got you," he said and began reaching into his pocket for the money.

"I said we straight," she said and pulled me by the arm away from Anthony and whispered in my ear, "How are you going to put me in a bucket of crabs with you? That was some tired shit. Don't ever carry me like that again."

She was moving her hands from side to side and bopping her head in an animated way. I knew she was pissed.

"I thought I had your back," I called after her as she walked back to the Mercedes. "Yo, who's that?"

She didn't answer.

As I began to walk back to her jeep, I stopped briefly to look at a few novels that I might want to pick up once we got back to Brooklyn. I usually bought my books from a local street vendor in the downtown area.

"My man book is coming out this fall," the young, slender, dark-skinned brother announced.

I turned around and looked him up and down. He had a certain swagger about him and a street stance that was undeniable. He looked straight 'hood, which was exactly my type of dude. In a split second too much was going on. I was too busy trying to figure out my next move as another jeep, a white Range Rover Sport pulled up to talk to the guy who was driving the CLS 500.

Quickly, I put down the book I was holding to walk toward Breezy when I overheard the book vendor say, "Kory, *Jane* is flying off the shelves."

My head swung around just in time to see the slender, dark-skinned brother leaving the vicinity in what appeared to be a Maybach. I trotted back to the book vendor and asked was that Kory the author and he said yes.

"Damn, why didn't you tell me?" I accused. "I love that motherfucker. His character Midnight and I must have fucked before because I'm telling you he was so on point with that."

Stupidly, he replied, "Oh, I thought everybody knew him. He a celebrity up in Harlem."

"I'm not talking about everybody. I'm talking about me," I yelled, suddenly annoyed at his stupid ass.

"Look, either buy book or leave," he retorted in his thick African accent, swatting his hands at me as if swatting away an annoying fly. "Stupid girl."

"Oh, you talking real greasy. You tough? Let's see how tough you are right now. Let me see your permit and vending license," I said through clenched teeth as I pulled out my badge, allowing him to glimpse my .357 that I had tucked in my waistline of my Cavalli jeans.

Immediately, his face twisted in disgust.

"Why are you giving me hard time? I'm black like you," he said, touching his skin for emphasis.

A small crowd began to gather as he told one of his workers in his native language to get the paperwork. Noticing the commotion, Breezy came rushing over and so did two uniformed cops. I identified myself to them and they immediately vouched for the vendor saying that he was cool. I decided to back down when I looked over at Breezy and she had a pleading look in her eyes. She hated when I showed out this way.

"Esha-kay, let's o-gay," Breezy said in pig latin.

I nodded my compliance and gave the street vendor a hard glare and hopped in Breezy's jeep. When she said that we were going up to Rucker's to watch some of these guys play ball, instantly I cheered up. Turns out that Breezy knew these guys from St. John's, and they were going up there to play some ball with a friendly wager. The real games were coming next month in July and we'd be there.

16

Nicoli

Gretchen had the weekends off. I stayed in bed for the most part and moped around the house. I spoke with my mother a few times throughout the weekend, and I could tell she was worried about me. She couldn't understand how I could still be in love with Black. I had only spent a summer with him, which most people would have considered a fling. Why was I not able to move on? Why was I still in love with a man who didn't love me?

Sunday morning I went to my church, Christian Cultural Center on flatlands in East New York, Brooklyn. The reverend preached on love and being stagnated. He said that we should stop looking back and move forward and how we have to know when to let go. He made reference to how we are creatures of habit and that we as women should stop sitting around for someone to rescue us because ain't nobody coming. He said that sometimes it's just you and God. He said that if you meet a person it should be love at first sight. If not, then you're compromising. He said that when you find that person, make him put a ring on your finger to profess his love. He made everything seem so simple as he emphatically preached his sermon. As if men with rings and commitment were easy to find. I'll admit that for the umpteenth time I prayed that God would lead Black back into my arms and for the umpteenth time Black had ignored me. I took the last part of his sermon to heart when he said that when God is gonna bless us, all we have to do is show up. God works through us....

That evening I made a Caesar salad, steamed shrimp and churned homemade vanilla ice cream. I rented two movies from Blockbuster and was just about ready to relax when the doorbell rang. It was just past six o'clock. I hadn't expected Black at least until nine. I buzzed him in and opened the door. I stood impatiently waiting, thinking about my food getting cold. I expected Black to toss the baby in my arms and turn back around as he'd done on so many occasions, but this time he came off the elevator, and when he saw me he smiled.

Is he smiling at me? I wondered.

"Hey, Nicoli," he said.

"H-H-Hey," I stammered.

"Our son is a trip. I took him to the Bronx zoo yesterday and he was already flirting with the pretty ladies. One lady walked by and he pulled the bottom of her skirt." He laughed.

My stomach squirmed the moment he mentioned other women. I wanted to trip out and say, "You better not have my son around your skank-ass bitches," but I knew that wasn't my place. Besides, Black would flip.

"Like father like son," I said dryly and reached out for Black Jr. who was sleeping peacefully in his father's arm.

"I got him," Black said, pushing inside the apartment. He walked to the back and put the baby in bed. He came out of the room and said, "Ummm, something smells good."

"I cooked," I replied as I sat down on the floor and pressed Play on the DVD player. I assumed that Black would show himself out.

"Since when you know how to cook?" he joked.

"It's an acquired skill," I said and realized he was towering over me. He'd actually been in my apartment more than five minutes. I didn't have a clue as to what he wanted until he said it.

"I'm starving. Would you mind if I joined you for dinner?"

I sat frozen as a deer blinded by headlights. He continued, "But if I'm imposing I could just take a plate home. You may be having company."

"No. I mean, no...there isn't an imposition. You can stay for dinner.

I've made enough," I said and decided to add, "I wouldn't have anyone around our son."

One part of me wished I hadn't said that last part once it came out. I don't know how he took that last line. Did he think that I was seeing someone but wouldn't allow them around our son or that I was pretending to be dating someone and said that line to get him jealous?

When I put his plate on the table, he said he wanted to join me on the floor in front of the television.

"Would you like Merlot?"

"Why not?" he said. "What movie you watching?"

"*Beauty Shop* with Queen Latifah," I said.

"I like her," he added.

"Me too," I replied, then there was an awkward silence.

As the movie progressed, we both laughed at the funny parts until we both had loosened up. When the white girl in the film dropped it like it was hot, Black burst out into laughter.

"She hasn't got anything on you," he encouraged. "Show her how to do it."

I knew that the Merlot was going to both our heads, but I couldn't resist being the center of attention again. I reveled in attention, and Black was the man I wanted to receive it. I jumped up and started dropping it like it was hot, but I was acting goofy. I wasn't taking his request seriously.

"No, not like that. You're playing. Do it like you mean it," he said and licked his full lips. My pussy started pulsating, and my heart fluttered. I hadn't had dick in almost two years, and I didn't know if my performance was going to procure me any, but I began dropping it like it was hotter than hell.

Slowly, I dipped to the floor and then came up slowly. I twirled around and stuck my ass in his face then began to grind. Black pulled me down to my knees and looked directly in my face. He brought his hands up and cupped my face. Then he turned it from the right side and then left, scrutinizing each inch.

"It's a miracle," he said incredulously. "Your scars are gone."

I wished Black would look deep in my eyes and see that I still love him. Make a move that would let me know that he was interested in fostering a relationship with me again, but he didn't, although this was the closest he'd come to spending any time with me or having any kind of contact with me. One part of the night gave me hope and the other made me feel the angst of wanting him.

"Yeah, I'm all healed," I responded.

Black let my face go and returned to watching the movie. I guess bringing up my scars reminded him of why we weren't together and killed his mood. He remained virtually silent for the rest of the movie then left shortly thereafter. I climbed in my bed and cried myself to sleep until I didn't have any more tears.

17

Jinx

We only had two air conditioners for the whole house, and they seemed to be on their last legs. It was just after 9:00 P.M., and I needed to cool off. I felt myself starting to perspire after I had a hard time looking for a pair of shoes I wanted to wear out that night. They were a pair of Pradas that I'd gotten in New York at a showroom two years ago. Retail, these shoes would go for six hundred dollars or more. I'd gotten them for $150. I usually had my pick of expensive shoes from showrooms because I had such small feet. I wore a perfect size 36 in European shoes.

Dexter was having a pool party at Prep high school on Van Siclen between Hegeman and Linden Boulevard for the Memorial Day weekend. Everybody who didn't go to Miami South Beach would be there, which should be cool. I had just taken out my Alicia Keys' hair extensions, and was back to rocking my Mohawk. After a nice cool shower, I had began getting dressed when my phone rang. Immediately I ran to it and yup, it was Shawn. Finally. After I'd spoken to Nana, I decided to listen to what he had to say and he took forever to call back. I must admit it was nice having a man beg and plead for me. I don't know but we as women can overdo it a little at times by being too stubborn. I wasn't holding out anymore. Shawn had been all I thought about since he gave me the bad news.

"Hello," I said with attitude. I guess I didn't know when to quit.

"What's up?" he retorted less than enthusiastically and I could tell that I had set the tone of the conversation.

"Nothing," I replied with a little less bass.

"Jinx, look, I fucked up, but I'm not going to keep playing this game. Either you can forgive me or you can't. It's not that hard to decide. If you don't want me to call you anymore, just say the word and I'll make it happen. Now, what do you want? Do you want to be with me or not?"

Damn…I don't like the way he was talking to me nor the way he just put me on the spot. Like, what am I supposed to say? Yes, I want to be with you. That would be so lame. And I couldn't keep bluffing and say that I didn't want to see him again because he seemed as if he'd had it with apologizing.

"Look, Shawn, if you can prove to me that you're really getting a divorce and that you're not living with your wife then I wouldn't mind starting all over," I said, and I wanted to pat myself on the back by flipping the focus back on him proving himself to me.

"Jinx, I'll do anything at this point. I told you that the papers were in. We just have to divide up our assets. I'm a man, and I'm going to let her keep the house and her car I bought."

Pangs of jealousy appeared, and I felt my stomach twisting up when he mentioned that she'd keep the house and car.

"That's what you should do," I said, although I didn't mean a word. We could use that house and car money. For the next hour I had to listen to him tell me about all the material things he'd bought her. The eighty-thousand-dollar engagement ring, the European car, furs, Gucci, Prada—he bought it.

"I'm a good dude…," he droned on. "A girl doesn't have to ever worry about having a problem with me because when I'm in a relationship I play by all the rules."

"Rules?"

"Yes. When I'm in a relationship there are things I don't do for fear of losing the person I love. For instance, I'm not running up in Sue's Rendezvous, the strip club while my girl is at home alone. I know how to play my position. I don't ask for much in a relationship, and I don't want much but loyalty. My girl doesn't have to work or cook if she doesn't want to.

I'm okay with that because I'm a man. I don't cheat—"

"You've never cheated on your wife?"

"Never."

"What about on a girlfriend?"

"I just said that I don't cheat. I don't have to walk down the aisle to be faithful. I've had three other relationships before my wife, and I've always been faithful. It's the other way around. The first time I got my heart broken, it was by the first girl I ever loved. I started noticing a change in her behavior. I'd invite her over, and she'd always have plans. One day my man said he saw her kissing another chick. I asked her about it, and she didn't deny it. That incident broke my heart. I mean I was really torn apart. I could never put someone out like that because I know how it feels."

Listening to him talk, my feelings started to grow. It was rare a man professing to being faithful with so much conviction that I believed him.

"But technically you're still married. Isn't what we're doing, cheating?" I blurted out.

"Jinx, I'm still a man. The moment my wife asked for divorce and I moved out, I don't feel as if I'm cheating. She feels the same way. She has a boyfriend."

"Are you jealous? Of her boyfriend," I asked.

"I'm over her. If I wasn't I wouldn't have left. Like I told you, we had already stopped living as husband and wife a year before I packed up."

"But why did you two break up? You never told me what happened."

"It was a series of events, but I started to realize that she wasn't the woman I thought I married. I don't know if I told you but my wife is white, and her brother would say little shit about me, and she wouldn't take up for me. She'd come home and tell me little shit and expected me to be okay with it."

A white wife? I thought. *If he likes white women why is he hollering at me?*

"Would he say racist things?" I asked.

"He'd say all sorts of shit. I started to realize there wasn't any loyalty there, and that's the one thing that I value most. You have to always be with me. Everyone else is against us," he lectured.

We'd been on the phone for so long Breezy was already knocking at my door and I wasn't even dressed. With cell phone still glued to my ear I crept downstairs to the door and opened it. I put my finger to my lips alerting her to be quiet. She looked from my naked body to the phone and her eyes immediately grew small. I knew she was pissed but she also understood that I liked this one. I chatted for another five minutes with Breezy glaring at me before I hung up.

"Don't tell me that was the broke, lying, married journalist."

"Breezy, he's not even like that. He explained everything, and I believe him."

"Okay," she said dismissively. I could tell she wasn't in the mood for me to defend him, but I wanted to.

"If I were him I wouldn't have told me the truth yet either. I mean, I had told him that I hadn't been in a relationship for three years."

"You told him that?"

"Yeah. It's the truth."

"That was stupid. Didn't anyone ever teach you not to let your right hand know what your left hand is doing?"

"What?"

"My dad taught me that when I was knee high. Never go into any relationship divulging all your secrets. He'll use it against you. For all you know he's already used it against you."

"Breezy, this isn't a game."

"Sure it is. It's always a game. One of you is going to get their hearts broken. And it seems that you've set the stage to be it."

"He's different. He's not like anyone I've dated in the past. You should listen to him speak," I pleaded then continued. "He told me all about how he's monogamous in his relationships and how he plays by all the commitment rules, that when he's in a relationship it's all about him and the girl. He pays all the bills because a women isn't supposed to come out her pocket."

"Jinx, it seems as if you have your mind already made up on what type of man he is. I'm just going to tell you to be careful because he seems like he's playing you. He may be a little over your head. I'm sorry if what I'm saying hurts, but I keeps it one hundred."

"I feel you, and I know you're just worried because how my last relationship ended. I know you love me and wouldn't want me to go through what I did with Jason. I'll be cautious with him. I promise."

"Get dressed," she said sternly. "You got all these men out here with money from East New York to Bed-Stuy trying to get with you, and you want to go for a married writer. What's up with you? You're not the Jinx I know."

"Breezy, all those guys spell trouble. I've been there. Having my dude stay out all night and then lie about where he slept. Having girls want to fight me simply because I got a man they want. Other girls wanting to befriend me simply because of the man I got. I just want a normal relationship. I'm getting older. I'm almost thirty. I'm not in my early twenties like you and Joy. I want to meet someone and settle down and have his kids."

When we pulled up on Van Siclen you could hear different rap selections blasting from different car stereos. Breezy pulled behind a navy blue .645 BMW with dark tinted windows. As we got out to walk toward the crowd we heard, "Wassup, playa, playaaa."

We turned around, and Joy had rolled down the passenger's side window. Unique was sitting in the passenger's seat. He leaned over and yelled out the window, "What's up, Jinx?"

"Ain't nothing," I replied casually.

"What's good, Unique?" Breezy asked.

"Just taking it day by day," he said humbly, which really meant he was balling out of control.

"Yeah, I saw your ass on *7 Days 7 Nights* looking really silly all hugged up with Inga," Breezy stated.

"Nah, it was the other way around. She wouldn't give me room," he said, pleading his case.

Unique had tried to holla at me on several occasions, but I never gave into his advances. He loves drama. His women are always fighting over him—breaking out his car windows and having his babies. I looked over to Joy to see if she felt a way with Unique giving me that shout-out but if she was angry her face didn't give her away. I guess she realized that we fit the same mold: pretty, light skin and sexy. She had her own personal style, which was loud and ghetto. I had my own style—artsy and reserved.

Even thought the pool party was inside, everyone had made their own party out in front. A few lame chicks walked inside with their bathing suits on. Joy purposely bumped up against one of the girls as she walked by and made her stumble. She didn't even bother to address the blatant disrespect. Joy was the most 'hood girl I knew—a girl who is good to have on your side and bad to have as an enemy. Although she'll deny it to anyone who listens, I believe she had something to do with her ex-best friend's face getting slashed. And with that on your résumé you can hardly be trusted.

An hour later and the whole block was littered with every expensive car you could name. Everyone was outside having the best time. At one point it felt surreal. At times like these I loved living in Brooklyn. I don't think I'd rather live anywhere else. Derrick had brought the liquor out-side, and we were getting drunk when a late-model Range Rover pulled up. It had to be circa 1996. When the uninvited driver stepped out everyone started whispering. It was Havoc, and his name was still fresh on the rumor mill for having murdered his ex-partner Craig and shooting Rachel in the face. She's still in a coma so police haven't been able to get a statement from her. The murder and attempted murder have been on the news every day all day for over a week. We tried to go and see her but her parents aren't taking any chances with visitors, and there's a po-lice guard stationed at her door.

As he walked up the pathway, this dark feeling came over me, and I knew he was guilty. I knew he was there.

"Shut the fuck up bitch," he yelled.

"Havoc, what are you gonna do?" she pleaded.

"Corey, shut that bitch up before I put both y'all to sleep. All I want is that gwap," he demanded.

"Man, you don't even have to go out like this. You know I got kids and shit," Corey pleaded as he was lead into his bedroom with a frightened Rachel trailing behind him.

"Havoc, you can't do this," Rachel begged. "You and I go way back. We used to make love when we were together. You know I can't die. I want to be somebody. I just got my acceptance letter for Brooklyn Law School. I'm a good person..."

Rachel was on the verge of hysterics. Her pleas fell upon deaf ears.

"Didn't I say ain't nobody gonna die up in this motherfucker? Now, lay face down and don't fucking move until I'm long gone. The first person who turns around is getting popped."

Sneakily he grabbed a pillow and put it over the back of Corey's head to muffle the noise. Corey didn't even resist or put up a fight. He knew he was dead the moment Havoc pulled out the burner. Silently he prayed that God watch over his kids....

"BOOM!"

"Noooooooooo," I screamed.

Everyone was startled at my outburst but not more than me. What had just happened? I stared at Havoc and lost my voice. My eyes began to tear up, and I started to walk backward away from him.

"Jinx, what's wrong with you?" Breezy asked.

"I-I-I have to go. It's late. I'm not feeling well. I'll just catch a cab on the corner."

"You just want to go and see that dude. You're not slick." She smiled.

I tried to smile back. I took off down the block in a slight jog and kept turning around to see if Havoc was following me.

I caught a cab instantly and hopped inside for safety. When I got in my room I tried to understand what had happened. How could I have seen those events? Did that really happen? It felt so surreal.

18

She giggled.

"I...think I've had too much to drinkkkk," she slurred then wobbled to my sofa. I watched as she had difficulty concentrating and had a hard time keeping her eyes open.

"What did you puuuutttt...my...drink," she stammered then hiccupped.

My face was stone as I stood with my hands stuffed in my pockets, towering above her. She began to ramble incoherently until she'd loss control of her muscles and collapsed on the floor.

I carried her farther inside of my apartment from the living room and lay her down on my bed. Earlier I had laced her drink with Gamma Hydroxybutyrate, otherwise known as GHB or Liquid E, the date rape drug. GHB is a clear liquid that's a bit salty to taste but mixed with any alcohol, it goes undetected. The reason I choose this predatory drug to help facilitate me in apprehending my victims is because if used in a large amount, it incapacitates your victim quickly. GHB metabolizes rapidly and is untraceable in the blood stream twelve hours after ingestion.

As I laid her face up on the bed, she grimaced, struggled for a moment then relaxed. Suddenly, she smiled openly and then past back out. I lifted her arm straight in the air, let go and watched it collapse.

Piece by piece, I removed her clothing. She was wearing a Polo shirt

pack of cigarettes and a Guinness Stout beer. I lost track of time speaking with the store owner. As I approached my block there was a car parked with two women standing outside. I looked in the back and there sat the adolescent. One of the women was about to get on her cell phone to call for assistance, and a small crowd had formed. Calmly, I walked over.

"Ma'am, what's happened?" I said. I could tell that the girl was still confused. I took a chance. "That's my daughter."

"This is *your* daughter?" the woman on the phone asked.

"Yes. Her school called, and some of her friends were suspended for sniffing glue. We just came from Kings County emergency room. She's supposed to be upstairs sleeping it off. They gave her a sedative and she's been grounded," I said sternly.

"Well that explains her behavior. She's really out of it. She was walking aimlessly down the block and we decided to call the police."

Inside the car she was mumbling and nodding back and forth. I reached in the back, and the woman helped me scoop her up. Calmly, I thanked the two women for their work and returned upstairs with the girl.

Once inside the apartment I stripped her naked again. I opened her mouth and jerked off. I needed to punish her for being a bad girl. That night I wrapped my hands around her neck and squeezed the life out of her. It was time for her to go. I had had her long enough.

I stuffed her body in a suitcase and put it in my car. I drove three hours to New London, Connecticut, and dumped her body. I wanted the authorities to think she was at least murdered in Connecticut. Let them look for a murderer dwelling in their state. I couldn't take a chance that she'd be identified by the same two women and have the authorities come knocking on my front door. I couldn't risk my freedom on a worthless cunt like her.

19

Breezy

When I turned nine years old, my father said he knew I was a precocious child and enrolled me in every thought-provoking hobby he could afford. When I entered high school, I spoke five languages fluently, played four instruments and had a full scholarship to four Ivy League schools. I knew I was every man's dream girl, but still I would vacillate between using my intelligence to carve out a lucrative career or to guarantee me a lucrative marriage. My father, who was my anchor and guidance made it very clear from my adolescence that he was pushing for the latter. He didn't want my being a woman to be my condemnation as it was for my mother and many other young girls growing up in poverty. He said that either I'd be a genius or he'd make me study hard and be something akin to it.

I had been honing the craft of chess every day, although after our last encounter Black hadn't been in touch. I called him the next day to tell him that I had a wonderful time at dinner, but he allowed me to go to voicemail. After leaving the message I knew better than to call again. Patience is virtuous, and I knew that he'd call—eventually. He was trying to confuse me and have me overthink our dinner together. He'd suggested that I come to his place, and I politely declined. In other words he's trying to tell me that if he makes that suggestion again, if I don't want to be put on punishment—or worst cut off completely—I'd better go with the flow. I wasn't worried about Black. I had been preparing for this encounter all my life.

Speaking of the devil, just as I was about to climb in bed for the night, my cell phone rang.

"Hello," I whispered in the phone as if he'd just awoken me from a peaceful sleep.

"Did I wake you?" he questioned.

"Who's this?"

"Black," he said, not disguising the annoyance in his voice.

"Yes, I'm sleep. I've had a long day. May I call you later on in the week?" I said dismissively.

"Yeah, sure," he replied then called, "Breezy."

"Yes?"

"I wanted to know if you were free for dinner this Friday. I've been really busy with work and I...um...missed you."

"I'll have to look at my calendar. I'll call you to follow up," I said and abruptly hung up before he could say another word.

At this point he was wondering how the conversation went the way it did. He was probably kicking himself. I'm sure he thought that the average woman would have not only snapped out of her grogginess but invited him over for a nightcap, booty call and full body massage. I knew not to second-guess my quick thinking. And the next day, slightly after two in the afternoon, his actions confirmed what I already knew when he called me again. I grinned and said out loud, "Didn't I say I'd call *you*?" I was only having fun with myself as I picked up the telephone.

"Hello, this is Breezy," I said with my mature voice in rare form.

"Hi, Breezy. This is Black," he said. "Are you busy?"

That was more like it. Tell me who you are. Don't just assume I know.

"No, I'm actually off today. How are you?"

"I'm doing well. Listen, I have to apologize for not getting back to you sooner. I was a little tied up."

"No need for an apology. I've been a little busy as well."

"Are you free for dinner this Friday?"

"Friday's no good for me," I said and purposely allowed a pregnant pause.

"I was looking for—"

"I was wondering if you'd like to go to the Metropolitan this Saturday evening."

"The Met?" he asked.

"Yes. Giuseppe Verdi is starring in *Rigoletto*, and I wanted to know if you'd like to accompany me. That's if you like opera."

"Truthfully, I've never been to the opera, but I'd love to go. What's the name of it again and I'll get us the tickets," he suggested.

"I invited you so I'll pay. Besides, the tickets are quite expensive."

He chuckled but didn't respond.

Black and I met in front of the Met thirty minutes before it was slated to start. I told him how strict they were. If you were late, you'd have to wait outside until intermission, meaning you'd miss the first half. He was shocked at the rules and regulations. I told him this wasn't hardly a ten-dollar movie. Before we entered, I told him the premise of the opera and that it was in Latin.

"If you don't speak Latin, they have a teleprompter in front of your seat and you can read the words in English."

"In Latin? All these people pay to read a screen."

"Not everyone is reading the screen," I said.

"I know most of us will be," he said then continued, "Right?"

"You're on your own with that."

"You understand Latin?"

"Yes. I speak and write Latin fluently."

Black stared in awe but said nothing. I knew he didn't want to barrage me with a slew of compliments. He didn't have to say it. I knew that was impressive.

As the lights dimmed and the spectacular stage lit up with the magnificent costumes and the opera singers bellowing voices, Black was like a child at the ice capades. He was so taken aback. I peeked over and his eyes were sparkling.

After the opera, Black and I walked a couple of blocks to a perfect little hideaway that I'd been coming to since I was a little girl. I had reservations for two at Cuisine Exquise, a French restaurant where the menu and wine list were only in French. Since this was my dime I wanted to spend it wisely. When we sat down, our waiter came over and said,

"Bonsoir, Madame. Il est si bon de vous revoir." He was greeting me and saying that he was happy to see me.

"Pierre, c'a été un long temps. Vous semblez wondeful. Et c'est mon ami, son nom est Black." I introduced him to Black.

"Monsieur Black, plaisir. Que dinerez-vous dessus ce soir?" He looked to Black and asked what he would be dining on.

"Nous prendrons le canard rôti, des bouts d'asperge avec de la sauce hollandaise des pommes de terre de bébé. Et quant au vin, nous prendrons le chardonnay."

I took the liberty of ordering us both roasted duck, asparagus tips with hollandaise sauce and baby potatoes.

"Merci beaucoup."

After I took the liberty to order dinner and our waiter had poured our wine, Black leaned in and grabbed my hand into his strong masculine grip and gently squeezed.

"So, you speak English, Latin and French? Anything else?"

I lifted my drink, playfully ignoring his question and said in German, *"Ein Toast zu unserer Zukunft."*

"You're amazing." Black chuckled then got serious and continued, "I think you're the most intriguing woman I've met in a long time."

"Why because I speak five languages?"

"Five? What's the fifth?"

"¿Cómo es usted?" I said while smiling.

"No, seriously, it's not just that. It's rare that you find a woman who's beautiful, smart, independent, no kids, and sexy who's not either a bitch or crazy or both."

"Let me guess: Your last girlfriend was crazy?"

"Ain't all women?" he challenged.

"I find that remark so unimaginative. All men say the same thing. Their exes were crazy. Did you *make* her crazy?"

"I didn't do anything but love her," he said, and there was despair in his eyes as he looked past me yearning for what he no longer had.

"Well perhaps you could rekindle the magic."

Black made a lemon-sucking face and his eyes grew smaller, making his thick eyebrows furl together, forming one line and said, "We tried that once. There are no encores."

Something made me wonder if he was being totally honest with himself and if Nicoli had what it would take to get back in his good graces.

Not if I have a say in his future, I thought.

"I'm the same way. I can't go back. If it's over, it's over. Whatever reason for the separation will pop up the second go-round."

After dinner, once again Black invited me to his apartment, and for the second time I politely declined. I wasn't making it too easy for him. Besides, all men love the chase. They're hunters by nature.

20

Jinx

Once Shawn and I worked through all my fears about his past, we were able to really click. He was the sweetest, gentlest, honest man I've ever met. One night, he invited me to his apartment in the Bronx where he was going to cook for me. I asked if he wanted me to help, but he said he wanted to do this for me.

It's been three months since we've been seeing each other, and for some reason I've been holding back with sleeping with him. Mainly because I wanted to make sure that he's not lying about him and his wife being separated. I know that when I get there he's going to want to have sex. He's been so patient. As I was preparing, I couldn't help but get a little nervous. Sex for the first time with a new person is always awkward. I hope he didn't disappoint me and vice versa.

After I showered, I decided to wet my Mohawk and leave it curly. I put on a pair of costume chandelier earrings, pink Lip Glass from MAC and pink eye shadow. I decided on a white jean mini skirt from Allen B. that I adorned with Swarovski crystals. I put my name, Jinx, on my ass in hot pink. A white wife beater T-shirt and a pair of Manolo Blahnik stilettos, circa 1999, completed my look.

Shawn called when he was out front and told me to come outside. The thing I didn't like about him was that he was such a private person.

He had yet to come inside to say hello to Nana. He said that he's not social and that I should respect that.

When I came outside and flung open his car door, he smiled with his eyes at my outfit but didn't give me a compliment. It's okay. I knew I looked good.

As his tires gripped the pavement on the Belt Parkway, I looked out the window at the lights illuminating the city. We were heading to the Major Deegan Expressway to take us into the Bronx. I didn't have a clue about anything in the Bronx. At some point during the ride he put on some freaky sounding music and began bopping his head to the beat. He looked so peculiar trying to keep one beat when there were about twenty different rhythms going on.

"What are you doing?" I asked.

"This my shit. Listen," he said and turned the annoying music up louder. *"Bitch, pop that pussy in and out pop it baby pop it pop it!"*

I screwed up my face and said, "You like techno music?"

He turned it back down.

"I love it. I grew up in a techno music area. The Bronx loves techno music. You should see them on the dance floor. They be blazin'."

"Blazing?"

"Yeah. You never heard that saying before?"

"No. What does it mean?" I asked. Without letting him answer, I said, "That they can really dance?"

"Uh-huh. I wish I could dance…" he said and drifted momentarily off into his own thoughts. "They got this new dance out where it looks like you're riding on a mechanical bull."

Shawn began gesticulating, trying to show me the moves while driving, and I laughed hysterically. He was awful. I hope his lack of rhythm didn't transfer into the bedroom because if it did we were in for a boring night.

As we drove down the dim-lit Bronx streets I couldn't help but feel a little intimated, and I couldn't understand why. Maybe it was because of the horror stories Shawn had told me regarding his area. We passed by small, decrepit houses and a tenement building with a large group of teenagers in front wearing ski masks, and it was eighty degrees outside. I couldn't believe it. Shawn saw the look of disbelief on my face, and he started in.

"All those little dudes are Crips," he explained.

"Why Crips?"

"Look at their back pockets," he observed. "They have blue bandanas in their back pockets."

I looked closely, and he was right. They did have blue bandanas to signal what gang they were in.

"That's so silly. You can only be tough if you have an army behind you," I huffed.

His forehead scrunched together into stiff folds. "Jinx, these little dudes put in work. The Bronx is known for not only originating rap music but getting that paper. They will run up in your house and kill your mother for that paper. They know how to let that thing go," he warned. He seemed almost proud that these young men were killers.

It seemed as if every block we drove down the lighting was almost nonexistent, creating a spooky atmosphere that was unnerving. I couldn't understand why I felt intimidated. I was raised in Brooklyn for the most part, and I know how we put it down out there as well.

"Let's stop with this tough-guy talk. It's giving me the creeps" I begged.

Instead of him listening, he twisted up his face defiantly and continued, "I'm telling you in my day I was a bad boy," he bragged.

Oh gosh, here we go…

"Let's let the past stay there," I pleaded subtly and turned up the radio for emphasis.

Shawn's apartment was fairly decent. He was renting the top floor in a two-family house and had access to the garage. The block didn't look as intimidating as the rest of his neighborhood. He opened his door to gray wall-to-wall carpeting and a futon on his floor.

"I told you that I'm just moving in. I didn't have a chance to go out and buy what I needed. I hope you don't hold this against me," he said sheepishly.

"Don't worry about it. In fact, I'm relived. When you kept putting off me coming to your apartment, I thought that you may be hiding something."

"I knew that's what you thought," he said, pursing his paper-thin lips together. "Jinx, listen. There aren't too many dudes out here like me. I play by all the rules. I would have never approached you if there was still a her and me. That chapter's over. I'm hoping to start a new chapter with you."

I walked farther into his apartment in my stiletto heels, which graced my tiny feet. I purposely took languorous steps, and as I walked my ass spread open. I was hoping he found this sexy. All men did....

One by one, I stepped out of my shoes and left them by the futon. He looked down at my perfect French pedicure and pretended to step on my toes with his Air Nikes. When I jumped he pulled me in close and kissed me. I pulled back to see if he really wanted it. The lust in his eyes confirmed any doubts I may have had. I inhaled his cologne and began to taste his skin. Gently, he put his hand behind my neck and kissed me softly. His kisses slowly moved down to my earlobe, then he began to gently suck my neck. He'd suck and then gently blow, sending a tickly sensation through my body. I stood back and pulled off my T-shirt and let it cascade to the floor. Following my lead he pulled his shirt over his head and let it hit the ground. We stared at each other in silence. Simultaneously he pulled off his jeans while I unbuttoned my skirt and stepped out of it. I stood there in my bra and panties, and he stood there in his boxers. His skinny legs appeared awkward as his boxers swallowed his small lower body frame. The two-tone patches covering his body popped prominently like a neon flashing light. My eyes were drawn to them immediately.

I turned around so that I could refocus, and he took this as a sign to unclasp my bra. My large breasts fell into my hands as he nestled behind me. I could feel his hard dick pressing against my lower back. Slowly, he turned me around to face him. I was still discreetly holding my breasts until he removed my hands and slid my bra off. He licked and sucked my pink nipples and paused for a minute to admire my large areolas.

"You have prefect breasts," he whispered and continued to suck on my nipples until my pussy began to tingle.

We made our way to his futon on the floor and playfully fell upon it with his heavy upper body weight on top of me. He removed his boxers then slowly slid my panties off, parted my legs and buried his face in my pussy. His wet tongue flickered rapidly beating my clit, and then he'd slow down and suck my clitoris while murmuring, "I've been waiting for this..."

I began to rock my hips back and forth, getting lost in the moment. I felt waves of pleasure cascading through my body, and my legs began to uncontrollably tremble. It had been so long since I had had sex that I was extremely horny.

I was silent as I came. The thick liquid gushing from my cave was the only evidence. As he lapped it up, he whispered, "Ummm…you taste so good."

I reached down for Shawn and pulled him up. Instead of letting him enter me, I turned him over to suck his dick. Not many women will admit it, but I will. I love sucking dick.

"Don't move," I commanded as I ran into his kitchen and began rummaging through his cabinets. "Got it."

"Got what?" he asked excitedly.

"Shhhhhh," I said as I covered my lips with my finger. "Close your eyes."

I started off slowly by pouring honey on the tip of his dick. As the gooey liquid slid down his shaft, I looked up to see a smile emerging on his face. At first, I teased him by sucking the tip. As his pickle-shaped dick went in and out of my mouth, I watched intently. I began slobbering all over it and making slurping noises. I arched my neck and opened my jaws wide to deep throat him. My jaws caved in and out, and his moaning encouraged me.

"Ummmm, baby, that feels soooo good," he murmured. "Damn, it feels good."

I went to his sweet balls. I took my left hand and continued to jerk his dick while my warm mouth took in both nuts. My tongue expertly flickered rapidly while pulling them in and out of my mouth. When he started babbling, I knew he was ready to release his juices. I took him fully into my mouth and sucked until he exploded. His cum erupted into my mouth, and I eagerly swallowed his bitter-tasting liquid.

I slid back up and laid on my back in the missionary position. I was extremely aroused as I remembered how much I enjoy sex.

"You sure you ready for this?" he asked and began stroking his juicy dick while towering over me.

"I can't wait," I purred and parted my legs, giving him easy access.

As he applied pressure, my tight cave resisted, and I could feel my body tensing. I began to relax as he methodically slid in. My wet pussy gripped his dick as our bodies moved in unison. We had sex in the frog position, doggy style then I flipped over and rode his dick. Finally, I was ready to cum as he pushed deeper and deeper into my walls. We both screamed out in ecstasy as we climaxed. I fell on top of Shawn, breathing rapidly as he wrapped his strong arms around my waist and held me firmly.

"Are you still in love with your wife?" I curiously asked.

He shook his head. "Not at all. I told you she's already seeing someone."

"Did you cry when y'all broke up?"

Laughing he said, "That's not how men do things. I mean I was hurt for a minute that we couldn't make it work. But sit down and cry—nah, that's not me. I'm not an emotional dude. Women are emotional. Once I knew it was over, I moved on—hung out a lot with my dudes, partied more than I needed to—but that's the extent of it."

"Am I the first girl you've been with since your breakup?"

When Shawn lowered his eyes, I screamed, "Don't answer that. It doesn't matter. I'm here now."

I was so tired that I thought maybe he felt the same way and was going to order out, but I was wrong. He jumped in the shower and told me not to move. He was going to serve me in bed.

"And you better not move," he demanded. "I don't want to have to spank you."

I leaned back on his futon and felt really good. I felt like he could be the one to complete me.

21

Kesha

Most of my fellow officers loved going to court to testify against the perps that they've arrested to ensure that they'd be put away for a long time. For me the process was so mundane and mechanical, yet I know how necessary it is. Working the narcotics unit, I participate in decoy cases, otherwise known as buy-and-bust cases, where a detective goes undercover as a drug addict, buys narcotics and then we swoop down and arrest the drug hustler. Most times we get the hustler and the hook. The hook is the person who will take the drug addict to the drug dealer and help facilitate the buy. The hook doesn't touch the drugs or the money and is usually an addict himself and will get paid in drugs when his shift is over. I wouldn't last five minutes undercover as a drug addict on the streets of Brooklyn. I'm too well-known. My cover would be blown within minutes. Bosco and I usually tread close behind our decoy detective and make the bust, which means a lot of paperwork and a lot of court appearances.

Today, I had to appear in criminal court to testify against a small time drug-hustler named Hector. We busted him on a humble with a half-pound of weed in the car and a half ounce of coke. We knew who he was working for, but he refused to roll over. He was only an eighteen-year-old kid and facing five to seven years in a state penitentiary. This was his second felony, and instead of copping out to a two to five he wanted to take his case to trial.

The assistant district attorney was fucking up big time. She kept stuttering and fumbling her words while making irrelevant objections. While prepping me, although I didn't need to be prepped, she admitted that this was only her second trial. She promised me that she was more than prepared to make grand theatrical gestures. Instead I witnessed a lackluster trial.

Grateful for my input to be over, I headed back to the precinct. As I walked out of criminal court, a mid-afternoon thunderstorm burst through the sky in violent, heavy raindrops that pounded on my shoulders mercilessly. I ran to my car, upset that my thirty-five-dollar hairdo was ruined.

"Just fucking perfect," I muttered while trotting through large puddles in an attempt not to get my shoes saturated in dirty water. When I got to the precinct the rain had stopped and the sun peeked through a few lingering clouds. I went in the locker room and changed my clothes then went to find Bosco, who of course wasn't at work yet. So I walked to the homicide unit and decided to see what my new lover, Darren was doing.

"What's up, D?" I asked as I propped my ass on his desk. He surveyed the room before he touched his dick and said, "You tell me?"

"What's really good?" I asked, which meant "When is your wife going to be missing in action?"

"Tomorrow, all afternoon."

"That's what's up," I said, nodding. I was off the next day, so it was all good.

"Cool," he retorted and began shuffling paperwork on his desk.

"What are you working on?" I asked. Darren always kept me abreast on all the homicide cases that came through. I was more interested in homicide cases than narcotics. I had requested a transfer but these things took time. I was sure that I'd be more viable in this unit because I was good at seeing what the average naked eye couldn't, and I was an excellent interrogator.

"This case just came in early this morning."

"The Brooklyn Butcher?"

"No. It's not connected."

"What's going on with the Night Strangler?" I asked.

"Between you and me, I think that both cases were committed by the same person. I have a strong inkling that the Brooklyn Butcher and the Night Strangler are the same person. I think that he's been in our midst for roughly ten years. He keeps switching up his M.O. for a reason. I just can't put my finger on it. I've been digging into cold case files and each victim, no matter the cause of death, is dropped on a highway in a suitcase. For some reason he wants to remain elusive. He's not ready to reveal himself. That's why he's switching up, going as far as copying other famous serial killers."

"Such as Ted Bundy?"

"Exactly." His voice rose high like a young girl's pitch. "He's clever...very clever, I can't lie. He hasn't slipped up yet, but it's only a matter of time. He'll get cocky. They all do..."

"Damn, I wish I could work this with you," I said, sulking. "These motherfuckers are taking too long to push my transfer through."

"And a lot of work it is. But back to this newer case I'm working. A lady complained that a car was illegally parked blocking her driveway on Hancock Avenue. Blues go over there, pop the trunk and there's a body in it. Thirty-one-year-old male shot twice in the back of the head, execution style," he said as he began pulling out the photos of the scene.

"Oh, you got a live one. Any leads?"

"Not yet, but I'm sure many people wanted to get at him. We ran his fingerprints, and he has a record."

While quickly flipping through the crime scene photos, my gaze stopped on the picture of the victim inside of the trunk of his car with a small opening wound to the back of his head. My throat immediately closed, and my hands began to tremble as Darren and I simultaneously said, "Rick Holman."

My mind raced back to the last day I saw Rick. How he professed his undying love for me and wanted to solidify our fling with marriage.

"Yeah, that's him. How did you know?" Darren asked.

I said nothing.

"Did you know him?" he questioned.

I continued to stare straight ahead.

"Kesha, are you all right?"

"No, I'm not alright," I shouted and began a roof-shaking temper tantrum. "Some fucking body is gonna take a dirt nap for putting my baby to sleep. I swear on my kids that I'm going to find who did this. They must have bumped their fucking head. Everybody knows that he and I go way back like Chinese slippers and jellies. How dare they disrespect me like this."

"Kesha, calm down. I'm sure this didn't have anything to do with you. Whoever did this probably doesn't even know you, and even if they did, I doubt they'd care," he spewed.

"How could this happen? Who would want to murder Rick...he only came up here to see me...to make me see how much he loved me," I mumbled.

"Kesha, what do you know about his murder? Did he mention any beefs? Who was he seeing? Maybe it's over a woman...or drugs. What do you know?"

"I know very little. Listen, I want you to follow up on a beef he had at Juniors Restaurant with some kid from the Bronx. That's all I know."

"That's a start. More than I had a moment ago. Okay, I have my hands full with the Brooklyn Butcher and Night Strangler but I promise you I'll make this case top priority and do everything I can to get justice for your friend," he soothed.

"Promise me that you'll let me ride with you when you put the silver bracelets on—"

"Kesha..."

"Please do this for me. He was a good guy...too good to have been handled like this. And, he wouldn't have even been in Brooklyn if it weren't for me...," I repeated. "I gotta do this. I have to avenge his death, and I need you to ride with me. Can I trust you?"

"Okay. I gotchu."

"Thank you. I have to go. Just promise me..."

"I'll do my best."

22

Jinx

I awoke to Nana playing her worn piano and singing her favorite church hymns. Her voice was melodic as her strong fingers glided across the keys. Whenever I heard her sing and play, it put me in an exceptionally good mood. It was just after nine in the morning, and I went into the living room and sat down next to her. She looked over and nodded to acknowledge me but didn't stop her crooning. It was a Kodak moment as I watched her lovingly massage the piano keys. Her concentration was so deep and freeing that it made her look deceptively young. We sat there for about another hour before she called it a morning.

"Nana, you have to let me record you one day so that I can keep it forever and pass it down to my kids."

"Chile, had you sat still long enough when you was a youngin' you would be able to play these hymns yourself for your own kids."

"I wasn't any good at the piano. My fingers are too short. You said so yourself. I needed long, slender fingers."

"I ain't never said no foolishness like that. You could have made a lot of money playing the piano. What's the name of that gal you look like. Emma…Emma…"

"Alicia Keys, Nana."

"Yeah. Emma Keys. Look at all the money she done made for her grandma. I bet she done bought her grandma a big ol' house."

"Nana, that piano alone didn't buy any homes. Let's not forget she has a powerful voice."

"So," Nana said, being as stubborn as only a seventy-seven-year-old Taurus could be. I looked at her with her hands perched on her hips and her lips pursed up toward the sky. Her silvery-white hair was in two plaits just as she liked, sticking up toward the sky. She had on a worn house-dress and a pair of pink slippers with her toes exposed. How I loved this old lady. I went and gave her a big bear hug and planted a wet, sloppy kiss on her face. She pretended to be annoyed but I knew better.

"Get off me," she protested. "You need to save some of them kisses for your young fella."

Now that she mentioned him, where was my fella? I hadn't heard from him since he called me early yesterday afternoon. He said he was going to pick up his son and that he'd call me in a few hours. I grabbed my cell phone as I went to take a shower and called. When I went to voicemail, a strange feeling came over me. I felt slighted.

Where was he?

I left a short message asking him to call me when he was free, jumped in the shower and headed to the gym. When I came out of the gym I had four voice messages. Eagerly, I listened and none of them were from Shawn. Concerned, I called his phone again only to go to voicemail. This time I hung up before leaving a message. I called Breezy back to tell her that I wanted to go with her and Joy to club Reign.

When I got home I engrossed myself in my work. I had sketched out this funky orange dress with a low neckline and spaghetti straps. Using my tailors chalk I made the style lines for the sloper then cut out the pattern. With my T-square ruler and stick pins, I draped the muslin over the man-nequins. I was making this for a perfect size-five woman, and I already had those specs. After I finished this, I decided to cut two more patterns. I wanted to make a pencil and a flare skirt for my showroom.

The more it irked my nerves that Shawn hadn't called me the harder I worked. When I finally looked up it was just past midnight. Although I was glad that I'd gotten a lot accomplished and that it had taken my mind off Shawn, I couldn't help but still be pissed that it was after midnight and he wasn't ringing my phone off the hook. Frustrated, I called again. And guess who went to voicemail?

"I don't know what is up with you not returning my calls but you better call me sooner than later," I screamed into the phone and slammed it down.

I didn't know if his actions had anything to do with a little incident we had the other day. Shawn has an annoying habit of keeping you on hold forever when you call. I called him yesterday and he placed me on hold. I sat on hold for over fifteen minutes and he never clicked back over. That wasn't the first time he'd done that. I hung up and he never called back to apologize for his blatant disrespect.

I shook off that assumption…he can't be that childish. Could he?

I was so glad to be going out or else I may have called a zillion more times. This time when Breezy came to the door I was ready. She already had Joy with her, propped up in the front seat.

"Wassup, playa, playaaa?" Joy smiled.

"Hi, gorgeous," I said jovially even though I was so angry my ears were burning.

As Breezy drove down Atlantic Avenue, I leaned way back into her plush bucket leather seats trying to block out what I felt was obvious. He was working. He had to be or else why would he treat me like this and I acted like a fool screaming on him like that. The only thing that made me feel better was the prospect of apologizing in the morning.

"What's up with the married writer?" Joy asked and I felt my pressure go back up.

"He's not married."

"Oh, he got the divorce," she pursued knowing full well that she was trying to be smart.

"Seen Nicoli lately?" I retorted.

"Nope. Sure haven't," she admonished. "But I did see Jason."

"Merry fucking Christmas," I said underneath my breath and was prepared to end it there when all of a sudden, I flipped.

"You're one miserable, silly dumb girl. Do you think I care about you seeing my ex? All you're getting is a lying, misogynistic, woman-beating deadbeat who just so happens to be a record producer. You think you got something? He don't give a damn about you. The only reason he's even messing with you is because he's still in love with me! He still wants me!" I screamed while pounding my fist on my chest for emphasis.

"Oh no she didn't," Breezy tried to joke to lighten the situation but it was too late.   "Bitch, are you stupid? Jason and I go way back like Now and Laters and Lemonheads. I fucked him before you. Continued to fuck him during you. And will still fuck him after you. Oh, you didn't know? You should have asked somebody."

Ain't that a bitch? I couldn't even get mad because he and I were through. In fact, her admission only makes my decision to leave him more warranted.

I swallowed hard, "All that fucking no wonder you're always second to number one. Your banged-up pussy don't have the strength to make it to first position!"

"Please don't make me sling this pussy on your new beat. Jinx, please, please don't make me do that to you," she threatened, then continued, "You're lucky he's broke…and married."

"Whatever."

I decided to let her get the last words. She could have Jason. Shawn was totally off limits. He wasn't in her caliber. He was too classy to be conned by a slutty piece of a woman like Joy.

When Breezy made the left onto Washington to go and park under the train trestle, she slowed down just in time to catch a full-on brawl. About thirty guys were thumping in front of the club. All you saw were punches being thrown, faces being pounded, guts being stomped out and then, yup, guns being fired. We ducked down, only for a second, then popped our nosy heads back up to see the rest of the fight. Most of the guys we knew from East New York and the Stuy. It was going down B.K. style, and nobody was breaking shit up. When we saw Butter hauling ass down the block and Chopper chasing after him we kinda figured out what was up. Butter had just started resurfacing into the limelight after he had snitched on more than a handful of niggas. Chopper's brother was one of them. Butter had given back thirty-four years of fed time, and it seemed that he didn't have one regret. He came home last year and had laid low. A couple of weeks ago his name started ringing again in the East—where he's from. He was driving around in the new CLS 500 and sporting all the obligatory jewels. We ran into a few dudes that his release didn't sit too well with. Whether they knew the men he snitched on or not, it was never acceptable to snitch in the 'hood. Rumor had it that the feds turned him loose to bring down even more drug dealers. Meanwhile, Butter was living the American Dream. I heard that he owned a few businesses and a huge estate out in New Jersey. He was stupid enough to take a few chicks there that came back and gave the full 'hood report.

The gun cannon sounded.

"Did you hear that shit?" Breezy asked.

"Hell yeah. It came from up the block," Joy replied.

At this point my eyes were popped open. As the blue-and-whites finally descended on the area, everyone scattered. Many bumrushed the door to the club and ran back inside, most likely to hide their weapons.

Two police officers pounced on Breezy's jeep with their weapons drawn.

"Turn off the fucking ignition and put your hands where I can see them," one officer yelled while the squad car had its lights beamed into the jeep. Breezy did as she was told, and we all put our hands in the air. Once he saw that we were women, it didn't stop him from cursing us out as if we were parasites.

After the barrage of insults, Breezy was able to give him her PBA card along with her license.

"My sister's on the force," she stated calmly.

"Who's your sister?"

"Detective Kesha Brown. Eighty-eight precinct," she lied.

"Detective Brown is your sister?" he said and finally lowered his gun. "Yes."

"Your sister is one of the good guys. Did you see anything?" Breezy shook her head.

"Just as we pulled up we heard shots. We ducked down and I called my sister. She told me to keep my head down and not to move until the shots stopped firing, then she told me to get the hell out of here, that she'd call the police."

"Okay, you did good, kid. Go home, we'll take it from here."

As we drove off we started giggling because we were amped up on adrenaline. Just as Breezy was about to turn right to take me home, Joy suggested she go straight where she'd seen Chopper follow Butter and heard the gunshots. We crept slowly down the block, and in between a red Camry and black Pathfinder was Butter shot full of holes. His whole body was leaking and his eyes were popped open. Half of his brain had been blown away. We knew Chopper did it. And we all knew that we wouldn't tell a soul. The rule is: Don't snitch. Right?

23

Breezy

I got up early this morning and went to my aunt's house. It was just a couple of blocks away. I knew that Nicoli dropped by every Sunday and brought the baby over to visit. I got there before Nicoli and waited.

"Hi, auntie," I said as she came to the door.

"Brooklyn?" she said as if she was unsure.

"Breezy, auntie. They call me Breezy now. How's everything?" I asked.

"Chile, come in and give ya aunt a hug. I ain't seen you since you were knee high with a nappy ponytail and acne," she said, and my stomach squirmed.

"Well no naps, no bumps and I've grown," I said as I pushed past her.

"Well I didn't mean to offend you. I just meant that I haven't seen you in a long time."

"I know what you meant."

"So what brings you around here? You know Nicoli don't live here no more."

"I didn't come for Nicoli. I came to see you. My father...I think he's sick. It may be cancer," I lied.

"Oh Jesus, Lord, no..." she said and held her chest as if she couldn't breathe.

"He won't talk to me, and I don't have anyone to talk to. I can't lose my father. Not after what happened to my mother."

"Chile, you ain't gonna lose your father. If I know my brother. He's a fighter. What the doctors say?"

"Well, I don't know if he's been diagnosed with prostate cancer but I know he went to get tested and ever since then he's been acting strange."

Just as I was in the middle of telling her my sob story, Nicoli walked in. She still had a key. We locked eyes for a moment before she broke the stare, smiled and said hello. You could tell that the initial reaction was hate. But then I guess she reminded herself that she's changed. Her face softened.

"Brooklyn, what are you doing here? I haven't seen you in a while. Is everything all right," she said as she struggled with the baby's carriage. I didn't bother to help. I examined the little toddler closely. For his mother to be stunning and his father handsome, he wasn't a cute little thing. His hair looked coarse and his small, beady eyes and pudgy cheeks made him resemble Stuart Little. He had two huge front teeth peeking out of his gums, which made it necessary for his mouth to remain gapped open. Saliva oozed down his shirt, and his large head kept lolling to the side of his stroller. *If this is the best-looking baby his father's sperm could create, I'll pass,* I thought.

"Brook—Breezy is here 'cause her daddy may be a little sick."

"Oh no, what is it," she said, trying to sound alarmed. Inwardly I wondered if her sincerity was authentic.

We talked for a while about my dad before we both loosened up in each other's presence. On the low, I inspected her face up close and personally, and you could hardly see the scars. I had to say, "Your face healed up nicely."

I saw her squirm in her seat. I'm sure the experience still haunts her.

"Three plastic surgeries later I'm back to about ninety-five percent of my regular self. I'll never be a hundred percent perfect but the doctors did a hell of a job. If you look closely you can still see the scars."

"Three surgeries. That must have been expensive," I probed.

"Well my son's father paid for each surgery."

"What's your son's name?" I asked and looked over at her baby.

"Black King, Jr. He wouldn't have it any other way," she said and laughed. I laughed, too, only I didn't find anything funny.

"Oh, so you guys are still together?"

"No. We went our separate ways before the baby was born, but I'm sure you knew that already," she said, and I saw a glimpse of the *old* Nicoli.

"If I knew I wouldn't have asked. If you didn't get the memo, I'll tell you. Nobody really cares about your personal business. I never have and never will. I was just trying to make small talk. I didn't come to see you anyway. I came to see your mother. My dad is sick if you've forgotten already," I said. I put heavy emphasis on my head and hand movement.

She played right into my hands.

"Breezy, I'm sorry if I was rude. I don't know why we dislike each other when we're first cousins. It shouldn't be like this," she pleaded. "I guess I'm still sour about not being with my son's father."

"I guess I can understand. I would want to be with my child's father as well. Especially if I still loved him. Do you love him?"

"With all my heart. When he comes to pick up the baby my heart aches. I can barely look him in his eyes from fear that I'll break down and cry."

"Well why you don't tell him how you feel?"

"I've done that on numerous occasions but he just doesn't care. I hurt him as a man, and he can't ever forgive me for that."

"Did you cheat?"

"It was a combination of things. I was still young wanting to make an impression on all my friends. At that time, I was truly immature, and I had to be seen all the time, whereas Black, he likes a flashy women but she has to put a curb on it. She can't run the streets wildly yet she can't be too conservative. Bottom line is that I didn't play by all the rules. I stepped outside, gambled, and in the end I lost the best man I'll ever have."

"So how did you get him in the first place?" I said and realized I was being too forward. I needed to clean it up. "I mean why did you get with him? You were so pretty you could have your pick at any man you wanted. Why didn't you go after someone much younger? Or did he come after you?"

"Both. I knew I wanted him the first time I laid eyes on him. I knew who he was and what he was worth. In the beginning it was only about money. There were a lot of players at the barbecue but I knew I wanted Black. He wanted me as well. He flirted the whole night, and I ended up in his bed."

"Y'all fucked on the first night?" I laughed.

"Did we," she said and paused as if she was reminiscing. "When I woke up the next morning he seemed content at keeping me around."

"Just like that? What did you do to him in that bedroom." I laughed, and she joined in.

"Well that's private. But when I tell you I miss the ground he walks on, that my heart hurts day and night. That when I look in my son's eyes sometimes I burst out into tears because he looks so much like his father. I'm not telling you a lie."

I sat listening to this dumb broad. She was speaking as if I should break out the violins. The bottom line was she had a good catch and was stupid enough to lose him. Don't cry now. The problem was that Nicoli thought she was too cute for a nigga to let her go. Black proved her wrong, and it's fucking with her ego.

I drilled her until I had gotten all the ammunition I needed to fully develop my personality to snatch Black up. I planned on practicing how to vacillate between Breezy, the educated girl from the 'hood to Breezy, the educated teacher with class. I needed to be less animated. No more hand and head gestures. I left and promised to keep in touch with my aunt and Nicoli who gave me her home telephone and asked for me not to be a stranger.

I'll call but only if I need to, I thought.

24

Nicoli

I tried being the born-again Nicoli who's left her scheming days in the past and that routine has run the gamut. It's already stale and dried up just like my sex life if I don't start being proactive in getting my man back. I mean, a little manipulation never hurt anyone. I was so depressed these past two years that I hated being awake. If it were not for my son, I don't know how I would have made it. Now, a scalpel, needle and thread has given me a new lease on life, and I'll be a smart girl in fool's clothing if I don't capitalize off my second chance.

As I sat around plotting my next move, I walked to the terrace and opened the doors to enjoy the soft summer breeze. I sat on my chaise longue and watched my sheer silk curtains billow in the wind. It was so soothing that I didn't realize how long I'd sat in the same spot staring off into space.

I need to foster a relationship with Black that exceeds past our son, I thought. *But how?*

I needed Black to remember how he used to feel about me. He used to love me once, and I needed him to remember the good and not the worst times we shared. At this point, his memories about us were toxic. I needed to connect to him again before it was too late. I'm sure he's seeing someone…I know someone is sharing his bed. And that's fine—

for now. I'm planning to have an emotional affair with Black because that's just as effective as a physical affair. Once I can get that bond back, I'll have Black back. And this time I won't take him for granted.

I had a little over twenty-four hours to come up with a plan to shamelessly make Black fall back in love.

After hours of pondering through my options and brainstorming ideas with my old pal Stacy, we finally came up with the perfect strategy. I realized that I'd be most endearing as a damsel in distress. If I were vulnerable and helpless his male instinct would immediately kick in. First, I'd try to be stoic but I was counting on him to try to overpower my objections and lay down the law.

"So, Stacy, this has to work," I gleefully announced.

"I hope so. What if he doesn't give a shit and leaves you to fend for yourself? Are you prepared to handle that?"

"I'll have to, but I won't give up. If this doesn't work I'll have to be more creative."

"I hear that. So how are you gonna pull off being sick? Don't you think he'll see right through that?"

"I haven't thought of that yet. But it'll have to be believable. Black's no dummy," I declared.

By nightfall, I had thought of a master plan. I turned down my central air conditioning to sixty degrees and then went downstairs and had a massive workout. I did ninety minutes of cardio so every pore on my body was open. Then I sat in the sauna room for another hour then went back up to my frigid apartment. I slept without any clothing or sheets covering my body. I gritted my teeth as I trembled throughout the night. When I awoke in the morning my throat was sore and I felt a sickness coming on, but I needed more. I called Black to tell him that I wasn't feeling well and asked if he could keep BJ until Monday. He sounded more skeptical than concerned but that was okay. I didn't have time to convince him—I had a plan to execute. I did this routine throughout the weekend and come Monday morning my body was screaming for relief. I had acquired a deep, haggard cough with runny nose and fever. I purposely pulled all of my cough medicine from the refrigerator and poured the liquids down the sink. I left just a smidgen of Buckley's in the bottle for appearance. Empty cough medicine bottles littered my dresser. I put a heavy quilt on my bed, turned off the air conditioner and put on the heat. I took my hair loose from my ponytail and left it wild and untamed on top of my head. I slipped into a sexy negligee with a matching silk robe to cover up my scantily clad body and waited for their arrival. Thirty minutes before they were due I took two Hydroxy diet pills that I'd had forever. I only used the pills once right after I gave birth to BJ. I wanted to get rid of my pregnancy weight, which ended up shedding off me naturally within eight weeks. But I remembered that those pills made me nauseous and made me sweat.

When Black rang the bell, I was no longer acting. I felt horrible and looked every bit the personification of sick. I dragged myself to the door, clinging to the walls for support. When I flung open the door, I kept my head lowered and my eyes on the floor. One hand tried to modestly hide my cleavage that was dangling out of my negligee. My little man was sound asleep in his daddy's arms.

"Do you mind putting him to bed?" I said barely squeezing out the words. My throat felt like sandpaper, and I winced in pain.

"You're really sick?" he admonished.

When I lifted my puffy, runny eyes to meet his I saw the concern in them. My eyes were weak, and I was sweating profusely.

"I told you I wasn't feeling well," I whispered then began a chest-rattling cough.

"I know but that was two days ago. I thought you'd be feeling better by now," he said, moving past me to put BJ in his room. Slowly I tried to make my way back to my room hoping he'd come in there to check up on me. The well-orchestrated plan was working better than I thought it would when I felt the sudden urge to throw up. As Black was coming out of our son's room, I ran past him and just barely made it to the toilet and regurgitated. Black was right on my heels as I kneeled over the toilet to throw up virtually juice because I had barely eaten all weekend. As my stomach muscles churned and contracted and my insides seared my throat I thought that I was going to die, I was in so much pain. As I sat crouched over the toilet, helpless, Black rubbed my back soothingly and for a split second I wished he would keep rubbing—only between my legs I was so in need of a good fuck.

When I finished throwing up I noticed the pills in the bowl and quickly flushed. When I tried to stand up, my knees wobbled, then buckled.

Black caught me and picked me up and took me to my bed. He laid me down and tucked me under the covers. I watched his eyes quickly scan all the empty medicine bottles. He put his hand over my forehead and said, "You're burning up. You should have called me to help you."

Black went inside the bathroom and got a cool cloth and wiped my forehead. Then he went inside the kitchen and began making me some soup. But not before he called down to his driver and told him to pick me up some cold and flu medicine. After Black fed me, his driver arrived with the package. I thought that he'd put the medication on the counter and leave but he didn't. He kicked off his shoes, gave me Alka Seltzer Cold & Flu and within a half hour, I was sleeping peacefully. I awoke to the television in the living room. I tried to call for Black but my throat was still on fire. I peeked over at the clock and it read nine-thirty. Shortly there-after, Black came into my room and fed me, medicated me and adjusted my pillows, which didn't need adjusting but I knew he was just trying to be helpful.

As I lie there the next morning trying to gather my strength to go in the room and get BJ so that I could feed him and take him to day care, I heard a key in the lock. There was a jangling before he finally found the correct key. My heart dropped. He was still here. He came walking in the room, and I pretended to just be waking up. When I looked into his dreamy eyes and milky skin I wanted to confess my love all over again but I knew that I couldn't.

"How are you feeling?"

"I guess okay," I lied. But I purposely lied unconvincingly and it worked.

"You don't look okay," he said and came to check my fever. When his hands slid down to my neck, I was soaked in sweat.

"Stay here. I'm going to run you a bath."

As the water was running he pulled open the drapes in my room to let the sunshine in then went to get me a glass of orange juice, soup and crackers.

"Here, eat this first and then I'll bathe you. You have to get your strength back."

After I tried to force down the soup and swallow the orange juice, which stung my throat, Black gave me non-drowsy Robitussin then leaned over, scooped me up and took me into my small, modest bathroom. He sat on the toilet and positioned me between his legs. Gently, he reached up and removed my robe. It glided down my shoulders and cascaded to the floor. My spaghetti straps on my negligee were the next to go. As Black's strong, masculine hands slid my clothing to the floor, I watched his eyes as he pulled past my breasts and then linger on my red pussy hair and finally my perfect French-pedicured feet. Black put both hands on my hips and guided me inside the tub.

"Is it too hot?" he asked.

"No, it's perfect," I said, my voice barely a whisper.

Black grabbed the washcloth and soap and began at my feet. He lathered the rag and began to wash in between my toes in slow, strong strokes. He was giving me a foot massage, and I almost drifted into a peaceful sleep. Then he moved from my calves to my upper thighs. His shirt got wet from bath water so he stood and pulled his vintage T-shirt over his head. His broad shoulders, firm pecks and ripe nipples beset his small waist and flat stomach.

"Stand up," he said and kneeled. Slowly I rose to my feet and stood with my pussy in Black's face, and I couldn't help but reminiscence about the first night he tasted my juices. We were on his terrace making love in the middle of a rainstorm. That night was so sensual and erotic that I still blush when I think about it....

Tenderly, he separated my legs and took the washcloth and began cleansing my inner thighs in circular motions slowly moving toward my cave. When he took the tip of the rag and parted my lips, he applied pressure, and as his fingers brushed my clitoris in a steady, firm motion, inadvertently I gripped his shoulders tightly trying to stop myself from shuddering. Black's eyes met mine, and he held my eyes for a long moment. I peeked down at his jeans and could see a slight bulge. Careful not to linger in that hot spot for too long, he moved up to my arms, fingers and the nape of my neck before making his way to my breasts. As soon as the intensity was overbearing, he pulled back. But only for a moment. Black turned on the shower and told me not to move. I did as I was told. When he began pulling off his jeans, boxers and then socks and stood before me completely naked, I moved over to make room for him in the shower. Neither one of us said a word as he reached for the shampoo and began lathering my scalp. His strong fingers stroked my scalp lovingly as if he were making love to me. With caution he tilted my head back and allowed the water to cascade down on my hair as I closed my eyes. He had his hand supporting the back of my neck and when he pulled me up I was surprised when he leaned in and kissed my lips, softly. My eyes popped open, and then he kissed me again. This time more aggressively as my eager lips welcomed him. I slid my tongue inside his mouth and we both began to grope each other passionately. Although, I felt weak and fatigued, I was up for this escapade. I had waited two years for this. Wet and slippery, Black carried me to my bed and gently laid me down. Finally he spoke as he climbed on top of me.

"Are you okay? Am I too heavy for you?"

"No, I'm fine," I said and reached up for him.

We started off slowly—long, deep kisses as he dug his hands deep inside my curly hair. Black sucked and licked my nipples until they looked like two copper nickels. I moaned as his strong hands groped my body. As he began to nibble passionately on my neck, I squealed with delight. When his dick pressed against the opening of my pussy, he applied a controlled pressure. When my pussy resisted, he pushed harder until the tip burst through. He teased me for a minute just rocking his tip in and out. As my pussy walls opened wider, he sunk deeper inside my welcoming cave. Black's strong pelvis rocked back and forth, keeping a steady rhythm. As he gently made love to me the moment felt surreal as I longed for the past.

As the moment intensified, I wrapped my legs around Black's waist, and we both gripped each other tightly.

"I'm getting ready to cum," he murmured. "Ahhhhh, I'm cumming."

"Me too," I crooned.

As Black came he whispered in my ear, "I love you, Nicoli…I love youuuuu."

The next morning Black got up to take BJ to school, only this time he didn't come back. He called and asked if I had enough energy to pick up our son. Of course after we'd made love I couldn't say that I was still feeling weak. Black sounded cold and distant on the phone, which worried me. Black remained a stranger for the rest of the week. When he came to pick up BJ on Friday I decided that we needed to talk.

"Why haven't you returned any of my calls?"

"I've been busy."

I let my head rock up and down as if I understood but I was doing this in a sarcastic manner trying to hold back my temper, which was brewing.

"I was thinking that we could do something this weekend—together as a family. If you'd like I could come to your house for the weekend."

"I don't think that's gonna work," he said as he walked past me to go get BJ. I was right on his heels.

"Why not?"

"Look, Nicoli, you know that it's not like it used to be with us."

"I do know that but I thought that you wanted to at least try to get it back to where we used to be."

"Why would you think that? Because we fucked?"

"Excuse me? Is that all I am to you? A fuck?"

"Look, stop yelling. Our son is in the other room. I'm not in the mood for a shouting match."

"Why are you doing this? You know how I feel about you, and this is what I get? You know that I gave you my body because I love you. And you greedily took it, not caring about the consequences."

"I can't take what I already had. The same record had been playing on the stereo after you fucked that lesbian dyke bitch. You and I could never, ever be a couple again. You fucked up, and you're gonna have to live with it. This will teach you to make better choices in the future."

"You know what…fuck you. I wish you a lifetime of misery. May you have to crawl over broken glass to find happiness."

"Likewise," he retorted and grabbed BJ who looked absolutely adorable in his New York Yankees baseball cap and T-shirt.

I lowered my voice.

"Look, I don't want to fight with you. That's not my intent. This is hard for me wearing my feelings on my sleeve and being this vulnerable, but I love you, Black. And I can't get over you even though I've tried," I said, fidgeting with my fingers.

"I'll bring him back Sunday. Be here when we arrive," he retorted and walked out.

25

Jinx

It's been nine days since I've last heard from Shawn. I've sent him text messages and left verbal messages on his phone but still he hasn't called. I don't have a clue as to what's up. I guess it's over but I just can't understand why. What did I do? I thought everything was going so well. Is this how we do it nowadays? Just walk away without so much as an explanation. No closure. I deserved better than this. I had cried all morning and refused to get out of bed. I had been sewing, cutting patterns, and sketching so much these past few days my fingers were cramped and my hands were swollen. I told Nana that I was tired from working so hard. I didn't want her worrying. If I told Nana what Shawn did to me she'd want to put on her tennis sneakers and whip his ass—at least she'd try.

Monday morning made eleven days and I hadn't gotten out of bed all weekend. I knew I had to get up for work or else Nana would grow suspicious. I purposely went to work looking a mess. I wanted to wear my pain on my sleeve. I wanted everyone to know that I wasn't up for small talk, nice gestures or office gossip. When my boss came out of his office to give me a demand for discovery to drawn up on a civil case, which demands the plaintiff's attorney to hand over certain evidence, his gaze stopped momentarily on my outfit. I had on a black winter blazer, pink summer mini-skirt and lime-green cowboy boots. I had braided my

Mohawk in one corn roll down the center of my head and was without any makeup. My sullen, puffy eyes told their own story.

"Jinx, come in and close the door."

"Yes, Mr. Zicarrdi," I said.

"Is everything all right with you? At home. How's Nana?" he asked in concern.

Mr. Zicarrdi was an aging sixty-three year old, robust Italian man who was genuinely fond of me. He was such a great boss.

"Everything is fine. Nana is fine. I just keep having a succession of bad dreams lately that I can't sleep," I said, which wasn't totally a lie. I did keep seeing crazy things lately that I couldn't explain.

"Oh, I know what you mean."

"You do?" I asked somewhat surprised.

"I can't keep watching the *Cold Case Files*. I've become too paranoid. I keep walking around my home checking windows and doors, looking over my shoulder. The other night I was watching Animal Planet and went to sleep and had a dream about alligators." He laughed and then continued, "I can't keep watching that crazy stuff. I'm too old."

I walked out of Mr. Zicarrdi's office assuring him that the next day I'd be back to normal. He was the only one who had confidence in my words....

As I walked out of the Euclid Avenue train station down Pitkin Avenue toward my block I decided to give it one more shot and call Shawn. Miraculously he picked up.

"Hello," he said.

"Shawn—"

"Jinx, hold on a moment," he replied, cutting me off.

I held on throughout my walk home and for another twenty minutes thereafter. Finally, he came back to the line.

"Jinx?"

"Yes?" I snapped, annoyed.

"See, that's my girl. You know how to *wait* for your man."

"Excuse me?" I asked, incredulously.

"What are you doing tonight?" he asked.

"What am I doing tonight? You've gotta be kidding me. Where have you been?"

"I've been covering a lot of music industry events and inundated writing articles for *Celeb* magazine. Do you want to go to a listening party in a few hours for singer Cammie?"

One part of me couldn't believe that my gut was right. He was teaching me a lesson for not holding on the line. The other part of me wanted to desperately go to the listening party for Cammie, the new R & B sensation. I agreed to go out with Shawn and he came to pick me up shortly after seven.

We arrived at club Crave in the meatpacking district in New York. The area was quite artsy and looked like a scene taken from a major motion picture. I was impressed from the moment we walked through the door. Celebrities came out to show their support to the young singer and I wished I could have brought Breezy to enjoy the festivities.

As I listened to each track I couldn't help but realize she was a talentless singer with a pretty face and nice dance moves. But it was interesting watching Shawn coexist in his element. He walked around greeting men with firm handshakes and women with brief kisses on the cheek. He never bothered to introduce me as I trailed behind. Still, I managed to have a nice time. When we got to his car at the end of the night a female walked over and he rolled down his window.

She had a natural hairdo, jeans and stilettos clutching a Gucci logo bag, circa 2002.

"So you about to get out of here," she asked Shawn.

"Yeah, I'm going in for the night. You need a ride?" he offered.

"Thank you. You sure you don't mind?" she asked, flirtatiously letting her hand linger on his shoulder.

"Not at all. Get in," he replied, without asking if I had any objections. It was already past midnight and we both had to work in the morning.

Feeling slighted, I decided to see if I could throw my weight around. I said, "Shawn, I have to work tomorrow and I wanted to go straight home. Perhaps your friend could get home in the same manner in which she came."

"Shawn, I see you got a live one. Where did you find her?" she said, while flinging open the back door and hopping in despite my objection.

I exploded.

"Honey, you're right about that. I'm so motherfucking live that your ass is getting out of this car!"

I jumped out the passenger's seat and walked briskly over to her car door. As I flung it open, she started objecting.

"Calm, down. It's not that serious," she pleaded, upon deaf ears.

"Guess what? Your mouth just blew your ride. Get the fuck out before I drag you out."

"Oh my gosh," she admonished while clutching imaginary pearls. "This is so ghetto."

"Ghetto?" I screamed. "Ghet—"

"Jinx, get in the car!" Shawn's deep voice ripped through the dry night air as his friend stormed out the car, walking towards the nearest train station.

"That was totally uncalled for," he continued.

"How dare she? Regardless of what I said I was talking to you. She should have stayed in her lane and played her position. That's why that bitch is walking," I said, while letting my neck roll. Somehow I felt a slight victory for standing up for myself.

"You think that was cute? She's right, you're acting ghetto."

"Look, I'm from Brooklyn. Take it or leave it," I snapped, and ignored Shawn for the rest of the ride home.

Shawn decided to play his little mind game again and I played right into his hands. I found myself going to voicemail, leaving messages to no avail. About one week later I got a text message. I looked at my phone and to my surprise it was Shawn. It read: *Jinx, I've been a little sad lately. You gotta feel me. I'll be in touch soon. Just give me space.*

Immediately, I hit him back: *Whatever you're going through, I'm here. Let me see you so that I can help. I miss you so much. I'm sorry about the other night…*

I waited for a response but none came. That night I tried to think of all the reasons he could be sad and why he wasn't calling me so that we could talk. Maybe I could help.

Two more weeks went by, and I was fighting off depression. It was like a dark cloud was looming over my head following me around everywhere I went. I found it hard to eat and equally hard to sleep. I didn't care how I dressed nor did I hang out with friends. Breezy thought that

Shawn and I were spending every waking hour together. Truth be told, he was nowhere to be found.

It was one full month later before I got that call. The call that I'd waited impatiently for. The call that I didn't expect to get. As his ring tone came blaring from my phone, Jay-Z's *Song Cry*, my heart dropped.

I exhaled and tentatively answered my phone.

"Hello."

"What's up, baby?" he casually replied, and my heart smiled first before a huge grin appeared on my face.

"Where have you been? What's going on? Why haven't you called?"

He laughed, "Slow down. I'm sorry, Jinx, that I wasn't able to call. I walked out my house, got into an argument with another motorist, which upset my day. One day led to thirty. I don't know what else to say."

That's it. All this time I'm thinking that there was going to be this big revelation and all he had to say was that he'd gotten into an argument. I wanted to curse his motherfucking ass out but I couldn't. Had he been Jason, I would have gone for the jugular. But he wasn't Jason. He was Shawn, and we'd never had an argument. He'd never raised his voice to me. He'd never put his hands on me. He'd never disrespected me calling me outside of my name. He was monogamous, religious, truthful Shawn. What was it about him that made me hold back my anger? I knew that I didn't want to open up a can of worms that I couldn't close. I don't know when was the first time Jason slapped me or if I had provoked it.

That's what he'd always say. That I provoked him to do the things that he did to me. I wanted so badly to have a functioning relationship that I kept quiet about Shawn's actions—or lack thereof.

Before I knew it all the uncomfortable feelings had subsided and we were on the phone chatting away for hours. It was past one o'clock in the morning and I had to get up for work the next day. None of those reasons were going to get me off the phone.

"What are you doing? I asked you the same question twice?" I asked when he failed to respond to a question.

"I'm playing with my dick while I listen to you talk in your sexy, sleepy voice."

I blushed. "You're so nasty," I encouraged. "I like it."

"You love it. You *love* this dick," he said cockily, and I smiled at his arrogance. The more brazen side of Jinx wanted to say I don't *love* your scrawny dick. I mean, it's okay, but the nice side of Jinx just continued to play my position.

At some point the conversation shifted in a drastic way. He asked what didn't I like about my ex-boyfriend and instead of me keeping my big mouth shut, I divulged.

"When I first met him he was a block-hugger. Making a few dollars doing hand-to-hand transactions. Although my nana taught me better, there was something about him that I couldn't stay away from. In my eyes he was no different than any other guy in my neighborhood. Most of the young guys sold drugs just to eat four chicken wings and shrimp fried rice from the Chinese restaurant. Instantly I was smitten. Overnight he'd gone from working for someone to having workers. He swooped me up when I was seventeen years old and moved me in with him. I didn't want for anything. He bought my clothes, shoes, food, tampons. At seventeen I was driving a convertible 535 BMW. It may all seem nice, like I was living the perfect 'hood fairytale, but the consequences were grave. While selling drugs he'd always make time to work on his favorite hobby, which was making beats. By day, a criminal. By night, a producer. It didn't take long for him to break into the music industry. Overnight, ask anybody did they know Jason and their response would be, 'from the East?'"

"Jason from the Hit Makers?" he asked.

"Yes, that's him."

"That was your last boyfriend? Like you had a real relationship with him?" he asked skeptically.

"I think what I just described constitutes a real relationship," I snapped. Silence.

"Oh, that's what it is then," he replied and then he continued. "If I was a girl I could never date a worker."

"What? What do you mean a worker?"

"Like how you dated Jason when he was selling drugs for the bigger nigga. I ain't never been the type of dude to work for another motherfucker. I'm always the bigger nigga. I'm telling you, Jinx, when I was out there I was a terror—a straight killer," he boasted.

"Huh? What are you talking about?"

"I'm talking about way before I met you. Long before I turned my life over to the Lord. In the eighties, early nineties, I had shit on lock. I remember one time in 1994, my man and I was coming out the barbershop. My whole crew was sitting outside supposedly watching my back. As soon as I stepped foot on the concrete four henchmen came and put a gun in my gut and took my re-up money that I had safety inside my knapsack. Now, only three people knew that I'd have that much money on me—my son's mother, my uncle and one of my men—so I know that one of them betrayed me, and all I keep thinking is that if I live through this somebody is gonna pay. After they take around two hundred, they make their biggest mistake. They let me live. I run back on the block and get my dudes and we shoot up the whole neighborhood. I then kidnap this kid that I know crossed me. I pull out my burner and I tell him to take me to where the rest of the stickup kids live. When he acts as if he doesn't know what I'm talking about I shoot him in his leg—broad daylight."

As Shawn is telling me this tall tale, I keep saying, "Uh-huh. Oh my gosh. For real?" In an attempt to hide my true feelings. Meanwhile, I'm laying on my bed with my lips twisted up in disbelief trying to figure out how my well-mannered, Christian boyfriend felt a need to tell me these things. I just told him what I didn't like in a man. How could he have not understood?

He continues for two more hours. "By 1997, my hands kept touching that paper. One day I ran into I.Q.—"

"I.Q.? Who's that?"

"And old dude with a lot of knowledge. He's like, 'Son, you know only a bitch would set you up like that. Better check those bitches you running up in."

"I'm confused. What are you talking about? What bitch? I thought you said that the guy did it and the only woman who knew was your son's mother."

"Yeah, me and the old dude were fly like that. When he pulled my coat I remember this bitch I used to fuck with and it all came together. That bitch had something to do with it."

At that point I was appalled. He'd never used that word *bitch*. And if at this time he was with his son's mother, and he's so monogamous, who's this *bitch* he just admitted to fucking with? I couldn't hold it back any longer.

"Weren't you with your son's mother at this time?"

"Yeah, but she ain't have anything to do with it."

"I know. The *bitch* did. My question to you is I thought you never cheated in a relationship."

"What I said is when I'm in a relationship I play by all the rules. My son's mother didn't play by the rules. She was fucking around with the whole town."

"So why did you marry her?" I asked, backing him in a corner.

"I'm not married to my son's mother. I married my wife. We don't have any kids together," he casually replied.

"What?" I screamed in disgust. "No, you didn't just tell me this bullshit. I thought that you and your wife were separated and that your wife had your son."

"No. I never said that," he replied calmly. "I said that I was married and that I also had a son. That's exactly what I said."

"Look, you can play all the motherfucking word semantics you want to play, but you won't be playing them with me. I know what the fuck you told me," I said and hung up on him. I was breathing so heavily from anger that it took me moments to calm down. Not only did he have a wife and a kid. He now also has a baby momma. This is absolutely too much drama.

If this wasn't a ghetto tale then I didn't know what was. Of course I was too hyped to sleep. I was seething. Not leaving well enough alone, I called back and he had the nerve to send me to voicemail. Me. Okay, I see how this is going down.

26

COLD CASE FILE TAKEN FROM THE DESK OF THE 88TH PRECINCT IN BROOKLYN REPORTED TO THE *DAILY NEWS*:

Police say that they may be getting closer to catching an elusive serial killer. Neighbors of 19-year-old Tanesha Washington of Flatbush, Brooklyn, say they saw an unidentified man fleeing her apartment with an executioners-style hood on just moments before her strangled and mutilated body was found slumped over her bed. The suspect is described as a light-skinned black male or Hispanic man. Between 6'1" and 6' 3", slim, athletic build weighing around 180 to 195 pounds. Authorities say that if you have any leads please call our hotline 1-800-555-TIPS. People in Brooklyn are in fear that we have three serial killers among them, The Brooklyn Butcher and The Night Stalker and now the Zodiac Killer. There was a note signed Zodiac Killer, with an astrological sign of Virgo left at the scene, which happens to be the victim's zodiac sign. Although there are several similarities, the original zodiac killer of the late 1960s was never apprehended and there were over 2500 suspects. The killings stopped but the letters taunting authorities continued until 1974. The original copycat of the zodiac killer, Heriberto "Eddie" Seda, was apprehended in

1994 and is still serving 236 years in a state correctional facility. Authorities will update us with details as they surface.

27

Breezy

I invited Black over to my apartment. I thought that better because I didn't want to be invited to his plush apartment whereas he could show off his wealth. I'd rather keep it on my side of town until he truly falls for me. This was both mine and my father's idea. Although my father taught me how to cook since I was a little girl, his cooking was a tidbit better, so he offered to make the food. He cooked steamed lobster, shrimp alfredo with penne pasta and asparagus tips and a Caesar salad. As an appetizer he'd made caviar on crackers and for dessert he'd made red velvet cake. After he cooked he cleaned the kitchen while I showered and dressed. We both thought it appropriate for me to wear a peach-color Roberto Cavalli dress with a pair of peach Manolo Blahnik stilettos. The dress gave me cleavage and fit snug around my butt and hips. I had my hair pulled up in a tight bun with a few pieces dangling around my face, and all I wore was a pair of emerald-cut diamond earrings.

My father left my apartment roughly ten minutes before Black arrived. My father opened the front door and introduced himself to Black as my older brother. The plan was to tell Black that me and my *brother* both own this brownstone and that our parents died in a car crash when I was just a baby. We decided that because we wanted Black to loosen up quickly and to not have to be mindful of parents.

Black gently tapped on my door, and my heart palpitated fast. I wasn't nervous about being in his company. I was nervous about playing him at chess. My father said my beating him at chess would give me the edge over any other girl he may be interested in.

"Hi," I said with a huge smile on my face.

"Hi. You look gorgeous," he said and gave me a kiss on my cheek.

"Please, come in," I said as I led him into my living room. I turned around quickly and noticed he was checking my place out.

"Nice place," he said.

"Thank you. My brother and I own it."

"That's nice. I just met your brother. He seems nice enough."

"He's really a great guy. He and his wife live downstairs in the duplex," I retorted.

"Do you rent out the first floor?" he asked as he took off his coat and handed it to me.

"No. Well, we use it for charity work. We find homeless kids and take them off the street and help them get their lives together. In the past decade we've helped close to thirty kids."

"Now that's impressive. I don't know of anyone who'd open up their home to perfect strangers."

"Those young girls need help and guidance. I tutor most of them, and my brother helps them find work."

He stared in my face for a long moment.

"I can't believe how young you look. You don't look more than nineteen years old," he said, shaking his head.

"It's in the genes." I gave my mature laugh, and I had him mesmerized.

When we sat down to eat, as he bit into each dish he'd look up at me and there was appreciation in his eyes.

"You're a wonderful cook," he commented.

"Thank you. I love to cook. It's my favorite pastime," I said.

After dinner, I poured us a glass of wine, and we went into the living room where I had a light fire going. I opened the window inside the apartment so it wouldn't get too hot. We sat on my sofa just talking, trying to get to know each other.

"You're a beautiful woman. Why aren't you married with kids yet?"

Bingo, I thought.

"Honestly, I've never wanted to get married," I said just as I'd rehearsed.

"Really? Why is that?"

"I don't think a man could meet my expectations. I think I have such an expectation for marriage that I'd ultimately get disappointed."

"That's a pessimistic way of looking at the union."

I shrugged, licked my lips then said, "That's a realistic way of looking at it for me. People don't realize that in order to make that union work you have to work just as hard at it as you would your career. I find many people become complacent once they've said their vows, and that leaves room for divorce. I believe how you met a person is how you could lose them, so if I start out by wearing sexy lingerie, running your bath water and giving you hour long blow jobs every night, then once we're married all of that stops, I could very well run the risk of losing you. And that's what usually happens. Honestly, that would ultimately crush me...to have my marriage fall apart, so I'd rather avoid the propaganda."

"I see what you're saying, and for the most part that's true. So you'll have kids without being married?" he probed.

"I hate to admit this because I don't know how you'll look at me—"

"Just say it naturally. No one is judging you," he assured. But I knew better.

"I don't want kids either," I said.

He put the most peculiar look on his face, then said, "Ever?"

"Yes."

"I don't think I've ever heard that before."

"I'm not maternal. I've never had a longing to have a baby grow inside of me, push it out and then raise it for the rest of its life. I know that may sound as if I'm a selfish person but I chose to look at it as I'm a focused person."

"You still have time to meet the right person who will change your mind," he said in a cocky manner.

"I've met beautiful men with morals and great occupations who always thought they could change my way of thinking. It is what it is. That's why I lay my cards on the table in the very beginning. That way no one is misled. And I need to add that not only do I not want kids, but I don't date men with kids either."

"What?" he asked incredulously.

"Precisely. I can't be bothered with the baby momma drama or the ex-wife calling me all types of bitches, hussies and whores." I laughed.

"You'd never date a guy with kids?" he pursued further.

"I love kids, don't get me wrong. But it's the mother that I can't allow in my life. People hate to admit this, but sometimes the parents are still in love with each other. It just didn't work out for whatever reason, so that spills into your current situation. My situation. My life and I can't—no, I won't tolerate—it."

He shook his head as if he understood, but I could tell he was in deep thought. He was struggling with whether he should tell me about his son. And purposely, I didn't ask if he had one.

I poured him a refill on his wine, and he relaxed even more. We were sitting adjacent from each other, and I had my legs crossed. My waist looked exceptionally small, and my hips were spread nicely. I watched Black's eyes look from my shoes up to my breasts then he stared directly in my eyes.

"Tell me about your last relationship. Why didn't it last?" he inquired.

"We dated briefly. It was a summer fling. I was in love, he wasn't. We were doomed from the beginning. Although I go to an occasional club, maybe twice a month to unwind, he'd party five nights a week—from Wednesday through Sunday night. I'd tell him it was too excessive, and he'd promise to slow down and be right back out the next week. Then I found out that he went out so much because he found what he was looking for in those clubs, which was someone to cheat with. When I found out, it crushed me. When you're in a relationship and you're monogamous and someone steps outside and cheats, the hurt is indescribable," I said, my voice barely a whisper. I could tell I had him thinking about his own past relationship with cheating-ass, partying-ass Nicoli.

Black leaned over and kissed me softly on my lips. I pulled back, and we looked eye to eye. Slowly he put his hand behind my head and pulled me in close for another kiss. This time I slowly parted my lips and let his tongue explore the inside of my mouth. His long tongue gently probed and sucked my lips. Again, I pulled back.

"You have a chess challenge awaiting you," I said.

"So you were serious?"

"You doubted me?" I said as if I was offended.

"I must admit...a little bit."

We sat down opposite each other in front of my father's custom-made chess set. Black was very impressed.

We started off slow, and I made a couple of bad moves. I looked up and I could tell he had a smug look on his face that made me step up my game. My father's words and instructions came back full force. I knew I couldn't let him down.

I moved my bishop and took his knight.

Black and I had an intense game of chess whereas we both were on the brink of losing it. Our competitive nature wouldn't allow either one of us to fold. Too much was at stake. I needed to win to earn his respect. He needed to win to stroke his ego. When I called checkmate, there was so much emotion.

Reluctantly he congratulated me and started making excuses about being rusty and not playing in ages. I knew better than to patronize him.

28

Nicoli

All I thought about was how Black and I had made love. It kept replaying in my head the whole weekend. I wanted to know what he was doing and if he had someone special in his life. I was practically counting the hours until he brought the baby home. I needed our conversation to pick up where it ended. Why was it so hard for him to forgive me? Men hurt women all the time. But hurt a man and they act as if it's fucking Armageddon. I wish we could just let the past stay in the past.

It was nearly eleven o'clock before Black brought BJ home. I'd actually thought he was going to call and say he was keeping him another night. When he rang the bell, I jumped up and ran to the door. I had *Teddy Pendergrass Greatest Hits* playing on my CD system. Teddy's aggressive voice resonated throughout my apartment and personified the mood I was in.

I sauntered to the door in five-inch Manolo stilettos. Over the weekend I finally went and got a professional hairdo. I got my naturally red hair highlighted with blond streaks and cut into layers with a razor. The cut and color cost Black six hundred dollars. I was wearing a baby blue, form-fitting pencil dress by Escada, and my face was tastefully made up.

I flung the door open with a glass of white wine in one hand and a look of determination on my face. Black looked me up and down and smirked his disapproval.

"Where've you been?" he asked as he aggressively peered around my apartment looking for houseguests.

"Put BJ in his room. We need to talk."

Black took BJ in the back then came out and walked into the living room with an attitude.

"Hot date tonight?" His words dripped sarcasm.

"Look, I'm twenty-two years old and the mother of your child. I told you that I love you, but I'm not going to wait with baited breath and put my life in your hands while you decide my future. I'm a beautiful *and* smart girl who can get any man she wants. Just so happens that I want you. Now I would hate to go back out there and find another man to take care of me and BJ, but I will if I have to," I threatened.

He exploded.

"Don't you ever threaten me about my son. I will put you in your grave before I let you let another man try to raise my son."

"Neo, step out of the Matrix and come back to reality. What do you think will happen if I fall in love with somebody else? They will move in here and help me take care of BJ 24/7," I reasoned.

"You already got someone in mind, don't you? Who you met, Nicoli? One of my friends…" he wondered.

"Look, my nights are lonely. I'm a young, sexual being. I can't keep denying myself happiness. Don't you think that I may want someone to hold me at night? Good girls need dick too," I sassily replied while taking a large gulp of my wine.

Without much provocation, Black came and tackled me. We both tumbled, and my glass fell, shattering against the parquet floor. He dragged me by my arms into my room and slammed the door shut. In a fit of rage he began to pull my dress up and commenced to ripping off my panties.

"What are you doing?" I screamed as I pounded my small fist into his back.

"Is this what you want, bitch," he yelled as he positioned himself between my legs and pulled out his dick. He had this wild look in his eyes as he rammed his dick into my pussy.

"Noooo," I screamed in pain as I tried to wiggle free. *Is he raping me?*

Black had both my hands pinned down over my head, and his heavy weight prevented me from moving. He began thrusting his pelvis into my resisting flesh—angry, quick thrusts of hate and rage silenced me.

"I hate you," he panted in my ear then aggressively grabbed my hair, making me look in his eyes. "You hear me…I hate you."

Inexplicably, I was turned on. The force, rage and passion had excited me. I grabbed Black's shirt and pulled his lips to mine and began kissing him. I began biting his lips while my body responded to his advances. As he aggressively pumped his ass in and out, I dug my nails into his back and pulled them down in a sinister yet sexy gesture.

"You hurt me," Black said as tears streamed down his cheeks. "You…hurt me." As he was nearing his climax, the strokes became harder and faster.

"I'm getting ready to cum…" he screamed as hot juices came gushing out. His body started shaking involuntarily then he collapsed on top of me, sobbing uncontrollably. Black lay on top of me for almost an hour, crying his heart out. I was silent as I rubbed his back. He was sweating freely and holding me tight. Soon Black pulled himself up from off the floor. He was unable to give me eye contact as he muttered, "I'm sorry, Nicoli…I…never…I…um…sorry if I hurt you. That wasn't my intent. It'll never happen again."

"Black, we need to talk through this."

"I just said that I was sorry. There isn't anything more to discuss."

"Yes, there is. We need to discuss us. Where do we go from here?"

"We continue to be parents to our child. That's it. That's where it ends."

"Look me in my eyes and tell me you don't feel the same, and I'll never mention this again."

Black paused at my bedroom doorway, took his left hand and aggressively grabbed my chin, tilted my head so we were eye to eye and said, "I don't love you anymore."

"Liar."

Tears flooded my eyes, but I refused to let them fall. I had strolled around here playing a wounded victim, walking on broken glass, sacrificing myself in the name of love only to have him degrade me. My weakness gave him strength. No more Miss Nice Bitch. I'm going to make his life a living hell.

29

Jinx

Once again, I was at a bad place. For one week straight I sat burning up over the lie that Shawn had told me. Was it a deliberate lie, or was it just a misunderstanding? Sometimes I think that I put him up on a pedestal and he keeps coming short of my expectations. What added insult to injury was that instead of begging for forgiveness, once again he shut me out and twisted everything around as if it's my fault and he's this victim.

After work I decided to go to Breezy's house to confide in her everything that's been going on with Shawn and me. She was in her room pulling out an uber amount of clothes, trying to get ready for her date. At first I thought she was only half listening because she seemed distracted, but once I finished my whole story, she sat down on her bed and gave me her honest opinion.

"Jinx, I can only say what it looks like on the outside looking in. Keep in mind that I may be wrong because I only have your side of the story to go on, but from the looks of things I don't think that he's digging you as much as you're digging him. What's that book, *He's Just Not That into You*? Have you heard about it?"

"Yeah. The authors were on Oprah."

"Exactly. Well the first thing that you did wrong was fuck with him—"

"I know. I should have never messed with a married man. I'm going to hell."

"Not that silly. That's his sin. And if he's as religious as he professes, he wouldn't be running around fornicating. He's one of those *'do as I say not as I do,'* Christians. We call them hypocrites in my book."

"But—"

"Look, no interruptions. I only have a minute to say what I need to and then I have to tend to my life. I think that he used you to get over his wife—if he's really even getting a divorce. Realistically, no one can be healed enough to start a relationship in four months. That's just not enough time. He may not have done it intentionally but that's the way I see it. And I also think that he knew a long time ago that he didn't want anything serious with you but he knew that he had to play you that way to get what he wanted. Now, he's flipping the script like slow down and the brakes been on. Y'all took months to fuck. He knew within that timeframe if he wanted you at number one or number eight in his life. You may be good for late-night conversations when he's bored and freaky fucks when he's horny but that's it. And I think since you believe so much in this façade that he's painted that he doesn't want to ruin it by blowing you off in a rude way—the way he's probably done so many chicks—so he wants to keep making you think that you did something wrong, that it's your fault that the relationship didn't work."

"Breezy, I hear you, but I think you're wrong. You're not there when we're on the phone or when we're making love. He's different. I just think he's going through something right now."

"Well you'll never know because he's not calling you."

"I know," I whined. "What can I do?"

"Go to his house. See what's up."

"He lives in the Bronx. I don't have car."

"Well I do. Take my truck and surprise his trifling ass."

"Would you really let me hold your truck?"

"Girl, I'm begging you to take it and get out. I have to get ready for my date. That's the luxury of dating men with money. They have their own rides. You remember that, right? Dating a man with money?"

I didn't even stay to answer Breezy's last remark. I grabbed her keys and flew out the door. Next stop: the south Bronx.

30

Nicoli

I had jotted down some of the most notable attorneys to represent me in the child support case that I was ready to file against Black. I was conflicted between Brett Kimmel who represented Misa Hylton-Brim in the case against Sean Combs and Alaina Kirshenbaum who represented most of the A-list celebrities in New York. After a long deliberation, I decided that a woman would be better suited to help me in my plight. A woman would and should understand that I was looking for blood. By the time I finished with Black, I wanted him to be drained and not figuratively speaking. I wanted him mentally, physically and financially drained. I wanted his dick to go limp every time my name was brought up. I wanted him so irritated that he snapped on all those around him. I wanted him to lose his mind and hair. I wanted him to go bald from the stress I was about to put on that ass.

I knew how Black was from the start and vice versa, but I ignored the signs that he was selfish and controlling, and he ignored that I was promiscuous, young and immature. Bad judgment on my part. Grave mistake on his....

Mrs. Kirshenbaum gave me an appointment for 10:00 A.M., and her office was located on Park Avenue and Thirty-seventh Street. After I'd taken BJ to school, I grabbed a taxi into midtown Manhattan. She was located on the forty-fifth floor. As I approached a large cherry wood door with huge brass doorknobs, I had to tell myself to relax. I needed to chill out and slow down. I was prepared to fly in their on my broom and do a complete swoop down, but I know I had to carry myself in a professional manner if I wanted her to take on my case.

Her secretary, a twenty-something attractive white woman with brunette hair seated me while buzzing Mrs. Kirshenbaum to alert her that I'd arrived. As I picked up a dated *People* magazine to leaf through, I also scanned the room. Three people. All women. All seeking something monetary...

Mrs. Kirshenbaum came out of her office promptly at ten. She was an unattractive woman in her mid-forties. She had a large Jewish nose, thin lips, pale skin and an unnatural-looking wig on her head. Her body was grossly out of shape as her breasts drooped low, and her child-bearing hips were too large. She had a firm handshake and penetrating blue eyes underneath thick-rimmed glasses.

"Please, have a seat, Ms. Jones," she said in a masculine, gruff voice.

"Thank you."

"So when my secretary screened your call you said that you're the mother of Black King's first and only child."

"That's correct."

"And he is the same Black King that made *Forbes* magazine?"

"Yes, ma'am."

"Are you currently getting court-appointed support?"

"No. I've never taken him to court."

"Does he acknowledge your son as his own?"

"Yes, he does."

"Please don't take this next question as disrespectful but I need to ask this. Is your son his? I mean, are you sure? Was there ever a paternity test taken?"

"Of course he's the father. They look just alike," I said and my voice rose a little unintentionally.

"Now if I had made a remark like that you would have called me racist. Most would argue most Black people look alike. My question is are you positive beyond any reasonable doubt that he's the father. Were you sleeping with anyone else at the time of this child's conception?"

Stammering for words, I inadvertently blurted out what I'm sure will come to light.

"Yes…well no. I mean…I was sleeping with someone else at the time but that person couldn't have gotten me pregnant."

"Prophylactics aren't a hundred percent safe," she said snippily. "That person could very well be the father."

"Listen, I'm twenty-two years old and know all about the birds and the bees. I've been fucking since I was fifteen and don't need lessons at this stage in my life. I know the person isn't the father because the he is actually a she. *She* is the reason that we broke up."

"I see," she said and cleared her throat. She looked down at her desk, and I could tell she was uncomfortable. For a split second I started to think I had made a mistake in choosing her. Surely, she should have heard worst than what I'd just exposed being that she deals with celebrity clients all the time. "Twenty-two years old in my book means you're still a baby, meaning you were just experimenting. And he couldn't forgive you for that? Well, we'll make him understand the old adage that it's cheaper to keep her, now won't we?"

I smiled at her humor and now feisty attitude. She and I were definitely on the same page.

"Just so that you and I are clear, I've read that the highest court order to date is thirty-five thousand a month. I want fifty, plus arrears for the past two years."

"I'm with you, but hold on a minute. Is he worth that type of judgment?"

"That and then some. He's co-owner of a basketball team, he now has four restaurants—New York, Los Angeles, Milan and Atlanta. All are doing very well. He has his own record label, which has produced several top-ten albums on the Billboard charts, a clothing line and movie production company. Since we've met his business has only flourished."

"Does he give you any support?"

"He's bought me a tired-ass apartment in Battery Park Towers worth $250,000 and gives me an allowance of twenty-one hundred dollars a month. He pays for our son's day care and all medical expenses. So you see, he's getting over like a fat, sloppy, dirty rat."

My disdain and disgust for Black was seeping through my pores and spilling out of my mouth.

"May I get candid with you?"

"Shoot."

"What's prompted you to come and see me if you've settled for these terms in the beginning? Was there some sort of change in your relationship with him? Another woman?"

"None that I know of but the status of our relationship did shift just last week, and I realized that he's been using me and being cordial not out of respect, admiration or love but as a calculated ploy to keep me complacent from seeking what is rightfully mine."

"You know he may ask the court to issue a paternity test."

"So be it."

"Okay. Fine. I'll get working on this as soon as possible. I'm going to file a motion with family court. I'll need all his addressees so that an officer of the court may properly serve him. He may try to contact you. Don't speak about the case and don't settle for empty promises. I've seen the most charismatic men in the world get their child's mother to drop child support cases with promises to buy fancy cars, jewelry, an allowance, and sometimes they even promise marriage. By the time she notices that she's been bamboozled years will have passed. Don't be a victim," she warned.

"I've already hung up my victim heels. I'm sporting six-inch diva heels."

She smiled, amused with my humor.

"I'll be in touch," she said while extending her hand in which I shook.

As I left her office my mind churned a thousand thoughts. This was only the beginning…a teaser. If Black wanted to play—we'll play. Everything is fair in love and war. Black and I are definitely at war!

31

Jinx

It was slightly after nine o'clock when I pulled in front of his house. I looked up to the window, and all the lights were on in Shawn's apartment. He had to be there. My heart felt as if it was easing up my chest about to burst through my throat. My palms began to sweat as I climbed out the Range and walked to the front door. I rang the bell once. No response. Twice. Nothing. Then I remembered a conversation we had, and he said that he never answered his door because he wasn't ever expecting company.

I got back in Breezy's jeep and called his cell. I crossed my fingers that he'd answer but of course he saw my number and allowed me to go to voicemail. Angry, I blurted out, "I'm downstairs, and I'm not leaving until you come outside and talk to me."

I was prepared to wait hours, days, weeks parked in front of his house. I was a chick on a mission. The mission was operation get my man back, by any means necessary...

Ten minutes went by before he decided to check his voicemail. He came jogging down the steps in a black Sean John sweat suit. His hair was freshly cut, and he had on a pair of new Nike Airs. He looked like he didn't have a worry in the world. Meanwhile, my once perfect French manicure was chipped, my once tight-fitting jeans were loose, and my once vibrant eyes were dull. There was definitely something wrong with this picture.

From the rip, he started off with an attitude.

"Yo, I don't go through this," he barked. He voice was low and menacing.

"Go through what?" I asked, perplexed.

"Having people show up at my house unannounced, that's what."

"Oh, you got somebody up there?" I yelled, angry at the prospect he could have someone up in his apartment so soon after our breakup. No matter how hard I tried to date a different man, it appeared that Shawn was turning more into Jason than I was willing to accept.

"That doesn't have anything to do with you. You made a decision the other night to break up so that's what it is."

"So easily? You can throw away what we have so easily? Are you glad that I wanted to call it off? I only said what I said as a defense mechanism. My feelings were hurt. I half expected you to put up a fight to keep me, to show some sort of emotion instead of always being so cold and distant."

"Jinx, I don't have the energy for this. It's too hard being in a relationship with you. You're always pressuring me for something in one way or another."

"Pressuring you? You've got to be kidding me. All I do is comply with your every whim. Look, if you tell me to leave and to never call you again then I promise that's what I'll do. All you gotta do is say the word, and I'll make it happen."

I was tired of being tired of this relationship. Maybe Breezy was right. He just wasn't that into me, and I should face it. Shawn opened up the jeep door and got into the passenger's seat. He stared ahead for a long moment, exhaled and then said, "That's not what I'm saying. All this arguing and drama isn't what I want anymore in my life. I left that when I left my wife. When I met you I was thinking this is a good girl. She's just right for me 'cause I'm a good dude. And then I listen to the things you say, and I back off. When you talk about dating this balling drug dealer or that your friend drives a Range Rover, I'm like, this is a gold-digging Brooklyn chick, but then I watch you and see that you get up every day for work and make it happen," he admonished.

At this point I was confused. I just kept shaking my head as he tried to explain why he was treating me the way he did. I'm not sure if he wanted to break up or not. Nor did I understand how I was being held accountable as a bad person because my best friend had a Range Rover and my ex-boyfriend sold drugs—the same profession he boasted about being in just a couple of weeks ago.

"As far as being a gold digger, what have I ever asked you for? Okay, you pick up the tab at dinner but aren't you supposed to do that? I mean you are a man, right?"

Why was he making me defend everyday normal activities? I mean, this was crazy.

"Ask any of my ex-girlfriends how much of a man I am. I've bought my ex-women European cars while I drive American. They walked around with fifty-thousand-dollar watches and eighty-thousand-dollar rings showing off to their girlfriends. Their shoe game was sick—all the Italian designers while I sported Nikes and Tims. Any chick that has come into my life lifestyle has been upgraded by me. And what do I get? Nothing, that's what. I'm not trying to put all my energy into you only to have it turn ugly."

Finally I had an understanding of why he kept pushing me away. He was afraid that I'd hurt him. I had to prove to him that I wasn't like all his other relationships and that we both wanted the same thing out of this relationship.

"Listen, Shawn, I want this to work. I'll back off as far as pressuring you if you promise me that if I call you, you'll always answer my call before the day ends. Do you think we can both agree to those terms?" I asked earnestly.

He thought for a moment and then nodded.

I looked at the time, and it was already close to eleven. By the time I returned Breezy's jeep and headed home it would be really late.

"Listen, I'll call you tomorrow. I should be going."

"Come upstairs for a moment," he suggested. "I want to show you something."

We both went upstairs, and he walked straight to his bedroom and opened up the door.

"See, you thought someone was here. I wanted to show you that I'm not seeing anyone. This isn't about a chick."

At this point, I didn't think someone was there. He was the man he said he was. Monogamous when he was in a relationship. What had distracted me was all the new furniture in his apartment. He'd gone out and bought a sleigh bed with marble night stands, dark brown leather sectional and a glass dining room set. I was impressed.

"I'm sorry about accusing you of cheating. That was my insecurities coming out."

"No need to apologize," he called out as he walked in the back to his room. I continued to look around.

"Shawn your furniture is really nice. When did you go shopping? I would have loved to go with you."

"That furniture cost me a small fortune," he yelled. "I spent over ten-thousand, easy."

"Wow," I said as I took a closer look at his sofa. On the back he'd forgotten to remove all tags. At closer glance I noticed a Rent-A-Center tag and I nearly gagged. Why would he lie? Next, I walked to his hallway closet and opened it.

"What are you doing!" he roared and scared me to death.

"Geez, what's wrong with you?" I screamed, holding my heart that was now palpitating at an accelerated speed. "I wasn't looking for anything."

"Good because nothing in there belongs to you," he said while shutting the doors. "Nothing in there but dirty laundry. Would you like to do your man's dirty laundry?"

He kissed me on my forehead and spun me around undoing the tension.

My curiosity was piqued. I wanted to know what he was hiding but I knew that I wouldn't find out tonight.

We talked for several more hours before I ended up falling asleep in his arms. He woke me up just after six in the morning, ushering me out so that I could get to work on time. Pretending that I wouldn't miss work because I wanted to lay up with a man, I reluctantly got up and got out.

32

Breezy

It was a still morning in my apartment. The orange-reddish sun had just risen, peeking through the clouds, and it was barely touching six o'clock. I peeked out my window to see the morning movement below. In the early morning hours, cars and people moved glacially. Groggily, I stretched, yawned and climbed out of bed. I walked into my kitchen and put a tablespoonful of hazelnut coffee into my Cuisinart coffeemaker. While my coffee was brewing, I pulled out my Pilates mat and began my morning Yinsuna yoga for twenty minutes. I loved yoga because it kept my muscles limber and was also a form of meditation.

After yoga, I had a pep in my step. I jumped in a quick, cool shower, drank my coffee and ate a bagel and sat down to read the *New York Times* when my telephone rang, startling me.

I peeked over at the caller ID and it was a private number.

"Good morning," I said perkily.

"Well good morning to you too," the husky voice replied. I knew immediately it was Black.

"How are you?" I asked.

"I'm doing well."

"That's good."

"Listen, what's your day looking like?"

"Nothing too heavy. I had a few papers I wanted to look over, maybe go out with the girls later. Why? Did you have something in mind?"

"Well yes...I'd like to spend the whole day with you. Does that sound like something you'd be interested in?"

"Sounds doable," I laughed.

"Great. I'll be there shortly."

Black arrived about noon and much to my amazement and chagrin he wasn't alone. He'd brought his almost two-year-old son.

"What a pleasant surprise." I beamed as I bent down to examine the little fellow closer. "Who's this little guy?"

"This is my son, BJ. I thought it was time you two met."

Up until now he had never mentioned he had kids. I decided to be calm about it.

"I didn't know you had any kids," I casually replied.

"That's why he's here."

"Right...smart aleck," I joked.

"He's so adorable," I crooned, reaching in to pick him up, which only caused him to burst out into a loud whine. His screeching voice irritated my ears but I didn't complain. I pretended to enjoy the moment and knew that this was a significant situation. Black stood there like the proud father as we all gathered in my living room.

"I know what you're thinking," he said.

"Do you?" I said, with tight-lipped resignation.

"I know you have reservations about seeing someone who has kids but I promise if you give me a chance you won't regret one thing."

"No. I'm actually thinking why you didn't tell me sooner...my feelings are involved at this point. How could I push you away?"

"I'm sorry if I seem deceptive but I knew you were special and call me selfish but I didn't want to lose you," he explained.

"Let's move forward and not dwell on the past. What's done is done. And how could I not be absolutely smitten with this adorable little being."

An hour into our afternoon, I had had enough. His bratty ass son was plucking my nerves. He wouldn't sit still or stop crying long enough for me to even enjoy the lunch I prepared for me and Black. It was obvious that his mother had spoiled him. Soon, Black said that he had to return his son to his mother but that he'd be back and he had a surprise for me. I tried to remain gleeful but I hoped he wasn't going to bring me to meet his baby momma.

Black came back sharply at four with a sly grin on his face.

"You ready?" he asked.

"Always," I retorted.

"You look beautiful."

"Always." I smiled, and he lightly slapped me on my ass as I sauntered out the front door.

The main good quality about Black was that he believed in chivalry. He was always running to open a door, pull out my seat and shower me with compliments. That coupled with his millions, I could understand why my cousin fell heart first in love with him.

As we proceeded down my parquet wood steps in my house, my father appeared at the edge of the lower-level landing. He tried to hide his surprise when he saw Black and me, but I knew better.

"Reggie, you remember Black, don't you?" I asked my father.

"Sure, sure. How are you?" he asked, extending his hand to Black.

"I can't complain." Black smiled.

"I see," my father said, referring to Black's chauffer-driven Maybach waiting for us in front.

"You ain't doing too bad yourself," Black commented on my father's Mercedes CL 600. I guess this was male bonding because Black invited my father out for drinks at a later date, and my father kindly accepted.

As I climbed into the deep-dished, buttery leather seat, I couldn't help but think about what surprise he had in mind. I was sort of eager, as a child would be at the unknown. Black and I indulged in small talk as we glided in and out of traffic heading toward the Brooklyn Bridge.

Ten minutes later his driver pulled onto East 34th Street heliport, and Black whisked me into a Sikovsky S76 US helicopter.

"Are you serious?" I squealed.

"What do you think?" Black replied and smiled confidently.

"Where do I sit?" I asked as I looked around at several empty seats.

"Wherever you'd like. I've rented this for our private affair."

"Is that all I am?" I asked coyly. "An affair?"

"You're far too intelligent, beautiful and sincere to be taken as lightly as an affair," he said earnestly and pulled me in close. He gently let his soft lips touch mine ever so softly then pulled back, as if to tease me. I must admit that it worked. *Nice trick*, I thought. I'd definitely try that one day.

"So the suspense is killing me. Where are we going?"

"To the beach. And that's all I'm going to say. We'll be there in under an hour. So re-laaxxx," he said, dragging his last word for emphasis.

I snuggled up closely under Black's arm, and we began discussing our lives while he massaged my scalp. I had my hair in loose drop curls that he kept twirling with his fingers. I was so relaxed as I looked out over the water and wondered how long it was going to take for him to ask me to marry him. There wasn't a doubt in my mind that I held his interest, but I had to make him feel as if he couldn't live without me. And I know this sounds corny but I needed him to feel as though I was his soul mate.

As the helicopter began its descent, I noticed that we were landing on a heliport in someone's backyard. There was a huge mansion up ahead surrounded by a beautiful white sand beach and perfectly manicured lawns. I swallowed hard and realized that I had to step up my game. How many women had he taken here?

We landed safely, and I noticed a small, motorized car coming toward us with an attractive, distinguished white gentleman driving and smiling brightly.

"Where are we?" I asked.

"Off the Southern coast of Cape Cod."

"Martha's Vineyard?"

"Best seafood in America."

Black grabbed my hand, and we walked toward the gentleman who was awaiting us.

"Breezy, this is Stabros. Stabros, Breezy."

I extended my small hand, and it was swallowed by his large, bony fingers with huge veins.

"Ahhhh, such a lovely sight." He beamed as he smiled broadly and gave Black a nod of approval.

"Thank you," I said graciously.

"Stabros is a financier and owns this beautiful property. He's a blueblood with old *dirty* money," Black joked and they both laughed heartily at the joke that I didn't get.

Stabros drove us to his mansion, and we sat outside on his sun deck basking in the late evening sun that was just about to go down.

"You know there's a lot of history to Martha's Vineyard," Stabros said aimlessly as he stood looking out at the ocean.

"I know. It helps create its mystique," I replied.

"Did you know that the island was named in 1602—" Stabros asked.

"Yes, by an English explorer…Bartholomew Gosnold," I retorted.

"Since then, the island is a great tourist attraction and also made famous by a few Hollywood films."

"Most definitely. There's also been a lot of infamy attached to the island from 1969 through 1999."

"The Kennedy's," he said knowingly.

We engaged in a brief conversation about the history of the island, and I could see that he was impressed.

Stabros walked over and gave me a big bear hug. "I love an intelligent woman. You better watch her Black…I may have to come up to New York and steal your lady."

"Watch it, old man," Black said.

It was cute watching them playfully bicker over me.

"Now will you two excuse me? I have an engagement to attend. Black, everything is set up. Enjoy. You'll have complete privacy."

After Stabros left, Black guided me to the left wing of the house, and we went through a side exit door.

"Take off your shoes," he said as he began to take off his. As we strolled down the beach, I could see that the servants had set up a little romantic picnic. There was a chilled bottle of Petron, two large rock lobster tails, beluga caviar, aged cheese and crackers.

I collapsed against the checkered blanket and felt the soft sand underneath. Black sat beside me and popped open the bottle. He poured two glasses of the expensive tequila and said, "Let's toast."

"Okay."

"Go ahead and make one," he urged.

I thought for a quick moment before bringing my glass up to meet his and said, "To new beginnings."

"To new beginnings," he returned, and we clinked our glasses together.

As we sat nibbling on our succulent array of food and watched the sun set, Black remarked how romantic the evening was turning.

"But," he noted, "romance can get dry. Let's add some fun in the mix."

"What are you suggesting?"

"You're not gonna go for it," he said sheepishly.

"Try me."

"You're a punk," he said, trying to bait me.

"What? I'm from Brooklyn," I said all gangsterlike.

The tequila made us giggle like two school kids.

"Okay, then bet. Do as I do. And you better not chicken out."

"Bet."

Black stood and I followed. When he started to unbutton his jean shorts, without hesitation, I stepped out of my linen shorts. Next, he pulled his T-shirt over his head, and I pulled off my fitted T. He stood in his boxers, and I stood in my lace bra and thong panties. His eyes penetrated mine as he drank in my sexy curves. I'm figuring at that moment he felt as if he'd scored. Truthfully, I'm not shy about anything. If I didn't have to play a role he would have seen the goods a long time ago. When he dropped his boxers and his huge dick almost touched his knee, my eyes couldn't help but give it away when they bulged from my sockets. I turned away and said, "That's all you get. I'm not stripping naked. Now what?"

"Last one in is a rotten egg," he screamed and ran toward the ocean. I gave chase behind him, giggling the whole time. As the cool, salty water crashed up against my baby-smooth skin, I felt rejuvenated. We splashed around in the dangerous, alluring sea water until our toes were wrinkled. I didn't even care that I had gotten my hair wet and that the salt water would surely ruin my relaxer. I was having too much fun.

As serious as Black could be, I was glad to see that he had a more fun, humorous side. At first we were just splashing around, waist-level high in the water.

"Can you swim?" Black asked.

"Like a fish," I replied, and we both dived head first into the waves. I took even, controlled strokes as my hands cut into each wave. Left, right, left, right, breathe. Left, right, left, right, inhale. I glanced at Black, and we were in sync heading deeper into the temperamental ocean. All of a sudden I got a cramp in my left leg and tried to kick it out. The undercurrent snatched me beneath the water, and I panicked. I had too much to drink and the treacherous waves wanted to keep me forever. As I fought to get back up I felt another sharp pain in my right side. I don't know what we were thinking by eating before jumping in for a swim. I couldn't see anything as I raced back to the top. As my head broke the wave, I let out a frantic yell for help but it was cut short when an angry surf pulled me back under.

I'm dead, I thought.

A strong, masculine grip grabbed my upper forearm and began pulling me up above the water. I frantically inhaled, gasping for air and clinging onto life. I began coughing violently and uncontrollably from the amount of salt water I'd swallowed. My stomach contracted involuntarily, making it harder for me to breathe. I knew enough to totally submit into his arms and let him get me back to safety. When we got to the shore Black picked me up and carried me past the blanket and back into the house. All you could hear while he carried me through the house was little sniffles involuntarily escaping from me. I was so traumatized from that incident that I went into distress for a moment. I was in shock as Black showered me and placed me in a king-size bed.

"I'm so sorry, baby," Black soothed as he ran his fingers gently over my face. "I should have never left your side."

Finally, I was able to speak. "It wasn't your fault."

"Shhhh, just relax. Get some rest and we'll talk in the morning. As Black climbed in the bed next to me, I drifted off into a deep, restful sleep.

When I awoke in the morning, Black was gone. I was amazed that he wouldn't wake me up since I was in a stranger's house. I looked over and on his pillow was a long, black velvet box. I knew it was for me. My surprise.

Excitedly, I reached over and opened the delicate box. On a bed of black velour was a beautiful pink diamond tennis bracelet. It was exactly what I deserved. Being a daddy's girl and being showered with gifts all my life, I knew quality and demanded the best. Black had gone far beyond any gift my father could buy me. It's amazing how a stone could bring so much joy to one's heart. My heart fluttered, my eyes beamed. I was absolutely flabbergasted by his generosity.

I slipped on my bracelet, hopped in a quick shower and washed my hair. I left a little conditioner in it with hopes of softening it up as I pulled it back in a tight ponytail. When I came out the shower I noticed that Black had brought my clothing from the beach inside the room. I slipped back on my clothes from the day before and went on my hunt for Black. I turned the heavy, gold-plated doorknob to a two-hundred-yard L-shaped hallway. I could hear a faint voice coming from below, and I knew it was Black. As I walked toward the voice his conversation became clearer.

"Me and Ms. Whitaker will be returning back to New York this afternoon," Black announced.

"When will you be returning, sir?" an unfamiliar male voice with a heavy Boston accent asked.

"I don't know if she's interested in coming back anytime soon."

"What about Ms. Nicoli and BJ? Are they coming up next weekend?"

"I'm not sure."

"We sure liked having you here with Ms. Whitaker. It feels good to have life in this house. This is a beautiful home, sir, if you don't mind my saying so, but it needs to be filled with children and happiness."

"I hear you, Kingsley. And you're right. I didn't spend this much money on this house not to enjoy it more often. I'll be back soon, and I'll stay a little longer. Keep everything together while I'm gone," Black said.

That little liar, I thought. *How dare he pretend that this was his friend's home....*

I crept back upstairs and waited for him to come fetch me.

When he opened the door, I greeted him with the succulent kiss.

"I see somebody got the bracelet," he said.

I hugged him tightly and inhaled his intoxicating cologne. I hated to admit it but I was catching feelings.

Black dropped me off and promised to call me later, which he didn't. I woke up the next morning pissed. I had fallen asleep waiting for his call, and when I woke up, reality hit me. Was he with Nicoli? When I called his phone and it went to voicemail, I knew I had to call in reinforcements. I needed to be put back into the right perspective by daddy dearest. I couldn't lose my cool or focus and blow it.

33

Jinx

Shawn and I were getting closer since our last breakup. Things were going smoothly, and I loved the fact that we talked about everything. One night after dinner I could tell that he had something on his mind. He was distracted the whole time we were at the restaurant. When we went back to his place and made love, it was quick as if he just wanted to release his anger or frustrations. I crawled under his arm, and as he began to run his hand through my hair he opened up.

"Did I tell you about the income tax business that I owned in downtown, Brooklyn?"

"No. I didn't know that you owned a business."

"Yeah. The only thing is that it's my business but it's in my wife's name."

I swallowed hard. "Why?"

"My credit was lousy and she had A-1 credit. She offered, and at the time I thought it was a great idea. I thought we'd be together until death do us part."

"So is she trying to keep the business?"

"Nah. She's not like that. Every month I give her a call and she pays all the bills—utility, rent, credit cards," he explained.

My heart started to beat faster because I didn't want to think about them communicating. "Well what's the problem?"

"It's not her that I'm worried about. She's a good girl. The only thing is that I'm afraid to mention divorce to her."

Does he realize that he's just admitted to yet another lie? Is it me or did he say from the first day we met that the papers were in for the divorce? I thought.

"Why would she get angry if a divorce is what you both want?" I said, weighing my words carefully. I didn't want to go through another few weeks of not speaking because I caught him in yet another lie.

"I gotta watch how I talk to her. She did it to me before. I could tell that she was angry with me because when I called her to pay the bills she was short with me. She has control of all of my money, and it makes me nervous. I mean right now it's cool, but what about when she meets someone? That very same man could have her thinking that my money is her money."

I didn't have an answer. And I wasn't sure if they were questions. I didn't have a clue why he brought up the subject or what message he wanted me to get out of this conversation, but what I would say is that it didn't sit well with me. And instead of trying to analyze it, I decided to erase it.

Several days later I decided to revisit the conversation with Shawn about divorcing his wife. No matter how I tried to forget it, I couldn't. He lied to me, and I wanted him to admit it.

"What's up, baby?"

"Nothing. Did you put the divorce papers in yet?"

Long pause, and then, "I told you that it's not going to be that easy."

"You also told me that you'd already put the papers in. So what am I supposed to believe? Which version is the truth, Shawn?"

"You don't even know what you're talking about. It's difficult filing for a divorce in New York."

"Bullshit. Filing for a divorce is simple when it's uncontested. Isn't your divorce supposed to be so amicable?"

"It's too expensive out here."

"Too expensive. Why? Are you Donald Trump and she's Martha Stewart? Is that the case? You have so many assets that it's going to be that expensive to separate? Stop taking me for a motherfucking fool because I'm tired of this shit. It's been going on way too long. The lies, Shawn. I'm tired. Tell the truth and shame the devil."

"First things first, I don't lie. I've been nothing but straight with you from the start, and I'm not going to keep explaining myself over and over."

"So what are you saying?"

"I'm saying for you to stop pressuring me about divorcing my wife."

Oh no he didn't.

"Pressuring you? I'm pressuring you to divorce your wife? Don't make this something that it's not. I would have never fucked with a married man. I was under the pretense that your marriage was a wrap."

"Stop peeking into my motherfucking window and mind your own business. All goddamn day all you do is nag me. You don't even know her and you're jealous of her," he spat and I could feel his forehead crease through the phone.

My voice rose to an octave I didn't recognize.

"Jealous? You must have bumped your two-toned head. Bitches are jealous of me—not the other way around. I upgraded you by merely being in your presence. You'll never find another Jinx."

"Bitches like you come a dime a dozen," he remarked, dryly.

"You're a fraud Shawn…a fraud! Don't be mad at me because you're not clever enough to keep your lies straight. If you thought you met a dumb bitch I'm sorry to disappoint you," I yelled into the phone and hung up. May I break all my fingers before I ever dial his motherfucking ass again. It's so over.

It was four weeks before I heard from Shawn. When I hung up on him I didn't expect him to call. The Shawn of apologizing was long gone. Now all that remained was a lying, cold and distant Shawn—a manipulative man with a lot of secrets. So it was shocking when I went to Lindenwood Diner with my girls and he was there.

In my drunken haze, I could still see the gleam in his eyes as I agreed to leave the diner with him. Shawn was speaking so softly to me as he drove over the Major Deegan bridge into the Bronx. Neither one of us mentioned our breakup, the conflicts or lies that were told. I sat back and closed my eyes until we pulled up in front of his house. As soon as we walked in, I felt that I'd made a mistake. Instead of going with my instinct,

I remained silent.

Shawn began kissing me softly as he gently unzipped my dress. I stepped out of it and stood in front of him in my stilettos, bra and panties. Quickly he undressed, and we made our way to his bed. There wasn't any foreplay other than the kiss we shared at the door. When he reached for a condom and wrapped up his dick, I didn't have time to think. He rammed his dick inside me, pumped a few times, and it was over. He pulled out of me and went to sleep. I was speechless.

That morning, his alter-ego appeared again and he was in rare form. Shawn basically walked around with an attitude from the time he woke me up, which was six-thirty.

"It's Sunday morning…like why are you waking me up this early?"

"I have somewhere I need to be," he spat with disdain.

"What is your problem?" I asked, jumping to my feet, sensing that something wasn't right.

"Jinx, I don't have a problem. I gotta go to the gym," he said.

"Six o'clock in the morning on a Sunday? Why are you doing this to me?"

"Doing what?" he asked incredulously.

"This. These mind games. Why did you invite me here?"

"Look, I thought there wouldn't be any strings attached," he calmly replied.

"No strings attached," I cried. "No strings attached?"

I began pulling on my clothes that I had only taken off hours ago. Tears streamed down my cheeks as I realized that I did this to myself. He showed me time after time in the beginning of the relationship that he couldn't be trusted, that he wasn't anything more than a liar. I ignored every tell-tale sign because I was so desperate to be in a relationship. It didn't matter that it was an unhealthy one. I compromised, swallowed my pride on too many occasions and kept allowing myself to be available to someone who only wanted to use me. I eagerly gave him my precious heart, and he stomped on it with Timberland boots, for fun. All I was was an ego booster, a test to see if he could get the pretty girl to fall in love. I was done with being faithful to these trifling men.

"Jinx, I don't need the headache. I didn't make you do anything you didn't want to do. You wanted it," he cockily replied. "You wanted to be here."

"Yeah, okay. I wanted to be here…in your lavish apartment that Rent-A-Center decorated," I spat. "With a married man who has a kid outside of wedlock, who lives in the past, professing to be a murderous, drug dealing, lying man. You're right, I did want it. I wanted the man you claimed to be not the man you are. You are not the man I met in the hospital. I guess that was your representative."

I could tell that my pain was absolutely invigorating to him by the way his eyes lit up when he spoke and the smirk he had plastered to his face.

"There must be something good about me you was all over my dick."

Finally, I was able to see what I refused. Calmly I replied, "You put on this façade as if you're really confident with this huge ego, but I know different. I know that you're an insecure man whose brain can't process how and why I'd be attracted to you—you, an unattractive freak of nature. Funny thing is that you're probably right. Maybe I don't really like you. Maybe I had been out of a relationship so long I've been fooling myself. I don't know, and I may never know, but what I do know is that you claim to be a good dude, I *am* a good woman."

I slipped on my Jimmy Choos, circa 2004, grabbed my pocketbook and bounced. He called after me, "Let me drive you home."

"Kick rocks, nigga. I don't fuck with you no more," I yelled back.

Thinking quickly, my sixth sense told me to scoop up his mail on his countertop before exiting.

After walking about forty blocks in the early morning hours, I finally was able to find the subway. I caught the six train, which was outdoors, heading to Manhattan. There I'd transfer for the A-train going into Brooklyn. Once on the train, I leafed through a few bills. Each bill was outstanding. His words about spending hundreds of thousand on his exes came flooding back. Then a letter caught my attention. I ripped it open and my hands trembled as I read her letter. It was from his wife and they weren't getting a divorce after all. She was in Iraq fighting our war. She'd been stationed there for eighteen months and would be home soon. Her letter spoke of her undying love and she couldn't wait to see the new place he'd gotten for them. I closed that letter and cried like a little baby. I didn't care if the bystanders looked. I felt like such a fool.

When I got back to my neighborhood, I dialed Breezy and began filling her in on what happened. As tears streamed down my cheeks, I listened to how she perceived the relationship.

"Jinx, don't cry," she soothed. "He just wasn't right for you. I'm glad he's out of your life because now you'll find the right man. He was a strange-looking man who behaved strangely and now you know why. He had a huge secret and he knew you'd find out sooner than later. Be happy that he's out of your life. He had too much baggage and you deserve better."

"How could he do this to me?"

"Jinx, if not you then someone else."

"I swear I wish I had someone to beat him down! Stomp his guts out and make him feel how I feel. I hate him! When I think about how he said I was jealous of his wife…like he had some sort of trophy because she's out saving the world. Like I'm nothing more than yesterday's trash," I sobbed.

"He used the oldest trick in the book to get into your bed: religion. Show me a man who's religious and faithful and I'll show you a hundred women all vying for his attention. That's our fantasy and he'd played into it. Don't be too hard on yourself."

"It's like the moment I showed him I liked him was the same moment he stopped liking me. At times it seemed as if he *hated* me."

"Jinx there isn't anymore I can say but be thankful that you at least no the truth. He can't hurt you anymore. You have closure."

Breezy was right, there wasn't anything else I could do except collapse on the bed and cry my eyes out.

34

Breezy

I sat listening to Keyshia Cole's CD, tracks one through twelve repeatedly all afternoon once I came in from class. It had been two days since Black and I left Martha's Vineyard. My father told me to fall back—that men hate to be smothered. It pushed them away. He said that Black made a statement with the bracelet and that I should just relax and wait for his call, but I had other plans. I had already devised a scheme that I wanted to execute sooner than later.

I went into the city to my cousin Nicoli's residence. Only, I didn't go inside. I staked out the building in the early-morning hours while everyone was sleep. It didn't take me long to figure out how to maneuver inside. I waited for the early-morning rush and walked in, past the doorman and got onto the elevator. I quickly glanced for the garage, which was on two lower levels. Once there I walked in search of Nicoli's car and Black's. I came upon Nicoli's car within the first five minutes but I never found any car that resembled Black's, but that didn't mean that he wasn't there.

Next, I went back out and parked my car, while keeping my ignition on, at the exit ramp of her building. I was sure that she'd be going out soon. And I was right. She came out slowly looking left, then right, before entering traffic. I pulled off slowly, keeping my distance. She dropped off her spoiled-ass kid to day care, went to pick up clothes from a nearby cleaner and then went to Forty-ninth and Fifth Avenue to shop in Saks Fifth Avenue.

"Enjoy it while you can," I said out loud, my words dripping with venom.

Nicoli was playing right into my hands and didn't even know it. Now that I could trace her whereabouts and was certain that Black wasn't with her, I left and put my plan into motion.

I went into a local Apple supermarket on Fiftieth Street and bought a dozen eggs. I pulled around to a secluded block, grabbed my switchblade that I keep on the side of my door for protection and carved the words WHORE. BITCH. SLUT. HOME WRECKER into my beautiful jeep's exterior. As I dug each word into my jeep, I prayed that this would play out the way I wanted it to. Then I took out a cheap Revlon red lipstick that I'd just picked up in the supermarket and scribbled all types of obscenities on my windows. The finishing touch was the egg. I showered my Range Rover with eggs then let it bake in the sun, which would surely ruin the paint.

I sat in the driver's seat for over an hour before I was ready for the grand finale. I called Black's phone hysterically. When he didn't answer it didn't stop me from leaving a frantic voice message.

"Oh, my gosh. Black…I think someone is trying to harm me…my jeep…they had a knife…" I sobbed into the phone and hung up. Two minutes later my phone rang.

"Hello," I screamed.

"Are you hurt?" he asked. I could hear the panic in his voice.

"I'm fine…I don't know what happened. Someone vandalized my truck. It's awful, and I think I was being followed all day."

"Vandalized your truck?" he asked in disbelief. "How?"

"Someone wrote all over my jeep calling me a whore and home wrecker. Me of all people," I wailed.

"Home wrecker?" he absently repeated.

"Yes, Black. I'm scared."

"Where are you?"

"I'm on Fiftieth and Fifth."

"What are you doing in the city? Okay, explain everything when I get there. Don't move."

Black's chauffeur drove him to meet me. He arrived within twenty minutes. As soon as I saw him I forced myself to cry again. When he saw my vandalized truck, he was furious. He read every word over and over.

"How did this happen?" he asked. "Where were you?"

"The college gives an alumni dinner every year, and I needed to get something to wear because I'm speaking. When I left my house this morning I could have sworn that I was being followed. There was a silver Mercedes that seemed to appear everywhere I went."

"A silver Mercedes? Did you get a look at the driver?"

"Not a good look. But it was a light-skinned female."

I could tell that I had him.

"Well, I go in Saks and while I'm waiting at a counter a very rude light-skinned female practically breaks one of my ribs when she elbowed me. It was too hard to be a mistake. I got away from her and continued to shop. I must have stayed in Saks too long because when I came out this is what I saw."

"How could this happen with all these people around? Didn't anyone see anything?"

"I asked but no one would say a word. Maybe I should call the police—"

"No. I mean that won't help any. You've been through too much. I'll handle it for you. Don't worry about it. Get in," Black demanded and jumped into my driver's seat. We drove to a midtown address and had his chauffer come and take my car away to a body shop.

"You'll have to borrow one of my cars until they've fixed yours. I hope you don't mind."

"I can't possibly do that. You've helped me so much already. I shouldn't have called but I was so frightened and didn't have anyone else to call."

"Don't be silly. You were supposed to call me. I'm your man, right? Even if you won't give me none," he joked.

I knew better than to play into the sexual suggestion because I was still supposed be upset about the incident. So I said, "Do you have any idea who would want to do this? Does the car and description I gave you sound familiar?"

"Why would you ask me that?"

"I'm sorry if I offended you but I'm not seeing anyone and someone carved the words HOME WRECKER into my car."

He shook his head. "I told you before that you wouldn't have to worry about my son or my son's mother. No baby momma drama. I don't have an inkling what's that about. Maybe someone got you mixed up."

"I'm so stressed. This is a bad time for people to be scaring me like this."

"How about you let me take away your stress?"

"Black."

"Not like that. You'll have to trust me," he encouraged.

Black handed me the keys to a silver Mercedes G55 truck. "Drive to the Brooklyn Promenade."

I got inside and drove to the romantic location. We sat there for hours uninterrupted just talking. We had both climbed into the backseat, and Black was massaging my scalp as I lay on his lap. Soon, his hand began to venture down my back and then stopped on my ass, which he began massaging. I said nothing as he began tracing the inner lining of my skirt. Next, he pushed me up. I leaned back in the seat as he pulled my panties to one side and began to taste me. I didn't resist. He sucked on my clitoris until I moaned softly. I was afraid to give him more of a reaction. Truth be told, I was a little terrified of getting arrested. As he aggressively began to nibble, suck and bite on my clit, I could no longer control my feelings. The spontaneity of the moment was sexy and erotic.

Black stuck my index finger in my pussy and twirled it around. Hot juices seeped onto my finger, and we both got excited.

"Play with your pussy while I watch," he commanded.

My ego wanted to arouse him. I began masturbating in the backseat of his truck while he watched. I positioned my finger inside my pussy to hit my G-spot while simultaneously massaging my breast. I began moaning sexily and chanting his name. "Black…you feel sooooo good," I crooned as I grinded my hips. Soon Black released his massive dick from his jeans and began to jerk off. I watched as he brought himself to a climax with his strong hands. Black reached forward and ripped my shirt open. My buttons popped off and flew everywhere. Quickly, he began to jerk off on my face and chest. Cum squirted everywhere, and I wasn't even embarrassed. The kinkiness of the moment was sexually gratifying.

"Take off your shirt," he asked.

Black took my shirt and began to wipe his semen off my body. I felt a connection as he pulled his T-shirt over his head and gave it to me to wear home. That night I knew that the relationship was moving in the right direction.

35

Nicoli

My grandmother used to say that a new bitch is made every day by a broken heart. I say a good bitch is born that way. I'm far from a new bitch and every bit a good bitch. Last year Black had given me a credit card for emergencies—plastic to purchase myself a few things but mainly for BJ to buy him clothes, footwear and toys. He stressed that I use this card modestly and like a stupid girl full of remorse, eager to please her ex-man, I obliged.

As I stood at the counter of Bergdorf Goodman, with ninety thousand dollars worth of clothing, I pulled out the champion of all credit cards…the one card that says you've made it…the American Express Centurion card, popularly known as the Black Card and slapped it on the counter. The sales assistant didn't need to call for assistance to verify I was the rightful owner. A gesture she would have surely done to any black female under these same circumstances. She had been seeing me for years only this time her commission would be a small fortune.

Quickly I scanned the luxurious items I felt I deserved. Badgley Mischka. John Galliano. La Perla. Prada. Gucci. They'd all get to know me a little more intimately once I got them home.

"Ms. Jones, could you sign here and then you're all set?" she said while smiling like a Kool-Aid campaign.

I took the sales receipt and scribbled my exotic signature on the dotted line. I loved doing that. I just couldn't wait until Black's accountant got the bill and called Black. He should lose a few strands of hair from this shopping spree alone. That coupled with the obscene amount of money I spent in the shoe section should push him over the edge, and I hadn't even begun to fight back. This would certainly teach him to not fuck with someone's feelings. The best way to get back at a man is to either get him in his pockets or have his enemy fall madly in love with you. I'm banking on pulling off both. Oh, I'm just getting started. This ain't over until I say it's over….

It took longer than I expected for Black to get the 411 on my shopping spree, but while I waited I started to enjoy our strained encounters when he came to pick up BJ. When his usual knock at the door sounded as if five-0 was looking for terrorists, I knew that only one of two things could have occurred. Either he was served or he got the bill. No sense in guessing when all I had to do was open the door.

I came to the door in full diva ensemble. My naturally red hair was wild and curly. I had applied a light green eye shadow from MAC cosmetics and a clear lip gloss. I decided to wear a pair of white fitted leggings from Cynthia Rowley and a white tunic shirt with Swarovski crystals. A pair of white-and-green Giuseppe stiletto heels adorned my feet. It takes work looking as if you didn't put any effort in choosing your outfit. That simple ensemble costs over three thousand dollars.

"What's your problem?" I yelled as I flung the door open.

"What's wrong with you?" he roared. "Do you think that my money is your money?"

"Is that a trick question?" I casually replied and sauntered back into the living room area disrespectfully turning my back on him.

"Why would you go and spend $115,000 on clothing? And don't try to say that that was for BJ because my accountant said that it was all from the women's department."

"Look, I'm grown. I don't have to tell little lies about what I spend my money on—"

"Look Alice, come from wonderland and let's start all over. Did you just say your money?"

"Yes. Did I stutter?"

"No. But when I punch you in your fucking mouth you may," he threatened. But I knew that that was all it was. Black wouldn't dare hit a woman, and most certainly not the mother of his child.

"Listen, where's my son? Why isn't he with you?"

"I left him back at my house so that we can straighten this shit out. I want you to return all of the nonsense you bought. You think I'm made of fucking money? You want shit, go out and get a job to get it."

Ignoring his snide remark, I yelled, "Who the fuck has BJ? He better not be with a bitch because I'll fuck her up. Don't be having my son around your ho-bitches."

"Oh, you think I'm playing with you? Where's the shit?" he challenged, running in the back toward my closet.

I panicked. "You touch shit in my house you're going to jail. Straight up," I threatened, prepared to call the cops at any second if he called my bluff.

Black pulled opened my closet and saw all the evidence. Designer tags dangling provocatively from my new garments. When he started tossing everything on the bed in preparation to take them with him I began dialing for help.

"I need assistance over at my apartment."

"What's the problem, ma'am?" the 911 dispatcher asked.

"I'm being robbed and I need help," I yelled. "Leave my shit alone."

"You calling the cops?" Black said, and his face twisted up in anger. He was amazed at my antics, and he didn't like how I decided to handle the situation. "Bitch, this is what you love?"

Black grabbed me by the back of my neck and shoved me face down into the clothing. I screamed out in fear that he'd finally lost his mind. When he went into the kitchen I could hear silverware jangling. He came back in the room brandishing a butcher's knife. My heart began to palpitate faster at an alarming rate but I refused to back down. I was in too deep.

I jumped up from off the bed, while I scanned the room quickly for a weapon.

My iron breezed past his head and smashed up against the wall. Black charged me, tossing me to the floor all in one gesture. When he lifted the sharp blade over his head, I ducked for cover. Cowering in the corner it took me long moments to get the courage to open my eyes. When I did it was already too late. He'd destroyed practically everything on the bed, cutting and tearing it to pieces—over a hundred thousand dollars worth of merchandise. I was floored.

"This is what you can't live without, you money-hungry, greedy bitch. Here, here," he said, smashing and trying to mush the torn and tattered material in my face. He was so aggressive that I was finding it hard to breathe. My face was stinging from coming into contact with zippers, buttons and crystals. Finally I was able to kick him off of me. When we both stood, we were both sweating heavily and our breathing was out of control and rapid.

When I heard a loud, thunderous knock at the door, it snapped me back into reality.

Police? I thought. But didn't have to wonder long before the officer identified himself. I ran to the door, almost leaping over furniture like a modern-day Superwoman. I flung the door open to the most beautiful sight ever.

"Ma'am, we got a call that a robbery was in progress," the young white officer said. I looked at both officers who were looking around the apartment, which was in disarray and both had their hands on their guns, ready to draw at any moment. When Black came out the room, both officers were on point. They had noticed that there was redness in my face from our struggle.

"My son's father has come in here and roughed me up, throwing me around and threatened me with a knife."

"What?" Black asked incredulously.

"Sir, step away from the lady, and put your hands over your head," the quiet officer said.

"Look, she's lying. She just ran up my credit cards without my permission. I just came over here to talk. That's all I did was talk to her. I never laid a hand on her. Nicoli, stop lying. They're going to take me to jail for this bullshit," he pleaded on deaf ears.

Tears began to stream down my cheeks, and I clutched myself. The white officer walked me over to the side and asked if I wanted to press charges.

"Yes, sir, I do. He's crazy. A maniac. And he also has my son. I'll need to get him, but I don't know where he is."

"Did he kidnap him?"

"No. He has him on the weekends. He was supposed to bring him home tonight but he hasn't," I said while tears streamed down my cheeks. "You've got to get him to tell me where my son is."

"Don't cry, ma'am. I hate it when a beautiful woman cries. Did he rip your clothes and bruise your face?"

Was he flirting?

"Uh-huh. I tried to stop him but he's much too big."

"You said something about him wielding a knife?"

"In the room."

"Okay, we'll need that as evidence."

I walked the officer into the room to show him the knife, and he said that he'd need to take it down to the station. Meanwhile, Black was trying to use his celebrity to get out of the situation. Both officers were uninterested in listening to his pleas. They knew exactly who he was, and they both were eager to put those silver bracelets on his celebrity ass.

"So you really gonna let them do this to me?" he said while his eyes pleaded with me for mercy.

"Where's my son?" I asked.

"He's at my house with my butler Alphonse…Nicoli…you're taking this too far. I'll replace all that shit. It's not that serious."

"Alphonse better have BJ and not some ho when I get there," I threatened.

"I stopped dating hos when I dropped you. I have an educated lady in my life. You know her…the one who you stalked the other day and vandalized her car."

"Oh please, Black," I said, rolling my eyes. "Stalk who? That bitch is playing mind games with your stupid ass."

I've known Black too long, and I knew that he really believed that I had stalked someone and vandalized her car. But who?

"Breezy's more woman than you'll ever be," he boasted.

Did he just say Breezy? As in my cousin Brooklyn? I felt my stomach get squeamish as my mind raced back to the unannounced visit to my mother's house after over fifteen years of being archenemies. Could she have really captured Black's heart? My cousin of all people. I wanted to flip but something told me not to. Breezy was plotting against me because she had the element of anonymity. I couldn't react emotionally at the moment. I needed to strategize. Besides, I wasn't sure we were talking about the same person but my female intuition said that I was right.

"Please. All that glitters ain't gold."

"You should know," he sarcastically retorted.

"Stop talking to the lady. We've seen enough to arrest you without her," the quiet officer barked.

"Man, fuck you. Who you yelling at? You ain't tough," Black shot back.

At six-one Black towered over both the average height men, but he didn't have a chance to put fear in them. He was clearly at a disadvantage.

Inwardly, I was enjoying the show. Listening to Black bitch up made me feel that I'd won at least one of many battles.

When Black realized that I was going along with locking his ass up he let out a litany of profanity that I didn't know was in his vocabulary.

"All you're good for is swallowing dick. I should have left you in the gutter with all the other hos but instead I gave you a shot. All you are is a bottom bitch with a decent shape and stale pussy. I bumped my fucking head when I took off the condom. It ain't over, you trifling tramp. Scheming, plotting pussy licker. I'll never take your contaminated ass back. I got a good girl. A smart, educated woman. Not an immature, lying, greedy gold digger."

The comment about Breezy had infuriated me but I was too slick to let it show. That was only giving me fuel to keep going at him hard.

"If her pussy is that good maybe we can do a ménage a trois," I suggested. Of course I didn't mean any of it.

"You make me sick to my stomach." He grimaced.

"Likewise."

As the police led him out he made one last remark about me going against the grain. I had already tuned him out. I couldn't wait to get on the horn to see if Stacy knew anything about Breezy and Black.

36

Jinx

After Shawn and I broke up I decided the best way to get over him would be to get out and see other men. I refused to spend another three years in hibernation. I ran around Kings Plaza Mall looking for the perfect outfit to wear out on my date. Since my main and only focus was opening up my boutique I put myself on a strict budget. I couldn't spend more than two hundred dollars on an outfit and that was my limit. I decided that I was going to be the next Kimora Lee and make Shawn eat his heart out.

I desperately wanted Breezy to come with me to the mall, but I feared if I asked her she'd have me in midtown Manhattan in Saks Fifth Avenue buying two-hundred-dollar jeans. She and I were typical Brooklyn girls. We studied hard to get our degrees, were focused on our futures, loved to party and loved fashion.

The reason this date was so important was because I was trying to get over my broken heart. I decided that before I fell into a deep depression that I'd date through pain. Men do it all the time.

I went into Macy's and tried on a pair of size 30 Von Dutch jeans and a wrap-around shirt, and my money was spent.

When I got home and looked in the mirror I looked no different than someone who had spent three times the amount I spent on my outfit. That, coupled with the fact that I pulled out a signature Gucci bag and matching shoes, I think I pulled it off.

That night I was going out with Rob. I'd met him two nights ago at club Exit. He was drinking champagne with his friends and sent me over a glass. We exchanged telephone numbers and talked every day.

Rob called my cell when he was downstairs in front of my house. I had to practically assure him that he'd be all right coming to pick me up in East New York. He claimed that he wasn't afraid but told me a long story about beating up a few guys so badly that he should lay low. Truthfully, I didn't believe his story but I just passed it off as him trying to impress me.

As I walked out my house I could hear him blasting "Dream" from The Game's debut CD. The music was so loud that he didn't hear me tapping on the window. When I tapped harder on the window it startled him, and he hit his head on the front glass from almost jumping out of his seat.

As much as I wanted to burst into laughter, I contained it. I would hate for the evening to start out on a bad note.

I climbed in the passenger's seat of his Expedition and took another look at Rob. This was my first time seeing him outside the club and under the influence of liquor. By society's standards he was a nice-looking guy. He was below average height for a man, I would say around five-eight. He weighed approximately 195 pounds and had chubby cheeks and hands. He had brown skin, sinister-looking eyes and two-toned lips as if he smoked. There wasn't any muscle tissue on his body. He was all fat. Truthfully, he wasn't my type. I prefer much taller men with a six-pack stomach and hard biceps. I wasn't that surprised that I took his number. I'd been feeling awfully lonely lately. There was no telling what you'll do when you're lonely, intoxicated and in a club full of men.

"So what you wanna do, Ma?" he asked.

I wondered how my name went from Jinx to Ma in one day, but I said nothing.

"I thought we were going to get something to eat."

"Oh, you didn't eat yet?"

"Well, no. I thought you said that's what we'd do."

"Well if you didn't eat and want to get something to eat then I guess we could do that…" his voice trailed off as if he was contemplating whether he should take me out to dinner.

"Well what did you have in mind?" I asked.

"I thought maybe a movie."

"Well it's early. Why can't we do both?" I suggested.

"Umm…well…I…umm…got shit to do. We can't do both. So what it's gonna be?"

"I guess we can go out to eat."

"You don't know how to cook?" he asked as I waited for him to put the car in drive so we could begin our date.

"Yes, I cook. Why?"

"Did you cook tonight?" he asked, and I looked at his chubby hands and cheeks. I didn't know where this conversation and I wasn't in the mood to entertain it.

"No, I didn't because I was too busy getting ready for this date," I said.

"You said you live by yourself?" he probed. I know there was a purpose to this line of questioning but at the moment I was at a loss.

"I live with my grandmother."

"Damn. Ain't rent like a dollar and fifteen cents in this neighborhood? You can't get your own crib?"

"What?" I asked incredulously.

"Nothing. Nothing. Hold up. I gotta make a call first."

He pulled out his cellular phone and placed a call while I sat impatiently waiting for our night to begin. I kept hearing Nana's voice in my head saying, *"Chile, always get what you want. Don't settle for less in a man. It leaves room for sin to sneak in."*

Nana was right. Rob was certainly not my type but for some reason I decided that one date couldn't hurt.

"Yo, man…I had to block my number for you to pick up," he said into the phone. "I need that money I loaned you. I got a lot of my money tied up, and I could use that five thousand I let you hold."

I listened intently wondering why he would loan someone five thousand dollars. That's too much money to risk not getting back.

"Nah, Bee…I can't wait. I'm going—"

Midway into his conversation his cellular phone rang. I looked at him. He looked at me and knew he was busted. I sank lower in my seat and turned my head out the window. For some reason *I* felt embarrassed.

He hung up the phone and said, "Yo, my phone company be buggin'. My phone is messed up. Sometimes I'm on a call and another call will come through and drop my call."

I didn't say anything. I just nodded as if I understood. After tonight, I don't think I'll be going out with lying Rob again.

We drove to the restaurant in silence. He drove to Applebee's on Rockaway Turnpike in Long Island. I must admit I was a little disappointed. Applebee's is a family restaurant or somewhere you go with your girlfriends. It's hardly an acceptable first date place. It states you're on a budget.

During dinner I had to listen to Rob drone on and on about million-dollar deals he's involved with. All of which are top secret. He bragged about his past cars, his past houses and his past women. And I nearly passed out.

When the waitress came around with the bill she placed it in the middle of the table and walked away. Rob pulled back out his infamous cell phone and began to talk, never reaching for the check. He didn't seem interested in it at all.

As he was on the phone he looked at me and said, "Ma, get the check this time, and I'll hook us up the next time," and continued to talk on the phone.

My heart dropped. I had never been played so cheap and been so disrespected in my life.

"Get the check? As in pay the bill?" I asked.

He exhaled as if what I'd said had gotten on his last nerve.

"Let me call you back," he said and slammed down his cellular. "Yo, could you get this?"

"No I can't," I challenged. "I can get me...but I can't get this."

"I see how this is going down," he said and reached for the bill. He pulled open his wallet and I saw a couple of bills. He didn't have more than sixty dollars in his pocket. Whatever the amount of the bill I knew it was more than the twenty-five dollars he threw on the table. Quickly, I looked at the bill and it read forty-seven dollars. This fat, broke, lying, fronting-ass bastard had only paid for his portion of the bill. I felt my face get hot. But before I could say anything he was already walking toward his car. He'd already gotten on his cellular phone as he bebopped out the front door.

My first night out after a miserable breakup and I had gotten played by Fat Albert. I remained calm and called Breezy. "Girl, come get me."

37

Jinx

I sat in the restaurant for about an hour, annoyed, as I waited for Breezy. Eventually, she pulled into the parking lot driving a luxurious Mercedes G55 truck. The silver exterior with chrome rims and trim complemented the vehicle. She was blasting "Cater 2 U," by Destiny's Child. As I climbed in, I inadvertently transferred all my negative energy toward her. I couldn't stand that she was always jovial and perky. I know that's she a phony bitch.

"Girl, this place is so far MapQuest don't even come out here," she joked, only I didn't find it funny. "You okay? You still seem pissed."

"That fat bastard really played me," I stated in disbelief.

"It happens to the best of us," Breezy soothed.

"No, things like this don't happen to you, so stop lying just to make me feel better," I accused.

"Okay, I see you like it rough. Shit like that doesn't happen to me and never will."

"I don't understand how you always get treated with respect and I get played like a groupie," I said, sulking.

"If I didn't know you I'd think there was a little resentment in your voice."

"I'm just saying I'm just as cute as you, and I deserve to have the fly things that you have."

"Excuse me?" she asked incredulously and slammed on her brakes. We were in the middle of Linden Boulevard, a few yards from my house. People started beeping their horns and flickering their high-beam lights. "First off I'm not cute. Cute is for dogs and cuddly cats. I'm a pretty girl who demands respect in any relationship I've ever been in. Don't hate because you settle for less. Your groupie-acting ass got just what you deserved. You were so desperate that night in the club, steady looking for a baller but instead got a bum. And you don't know shit about what I have to do to get and maintain my 'fly things,' so I'm only going to say this one motherfucking time: Stay out my business and stop comparing you to me. You'll always lose."

It took a lot for Breezy to get upset. She was always happy go lucky, so I knew that from this outburst she was really pissed with me.

"All I'm saying is that things come easy to you whereas the rest of us have to work really hard."

"Scabeatit with that shit…," she smirked. "I'll skip over the body of my dead mother to get what I want!"

Her remark unnerved me.

"Damn, girl, it ain't even that serious for you to be screaming and acting all silly," I said, trying to downplay my role in her outburst yet still wanting to get her pressure up. We were still sitting in the middle of the boulevard.

"Bitch, are you stupid?" she yelled, and I saw a glimpse of her dark side. She was moving her head rapidly and talking with her hands. "I got out my bed to come and rescue your stranded ass because a nigga didn't think enough of you to drop two twenties on your restaurant tab. And you got the nerve to sit up in my motherfucking face and say little slick remarks like a bitch don't deserve what she got. I got too many bitches out here quiet hating on me to let my best friend pop shit because she thinks she can without repercussion. Jinx, I am not the one," she warned, and I got the message.

Every since I've known Breezy she will give you the shirt off her back. The last ten dollars in her pocket and even pick you up a shirt or two while she's shopping at the mall. She was really nice to those she called her friends, but there was something embedded deep down in my gut that said she was phony, that her actions were calculated decisions to make you *think* she was this nice, sweet individual when in reality she wasn't. On a few occasions I'd seen her darker side. And it's not just a bitch with an attitude as some may think. I could actually feel negative energy seeping out from her pores that my hair stood up on the back of my neck. I told Nana about it, and she told me on numerous occasions to leave Breezy alone. She said that that's my intuition kicking in. That God gave me the gift of clairvoyance and if I felt an evil spirit surrounding Breezy's aura that I had better take heed. Nana was from the old school so I could hardly take too much of what she said seriously.

"Breezy, I was only joking," I lied. "I was trying to get you to flip out. I love seeing you perform—tossing your head from side to side with that melodramatic brat shit you do."

"Jinx, you had a bitch pressure up," she admitted. "You should have gotten that broke-ass nigga pressure up for trying to play you," she joked and started the car back up.

"I only went out with him because I was tired of being out of the loop," I reasoned.

"Don't make excuses for what happened tonight. Fuck it. You learned something tonight and it only cost you thirty dollars."

"Yeah, I guess you're right," I said as she pulled up in front of my house. "What's up for tonight?"

"You wanna have some drinks at your house?" she asked.

"My house? Hell no. Let's go back to your house."

"Okay, but you're going to have to spend the night because I'm not driving you back home tonight. I feel like getting fucked up. Let's call Joy and make watermelon martinis."

As the Mercedes Michelin tires gripped the pavement, I took pleasure in how my body sank into the plush leather seats.

"Did your father buy this for you?" I asked.

"No. I had to borrow this from a friend. It goes back in a few days," she said evasively and I decided not to probe. Then I thought about her beautiful jeep that he daddy did buy her. She had wood-grain interior, a navigational system and TVs in her headrests, all compliments of her Mr. Whitaker. Breezy's father does import and export via the Internet. His company made lots of money in the early nineties and has flourished ever since. He purchased a beautiful brownstone house in Bedford Stuyvesant a few years back and that's how Breezy and I met. My beautician is on Lafayette, not too far from where Breezy lives.

Breezy doesn't talk about it much but her mother was killed in a car crash when she was just a baby. Breezy said that her mother was going to confront her stepmother when she lost control of the car and crashed. Breezy was in the car, too, but came out unscathed. The irony of her story is that we share almost the same fate. But our lives have turned out totally different. She has a great father and a loving stepmother. And all I have is Nana who is wonderful, don't get me wrong, but it's nothing like losing both your parents to a tragic accident.

Breezy had to get out and open the gate to her driveway. She pulled in next to her father's SL 600 Mercedes Benz. The car suited her father. It was sophisticated, sleek yet masculine. I never admitted it to Breezy, but I had the biggest crush on her father. He looks like he could do damage in the bedroom. Although he's polite and is really sweet to us, there is something street about him. I've grown up in the 'hood all of my life, and I know when a person's down. But Breezy swears her father grew up in the suburbs and that he's a square from nowhere. She said they moved from Fort Lee, New Jersey, when she was ten years old, and she'd never go back. She loves Brooklyn, but doesn't everyone?

We walked up her cobblestone steps and entered the newly renovated brownstone. Every time I enter her house, I lose my breath. No matter how many times I went there. When you walk in there's a foyer with a high ceiling. Off to the right is a family room. Each room in the house has large storm windows and antique fixtures. Every floor has a beautiful marble working fireplace. The first floor has a living room, a kitchen, large bathroom and three bedrooms that are rented out to homeless girls that don't have any family. Mr. Whitaker helps them enroll in college or finish high school, find jobs and even tutors them if they need it. They pay a small, nominal fee to live there every week and help out around the house. Mr. Whitaker takes pride in watching the progress the girls make but that is only short lived. It never fails. Once they get on their feet they disappear. They run off back into the streets without saying so much as a thank you. This year started off with three girls. The other two left on different occasions, and there is only one girl left named Susan. She's eighteen years old.

The second and third floors are a duplex where Breezy's father and stepmother live. The top floor is Breezy's. She has two bedrooms. It used to be three bedrooms but she had her father pay to have one of the smaller bedrooms turned into a walk-in closet. She also has a fireplace with a huge naked picture of herself adorning it. Her kitchen is decked out in granite countertops and the floor match. Each bedroom has cherry-wood floors, and the living room has a plush peach carpet. Oversized leather sofas decorate her lounge area and a romantic canopy bed graces her bedroom. When you walk into her house you feel like a princess, which is exactly how Breezy's father treats her.

While we were upstairs waiting for Joy and her cousin Kesha to come over we made the martinis and began to drink when Breezy's cell phone rang. She looked at the number, smiled then let it go to voicemail.

"What's that about?" I inquired.

"That's my new friend. Jinx, when I tell you he's filthy rich believe what I say. I predict that he's going to be my future husband," she assured.

"Who is he? When did you meet him?" The questions tumbled out.

"Don't worry about it. I'll let you know when it gets serious."

I knew if Breezy wanted him she'd most likely get him. Inside I had to fight off pangs of jealousy, and I prayed that my face didn't give me away. As much as I love Breezy, her plush lifestyle and great luck with men was slowly wearing me down. Why couldn't some rich man come and sweep me off my feet? Isn't that every girls dream?

The girls came over and we drank, laughed and talked shit for the rest of the night until Joy and Kesha left.

In the morning we went down to Breezy's parents' apartment for breakfast. Her dad was an excellent cook. He'd made sausage, bacon, French toast, grits, scrambled eggs and biscuits. Breezy and I eagerly set the table like two schoolgirls.

"Everything tastes so good, Mr. Whitaker," I said.

"Jinx, thanks. Say," he said, "how's school going for you?"

I put my head down as I spoke. "I had to drop out. It was becoming too difficult going to school full-time and working full-time. I couldn't find time to do homework and study for exams."

"I hear you," he empathized, "but education is key to securing your future. Can't you work part-time at the law firm and go to school full-time?"

"Well, I don't want to work part-time because I need the money."

"Don't you live with your grandmother?" he questioned.

"Y-Y-Yes," I stuttered because I knew what he was getting at.

"Well then your overhead bills can't be that taxing. I'm sure you can survive working part-time at least until your studies are done."

"I'll think about it," I said to close the subject.

Although I loved Mr. Whitaker, it was hard being told what to do. Since my parents were killed I didn't have an authority figure overseeing my decisions. Nana has always loved me but she never really enforced any rules for me growing up. Luckily, I didn't turn out like the other two kids she raised.

"Breezy, how are you doing in class?" he asked.

"Very well, Papa," she said, stuffing a forkful of French toast in her mouth.

We all sat around the breakfast table talking long after we'd eaten. Mr. and Mrs. Whitaker drank coffee while Breezy and I told them all about my horrible date the night before. Mr. Whitaker was so mad that he said he would go and tighten him up for disrespecting me. He had a thing about how women should always be treated with great respect and doted upon. And it was evident in the way he treated Breezy and his wife. I sat there in awe as I envied their close-knit family. If I had half of what Breezy had I could die today and be satisfied.

38

I lit a few scented candles to accentuate the mood.

"Yeah, baby, give it to me good," I said and pumped my ass in and out. Sweat rolled down my body as I gritted my teeth in preparation to cum. "You fat, black whore bitch, give it to me good," I demanded and got myself even more excited.

I was jerking off to a photo of the latest victim in the New York *Daily News*. Her name was Latisha. I was in my apartment with all the lights off. As deep waves came flowing through my body, my hand moved more rapidly bringing me to my climax. The sharp butcher's knife that I held steadily in my left hand dug deeply into my skin and cut the surface just as I exploded all over Latisha's face.

"Take that, you smug bitch," I said and collapsed on my sofa. I lay there for moments breathing heavily with my legs and arms stretched out. My athletically wrought naked body felt fatigued. I'd been at this for hours, and that last climax had drained me. As my own blood dripped on my carpet, I felt euphoric.

As I reveled in ecstasy my cell phone rang. Since I had selected different ring tones I knew exactly who it was. He's the only nigga that I'd pick the phone up for at this moment.

"What up?" I asked.

"I need you to come over tonight for a meeting. We got important shit to discuss," Reggie said.

"I'll be there in thirty minutes," I said and hung up.

I showered quickly and wrapped my hand in a gauze bandage. I threw on a black Rocawear sweat suit, black Prada sneakers and a fitted cap. I jumped in my Tahoe jeep and headed straight over. When I pulled up to the brownstone, I noticed all the cars were in the driveway. Something had gone down for Reggie to call an impromptu meeting.

I walked in with a key and went straight upstairs. At the kitchen table there sat Reggie, his wife, Lisa, and Breezy. They all had long faces.

Reggie came to shake my hand when he noticed the bandage.

"Old habits are hard to bury," he observed.

"I do what's best for me," I retorted.

Reggie and I go back almost twenty years. He practically raised me. I lived on Herkimer Avenue, a block that he used to hustle on. I was no more than ten years old and he was twenty-one. He was making hand-to-hand transactions, and I would watch him every day. He'd kick it with me and drop jewels on me that at the time were over my head. When my father murdered my mother and then killed himself he paid for both funerals. He was the first person to tell me to suck it up. "Shit happens," he stated. "Some bitches ain't shit. Weed them out and find yourself a good girl that will ride or die for you and you'll be straight. Your mother played the game and lost. She paid with her life. That's how shit goes. Don't shed too many tears, little man. She didn't think about how her actions could fuck up your life, so don't cry over how she lost hers."

That was his advice to a ten-year-old boy, and I took heed. Every day I had to live with my aunt and her miserable kids, I thought about how it was my mother's fault. How she'd rather fuck than give a fuck about how her actions would affect her only child. A deep-rooted hate for women was embedded in me, and that filtered out to every woman with whom I'd ever come into contact. God help these bitches when they crossed my path…

Herkimer Avenue is where Reggie had met Michelle, Breezy's mother. They fucked around for a while but Reggie knew not to make her his main girl. She had already fucked the whole block and then some. By the time Reggie and Michelle hooked up, I was thirteen and Reggie had left the block and moved to New Jersey. The only time I'd see him was when he came to fuck Michelle. Soon she was pregnant, and I couldn't understand how he let himself get caught up with a ho like her. Truthfully, I was a little disappointed in him. What about all the rules he had schooled me on? Just when I was about to lose faith in my mentor, Michelle went and got herself killed. Luckily, his daughter, Breezy, survived. Reggie never went to the funeral nor did he pay for it. He never shed one tear. His philosophy was that the bitch knew her place.

"Wassup?" I greeted Lisa and Breezy by giving them pecks on their cheeks. They were the only two women I'd ever let my lips touch.

"Nothing much, Uncle," Breezy stated. She simply called me Uncle. No one except her father knew my name. I'm a man of many aliases.

"Okay, let's get down to business," Reggie stated. "Susan left. She's gone. She snuck out in the middle of the night and hasn't been back since. She left a note saying she appreciated everything we've done for her but that she felt something strange in her bones and knew she had to leave."

"What?" I asked incredulously. "All the time that went into finding her, investigating her past, setting up the policy. If only she'd waited one more week we'd all be in the clear."

"Listen, we can't dwell on how close we were to sealing this deal. All that matters is that it fell through. Now we need to get back out there and find a replacement. I've done some research and there's an insurance company that doesn't have the one-year restriction. They pay out forty-eight hours later if someone is deceased, murdered or dies of natural causes."

"Do you have anyone in mind?" I asked.

"No, I don't," Reggie said, shaking his head.

"What about you, Breezy? Any friends?"

"No, Uncle. I can't think of anyone."

"Well, we all better scour out and find some more girls to occupy downstairs or we'll all be singing the blues. Susan was a half-a-million-dollar pay date, and she just vanished right before our eyes. We're slipping. We're all too relaxed. Let's not forget that we all have bills that need to be paid. And we're all $125,000 poorer, so we'd better find another victim—and soon. I can't risk what we already have," Lisa lectured.

Reggie and Lisa had put a $250,000 insurance policy on Susan. If for any reason she was in an accident and died or was murdered the policy had a double indemnity clause. The payoff would be $500,000. The one-year restriction on the policy matured last month. This weekend was going to be her date of death…

That's where I came in. I was carrying out murders for Reggie since I reached my eighteenth birthday. My specialty was taking a wire and strangling my victim. Sometimes I squeezed so tight that I'd nearly decapitate my victims. In the early nineties Reggie left the drug game alone. He'd made a lot of money and realized the risks were too great. He'd either end up in jail for the rest of his life or either one of those younger punks would try and leave him leaking on Route 280 full of bullet holes. But it was Lisa who came up with the insurance scam. She realized that there were lots of young teenage runaways that nobody cared about. Most were prostitutes or drug addicts who either didn't have any family or didn't have any family that cared. The screening process Lisa did was laborious. She had to make sure that the victim wouldn't be missed, that nobody would come snooping around trying to figure out how their daughter's body was found ditched on the side of the road and want to demand an investigation or why their child had an insurance policy out on their life payable to a complete stranger.

Thus far we'd successfully carried out eleven murders in the past ten years. It's made all of us a lot of money. At first we'd split the pot three ways—Reggie, Lisa and myself. When Breezy got old enough to understand the game, Reggie said he wanted her in. At first, I was a little hesitant about giving my approval. I thought Reggie was just being greedy by wanting his family to take three-fourths of the cut when I ultimately did the dirty work. But I was wrong. Breezy turned out to be an asset. It was easier for her to move around and scope out troubled teenagers. She'd gain their trust and reel them in. Out of the eleven victims, Breezy brought in six.

I left there that night in a rage. That slick bitch Susan had outsmarted us, and it didn't sit well with me at all. I told Reggie to continue to pay on her policy because the little bitch-ho might show back up at their door. And the minute she walked through, even if it was ten years from now, she was a dead woman. As I thought about her I squeezed my left hand together with all my strength and burst my cut back open. Blood oozed down my arm and dripped onto my sweat suit. The pain felt exhilarating as I sped across Nostrand Avenue on my way home.

We all needed to spread out and find another victim—and soon.

39

Jinx

I'm not a virgin, but that hardly makes me a ho. Yesterday morning, on my way from the hair salon, I met a man named Kelsey. He was a nice enough individual who stopped his jeep, jumped out and proceeded to walk side by side with me for five blocks until I reached the train station. We exchanged telephone numbers, and he promised to call. He called last night and asked me out on a date. Since my last encounter, I wanted specifics. He said that he wanted to take me to eat in the city to a place called Bar 89. I know the place well. It's a quaint retro bar that serves appetizers. It's a great place to get to know someone better.

"Nana, I'm going out tonight," I said as I pushed open her door.

"Let me see whatchu got on," she said, struggling to sit up properly. I was wearing the exact same outfit I'd bought last week and wore out on the date with Rob.

"How do I look?" I asked.

"Oh…don't you look stylish. Like a little doll baby. Pumpkin, do you like this one?" Nana asked and I saw concern in her eyes.

"I don't know, Nana. We've just met. I like his telephone conversation, and he seems nice enough. Respectful."

"That's good, sugar, 'cause you're too young to compromise and settle on just any man. You deserve the good life. Always remember," she paused and I chimed in, "Always get what you want. Otherwise it leaves room for sin to sneak in."

We both laughed.

Kelsey called when he was downstairs in front of the house. As I walked out I saw his black jeep parked right in front. The only difference was that he wasn't obnoxiously blasting rap music. Instead, he was listening to slow jams. He was softly playing Pattie LaBelle's rendition of *"If You Don't Know Me by Now."* I almost sang along as I got in the car.

"Hello," I said cheerfully.

"Hello, gorgeous," he said and looked me from head to toe. "Nice outfit."

"Thank you," I said with a cheesy grin on my face.

Just as he said we would, he drove us to Bar 89 in lower Manhattan. In the car we engaged in small talk. He asked about my childhood, my family environment and then my parents. When I told him about the plane crash I could visibly see the pain in his eyes.

"I'm sorry about your loss and your ordeal," he said and gently placed his right hand over mine.

"Thank you," I said and felt he was genuinely sorry for my loss.

Inside the restaurant, I took another good look at him. He stood about six-two, which I loved. He had a muscular physique, light skin, curly hair, broad nose and full lips. He wasn't what you'd consider handsome but he had nice features. Although, he was wearing street clothes, a sweat suit and a pair of Nike Air Ones, there was something square about him. Truthfully, he wasn't exactly my type either but he was more appealing than the clown I went out with last week.

During dinner he didn't want to open up about himself. He probed more into my life than anything else. I could tell he was just nervous.

"So you live with your grandmother?" he asked.

"Yes. Sometimes I worry so much about her. She's not in the best of health, and the doctor has warned her to quit smoking and to change her diet, but she won't listen. She said she didn't live to be seventy-seven listening to doctor's orders."

"Do you have siblings? Anyone you're close to in your family that you could talk to?"

"In my family? Please. My family is a hot mess. My aunt is a drug addict and my uncle is a nineteen-year-old lazy, womanizing bum. They don't even care that I exist," I said and got really sad that it had to be that way.

"Sure they do," he said, trying to cheer me up but it was too late. I was already down talking about my parents and my dysfunctional family.

"Enough about me. Where do you live?"

"I live in a brownstone in Bedford Stuyvesant."

"Nice. My friend lives down there as well. Where do you work?"

"I work from home. I make and sell candles via the Internet."

"No way," I exclaimed. "How creative. Does it pay the bills?"

"And then some..."

"Wonderful. I want to open up my own boutique in the near future. Perhaps you could give me a few pointers on running a company."

"I would love to."

"What did you do today?" I asked.

"Nothing too heavy."

"No church? Are you religious?"

"I'm Hebrew. I'm an Israelite."

"I've never known anyone who's Hebrew. What does that mean?"

"Oh, we have a few rules. My lips are never to touch the skin of a woman who's not my wife. I can't have intercourse until I'm married...you know things like that."

My face dropped and fell in my lap. He looked damn near thirty years old and he couldn't even kiss my needy lips? What had I gotten myself into?

Another dud, I thought.

"How long have you practiced this religion?" I said, hoping maybe he bent the rules as hypocritical Shawn did.

"All my life. I grew up in a Hebrew home."

"I see..." I said, and my voice trailed off. "Could we order something to drink?"

"I don't drink but you can order whatever you like. I'll call our waitress."

As I took large gulps of my white wine I could feel him staring at me. For a brief moment I was intimidated and didn't want to return his gaze. Finally, I looked up into his eyes, and he put the most adorable smile on his face, and my heart melted. What was

I afraid of? Meeting someone who worshipped differently than I did? I was turned off because he didn't bend the rules in his religion as I did mine. I went to church on Sunday and professed to be a Christian. But that didn't stop me from fornicating, drinking, cursing, having envy and jealousy in my heart not to mention an occasional lie. Maybe it would be nice getting to know someone who played by all the rules.

During dinner, Kelsey began talking about our Black history and the civil rights movement. By the end of the night he'd certainly left an impression on me. I wanted to get to know him better. He seemed like an intelligent man with a wealth of information he was willing to share, but not in a patronizing way.

He dropped me off and promised to call me the next day. For some reason, I couldn't wait. What I liked is that I didn't fall head over heels within the first hour. I mean, I thought he was cool, but that was it, which was a change. I'd give him a chance, but I wasn't saving it for marriage to speak frankly.

40

Jinx

My heart raced as I walked to my blue Mitsubishi rental car. I had rented it to drive to Long Island to visit my parent's grave and decided to keep it an extra day to party. I jumped in the passenger's seat and threw the key to Kendu who usually pushed a CL 500, but had recently crashed it on the Southern State Parkway on his way home from a club. He said he'd fallen asleep at the wheel and was lucky to be alive. I could still see the look on Breezy's face as we exited the club together. She thought she'd be leaving with him and not me, but he didn't want her. He chose me over Breezy. Briefly, I thought about my new friend Kelsey and wondered how he'd feel knowing that I'd left the club with someone else. *Men do it all the time,* I thought. Besides, it wasn't like I was his girl. We were just friends. At this point he was like a brother to me.

I sat back and relaxed as he drove through the midtown tunnel on our way towards Queens. I imagined we'd be going to his house. I heard he had a lavish mini-mansion out on Long Island with six bedrooms and a spiral staircase that led to his bedroom. In the 'hood we talk about everything. Nothing is sacred and everything is newsworthy.

Kendu leaned over and squeezed my leg, which startled me. I looked at him and smiled. I was in a daze trying to figure out if I'd have sex with him or not. If I'm not going to give him some then why did I leave the club with him? Even if I didn't want to I knew I had to. These type of brothers didn't play any childish games. He could have left with anyone, and he chose me. I was flattered to say the least.

I watched as Kendu exited the Belt Parkway and drove into the parking lot of the Sheraton hotel in Queens. My heart sunk.

"I thought we'd go back to your place," I said, my face displaying disappointment.

"Nah, ma. I had a flood in my bathroom. I can't take you there with shit fucked up like it is. I promise I'll take you to my crib in time. This ain't our last night together, is it?"

"I hope not," I said reluctantly.

"Stop acting silly," he said and jumped out to get a room.

He came back momentarily, and as we walked through the lobby he grabbed a handful of my ass cheek and squeezed. I mean I was drunk but not drunk enough to not feel slightly disrespected by his behavior.

I pushed open the door to a neat, small room with two double-sized beds, a television, table, chair and bathroom. I started fidgeting as soon as I walked in.

"Do you want to get in the shower first?" he asked.

"S-S-Sure," I said. I put down my pocketbook and walked straight into the bathroom. There I looked in the mirror and smiled. I had waited for an opportunity like this all my life. I had been hearing about Kendu since I was knee high. The streets told his story. They spoke about his cars, money, women and run-ins with the law, all of which intrigued me.

I never dreamed that I'd ever get this close to him. I figured he had to be in his early forties. His skin was the color of hot chocolate, smooth and creamy. He had round, expressive eyes with long eyelashes that added innocence to a sinister face. His strong jawbone, scar on his left cheek and broad nose gave him character. He stood six-one without an ounce of fat on his entire body. He had a wide chest and pillars for arms. He looked like he bench-pressed three hundred pounds.

After I showered I didn't know if I should put back on my clothes to come out the bathroom or come out naked. I decided neither was appropriate so I wrapped myself with two towels—one to cover my bottom and the other for my top—and I inched out the bathroom. He was collapsed on the bed, snoring.

"Kendu," I said softly. No response. "Kendu."

He struggled to open his eyes, and when he focused on me he smiled. That made me feel good.

"Come here, sexy," he said and reached for me. I hesitated then took baby steps toward the bed. He reached up and yanked me down on top of him, and my towels fell off exposing my nakedness. He immediately started to grope my breasts and ass so feverishly I almost told him to calm down.

"Tonight, I just want to lay back and get fucked," he breathed in my ear. "I don't want to do shit. You do all the work."

I wanted to ask him if he was going to take a shower but I realized that wasn't going to happen. He was ripping off his clothes in a frenzy. When he was completely naked just as he said, he laid back with his arms propped behind his head and expected for me to give him pleasure. To say this was challenging was an understatement. I barely knew him so pleasing him was going to be a task. I didn't know where he liked to be touched or kissed.

I started off slowly kissing his neck then moved down toward his hairy chest. I didn't get a reaction. I moved up and started to gently bit on his ear then I sucked on his lobes. Nothing. I reached down and his dick was still limp. I mounted him and slid my tongue in his mouth. It took a moment for him to respond. Slowly our tongues explored each other as I grinded my hips on his dick, but still I couldn't get a rise out of him.

"Kiss it," he suggested.

I ignored him.

"Kiss it, ma. Do that shit…make Daddy feel good."

As I contemplated whether I should go down on him he decided to speed up the process by pushing me toward his limp dick. By the time my face was within one inch of his dick it began to grow. It stiffened slightly, and I could tell this was his pleasure. Reluctantly, I opened my mouth and began to suck the tip, gently at first as he dug his nails in my hair and began guiding my movements. He pushed down hard when he wanted me to deep throat then pulled me up slightly when he wanted me to concentrate on the tip. He rocked his hips back and forth but he remained silent. He never said a word—no oohs or ahhs, nothing to give me encouragement that I was on the right track.

As I sucked his slim penis I must admit that I was already disappointed. Kendu was a big dude with a big name. I thought he'd have a big dick as well. At some point he grabbed my hair and pulled so hard I thought he'd pop a few strands. I knew he was about to cum. I released my mouth and mounted him. I let him enter me and rode his dick as best as I could but my pussy was drowning the nigga. I pretended to be in ecstasy but in reality I couldn't wait for him to cum so we could get this over with. A few more pumps, and he exploded inside of me. As his hot juices squirted in my vaginal walls I knew I'd fucked up. I wasn't on any birth control, and there are too many diseases out here to not have used a condom, but it was too late for regrets. What was done was done. It happens to the best of us, as Breezy would say.

I collapsed on top of Kendu, and I tell you no lie, he'd fallen asleep in two seconds flat. He let out a hearty snore and damn near woke up the whole hotel. I eased out of him and went to take another shower. It was nearly daybreak, and I was exhausted. I gently climbed in bed next to him and fell into a deep, peaceful sleep.

41

Nicoli

Black was released from central booking's holding cell the very next day. The police wanted me to go down and sign an order of protection against Black stating that he stay within one hundred feet of me but I refused. I had already won that battle. I had more important shit to follow up on. I went into Brooklyn with little BJ and scooped up my mother. I told her that I wanted to go to her brother's house to see how he was doing and so he could see BJ.

"Mommy, we don't have much family. I think it would be nice to go and see your brother," I said persuasively. I hated to lie to my mother and use her this way but I was a desperate woman on a mission.

"But Nicoli I don't want to go. Reggie and I aren't close. He was raised by his mother, and I was raised by mine. We didn't find out we had the same father until our father's funeral. I can count the number of times I've seen Reggie on one hand."

"That's not nice, Mommy. You said that Breezy mentioned that he may have cancer. We should at least go by and say hello. You live so close, and it should be fun. If not then we'll leave. I promise."

Reluctantly she agreed.

We arrived at the historic landmark brownstone that my uncle owned. It was a beautiful piece of architecture nestled behind a beautiful array of shrubs, a sycamore tree and weeping willow with huge branches. The driveway held three vehicles: Mercedes S 430, Mercedes SL 600 and a Range Rover.

My mother, BJ and I climbed out of my silver Mercedes CL 600, and I wondered if I would be able to hold back my contempt for Breezy. I led the way up the concrete steps and rang their bell. I noticed that they had the melody *"Flight of the Bumblebee"* as their tune.

Breezy came to the door, flung it open and couldn't contain her surprise. Her mouth fell open as her eyes protruded from their sockets. Quickly, she regrouped and began to stammer, "Nic…Nicoli…ummm…why are you here? I mean, it's nice that you are but I wasn't expecting you."

I quickly examined my trifling cousin and remembered when I used to be just as trifling. As she'd gotten older, I must admit that she'd grown into a pretty girl—nothing on me, but pretty nonetheless. Her dark chocolate skin had hints of bronze, which gave her a glow. Her jet-black hair was sprinkled with gold highlights cut provocatively into layers. Her once skinny, awkward body was fully developed and curvaceous. But what caught my eye was the pink diamond tennis bracelet adorning her small wrist. It had to be at least eight carats and most definitely compliments of Black.

Their relationship may be more serious than I expected. But how long has it been going on? I thought.

"Well we decided to do as you do. You know…drop by unannounced. I hope you don't mind but we were concerned about your father and also wanted to catch up on old times," I said. I decided to smile warmly because she still hadn't invited us in.

"Ohhhh, okay," she retorted with skepticism.

"May we come in?" my mother said, finally interjecting and breaking the tension.

"Sure. How rude of me. Please come in and sit in the foyer. I'll go and get my father."

We sat in the front foyer with huge ceilings and large storm windows for approximately ten minutes before Breezy returned with her father. She was no longer sporting her bracelet, which only confirmed my suspicions that Black had bought it.

Reggie came with his arms extended for a hug and a kiss from my mother and then me. Next, he scooped up BJ and began to besiege him with compliments. Breezy stood at a distance, close in proximity of her father, as if he would shield her from whatever unleashing she thought I had planned, but I made nice, and quickly they both relaxed.

"Gail, it's been too long since we've seen each other," Reggie acknowledged.

"I know and that ain't right. We shouldn't be that way. After your chile came over to see me, I started feelin' guilty and told Nicoli to bring me here to see my brother. I gotta see how's his health," my mother lied.

My mother wasn't a stupid woman at all. Somehow she picked up that my wanting to come over here was calculated and played the situation to the hilt. Inwardly, I smiled. If she had said it was all my idea it would have certainly showed motive on my part.

Reggie decided to make us lunch and we sat around talking for hours. When I went into the bedroom to change BJ, Breezy followed. I knew she would.

It didn't take her but a moment to get to the point.

"So, how's everything with his father?" she casually asked as she passed me a Pamper out of my baby bag.

I shook my head as if I was defeated. "As I told you before everything is horrible. We can't get along and only tolerate each other for the sake of our son."

"Do you still want to get back together with him?"

"Sometimes yes…sometimes no."

"When was the last time you guys were together? I mean, maybe there's still a chance."

"Not in this lifetime. If you don't mind I don't want to discuss Black. It's too painful."

"I understand."

"What about you? How's your love life?"

"Nonexistent."

"You? Don't have a boyfriend?"

"Nope. I'm just concentrating on finishing school."

After I finished changing BJ, I said, "Do you mind holding him for a moment while I go to the bathroom? I'll be out in a moment."

"Give me that adorable little thing," she said while reaching for BJ who ultimately began to cry. She began rubbing his back while I went into the bathroom to wash my hands. When I came back everyone was in the living room, and it was time for me to do what I came to do. I pulled out my cell phone and began capturing images of Breezy holding BJ without her knowledge. I pretended to be searching for a number and no one paid me much attention. Each picture was clear and crisp. Next, I sent those images to my computer, which I would later put on a disk and take to get developed. This was way too easy. After I had what I needed, I was ready to go. This was only half of the plan I wanted to execute.

We all said our good-byes and promised not to be strangers. I dropped off my mother and ran home to begin commencing phase two.

42

Jinx

I'm not an oracle, although Nana would like to think that I am, so when I awoke alone the next morning and Kendu wasn't in bed, I didn't have a clue where he'd went.

"Kendu," I called.

Nothing. I jumped up to make sure he wasn't in the bathroom. It appeared that he'd already showered and all of his clothing was gone.

He must have gone out to get us breakfast, I thought.

I waited patiently for him to return or call but neither happened. When the hotel's front desk called and said it was check-out time, I panicked. Kendu had taken the key to my rental, thus I had no way of getting back home. I only had ten dollars in my wallet and a cab from Queens would cost more than that.

I showered and dressed and decided to wait in the lobby for him to come back. I sat impatiently, pacing but he never showed up. By five o'clock in the afternoon, I took the situation for what it was. I got played. I had the hotel call me a car service because I was too ashamed to call Breezy to rescue me. Although I knew I'd tell her what happened, I just wasn't ready to tell her at that moment.

The car service was skeptical about driving me to East New York, Brooklyn. And when I named, Pink Houses projects he wanted his money upfront. After I assured him that I wouldn't stiff him for his fare and also gave him stimulating conversation the whole ride, he relaxed and trusted me. We pulled up to the projects, and everyone was outside. I told the cabdriver that my brother would pay and was waiting outside for us. It was a hot summer day and I knew that I'd know someone. Just as I thought, I spotted Jock, an old high school classmate.

"Yo, Jock," I called. He spotted me and started bebopping toward me.

"How much?" I said to the cabby.

"Thirty-five dollars," he said and smiled.

When I opened the door I saw the panic in his eyes.

"I'm going to get the money from my brother—" I said and walked slowly toward Jock, then I took off down the pathway. I dashed past Jock like a maniac. I turned around to see the cabdriver struggling to get out of the driver's side. Jock moved out of my way and blocked the cabdriver from gaining chase. I dashed in the building and ran up six flights of steps nonstop to my cousin Kelly's house. When I was safely inside I looked out the window and the cabdriver was still there. He was yelling at the top of his lungs. He was irate and had called the police. They'd arrived within minutes. I peeked out the window for as long as it held my attention and then snuck back downstairs and out the back door. I needed to get home. I went into my room and burst out into tears. How could Kendu do this? Why would he do this? There must be some sort of explanation. Maybe he went to get breakfast and had gotten hurt. Or maybe he'd gotten arrested. I needed to give him the benefit of doubt before I jumped to any conclusions. The worst part is that I didn't have a cell number to get in contact with him. By the time nightfall came, I needed to confide in someone. I called Breezy.

"Girl, I need to talk...."

43

Breezy

"She knows," my father declared.

"Papa, I don't think so."

"Breezy, trust me. That girl didn't come over here for a family get-together. It was contrived, and her mother was in on it too."

"They came over here because I went to them first."

"Exactly. She's put the pieces of the puzzle together. You went over there with a motive. She's returned with hers."

My father's eyes had hooded over and the veins in his temples were bursting through his skin. He was aggravated.

"I'm telling you I can read body language. When I was grilling her in the room I could tell that she was totally clueless. I don't have a thing to worry about. Let's just stick to the plan and by the time she figures out anything I will have stolen Black out from under her."

"What you're going to do is go upstairs and call Black. Talk to him casually and mention that your cousin came over today and that you all hadn't spoken in years. She had her son with her and you realized that he's the father. Be stern and shocked, hurt and confused. Make him feel as though he's at fault. Attack him offensively until he has no other choice but to be defensive about his baby momma."

"I can't do that. That'll ruin everything," I screamed. I couldn't tell my father that I couldn't do that because of the stalking car vandalism scheme I had concocted. I said that the girl bumped me and elbowed me in my ribs. How could I come back now and say that it was my cousin all along? He'd know I was a liar.

"Are you defying me?"

"You don't know what you're talking about," I shouted stubbornly.

In the blink of an eye, my father grabbed me up from off the sofa by my collar and brought me closely to his face. I felt his breath as he aggressively spat, "I'm far smarter, stronger and wiser than you. I've carried you this far without error. I will not live out the rest of my life in this same tax bracket. In order for me to retire a millionaire, you're going to have to not just sleep with one but earn his trust and get him to marry you without a prenuptial agreement. You're not getting any younger. You're at your prime. Don't fuck this up."

We stared eye to eye. One Whitaker to another. I was tired of my father's overbearing and controlling ways. Sure, he had always taken care of me but I'd been proactive in my future as well. He wasn't the one who would have to fuck Black or suck his huge dick nor did he go out on the streets scouring looking for victims for our insurance scams. I'd done more than my share. I'd done more than Lisa had ever done and she got a part of our profits. I didn't see him yoking her up and threatening bodily harm. All he did was walk around like a tyrannical dictator. Not anymore. I was ready to reclaim my life. I was running this show from here on out. May the best Whitaker win.

44

Jinx

Two weeks later I was aghast. I still hadn't heard from Kendu nor had he tried to return the rental. I now owed fifteen hundred dollars on my American Express. This morning I felt a little sluggish as I got ready for work. I'd been in a bad mood ever since the incident. I couldn't tell Nana what had happened because she'd want to go and knock on doors. His momma's door, aunts, uncles…she wouldn't care. She didn't tolerate people taking advantage of her loved ones. I told her that work was stressing me out.

After I got out of the shower I went to pee and let out a little scream. When I urinated it burned. I went to wipe myself, and there was an obsessive amount of green-colored discharge with small traces of blood. I didn't know what I had but I knew I had something.

I called out sick from work and went into my gynecologist. Four hours later I was told that I had syphilis, a sexually transmitted disease for which I needed to take antibiotics.

After the doctor's visit I went home and crawled in bed. I called Breezy some time after 2:00 P.M. I knew she'd be home from class.

"Breezy," I cried, "I need to talkkkkk."

"What's wrong?" she said and I could hear the alarm in her voice.

"This nigga just won't quit. Not only did he rob me for my rental, I just came from the doctor and my pussy is burning. I got syphilis."

As soon as I said it I knew I'd fucked up.

"Wait. I thought you said you didn't fuck the nigga," she accused.

"I didn't," I lied. "He put his sick dick next to the opening of my pussy and his contaminated discharge must have seeped in. The doctor said this is common."

"Oh," she replied. I couldn't tell whether she fell for my lie or not. "That nigga needs to get fucked up."

"Who you telling?"

We spoke for hours until Breezy said she was going out with Joy that night. She asked if I wanted to go but I declined. I wasn't in any mood to be social.

Shortly after 11:00 P.M., Breezy called my cell phone. She whispered, "Jinx?"

"Yeah, what's up?"

"That thieving, contaminated dick nigga is in the diner right now with this *pretty* bitch."

"What?"

"Kendu is in the diner with Cherise."

"What Cherise?"

"The Cherise that used to fuck with Jamaican Rob."

"Really?" I said as my heart sunk then reemerged as it filled with anger. "You see my car?"

"Yeah. It's parked outside."

"What diner you at?"

"Lindenwood on the boulevard."

"I'm hopping in a cab. Don't let him leave."

I reached the diner in five minutes. I saw my car parked out front as well as Breezy's Rover. When I walked inside it was packed. It was a Friday night, and it was always popping during the weekends. I spotted Breezy first. She came running to me.

"He's in the back with Hassan and those niggas from Tompkins," she said.

"Yo, whatever you wanna do, I have your back. That was some bullshit he did to you," Joy said.

Although I was glad that Joy had my back I was a little annoyed that Breezy had told her my business. Breezy needed to realize that she's my friend and Joy's her friend.

We all stepped accordingly into the back of the diner. My face was stone as I looked at Kendu laughing and having a good time. Cherise had a plate of lobster and a glass of champagne in front of her. As soon as he recognized me his face straightened up. No longer was he sporting a cheesy grin.

"Motherfucker, where the fuck is my girl's car?" Joy blurted out and set it off.

"What?" he said as if he didn't hear her correctly.

Joy looked to me to step up.

"Kendu that was some bullshit you did. Give me my motherfucking car keys."

He reached in his pocket and tossed the keys in my face. They hit me on my cheek and fell to the floor. I was never so disrespected by one individual in my life. Breezy bent down and picked up the keys to save me the embarrassment.

"You're a crab ass!" Joy pursued. I could tell she wanted to fight and set it off up in there. She was intoxicated.

"Yo, get outta my face with that childish shit. You see I'm up in here with my girl," he countered. The whole room was quiet waiting to see what the bickering was about.

"Fuck your girl," Joy said, picked up Cherise's champagne glass and tossing the liquid in her face. Without hesitation, Kendu lunged toward Joy and I leaped towards him. Kendu back-slapped me , and I stumbled backward. Before I knew it Joy was beating down Cherise, and Kendu was whipping my ass. He was literally stomping my guts out as I screamed for help. I tried to crawl underneath a table but he pulled me back out by my feet. Everyone moved out of the way as I kicked and screamed for my life. I kept hearing Breezy scream, "Break that shit up. Break that shit up."

At some point one of the guys told Kendu that the cops were coming. He pulled Joy off Cherise, and they exited the diner rapidly in Cherise's car.

I could barely stand I was so fucked up. The inside of my mouth had cuts from my teeth bearing down on my gums. My right eye was swollen, and my wrists were sore.

"It's not over," I kept repeating. "He gonna get his."

I had Breezy and Joy follow me to Breezy's apartment where I parked the rental in her driveway. I knew it would be safe until I returned it to Enterprise the next morning. Then I did something totally out of my character.

"Breezy, go inside and get your gun."

"What?"

"You heard me."

"This bitch done lost her mind. Whatchu gonna do with her gun?" Joy asked.

"Don't worry about it. Either you stepping with me or you're stepping out of my way."

"I'm down for whatever," Joy stated.

Breezy looked in my eyes and could tell I had something to prove. She ran upstairs and grabbed her .380 her father had given her. We jumped in her Rover, and I told Breezy to drive me to Boulevard projects. That's where Cherise lived and that's where I was sure Kendu was.

Breezy and Joy remained silent the whole ride. If either one of them were scared they didn't show it. If at any point we'd gotten pulled over we'd all be going to jail for that gun, but I didn't care. My feelings were hurt beyond repair.

Breezy crept inside the outdoor parking lot doing about five miles per hour. As soon as I saw Cherise's car, I yelled, "Stop."

Breezy threw on her brakes and stopped right next to Cherise's car. I pulled out Breezy's .380 and then gave her instructions.

"I'm about to light this fucking car up. As soon as I empty this clip, don't speed out of here. Drive slowly as if nothing happened. Do you hear me?"

"You sure you want to do this?"

"Do you have my back?"

She looked at me through her side-view mirror. "You know I do. You're my girl."

"Wait," Joy interjected. "Why are we fucking up Cherise's car? I thought you were gonna shoot Kendu."

"What I look like?" I screamed. "I ain't shooting anybody. The next best thing is something materialistic. Since Kendu's car is in the shop his girl's car gotta get it. Most likely he'll end up footing the bill."

I inched up out of my seat, rolled down the window and stuck the gun out. I thought my hands would tremble handling a gun for the first time but they didn't. I aimed at Cherise's BMW X5 and squeezed the trigger. Nothing happened. Then I remembered I needed to take off the gun safety. I did and aimed again. I gently squeezed on the trigger.

Boom! Boom! Boom! Boom! Boom!

Five shots entered the engine of Cherise's car. You could hear people running for cover. I leaned back inside the car and calmly said, "Okay, let's roll."

Breezy remained composed as we drove out of the parking lot. The whole ride down Atlantic Avenue I sat trembling. What had I done? What would the repercussions be?

Once we were back on Breezy's side of town in her house we burst out into laughter and recapped the whole evening. Breezy bragged about being the getaway driver while Joy rode shotgun. They started calling me Psycho Bitch.

About an hour into our night my cell phone rang. The telephone number was private. I picked up.

"Hello."

"You're going to jail."

It was Kendu. I could tell his voice.

"Fuck you," I said calmly.

"Never again. But you're going to jail. Somebody got you and your stupid friends on camera. The black Range Rover…you shooting up Cherise's truck…"

My heart sank but I had to play it to the hilt.

"Whatever, nigga. That was a warning. You better pay for that rental—"

He hung up.

"What did he say?" Breezy said and I could see the fear in her eyes.

"He said that somebody got us on camera and that we're going to jail."

"What?" they both said in unison.

"But he's lying. Ain't nobody got us on camera…right?"

"I don't fucking know. Listen I'm not going down for this bullshit. That bitch-ass nigga snitched. Don't tell me he's a bitch *and* a snitch," Joy assessed, then she continued, "I'm calling my cousin, Kesha. She'll help us out. She has to."

45

Breezy

I sat on my bed and watched how the situation was unfolding. I realized that we all could be in a whole lot of trouble. Joy and I would be guilty by association if it came down to the wire. My father would kill me if he knew how I put myself in a vulnerable position without strategizing. I don't know what made me roll out with Jinx and her situation. I knew she had something to prove because she was tired of getting disrespected by men. If not Kendu then it would be the next nigga. I'd never been around Jinx with any of her boyfriends but her relationships never lasted. She could never keep a nigga. They all ended up despising her. I watched as she bit her bottom lip and paced around my bedroom floor. I waited impatiently for her to say what she was supposed to. When she didn't, I spoke up, "So, if this gets ugly, what are you gonna do?"

"What do you mean?" she asked.

"If that nigga snitched on us, what are you gonna do?" I repeated.

"What can I do?" she asked and had the stupidest look on her face.

"You can take the weight."

Her eyes grew big, and she immediately caught an attitude.

"If he tells on all of us, what am I supposed to say? That it was only me?"

"That's exactly what you're supposed to say. Joy and I don't have anything to do with this bullshit. I'm not getting locked up for your shit. This nigga ran up in you with a sick dick and stole a car you don't even own. This is your beef. Handle it like a woman," I yelled.

Joy understood exactly where I was coming from and immediately caught an attitude.

"Jinx, if my cousin can't help us out with this shit, ya better be ready to take the weight or take an ass whippin' from me. You chose..." Joy stated as she dialed Kesha. I could see the hate in Jinx's eyes. She couldn't stand Joy and me right now, but who cared. I'm too pretty to be sitting in somebody's jail. Especially over some shit that ain't even my situation.

"Kesha, whaddup?" Joy said. "Yo, we got a situation. Come over to Breezy's. Not now but right now."

Kesha was still on duty when she came over. She had her partner wait in the car, and she ran up to my apartment. When she walked in she saw the sullen looks on all of our faces.

"What y'all done did now?" she asked. "And hurry up and tell me. I'm on duty. I don't have all day."

I looked to Jinx to explain her story but she sat there with her lips poked out, so I stepped up.

"A couple of weeks ago Jinx went to a hotel with Kendu—"

"What Kendu?" Kesha asked.

"Kendu from East New York."

"I know him," she replied.

"Everyone does," I said, a little annoyed, then continued, "Kendu fucked Jinx, burnt her—"

"Didn't I tell you we didn't fuck," Jinx yelled, and I ignored her. She'd lost all of my respect at that moment.

"Miraculously, Jinx claimed they didn't fuck but in any event she's walking around here burning."

"Say word?" Kesha said, and I could tell I had her full attention.

"Word. So tonight Joy and I are at the Lindenwood Diner, and we see the nigga up in there with a bitch," I explained.

"What bitch?" Kesha asked. For someone who was on duty and claimed she was in a rush she wouldn't let me get the story out without interruption.

"Cherise from Boulevard."

"That bitch think she cute. Didn't she used to fuck with Jamaican Rob?" Kesha asked.

"Yeah, that's her. Anyway, Jinx roll up in the diner and they get into it. Joy set it off and start fucking up Cherise. Meanwhile, Kendu stomps a mud hole in Jinx."

"That nigga put his hands on you?" Kesha said and went to inspect Jinx's face. "I ain't worried about you, Joy. I know you can handle yourself."

"You know I'm nice with mine," Joy bragged. "I beat that fragile bitch *down*."

"Kesha, you have to let me finish the story. You know all the players. Now, just listen. After Jinx caught a beat down we all came back here, and Jinx took my .380—"

"Ohmigod. Please don't tell me y'all stupid bitches done did something crazy," Kesha exploded.

I nodded.

"We drove down to Boulevard in my truck and Jinx filled Cherise's car full of bullet holes. Kendu called her cell phone and said we're all going to jail. He said they got us on camera."

"Jinx," Kesha asked in amazement. I'm still amazed myself that scary Jinx had the heart to do something so brazen.

"I had to do it," Jinx said as tears slid down her cheeks. "My pride…"

"Boulevard Houses, that's the 75th precinct. I got a few connections over there. I'll get on it right away and see what I can do. Jinx, spend the night over here. I'll call you guys as soon as I get something."

Kesha left, and Joy decided to spend the night as well. Only we didn't get any sleep. Everyone tossed and turned all night. Finally, Kesha called at seven in the morning and said that the housing development had given the videotape to the police. Two rookie cops took the call. Kesha managed to get them to turn over the tape to her, and since neither Cherise nor Kendu had gone down to the station to make a report, her connection in the precinct agreed to turn the other cheek for Kesha.

I woke up the girls and told them the good news. Joy and I were relieved. But I could tell that something was still bothering Jinx.

46

Jinx

It's been two weeks since the Kendu incident and I was desperately trying to put my life in a better perspective. It was a Sunday night, and I was on my way to bed. I had been seeing Kelsey for over a month, and things were progressing nicely. I had decided to put my past bad relationships behind me and try to focus on someone who was older and stable and most importantly not a liar. I must admit that I didn't like him romantically at first, but I loved his conversation, which had led me to have feeling for him. As much as I wanted to, we hadn't slept together yet. He hadn't even kissed me. You would think that all we had was a friendship but it's more than that. I respected his religion, and he respected me. And he was more of a gentleman than any other male I'd ever dated. I hadn't mentioned him to Breezy or brought him around my family—not yet. I just wanted to lay low for a while until I knew that we were going to last.

I'm serious. I was really banking on this to work after the humiliation I'd suffered with Jason, Shawn and Kendu. Now that it's clear that I'm not going to jail behind my impulsive reaction, I'd decided to put things in the right perspective and find a nice man to settle down with and have lots of babies.

I was about to go to bed when I heard Nana laughing hysterically. If I wasn't so tired I would have joined her and got a little chuckle before turning in. I don't know what she'd do without cable.

"Nana, do you need anything before I go to bed?" I asked as I pushed open her door. She had her covers pulled up high, just reaching her neck. All I could see was her small head peeking out. Her gray hair was in two braids, which were pointing toward the ceiling. I loved this lady so much. She was the most adorable little thing.

She grinned a toothless smile. "Nana alright. I'm just gonna sit here and watch *Dynasty*. This is the episode where Alexis and Crystal get into a fight. I love it when Crystal whips Alexis li'l ass."

I laughed.

"Don't stay up too late. Now that we have cable you're up all night."

"I won't, pumpkin," she promised.

I went to my room and got in bed. Within minutes I was sound asleep.

I tossed and turned all night and had horrible dreams. The kind that you can't remember when you wake up but you know they were bad. I slept horribly. I woke up shortly past 6:00 A.M. and went to get some orange juice from the kitchen when I realized Nana was still up watching television. Either that or she never turned her television off from last night.

"Nana," I said and pushed the door open, not waiting for her to respond. She was still sleeping, and it was freezing in her room. I crept over and clicked off the television and closed the window. The early morning breeze was brisk. I walked in the kitchen when I felt a chill go down my spine then I knew. I ran back to Nana's room and pulled back the cover. She lay there peacefully sleeping only she'd never wake up.

"Nana," I screamed and collapsed on her bed. Her body was stiff. Rigor mortis had set in. "Oh, Nana…noooo…don't leave me…I need you. I need you, Nana," I cried.

I must have laid in the bed with Nana for hours just talking to her. Finally, I got up and called 911. They said they'd send someone out to collect her. Next, I called my job. They were worried sick. It was already noon when I called to tell them what had happened. Last, I called Corey and told him about his mother. I could tell he was hurt but tried to sound like a man. He said he'd try to find Kim and that they'd be over as soon as possible.

Before Corey and Kim came I gathered all of my personal belongings that I had lying around the house, tossed everything in my room and locked the door. I even went through Nana's personal belongings and gathered what I wanted to take as keepsakes. She had this beautiful broach that she'd had several pictures in. She said that my mother's father had bought it for her while he was in the army stationed in Japan. I also took a vintage bracelet that she loved. My mother had bought it for her before she died. I knew that Corey and Kim would come and take everything else.

Corey and Kim made it to the house just in time to see the coroner taking away Nana's body. Kim threw a fit and started punching, kicking and spitting at the two men.

"Give me my mother," she wailed. "Give her to me."

It took Corey and me to restrain her and also the threat from one of the coroners to have her arrested for assault if she didn't stop. Eventually she calmed down. That's when the bullshit began.

They both ransacked Nana's room, looking for money, jewelry and anything of value. They stopped only briefly to ask me if she had an insurance policy.

"I don't know. Look through her paperwork," I said.

An hour later, I heard Corey say, "Bingo."

They'd found an insurance policy for five thousand dollars. Kim was the beneficiary. Obviously, Nana had taken out the policy before Kim had gone on her drug missions.

Shortly, thereafter, Kim left with a bag full of Nana's things. I stopped her at the door.

"Where are you going with Nana's things?"

"Get out of my way, you bum bitch," she challenged. And I couldn't believe the audacity of this crack head.

"You're not going to run out and sell your mother's belongings to get high. Her body isn't even cold yet. How could you?"

"She was my mother not yours," she spat. "I'll take whatever I want. Everything in this house is rightfully mine."

"I said let it go." I reached for the bag as she pushed me up against a wall. I swung wildly in the air, and she ducked. She followed up with a swift kick in my knee, and my leg went limp. I reached up and dug my fingers in her hair and pulled her down with me. We fell to the floor. I was somewhat heavier so I threw my weight on top of her. I began to punch her as hard as I could on her head while she reached up and dug her nails in my face. We called each other a million bitches and fought hard without interruption. Every now and then I'd see Corey still coming out with more bags that he was taking. He rummaged through Nana's room for the remainder of our fight. Finally, he decided to come and break it up.

"Y'all need to stop disrespecting my mother's house," he spat as he pulled us apart. She only been dead a few hours, and this is how you two show respect. Now Jinx, Kim can take whatever she wants. Don't forget that Nana was her mother, and she's gone now. This means she doesn't have any use for that stuff. I'm taking Nana's house keys, and I'll be back tonight to move my things in."

"You're moving in here?" I said in bewilderment.

"Yes. I'm moving in Nana's room. But what you gonna do?"

"Me?"

"Yes, you. My mother didn't leave a will, so this house is mine and Kim's. Now, I'll let you stay but rent is due to me on the first of each month. I'm charging you six hundred dollars a month if you want to stay. If not, you can get the fuck out by the week's end. But remember, you can't find an apartment for cheaper rent."

I stood there dumbfounded. How had my life changed so quickly? All I could do was blink rapidly. Meanwhile, Kim and Corey had gathered up Nana's belongings and were gone…

47

Jinx

It was a somber moment in my life. There was a cold, biting rain on the day we put Nana's body to rest. She had a beautiful ceremony at Ponce funeral home on Atlantic Avenue not too far from where we live. Breezy and her father bought a beautiful bleeding heart from their family. The funeral home was filled with nothing but flowers from my friends, my job and me. When I saw her large body, snuggly fitted into her casket my breath emptied from my lungs. I stood before her with my tear-soaked shirt and wet eyes and begged her to come back.

A local singing group from Pink Houses projects came out to sing the Boyz to Men rendition of Cooley High's *'How Can I Say Goodbye to Yesterday.'* As her casket was being carried out to her final resting place I clinched the edge of my chair in despair. I couldn't believe she was really gone. My Nana....

I ended up having to pay for Nana's funeral. It cost me $6,500 out of my savings. I buried her in her favorite color lavender dress. Kim had gotten the insurance money, and it was rumored she went through it all in one day. She didn't even care that the money was to bury her mother.

After the funeral, black-clad mourners came back to our house. Corey and his baby's mother had already moved in from out of her mother's house. She was seventeen years old with a one-year-old daughter who cried the whole night. All of our neighbors brought food over and every-one sat down to eat. Kim started her performance, crying hysterically and yelling that it was my fault. I was the family jinx. I just couldn't take it anymore. I went to Breezy. "Can we get out of here? Can I go back to your place and spend the night? I need to get away from here."

"Sure…sure…anything you want. Go get your clothes and we're gone."

I went to Breezy's house and crawled in her bed and immediately went to sleep. I usually did this when I'm depressed. I woke up early the next morning and Breezy was already awake.

"Do you want to go downstairs to my father's and get some break-fast?" she asked.

"No. I don't feel like being around too many people right now. Do you think you could bring me something up?"

"Sure. I'll be back shortly," she replied and kissed me on my cheek.

When Breezy left I buried my head deep into her pillow to stifle the gut-wrenching moan that had to escape. I poured all of my emotions into that cry and then went back to sleep.

48

Kesha

It was a rainy Saturday morning, and I expected my husband to have made me breakfast in bed. Instead he'd taken the kids out and left a brief note on the refrigerator stating they'd be gone for a while. I was a little insulted that I wasn't invited to join them on their excursion, especially since he knew I had the day off.

I moped around the house for a little while, not quite knowing what to get into. I sat on the edge of my bed and stared at the green Rolex box that had my watch in it. I was amazed and disappointed that no one had mentioned it. I saw my husband glance at my wrist but he said nothing. And Darren looked as well…nothing. But I knew that wouldn't be the case going around Joy or Breezy. I knew they'd spot the watch a mile away. Some part of me wanted to confide in at least Joy and tell her where I'd gotten the money from. I knew I felt this way because I wanted to relieve some of my guilt by sharing what I'd done, but I knew I could be putting Joy in danger. If for any reason I was to get busted, it was better that no one be able to admit that I'd told them where I'd gotten the money. They'd just feel awful having to roll over on me. I pushed those bad thoughts to the back of my mind. Nobody was getting caught for anything. We just lifted a few dollars off some drug dealers. There wasn't anyone to tell on us.

I got back up and put my watch on. I looked at how it adorned my small wrist, and I felt complete. I know that sounds stupid but it's real. I never thought anything but diamonds could make me this happy. How wrong was I?

I sat sipping on hazelnut coffee when Joy called. She said that she and Breezy wanted to go to Bloomingdale's to buy some shoes. They had this great sale going on whereas you buy a pair of shoes and get the second pair for fifty percent off. No strings attached. They wanted to tear up the Chanel section. I looked in my wallet, and I had ninety dollars. What could I do with that? All of our credit cards were maxed out because of shopping sprees like this one. I was still paying for the kid's back-to-school clothes. Not to mention my husband needed to shop for his clothing, groceries, toiletries—everything gets charged to our cards.

As I was still on the phone trying to decide whether I should go just to have something to do, I opened the drawer in the kitchen and our rent money was lying there. I looked at the twelve hundred dollars and couldn't resist. I had a week to replace it...

"Joy, I'll pick you up in one hour," I said and hopped in the shower.

I know this was a little irresponsible of me but sometimes I need a break. It gets daunting paying all the bills around here. Sometimes I just want to splurge. Sometimes I get the credit card statements, and I'm blown away. My husband can spend an obscene amount of money at any given moment. At those times we get into our biggest arguments because I can't ever see the merchandise that he's bought. I'll get a three-thousand-dollar credit card statement, and I'm like, "Damn, when did you do this?"

I hate arguing with my husband because it seems he enjoys it too much. He's always ready with a slick remark that will just get underneath my skin. If he says something too slick I'm almost tempted to bitch-slap him as I do my perps who give me lip. But then I calm down and realize that he's the man around the house—my husband—and that I still need to respect him.

I hopped in my Camry and drove over to pick up Joy. She came downstairs wearing the cutest Christian Dior rain boots with the jacket to match.

"You look so cute. When did you get those boots?"

"This kid named Paul took me shopping the other day," she retorted as she adjusted her seat belt.

"That's a good look. He got any friends?" I said jokingly.

"I wish he did have friends instead of wanting to be up under my ass all day. A nigga won't let me breathe. Ever since he dropped a coupla dollars on a bitch he's gotten a little possessive. The other night he wanted to come over so he could hit it, and he's like 'put on something sexy before I get there. I want you do dance for me.'"

"Dance as in the girls from a go-go bar? A striptease?"

"Yeah," she said and rolled her eyes, "I'm like, 'nigga this ain't Burger King. You can't have it your way.'"

We both started laughing.

"But that's how men are. They buy you a pair of boots and they think they not only own your feet but the body their attached to. That's why I don't fuck for money," I stated.

"Wait. Hold up. You just tried to play me. Who fucks for money, Kesha? To set the record straight, I fuck and I *get* money. There's a difference," she countered. Joy was always too sensitive. She'd spend the whole day setting records straight. Since I didn't feel like entertaining this argument, I said, "I hear that."

We called Breezy when we were five minutes away from her house, so she came out and waited for us in her truck. When we got there I parked my Camry, and Joy and I both jumped in the Rover.

"What's up, girl?" I said as I jumped in the backseat. I pecked her on her cheek and she smiled.

"Nothing much. I'm just chilling and working hard in school. A chick can't wait until this semester is over," Breezy said.

"Are you taking summer classes?" Joy asked.

"I didn't want to, but my dad wants me to take two classes. He said it's only for six weeks and I'll get closer to graduating. He thinks I should graduate in three years instead of four," she sulked.

"Mr. Whittaker puts a lot of pressure on you, Breezy. I like your dad but sometimes he goes too hard," I commented. I wondered if I'll be that type of parent when my kids are older. I know my husband isn't like that. He'll encourage them but I'm sure whether they want to take extra classes in school will always be their choice.

"He just wants the best for me, and he hasn't steered me wrong yet. He's so clever and analytical that sometimes I listen to him speak and I'm left in awe," she bragged.

"I don't know about all of that," Joy interjected, "but he does look like he can fuck the taste out my mouth."

"Joy, you're so nasty." Breezy laughed. "My father would fuck you numb, and then my stepmother would beat you numb."

"Please, I'm nice with my hands. Don't let the stilettos fool you," Joy spat back.

We parked on Third Avenue and ran inside Bloomingdale's to a shopping frenzy. Lines were almost around the corner. Everyone had their coupon booklet, and we ran to get ours. It had coupons off items anywhere from fifteen to fifty percent off. The best deal was the shoe deal. We took the escalator up to the fourth floor and walked to the front where the expensive shoes were located. We marched right to the Chanel section. It wasn't a large selection but it was enough. I focused on the pink suede pair with the wedge heel priced at $395 and a pair of black flats with the white CC's priced at $535.

Breezy came over and explained in order for me to get the best deal I should pick two pairs that were close in price, and I understood her logic, so I put back the black pair and found a red suede pair for $375. When I went to the register I paid full price for the $395 and got half off the $375 pair. Joy and I both bought two pairs of shoes but not Breezy. She purchased eight pairs with her daddy's money. I knew I shouldn't feel slighted but sometimes I did. I have a career and Joy has a job but we can never outdo Breezy. We can't out shop her. Out drive her. Or out live her. And all she has to do is go to school and get good grades.

After we purchased our shoes we went down to the second floor—the urban floor—and started trying on jeans. I picked out a pair of Jo jeans, Paper Denim & Cloth and Citizens. Combined the grand total was six hundred dollars. There wasn't a sale on this shit. I hate spending so much money on jeans but for the past four years that's all that's in—a sexy shoe and a pair of jeans. And these jeans fit your butt the best. Makes almost any ass look sexy.

As we were in the dressing room trying on our jeans Breezy noticed it first.

"Hold up. Is that a Rolly on your arm?" she inquired as she came closer.

"Oh, this?" I casually replied.

"That's really cute," she remarked after she looked. "Who bought it?"

Before I could respond Joy came running from her dressing room to take a look.

"Say word?" Joy said. "Why didn't you show it to me?"

"I forgot," I said and shrugged. I noticed that the watch didn't hold Breezy 's attention for long. Truthfully, she'd lost interest in a matter of seconds. She had an array of watches compliments of her dad so my having this watch was hardly going to knock her off her feet, and it wasn't a jealousy thing either. She went back to trying on jeans while Joy was going crazy. She wanted to try it on. She even asked to borrow it.

"How did you get this?" Joy asked again.

"I bought it. You know that I'm making more money now."

"But you have a lot of overhead paying all the bills in your household. Anyway, I thought the more money the more problems," she joked.

"That's true." I laughed.

After we shopped I went home, and my husband still wasn't there. I climbed in bed and drifted off into a peaceful sleep.

49

Jinx

I had been paying Corey on time each month and still I had to hear his mouth every morning before I went to work and every night when I came home. The house was always filthy no matter how much I cleaned up behind Corey, his baby mother, Alicia, and his child.

Alicia always left dirty Pampers on the kitchen table even though the garbage was a few feet away. The sink was always piled high with dishes, and the bathroom was disgusting. Corey's aim for the toilet was always off so sometimes I'd come in the bathroom in the middle of the night without any slippers on and step dead into a puddle of piss. Not to mention neither one of them bathed. They had the apartment reeking like cat piss, and we didn't own a cat. I was so self-conscience now thinking that the awful smell would seep into my clothing and people would start thinking I was a funky monkey who didn't bathe that I kept air fresheners in my room and kept the door locked.

Since I had exhausted most of my funds on Nana's funeral it was a little difficult for me to move. I was trying to save money but it was hard. When Nana was alive I didn't have to pay rent. I just took care of the food shopping, toiletries and telephone bill. That allowed me to save so quickly. Now, I had to pay Corey six hundred dollars, plus pay my cell phone bill. Our house phone went off four weeks after Corey moved in when he and Alicia ran it up and didn't want to contribute to paying the bill. Corey had accepted a collect call from almost every inmate in the correctional facilities, and I refused to go food shopping and let them eat up all my food while I was at work all day, so now I mostly ate out, which was taxing.

I came from work one evening exhausted. I really wasn't up for Corey's slick mouth and his dumb broad cosigning every stupid thing he had to say. I decided that I'd go home, grab a few things and go spend the night over at Breezy's. I came home and immediately realized that my room door was open. The lock had been broken, and no one was home. I flew inside my room and noticed that almost everything was gone. My closet had been raided, all my garments for my clothing line, television and DVD player were gone and my small jewelry box was missing as well. I flipped out. I ran downstairs looking for Corey but no one had seen him. I sat waiting in front of the house for hours when he came bebopping down the street. He didn't have Alicia or his kid with him. Immediately, I confronted him.

"Corey, you going to jail, motherfucker," I screamed.

"Whatchu talkin' 'bout?" he asked and raised his eyebrow in shock.

"Where's my shit?" I screamed and tiny tears escaped my eyes. I was furious. I wanted desperately to knock him upside his head but I knew I couldn't beat a man. No matter how small Corey is he's still a man, and his punches hurt.

"What shit? Don't tell me…did Kim steal your shit?" he asked, and my stomach dropped.

"How could Kim steal my things? You had in her the house?"

"Yeah, she came by earlier. She had been up all night and needed to get some rest. I told her she could get a few hours sleep on the couch but she had to be gone before you came home because I didn't want to hear your mouth."

"Why would you let her in?" I yelled, on the verge of hysterics.

"Yo, Jinx, no matter what she's still my sister…" he said and his voice trailed off.

"She stole all of my things," I cried and felt hopeless. "How did she do it? Weren't you home with her?"

"Alicia and I had a fight, and I had to run behind her. She stormed out. I thought I'd only be gone for a few minutes. I'm just getting back."

"You should see upstairs. She took everything! All my years of hard work for Spoiled are gone."

"Did she take my shit?" he asked, alarmed.

"What shit? You don't own shit," I corrected.

"Oh, my bad," he said as we walked toward the house. I didn't even want to go upstairs. I turned around and left.

"Jinx, where you going?" Corey called behind me, but I ignored him.

I walked to Pink Houses projects where I knew Kim used to hang out. There I found her. She was sitting on the bench with a few people. They were all watching a couple of guys shoot dice.

"Kim!" I yelled and she looked up unaffected by my outburst.

"Kim, what you done stole now," someone said.

"Bitch, pah-lezze. I ain't stole shit. If I did would I be sittin' my ass here? This bitch is trippin' as usual," she stated.

I had to admit she didn't look high off any drug, but still I pursued, "Where's my shit, Kim? I want it all back—now," I yelled and grabbed her up by her collar. Everyone moved to the side in anticipation of a fight.

"Get the fuck off me," she yelled and pushed me off her. "I ain't stole your shit."

"Liar. Corey said he left you in the house alone and now all of my shit is gone."

She laughed a hideous cackle, sucked her teeth and scratched her shoulder blade before ultimately saying, "That mutherfucker ain't gonna put this one on me. What was I supposed to steal?"

"Does it matter? I want my television, DVD player and clothes—everything—back."

"Damn, he hit payday and that lying little mutherfucker didn't put me down?" she said, and I could see she was furious. "I was sitting here all day. That little punk won't let me in the house. And how the fuck can I carry your big-ass television, DVD player and all that shit? That was Corey's doing…he probably had Karon and them dudes from Stanley help him rob you."

What she was saying was making sense. Then, a few guys started dry snitching, "Oh dip, I heard they were trying to sell some shit to light-skinned Nita earlier. That's my word."

This news had me crushed. I was living in the middle of a war zone

right in my own house. Defeated I walked away. I cut through
the projects until I reached Grant Avenue train station. I needed
to go to Breezy's for peace of mind.

I ended up staying at Breezy's for the rest of the week and
went to work from there. By the time I decided to go home most
of my anger had past. I decided not to replace anything that was
stolen and just continue to save my money in the bank. I planned
on telling Corey that I wouldn't be paying him rent for the next
year to compensate for part of my things he'd stolen. That way I
could save up a few dollars to go to a real estate office and find
me my own apartment. Breezy helped me come up with this idea.
I'd invested thousands into my clothing line and countless hours
of labor for it all to be gone in sixty seconds.

I got out of the cab and hesitantly went towards the house. I
dreaded going back but for now I didn't have a choice. As I got
to the door I noticed a large padlock on it. I rushed closer. There
was a note affixed to the door stating it was a dispossess. I was
numb. That little, lying bastard took my money faithfully and never
paid the property taxes. How could I have been so stupid?

With nowhere to go, a few dollars in my wallet and only the
clothes on my back I ended up at Kelsey's. Hot tears streamed
down my cheeks as I fell into his arms.

"I can't take it anymore," I cried and collapsed into his arms.
He calmed me downed with a cup of hot tea, and I told him everything. The truth. He told me that I could stay the night and the
next morning we'd come up with a solution. I loved how he said,
"we." That "we" enabled me to get a good night's sleep. I slept
in his bed, and he slept on the sofa in his living room. He was
always the perfect gentleman who treated me like a lady. Even
though I wouldn't have complained if he fucked me and treated
me like a whore. I needed some excitement in my life of a different kind.

For the next couple of weeks I spent my nights between
Kelsey's and Breezy's while I saved money. Neither one of them
asked me for rent because they knew my circumstance. When I
think about how my life changed so rapidly it makes me fear to-

morrow. Not knowing what the future holds is daunting. I feel so alone in this world and I miss Nana so much that my heart hurts. I keep asking God why take both my parents? Why take Nana? How much more can He take from me and still expect me to remain stoic? I have nothing. No one…except Breezy.

50

Jinx

I had been planning this trip for six weeks. Kelsey's birthday was coming up soon, and I wanted to do something special. He'd told me on numerous occasions that nothing really surprised him or gave him real joy. He'd never been able to explain exactly why he felt that way but I think it had a lot to do with his childhood. He'd told me that he's thirty-nine years old and has never been outside of Brooklyn. Even I've traveled more than him by taking trips with my girlfriends to Atlanta for All-Star Weekend or Cancun for Memorial Day Weekend, but I'd never been to Aruba, and I was hoping he'd like it as much as I'm sure I would.

I called my travel agent and booked us a room in a five-star, all-inclusive hotel. I even planned outdoor activities such as snorkeling, using a Jet Ski and swimming with dolphins for each day we'd be there. But the best part of the trip was the surprise element. He has no idea what I had in store for him. I was thinking that if I told him to pack a suitcase for five days, four nights, it would ruin the element of surprise. Even though he wouldn't know where we were going, he'd know that we were going somewhere, so being as clever as I claim to be, I went to Macy's and purchased him a full wardrobe—a few Polo shirts, jean shorts, underwear, Nike Air Trainers, sandals, socks, cologne—the whole works. The trip in full was costing me a pretty penny, and I had to dip hard into my savings. With paying for my grandmother's funeral and now this trip, I had nine hundred dollars left in the bank, and I'd need that as pocket change for the trip. I didn't want Kelsey paying for anything.

On the eve of the trip I spent the night at Breezy's house but I told him that I'd be at his house at 7:00 A.M. sharp and that he should already be dressed. Our plane was to leave at 10:30 A.M., and I didn't want to miss it. We were leaving out of John F. Kennedy airport in Queens, New York.

That night I couldn't sleep. The anticipation was killing me. I couldn't believe that I was really going this far for a man. What was it about Kelsey that I liked? Could it be that we'd been dating for months and he'd never laid a hand on me? Was that factor alone a challenge? Inwardly, I was hoping that this trip would be romantic enough that he'd want to push his religion to the side for the moment and make love to me. At night I thought about his masculine body and yearned to wrap my legs around his small waist. I wanted to feel him deep inside my cave exploring my walls and tasting my juices with his thick, pink lips...

I had the car service arrive at 6:15 A.M. sharp. He helped me load the luggage inside the trunk then I gave him Kelsey's address. I sat fidgeting the whole ride. What if he refused to go? What if he thought I was being too forward? What if I lost all my money on this damn trip? The reality of the situation was that it was too late to turn back. And since I'd never been a risk taker, this seemed like an appropriate challenge. I kept thinking that Nana would be proud to see me going after something I wanted.

When we reached Kelsey's apartment I called his house from my cell phone. He answered on the first ring. "Good morning," he sang.

I smiled.

"Good morning. Happy Birthday."

"Thanks. Thanks," he said, and I felt him smile through the phone.

"Are you ready for your gift?" I questioned.

"As ready as I'll ever be."

"Good, come downstairs. I'm waiting for you in a cab."

"Now?" he asked as he looked out the window and saw me looking up at him. He waved.

"The meter's ticking." I laughed.

"I'll be down in five minutes," he said and hung up. For some reason I felt like this was going to go off without a hitch.

Kelsey climbed in the cab and took my hand and kissed the inside of my palm. Still no sweet kisses on my lips.

"What's the big secret?" he probed.

"Can't tell you. Just sit back, relax and enjoy the mystique."

After we came off the Belt Parkway eastbound he noticed we were entering John F. Kennedy airport. I could see the twinkle in his eyes but he was a sportsman and knew how to play the game. He knew I wouldn't tell him where we were going but he knew we were going somewhere. He remained calm.

We exited the cab and the driver came around to help us with our luggage. Still he didn't question anything. He just smiled. I took him by his hand, and we walked to the ticket counter for Continental Airlines. It wasn't until then that he knew of our destination. We both went through a few check points and walked to gate ten, which was where we'd board the plane in less than two hours.

"I must admit that nothing surprises me. I think I told you that before, but not only am I shocked, I'm also flattered. No woman has ever gone out of her way to treat me with this level of fondness. If I forget to tell you, I want you to know that you've made a difference in my life," he said and squeezed my hand.

"I'm doing this because you've made a difference in my life. I love spending time with you, and I wanted to show you my appreciation."

We both slept for most of the five-hour plane ride. We woke up in Aruba. It was 2:30 P.M., and the sun was shining. We both looked out the window from the plane and put huge grins on our faces. My heart was racing, and the eagerness showed on both of our faces. Soon we cleared customs and were ushered off to our hotel. We were staying at the Hyatt Aruba. It was a beautifully decorated hotel with marble floors and crystal chandeliers. There was an indoor and heated outside pool with a waterfall. There also was a swim-up bar, beach and all types of water sports. We raced up to our room, which had a balcony, separate shower, Jacuzzi and cable television. We didn't stay long. I thought that Kelsey would be a little stiff but he was a completely different man. I took my shower first and put on a sexy, two-piece Calvin Klein bathing suit, and he hopped in the shower right behind me and put on the Polo swimming trucks I picked out for him.

He was amused looking through the suitcase at the outfits I selected. He said that he liked everything I bought and that I had good taste.

Our trip flew by rapidly. We went from horseback riding to the bat cave to wind surfing, and Kelsey was like a kid again. I've never seen him so jovial. I can certainly say that the trip brought something good out of him that lay dormant for years. When it was time to leave he was almost sullen. He said something about not wanting to return to his life back in Brooklyn, and I didn't understand. When I asked him to explain what he meant he just shrugged it off and shut down.

From the airport we went back to Kelsey's apartment and I wanted to readdress the comment he'd made in Aruba about not wanting to come back to his life in Brooklyn.

"Kelsey, I've shared so much with you about my life, my secrets and I wish you'd do the same. Is there something bothering you? Maybe I can help," I asked, as we started to unpack. I turned around to face him and looked deeply into his face. Up until now I never noticed Kelsey had shark eyes: dark, shallow and cold. I shuddered and felt a slight chill in my bones.

"Jinx I was being selfish. I'd had such a good time and I didn't want to come back to the blaring car stereos, busy city streets and cracked concrete," he said, earnestly.

"You sure?" I asked, skeptically.

"Would I lie to you," he grinned, and embraced me.

I exhaled and was glad that he didn't have any looming problems awaiting him in Brooklyn. I don't think I could take any more bad news.

51

Breezy

Tonight will be the first night that I'd give into Black's advances to make love. I had already gone to Victoria's Secret and bought the cutest two-piece negligee I could find. It was black lace with the nipples cut out. Two pink bows made a connection over my areolas, and the panties were lace with the crotch cut out. Women call these "eat me" panties, and that's exactly what I wanted him to do.

At first I was skeptical on how far I could let myself go in the bed-room. Should I take it easy and play timid or should I fuck his brains out and have him screaming out my name? I decided to go with the latter. They say you only get one chance to make a first impression. The only thing I decided not to do was suck his dick. While there in the moment men love when you do that shit but the next day they sit back and wonder just how many dicks you've eaten in your life. And since my sucking dick game is out of this world, I could mess around and definitely send the wrong message.

Since I'm an analytical perfectionist, I had everything planned to the last detail. But instead of it coming off as rehearsed, he'd think it was purely impromptu. I had my dad prepare roasted chicken, baby potatoes and steamed carrots. I purchased a bottle of Dom Perignon and pre-pared peach cobbler. He just mentioned that it was his favorite.

He was supposed to arrive at 8:00 P.M. but the time came and went. I called his cellular phone, and he kept sending me to voicemail. It took all my strength not to curse his ass out. How fucking dare he play me like this? Somewhere around 10:30 P.M. he called.

"Hey, sexy," he sang.

"Hey, I was starting to think you forgot about me," I said as calmly as I could project. I didn't want him to think that he'd even ruffled my feathers.

"No, no, I got caught up handling some business. Listen, I need to take a rain check on tonight. Is that all right with you?"

"Sure, not a problem. I'll give you a call tomorrow. Be safe," I replied and began to hang up.

"Wait. I mean I can make it but it won't be for another thirty minutes. I hear the disappointment in your voice, and the last thing I want is for you to be mad at me."

I saw what type of game he was playing. I actually thought he wasn't into the mind games. He needed to recognize he had to get up early in the morning if he planned on getting over on me.

"Mad? No, no…I'm the last person who'd want to stand in between you and business. I have my own work ethics that I take seriously. Handle your business and call me tomorrow when you have a moment. Maybe we can do something next week."

"Didn't you say you cooked?" he asked, and I could hear the panic in his voice.

"Yes. Yes, I did."

"Okay, sit tight. I'm on my way."

Before I could object further he hung up. He was ringing my bell in less than twenty minutes. He'd probably ran every light just to get there before I called back to cancel our night.

He came inside in an exceptionally good mood. He was probably glad he didn't fuck up tonight as he almost had. We ate dinner by the fireplace and talked about our days. He told me the truth, and I lied my ass off.

"Breezy, when I look at you I see an ambitious, educated woman who's taken me by surprise. I don't know what it is about you that makes me think about you all day when I'm not with you."

I avoided eye contact and put my head down as if I was blushing. He took his hand and lifted my head back up. We looked deep into each other's eyes, and he leaned over and kissed my lips gently then slowly he slid his tongue in my mouth. We softly kissed by my fireplace. He went down and sucked on my neck, then my shoulder blade and was hesitant about caressing my breasts. I knew he didn't want to get too aroused only to be told no.

I stared in his eyes and gave him a look that allowed him to go further. He tried to unbutton my shirt when I stopped him. I could tell he was frustrated and about to say something harsh when I said, "Not here. Let's go to my room."

I walked slowly in my bedroom with him right on my heels. I stood back and began to slowly undress. I unbuttoned my shirt and let it cascade to the floor. Next, I unzipped my skirt and stepped out of it. There I stood as sexy as any man could ever want a woman to be with my hands covering my breasts. I needed to play bashful yet be alluring, and I could tell it was working. His large dick bulged through his jeans, and I hadn't even touched him. I sashayed over to Black and stood on my tiptoes to kiss him. He leaned over and met my lips, and we began to passionately kiss. His soft tongue expertly maneuvered inside of my mouth and left me breathless. He pulled me in closer, pressed his pelvis up against my pussy and began to rock in and out while he gently cupped both breasts and began to playfully lick my areolas. I moaned my pleasure, leaned my head back and got lost in the moment. Black picked me up and walked me over to my canopy bed and gently laid me down. As I lay looking up at him he began to undress. Layer by layer he took off each piece of clothing and tossed it to the ground. When he was completely naked his ripe dick stood at attention, and my pussy got wet just from anticipation. Slowly he crawled on the bed, and I parted my legs hoping he'd start there. Instead, he started with my toes. He grabbed my petite, size-seven pedicured feet and began to lovingly suck each toe. I could tell this was going to be a lovemaking session. I saw the intenseness in his face. As his warm, moist tongue sucked each toe, I laid back and enjoyed the moment. He was taking his time as he made his way to my inner thigh and then to my clitoris. Expertly he performed cunnilingus in a controlled manner. He concentrated on one area instead of being all over the place.

Twenty minutes later he was still eating my pussy. I was rocking my hips in a sensual method, and I had to literally bite down on my hand to keep from screaming out. As my legs trembled, it seemed to turn him on. He was making little love sounds as if he was enjoying it just as much as I was.

When the feeling got too intense, I reached down and gripped my silk sheets as strong waves of pleasure came pouring out of me like a waterfall. He'd pleasured my most sensitive area then began to trace my erogenous zones with his tongue. My body was hot and moist as he tantalized and tickled my most sensitive areas, bringing me to feel a host of new sensations.

Black grabbed a condom and positioned himself to enter me.

"I'm just going to give you a little bit," he whispered in my ear. "I promise."

I lay in the passive position as he applied pressure. I felt as if he was dominating my body as my pleasure intensified. I wrapped my legs around his sexy waist, our limbs entwined, and we began to make love. Each deep stroke opened my resisting walls. I gritted my teeth to take the pain.

Black amazed me on how long he could prolong his climax. I had multiple orgasms, and he was still maneuvering me through erotic positions. We tried everything, and I enjoyed every minute.

When I awoke the morning he was still sleeping peacefully. I went to walk to the bathroom, and I had to almost crawl. He had bruised my swollen pussy so bad that when I pissed it stung and I almost moaned in pain.

When I crawled back in bed, he woke up for a moment and reached for me. I nearly panicked thinking he wanted more.

"Do you want breakfast?" I asked and gently kissed him on his cheek. He just smiled and nodded.

Now, I can get busy in the kitchen as well as my father. I made Belgian waffles, beef sausages and eggs over easy. I brought him his breakfast in bed and as we ate he confided in me.

"That was so good last night, wasn't it?" he asked.

I blushed and said, "I think we woke the whole block up. I can't imagine what's going through my brother's mind."

"He was probably cheering saying, 'finally she gave a brother some,'" he joked.

I laughed. "You think so?"

"You took forever to let me taste you," he said with a sheepish grin.

"I did not," I protested.

"Yes, you did. I don't know if I should even tell you this, but lately if I meet a woman and if she doesn't sleep with me within two weeks, I leave her. And if she does sleep with me within two weeks, I'd leave her."

"That's a double-edged sword."

"I know, but I was protecting my heart. I was in a relationship where we got together quickly, and I ended up getting my heart broken. I can't go through that again, so I'm glad you made me wait."

I knew he was taking about Nicoli, and his response also confirmed that I had him. Bingo. I'd come a long way, and I knew I couldn't mess it up.

Black and I stayed in bed all morning lazily talking and canoodling. He left in the early afternoon with promises to call me later. I took the remainder of the morning contemplating my next move.

Checkmate...

52

Jinx

Every year the first week in June, Breezy's father throws a barbecue in the park located at Tompkins Avenue. Everyone from East New York, Brownsville and Bedford Stuyvesant show up with their best clothes and the best cars. I looked forward to this event every year. I went to Bloomingdale's and bought a pair of jean Citizen Capri jeans. They cost $165 with a pink retro T-shirt with rhinestones. The T-shirt cost seventy-nine dollars. At home I already had a pair of pink Gucci sandals that matched the T-shirt perfectly. The night before I had gone to Harlem and gotten my hair braided going back with the sides in a zigzag shape with beads on the ends. After I got dressed, I put on a sheer pink Lip Glass from MAC and a pair of sterling-silver hoop earrings.

It was nearly six o'clock by the time I had gotten ready. I looked out the window, and it was a perfectly sunny day. I was already late. I was supposed to meet Breezy at her house thirty minutes ago. My cell phone rang.

"What's up, girl?" I said when I picked up. I knew it was Breezy from her ring tone, the Pussycat Dolls. When she called you heard, *"Don't you wish your girl was a freak like me...don't cha."*

"Where you at?" she asked impatiently.

"I'm still home." I was now permanently living with Kelsey.

"I'm out. You gotta meet me there. I'm already late waiting on you."

"That's cool. I'll meet you there. Where are you going to be at?"

"I don't know. Find me," she snapped. "You know I'll be wherever the crowd is."

"Okay. I'll be there in forty minutes," I said and hung up.

I was running late so that meant that I had to take a cab. I originally was going to take the train to Breezy's house, and she'd drive us in her jeep to the barbecue, but I couldn't come walking from the train station, not when all the major players would be out there.

I was three blocks away in the cab when I heard the music blasting. The deejay was bumping T.I.'s *"You Don't Know Me."*

I started bopping my head to the music, snapping my fingers and singing along. The cabdriver looked back and smiled. He could see I was excited.

"You going to the barbecue?" he asked as he made a right off Atlantic Avenue onto Bedford.

"Yeah."

"I hear good things about the guy who throws this. He does it every year for the neighborhood, doesn't he?"

"That's my best friend's father," I bragged. "He's filthy rich and gives back to his community."

"He sounds like a great guy," the cabdriver said. "That'll be ten dollars."

I reached inside my pocketbook quickly and pulled out a ten. I could see Breezy and Joy surrounded by a few dudes. It was Hassan, Begal, One-fifty and Doc. They were all shooting dice, and there was lots of money on the ground. I approached slowly.

"What's up?" I asked the crowd.

"What's up, girl," Breezy shouted and got everyone's attention. The guys turned around briefly from gambling to acknowledge me.

"What's up, Jinx?" Begal said. "Come here and blow on these dice and give me some luck with your sexy self."

I walked over seductively, wrapped my hands around his and blew on his dice. He looked me in my eyes and smiled. He knew I was flirting. He shook up the dice and tossed them.

"Yeah, baby," he yelled as the dice stopped on 5-6. Begal reached down and picked up what appeared to be about a thousand dollars. He pulled off a few hundred and handed it to me. I smiled politely and stuffed the money quickly inside my wallet. I could see Joy staring with envy. She used to fuck with Begal last summer but they're just friends now. Despite what Joy might be thinking I would never fuck behind her. Even though we're not as tight as her and Breezy, I still wouldn't violate the code by fucking with Begal.

"Jinx, here," Breezy said and handed me a glass of Hpnotiq.

As we sat there getting fucked up the deejay was going bananas. He was blasting old school Lil' Kim. *"I know a dude named Jimmy used to run up in me."*

We were all dancing seductively to the music. Even the guys were singing along. *"Night time pissy drunk off the Henny and Remy..."*

Then he started mixing in classic Foxy Brown and the crowd lost their minds. *"Let me tell you where I grew up at, threw up at...Brooklyn beef who want that?"*

Breezy's father was walking around like the President of the United States. Everyone was showing him mad love. He was walking around and shaking hands like a politician meeting and greeting the public. I felt honored to even know him personally. Mr. Whittaker made his way over to us. He shook the guys' hands and wrapped his arm around Breezy.

"Everyone all right over here?" he asked.

"Yeah, it's lovely," Hassan said. "Reggie, please keep doing it real big."

Kesha rolled up shortly after 10:00 P.M. She was on duty but you would never know. She had on a tight pair of Citizen jeans with the jean jacket to match. Underneath the jacket she had her .357 in a holster. A pair of Nike Air Force Ones were on her feet. She was loud as usual. When One-fifty saw her coming he mumbled, "Goddamn, here comes Kesha. That bitch about to hop on my dick."

"Excuse me," Joy challenged.

"You heard what the fuck I said," One-fifty barked.

He got tired of Kesha always harassing him. It was no secret that he fucked Kesha on some one-night stand shit, but Kesha didn't want it to be that way. Every since then she was always running his plates, pulling him over and searching his car. If he had so much as a spliff of weed in his car she sent him through the system. She just wouldn't leave him alone.

"What's up, Fifty?" Kesha asked with a snarl on her face.

"Fuck you, bitch," One-fifty said without hesitation.

Kesha just laughed and ignored his snide remark. She walked over to the bench where me, Breezy and Joy were sitting and drinking Alizé mixed with Hpnotiq and Malibu. We called this drink Fuck Me because it tasted so good that before you knew it you'd have drank way past your limit, thus leaving room for you to get fucked.

"You still on duty?" Joy asked.

"Yeah, I'm on until 3:00 A.M."

"Kesha, why didn't you take off? You knew it was my father's barbecue," Breezy whined. We all wished Kesha could hang out. Once she got drunk she was the life of the party.

"Breeze, I got bills to pay. I can't be taking days off to just sit and chill. Besides, I party with ya'll enough. And you'll fill me in on the highlights tomorrow."

The barbecue ended in the early hours of the morning. Joy rode with Breezy to take me home. Joy was pissy drunk talking junk.

"Please, this is Unique callin' me in shit. I ain't even pickin' up for that motherfucker," she said.

"Why? Ya'll was all hugged up at the pool party last month. What happened?" Breezy asked.

"He be buggin. Last night we fucked and he's like, 'yo, suck my dick.' I ain't sucking that dirty nigga dick. He won't have me on blast talkin' 'bout I swallowed his kids."

We all burst into laughter. Joy was too crazy. I crawled out of Breezy's jeep and promised to call them the next day.

"Love you," I said and gave her a kiss on her cheek.

"Love you too."

53

Breezy

In the days after Nicoli's unexpected visit, I hadn't really been able to spend any time with Black. He called to check up on me but was always distracted. When I thought we were getting closer, he pulled away. He was consistently inconsistent and it was driving me crazy. He was hard to figure out, and I couldn't read him. I didn't want to run to my father every time Black didn't behave the way I'd like because I needed my father to believe that I had everything under control. Black called when he wanted to and rarely took initiative on making a date. I always had to suggest that we see each other. When I asked if there was something on his mind or if he was going through something he always denied it. So I wondered if everything was so perfect in his life and if he liked me the way he said he did, why he didn't ever want to spend time with me or call me.

Just when I was about to get paranoid that I'd made the wrong decision to not tell Black about Nicoli and I being cousins, I stumbled upon a breaking news story on *Entertainment Tonight*. The news correspondent stated that Black King was being sued for child support by his estranged child's mother, Nicoli Jones. They showed a clip of Nicoli emerging from family court with paparazzi everywhere. Lightbulbs were flashing as she held up her hand to block out the camera lenses. Large Jackie Onassis dark shades hid her small, pale face as her lawyer whisked her away in a black Tahoe jeep.

I was floored.

I didn't know if I should be elated that they were really over or upset that she was trying to get her greedy hands on Black's money.

I sat back with my feet up on my sofa watching *E.T.* on my fifty-two-inch plasma television when my cell phone rang. As I went to answer it I wondered why no one ever called on my home phone anymore. I looked and the number was private.

"Hello," I said.

"Hey, baby girl." It was Black.

"How are you?"

"Doing better now that I'm talking to you."

"Glad I could make your day."

"So what are we doing tonight?"

"Ummm, I don't know. What do you want to do?" I said, shifting the pressure back to him. I was tired of taking the initiative. I needed him to be a little more decisive and act as if he had an interest in this relationship.

"How about you come over to my place tonight? I want to cook for you," he suggested.

"How nice…What time did you have in mind?" I said, trying to play it cool when I was really flattered.

"How about eight o'clock?" he said.

Black and I agreed that I'd come over and he'd cook. He then gave me his midtown apartment address, and I hung up and realized I only had a few hours to prepare. As I got ready, I wondered what made him want to do this for me. Were we getting closer? Did he miss me and think about me when we weren't together?

For the occasion, I decided to wear an orange John Galliano dress with a pair of gold Jimmy Choo stilettos. I had my hair swept up in a loose bun with spiral curls dangling over my face. I put on a pair of eighteen-karat gold hoop earrings with my gold presidential Rolex watch. For makeup, I applied Chanel bronze powder, sheer orange MAC Lip Glass and false eyelashes. I looked as if I had been tanning in the Caribbean for weeks.

When I arrived at his building the doorman let me in. I had to be announced at the front desk and given permission to enter the building. I took the private elevator up to Black's penthouse apartment. When I arrived, he opened the door wearing an apron and chef's hat. He looked adorable. I smiled.

"Don't you look festive," I said as I entered his apartment.

"And you look simply gorgeous," he said, and I blushed.

"This is for you," I said, handing him a gift I'd picked up.

"For me?" he admonished. "What a pleasant surprise."

Black put down his gift and led me into his massive living room with ten-foot windows that led out to the terrace with a panoramic view of the city. The living room was professionally decorated and beautiful. His wine-colored walls were trimmed in dental moldings. Oversized deep chocolate leather sofas sat neatly on top of Persian rugs. Antique vases and priceless paintings added to the rich décor.

"Make yourself at home. Let me turn the food down to simmer."

"Your home is beautiful," I complimented.

"Let me show you around."

He walked me into his kitchen that had a granite island in the center that matched the countertops and floors. Stainless-steel Viking kitchen appliances stood out against the deep hunter-green hues. There were two full bathrooms on the first floor and a marble fireplace. Upstairs, he had three bedrooms with one master bathroom and two smaller ones and a den. I could tell he kept peeking over at me to see if I was impressed but I wasn't. He was wealthy; he supposed to live this way.

How could Nicoli mess this up? I thought.

Back downstairs, I got cozy on his sofa. Black came out of the kitchen to check on me and to give me a glass of champagne. His apron was covered with grease and flour. Secretly I wondered what he was cooking. I couldn't make out any distinct smells coming from the kitchen.

"*Mu-ah*," he said as he kissed me full on my lips. "You taste good."

"Thank you." I smiled. "What are we eating?"

"Well I'll be eating you," he joked. "And hopefully you'll be eating—"

"Don't you dare say it." I laughed.

Black went back into the kitchen, and my gaze roamed around the room. He had beautiful paintings adorning his walls. A Monet hung over his fireplace. There weren't any photos of him or family members. He was such a private person and didn't really open up. Truthfully, I didn't really know much about him, his family or his background. I thought it wise not to ask. When he was ready to open up he would. Finally, Black came out of the kitchen.

"Dinner's ready," he announced. "Let's eat outside. It's a beautiful night."

We both walked out on his terrace, and I sat down at a table that he'd already set. He ran back inside and came out with two plates. He placed one in front of me, and I burst out in laughter.

"Franks and beans?" I laughed.

"What? Don't tell me you've never had franks and beans."

"I've never eaten franks and beans," I said seriously.

He looked in my eyes and knew I wasn't lying.

"You've got to be kidding me. You don't know what you've been missing."

"Oh, poor, poor, Breezy," I joked. "So I guess the flour and grease on your apron was a ruse?"

"Clever huh?" he nodded, knowingly.

Black ran back inside and brought out the bottle of Clicquot. We sat down to dinner eating franks, beans and drinking champagne. I must say he was original.

Now it was my turn.

"Why don't you open up your gift?"

"You know I really don't deserve a gift. I've been a horrible boyfriend," he admitted. "I've been so inundated with work that I've been neglecting you. Don't think that I haven't noticed. I'm glad that you've given me a chance and that you're patient with me."

"You were patient with me," I reminded him.

"That I was," he said, smiling sheepishly.

We both walked inside, and I gave him the box, expensively wrapped with an elaborate bow on top. I could see the gleam and excitement in his eyes as he jiggled the box to see if he could guess what it was.

"Just open it silly." I laughed.

Tearing into the gift as a young child would, he stopped short when he saw the colorful letters staring back at him.

"Twister?"

"My favorite game of all time. I'm the all-time champion," I said, snatching the game from him.

"That's impossible because *I'm* the all-time champ," he challenged.

"Well, we'll just see about that."

He kicked off his shoes as I went to set up the board on the floor.

"You ready for this ass whipping?" he asked while cracking his knuckles.

"If you can stand getting beat by a girl…again!"

"Ladies first," he laughed.

"Not so fast. We're playing Brooklyn style."

"That means you're gonna cheat," he mocked.

"Cute," I replied and kicked off my shoes. "Strip."

"Strip?"

"This is *naked* Twister."

We both stripped and began our game.

"Right foot yellow. Left hand purple," I said as I stretched my body in contortions I didn't know I could after spinning the wheel. Black and I were intertwined with each other in the most erotic positions one's imagination couldn't have imaged. When he had to move into a position that allowed him to tower over me and my lower back brushed the tip of his penis, it immediately grew hard. Black reached up and ended the game by grabbing for my breasts. I was wondering what had taken him so long.

"Let's get in the shower," he suggested.

The hot water cascaded down my face as I submerged my body underneath the powerful showerhead. The steam was so thick, I couldn't see my hands. I let the soothing water drench my hair and face as Black came in from behind and pressed his hard body up against my backside. His masculine hands started lathering my back. As the soapy rag traveled along the nape of my neck, tracing my hips, my ass and then lingered in between my thighs, I shuddered. I turned around to face him, and we began kissing passionately. Black began to slowly lick my earlobes while massaging my erect nibbles with his fingertips.

Black sat me down on the stool located inside his shower, got down on his knees and parted my legs. He pulled me to the edge of the stool and opened my nether lips with two fingers. My ripe clitoris entered his warm mouth eagerly. As he began sucking my clit, I wrapped my legs around his neck and held onto the shower walls for support. He traced the creases outlining the walls of my vagina with his tongue, causing me to quiver involuntarily. Black nodded as if to say he knew he'd hit the right spot. Our silence was unequivocally erotic.

Black pulled back and stuck his finger into my inflamed flesh and began twirling. Hot juices seeped out onto his hands, and I encouraged him by moaning. He then pulled me up. Black sat down and positioned me in front of him. He leaned me over, spread my ass and began lowering me on top of his dick.

"What are you doing?" I asked in astonishment. He didn't say a word. Black began to aggressively massage my breasts in a circular motion while placing wet kisses on my spine that were driving me crazy. Inch by inch, his massive dick began penetrating my anal cavity. The sensation was exquisite. I began rocking my hips seductively as the sensations began filtering through my body. Finally, he had entered me completely. The pain mixed with pleasure was a little overbearing as our slippery bodies became one. As Black held tightly onto my hips, pumping in and out, I moaned my pleasure.

"You…like…this?" he moaned. "You…like…this…big…dick?"

"Oh, yesssss," I agreed. I was *loving* his big dick.

"Tell me what you want?"

"I want you to fuck me harder," I demanded.

"Like this?" he asked through clenched teeth as he began to mercilessly ram his dick in my ass.

"Yeeesssss," I screamed, still gripping the shower door for support.

"I want you to play with your pussy," Black commanded.

I began massaging my already swollen clitoris as Black continued to guide his long, thick dick in my backside. The combination was explosive as I felt strong waves of pleasure cascading through my body. I braced myself as my muscles tensed up. We both exploded and screamed out in unison. For long moments we both breathed in and out trying to catch our breaths. I had never experienced anything like that in my life. Soon Black eased out of me, and I thought that I wouldn't be able to walk straight for a week.

Black continued to do what he started, which was wash my body. He seemed to enjoy washing my fingers, arms, feet and intimate parts. Next, he carried me back to his bed where he laid me down and slid his tongue in my mouth. We began kissing softly, which soon progressed to slow, passionate kisses. When I felt him get aroused, I couldn't believe it.

My body was yearning desperately for him to enter me again. I arched my back as he aggressively sucked my breasts until my nipples were erect. I wrapped my shapely legs around his trim waist, and he entered my pussy gently. As he pumped his dick, I pushed my hips back, meeting each thrust. It felt as if his penis was growing bigger inside of me as I dug my nails deep into his masculine shoulders. I began to nibble on his neck before I flipped him over and mounted him.

I expertly rode his dick while his hands guided my waist.

"Go ahead get yours," he crooned. I looked down and saw pleasure all over his face. I began sliding up and down on his dick while contracting my Kegel muscle, which drove him crazy.

"Is it good?" I said.

"Oh, baby, you got some good pussssyyyy," he moaned.

As my pussy began to contract involuntarily, I sped up my rhythm.

"I'm about to cummmm," I yelled as Black grabbed me tightly. We both exploded for the second time. Sweat poured from both our bodies as I collapsed on top of his broad chest.

We made love five times from the shower to the bed in one night. I must admit that was a record for me. The last time I came so hard that I was physically drained and exhausted.

Before I could drift off into a peaceful sleep, Black went inside his closet and came out with two sleeping bags.

"You've got to be kidding," I stated.

"We're having a sleepover. Here," he said and tossed me a pair of his pajamas. I was totally enamored. I decided to play the game. We both went back downstairs and crawled in our sleeping bags while the fire crackled. It was so romantic as he looked in my eyes. As we lay together, I watched him sleep peacefully. I then noticed something that I hadn't before—a round, deep burgundy hickey was proudly plastered on his neck and I knew that I didn't do it. I didn't give nor did I receive them. Sharp pangs of jealousy shot through my body. If not from Nicoli, then who? I crawled out of the bag, tiptoed around downstairs and pulled his cell phone out of his jeans. I went through his recent call list and name after name appeared: Nicoli, Cheryl, Stacy, Lisa, Kim, Crystal, Katrice, Ellen, and the list went on.

I wondered how many pink diamond tennis bracelets were floating on the wrists of women in New York compliments of Mr. Black King.

54

Nicoli

After I had gotten Black arrested I was officially on his shit list. No matter how many ways I tried to casually get him to come up to my apartment, he refused. He wouldn't answer my calls and had Alphonse come to pick up BJ for his weekend visits. I had gotten the pictures that I had taken of Breezy hold BJ developed, and I wanted to leave them casually around before Breezy could make another allegation against me. Holding all of this in was killing me. I couldn't stand another day with Breezy and Black being together. I was going to win. I was determined to get Black from her clutches.

God was definitely looking out for his baby girl when Black called to announce that Alphonse had called out on an emergency and he needed to come and pick up BJ.

"When I call just bring him downstairs," he demanded.

"Look, I'm not lugging all of his things downstairs. He's your son. Come up and get him."

Black slammed down the phone in my ear. I couldn't help but chuckle. It was so easy to get his pressure up. He'd better watch out. A man his age is prone to stress-related heart attacks.

As planned, when Black arrived I was soaking wet from a shower. I had the shower running and shampoo in my hair. I ran and opened the door and dashed back into the shower.

"Show yourself out," I yelled as I dashed back into the bathroom and locked the door.

BJ was asleep in his crib, and I purposely didn't pack his overnight bag. I had his clothing laid out on my bed and mixed in with our clothes were the pictures. There's a little bit of curiosity in all of us so I knew that Black would snoop. Within minutes he was banging down the bathroom door.

"What?" I yelled in aggravation and had to hold my mouth to keep from laughing out loud.

"Get your ass out here," he commanded.

I slowly rinsed, letting him simmer, then came out.

"What the fuck are these?" he asked as he tossed the pictures at me. They dangled mid-air until finally resting at my feet. I took a look at them then at Black and replied, "That's my cousin Breezy and my uncle Reggie. What? Did you think I had our son with strangers? You're crazy."

Black's face personified shock. He backpedaled to my bed and collapsed with his mouth gapping open. I knew I had to hammer it home.

"Growing up she's always hated me, so it was a shock when she came around and wanted to be in my life as well as BJ's. If you and I were on better terms I would introduce you guys...she keeps asking about you."

"No...no, that won't be necessary. Have you ever left her around BJ alone?"

"Why would I do that? I don't trust her like that. I just told you the girl hated the ground that I walked on. She was always calculating and vindictive as a child. Do you think I would just trust her overnight with my most prized possession?"

"How much older than you is she?"

"We're about the same age. She should be around twenty-one or twenty-two, somewhere around there. Why are you asking so many questions about her?"

"I just want to know who you got our son around, that's all."

"And I just told you. Do I question you to that length about the girlfriends you have our son around?"

"That's because I don't have a girlfriend, and you know that. Ain't no girl out here worth me giving my heart to," he spat.

He sounded so defeated I almost felt sorry for him. I helped him pack the baby bag, he gathered up BJ and left.

Oh, how I wish I could be a fly on the wall to see it unfold with Breezy and Black. I wondered how he was gonna confront her. Would he tell her that he caught her in a lie? I doubt it. That's not Black's style. He'd just cut her off and have her go crazy trying to figure out why. He hated confrontations and arguments.

55

Jinx

I'd been seeing Kelsey for what seemed like a lifetime, and he still hadn't touched me. Although I respected his religion, my body was yearning for him to enter me. One night we went to Blockbuster and got a movie, and he also cooked dinner for me.

I arrived just past eight o'clock from work, and dinner was just about ready. Kelsey kissed me on my forehead and took my shawl. He was different from the other guys I dated. He was older, more mature and respectful. It wasn't about booty calls for him. He truly enjoyed my company, and I was appreciative.

"You look gorgeous," he said.

"Thank you," I replied as I sat down at the dinner table. "What did you cook?"

"I hope you like calamari and filet mignon," he said as he brought my plate to the table.

"Oh, I love it. It looks delicious," I said.

As we ate dinner I couldn't believe how wonderful a cook he was. The food melted in my mouth like butter.

After dinner we sat around talking while I drank Merlot and got a little tipsy. We began to talk.

"Tell me about your childhood," I asked.

He placed his eyes downward and said, "I don't talk about my past. It hurts too much."

"I understand. I used to keep my memories of my childhood bottled up inside as well until Nana told me that I had to let it out or else those memories would rot inside me and make me bitter."

"Is that right?" he said and refilled my wineglass.

"That's right," I said, then changed the subject. "Do you know how to play poker?"

"No. I've never learned."

"What about pity-pat?"

"Yes, I can play that. I have some cards in the drawer. I'll get them, and we'll play on the floor."

"Perfect," I said. "But we're going to play strip pity-pat. Are you down, Kelsey?"

"Strip pity-pat? There's no such game."

"There is now." I grinned. "And you better not cheat."

Before the game, Kelsey and I put on all of our clothing. I pulled on my shawl and put back on my sandals. And then we began.

The first round, I won. He took off his fitted hat. The second round, he won. I took off my shawl. An hour into the game he was beating the pants off me—literally. I was sitting in front of him with my bra and thong panties still on. The next hand would decide it all. That's when Kelsey wanted to quit.

"I think we've played this long enough. You should put back on your clothes," he said, never giving me any eye contact.

I leaned over as if I was going to grab my clothes and fell on top of him. Sneakily, I slid my tongue in his mouth. He tried to resist but I was too much for him. All the passion I had bottled up inside came bursting out. My tongue explored the inside of his mouth and his earlobes, then I moved down to his neck. I sucked gently on his neck until I heard a faint moan. I grinded my hips up and down, and I felt a bulge, which excited me. I got more aggressive and reached inside his boxers. Once my hand touched his penis it grew to an enormous size. I almost backed out from fear of what he was packing.

Soon, Kelsey started to respond to my gestures and began making love back to me. He gently caressed my back then his hands traveled around to my bra. He gently unclasped my bra, and my breasts spilled out. He opened his mouth and took a mouthful. He sucked until my nipples were like two ripe fruits. We switched positions until I was lying flat on my back and we were in the missionary position. I parted my legs slightly, and he eased my panties off. He looked in my eyes and I think I saw love. Next, he went down and tasted my juices. He sucked on my clitoris with his skillful tongue until I felt heavy waves cascading down my body. I grabbed him by his shoulders and pulled him back up.

"Enter me," I breathed. "I need you inside of me."

He steadied himself on top of me and gently pushed against my stubborn walls. I was so wet you could hear soft love noises as he pushed the tip of his dick in and out. My pussy wouldn't allow his dick to go farther. It took steadied, consistent strokes in order for my pussy to open up and allow his dick to completely penetrate. He took one deep thrust, and I screamed in pleasure mixed with pain.

"I'm sorry, baby," he crooned in my ear.

"Don't stop…Kelsey, it feels so good," I whispered.

I was grinding my hips to his rhythm, and the feeling was sensational. When the feeling got too intense I bit down hard on my bottom lip to keep from screaming out. Instead, I dug my nails deep into his back. He didn't let up. He kept pumping his ass in and out then in circular motions. Then he'd go hard until tears streamed down my cheeks then he'd slow it up and go softer…and softer…

I was losing my mind. It felt like we were making love for hours. Just when the feeling couldn't get any better Kelsey started making love to me faster and faster. Deep waves came cascading down my body until it reached my toes. My whole body shuddered as I came with such a force, I yelled out in pleasure. Hot juices entered my body and seeped down my leg. Kelsey lay inside of me for a long moment just breathing. Finally, he eased out of me, and we both fell into a peaceful sleep.

56

Kesha

I woke up on the wrong side of the bed. Not anything in particular was bothering me, I just felt a little agitated. I went into work on time and caught roll call. Our unit usually had informal roll calls, but still they were informative. After I listened to the color of the day wrist bands that the undercover detectives are to wear to identify them from civilians, Bosco and I set out on the street. We drove around aimlessly just wanting to catch some action. I was driving when I saw Jock. He was double parked outside of this chick named Candy's crib. I hopped out immediately and started writing him a ticket. Within moments he was coming down her stairs.

"What you doing in New York with North Carolina plates on your truck?" I said.

"Yo, Kesha, why you writing me a ticket? You not traffic police. Don't you have better shit to do than to harass me?"

"I thought you were a baller. A baller can't afford New York insurance, so you have to drive your shit a thousand miles to get cheaper insurance," I spat. I could tell I had plucked a nerve.

"Yo, get off my dick," he yelled and grabbed on his waist as if he had a gun. I pulled out my .357 and pointed it to his head.

"Don't move, motherfucker," I yelled. "You were going for a gun?"

Bosco jumped out the car, slammed him up against his jeep and started patting him down in hopes of finding a gun.

"He's clean," Bosco said.

"Yeah, I'm clean. Why wouldn't I be?" he sarcastically replied.

"So what you be doing down in N.C.? You making money down there? Maybe fuck a few country broads? You got any baby mommas down there?" I asked.

"Kesha, if you keep fucking with me I'm going to the precinct and file harassment charges on your crazy ass," he threatened.

I tossed his ticket in his face and got back in the car with Bosco. We rode up on Nostrand Avenue and got out to get a slice of pizza. A few younger girls were outside jumping double dutch. I jumped in and did a few moves I remembered when I was little. I played around with the girls for a moment until Bosco came out with our pizzas.

"Come on, Kesha. One of them may be your future collar," he joked.

I hated when Bosco made such racial jokes. That got under my skin, and I had to set his white ass straight.

"Don't play with me, motherfucker, 'cause we can drive down to Crossbay Boulevard and pick up a few of your loan-sharking, mob-affili-ated, extortionist cousins."

"Stop being so sensitive. I was only joking. And for the record I'm Jewish remember," he replied as we got in our undercover car.

As we sat there eating pizza we couldn't believe our eyes as we wit-nessed a drug deal go down. Two cars drove onto Macon Street. One guy got out holding a shopping bag, looked around, then got into the other car. They sat there for about ten minutes before the guy got out of the car holding a duffle bag. Bosco and I were dead on it. We rolled up with our sirens blaring. We both jumped out with guns drawn. The driver in the black Impala gave up without incident. But the driver in the Nissan Maxima gave chase. He didn't get far before Bosco pounced on him.

I looked inside the duffle bag and there was at least a hundred thou-sand dollars in there. When Bosco brought the other perp back to the car we checked, and he had five kilograms of cocaine on his person. They were both going down. We handcuffed both perps, and before I could call it in, Bosco peeled off thirty thousand dollars of drug money and stashed it in the back of our patrol car.

"We're gonna split it fifty-fifty," he whispered and I nodded.

We called the bust in and called for NYPD tow trucks to tow away the cars and process the scene. When we made it back to the precinct we were heroes.

"Nice work, Kesha," my C.O. said. "You, too, Bosco."

We both had the cheesiest grins on our faces.

About two weeks later my commanding officer called Bosco and me into his office. He said that one of the perps from our bust had cut a deal and wanted to testify against his co-defendant as well as give us a few other cats.

"That's great," Bosco said.

"Yeah, but he's also made an allegation. He said that there was a hundred thousand dollars of drug money in the duffle bag. He said he sat in the car and counted it out right before you two busted him. Only seventy thousand dollars was recovered. I.A.D. wants to know what happened to the other thirty thousand."

"You've got to be fucking kidding me," Bosco exploded. "How fucking dare this fucking scum bag try to tarnish our good names. This guy is a joke. Do you believe him?"

"Bosco, I don't believe shit that comes out of his snitch mouth. I'm just pulling you and Kesha's coat. Internal Affairs is going to come around snooping, and they better not find so much as a hair out of place. They're going to want to question you two separately. Don't go in there without your union attorney by your side," he warned, and we both took heed.

Bosco and I were both too afraid to talk about the situation in the precinct or in our patrol car. We waited until we took a stroll to get something to eat before we said a word.

"What do you think they got?" I asked.

"They ain't got shit. They got this canary's word against the word of two upstanding officers. Trust me, this'll fly. Don't talk about this to anyone—not your girlfriends, your cousin…no one. Keep quiet, and we'll beat this thing."

"No doubt," I said and pretended to be tough, but inside I was nervous. That was a heavy accusation, and I.A.D. didn't take shit like this light. They hated dirty cops.

"Whatever you do, go and get that money from out of your house and put it up somewhere safe. Don't upgrade your car and don't buy any new jewelry. They look at shit like that," Bosco coaxed.

"I'm on it tonight," I said and wondered where I would hide fifteen thousand dollars without detection.

Hours later I still didn't know what to do with the money I had hidden inside my Prada shoebox. Every night I'd secretly count it to make sure my husband hadn't found it. I.A.D. called Bosco and I in for a separate interview just as my C.O. said. I went in with my attorney, answered a few questions and was told that they would follow-up. After about a week the heat died down, and I decided to go to the car dealership. I was too smart to leave a paper trace. I traded in my Camry for the Mercedes Benz truck with no money down. I had a seven-hundred-dollar a month car note but I knew I could manage it because I still had money in the stash. When I pulled up my husband flipped.

"You've got to be kidding me," he barked. "We've got outstanding credit card bills, you've paid our bills late for the third month in a row and you go and get another expense. Please tell me that this is Breezy's."

"Breezy's," I spat. "Since when do I borrow shit from other people? I've always worked hard for mine and I deserve this truck."

"Kesha, we have three kids who'll need to go to college one day very soon. As parents we should be developing a portfolio and investing our money wisely. They have IRAs that are specifically for education. I can't sit back and watch you splurge and live out your ghetto-fabulous fantasies. First the Rolex now the Benz. What's gotten into you lately?"

So he did notice the watch, I thought.

"Daniel I've been carrying this family for the past few years and I'm not going to let you or my kids down. I promise I'll have the credit cards paid off within a week. Just trust me."

"In a week? Where would you get that type of money?" he probed.

"Just trust me," I replied and stormed back out to go and show off my truck. I decided that I'd use the stolen drug money to pay off all our debt. If someone comes snooping, I'll just say that my father gave it to me as a loan.

When I rolled up in my truck Breezy and Joy went bananas.

"Girl, what are they paying you at the precinct?" Joy asked. "I need to join the force so I can get out of my Honda."

"They ain't paying me shit. I got this on credit, something Black people need to worry more about," I preached.

"Kesha, what have you been doing to Jock?" Joy asked, changing the subject. She had a serious look on her face. "He's running around telling anyone who will listen how you're on his dick and be harassing him all the time."

"No that motherfucker didn't say that," I said.

"Hell yeah. He said you be riding him," Breezy said.

"He ain't nothing but a wannabe. He mad because I won't give him none. He's been trying to get with me for years," I explained.

"Oh that's what's up," Joy asked.

"True. Hey, whatever happened with that job interview you went on at the insurance firm? Did you get it?"

"You know I did," she bragged. "Soon, I'll be ridin' on dubs. I'mma trade in my Honda for the new Lexus jeep."

"That's a good look," Breezy stated.

"Come on let's take a ride in my new truck," I said.

Breezy and Joy jumped in, and we cruised around the neighborhood. We were heading downtown to Juniors Restaurant to get some cheesecake when I passed a white Mercedes SL 430.

"Stop the car," Breezy yelled.

I slowed down then stopped. Breezy jumped out and ran up on the driver. They embraced.

"Who that?" I asked Joy.

"That's Little Wayne from Sumner. You don't remember him?"

"Nah. What he do? What he into?"

"What you think?" Joy said as we both looked on. I locked his name and his car in my memory bank, as I did with all the ballers in Bed-Stuy. It was my job to know everyone and what they're into. We kept it moving.

After we left Junior's I dropped my girls off and headed into the precinct. I pulled up just as Bosco did. We looked eye to eye and he gritted his teeth, rolled his eyes and got out in disgust.

We sat in roll call not saying anything to each other. When we got in our car I went to say something and he silenced me with his hand. When we went to get something to eat he started.

"Didn't I tell you not to go out and buy shit with that money? I'm not going down for your bullshit."

"Calm the fuck down, nigga. I didn't use the money to buy the truck. I traded in my Camry and got the truck with no money down."

"It still looks fucked up," he screamed.

"So let them snoop. When they go sniffing up my tree they'll hit a dead end. They'll be on a paper trail and will realize that if I had paper I would have used it. The fact that I traded in my old shit and got something with just credit will amaze them," I reasoned.

"You better hope they look at it like that, Kesha," Bosco said, and for the rest of the night he didn't have too much more to say to me.

57

Breezy

I really didn't have time for Black's bullshit. One minute he was all over me and the next he was putting me on the back burner. I needed to speed things up regarding my financial status. My father was constantly nagging me on what progress I'd made, if any. I decided that I needed a little attention. This time I was going to pretend that I'd been receiving threatening phone calls, muffled voices saying that they're going to slash my pretty face. Yeah, I thought that would work. Again, I decided to keep this bit of information from my father who'd undoubtedly tell me that it wouldn't work.

One morning I breezed through two exams at school then headed home. Jinx called excitedly to say that she was pregnant. I wanted to ask her if she knew who the father was but I didn't. I pretended to be happy for her, and she promised to come over and tell me all the details and about the baby's father. I was so uninterested in what was going on in her life at the moment. I had too much on my plate. Besides, that girl was confused that it almost seemed logical to put her out of her misery. But then she ended the phone conversation by saying, "I love you."

Automatically, I replied, "I love you too."

After I hung up I thought about those words. Did I love her? If so, how could I let her be next on our list of victims? Instead of heading up to my apartment, I went to see my father first. Lisa wasn't home, and I was glad.

"Hey, Papa," I announced as I walked into his apartment. He was watching CNN and playing against himself in chess. Immediately, I sat down and began to pick up on the chessboard as we both made small talk.

"How are your studies?"

"They're going well," I replied as I moved my pawn to protect my queen.

"How are things with our millionaire?"

"We're moving along nicely," I lied.

Feeling my apprehension he asked, "Are you sure? You're not being too pushy or smothering, are you?"

"Not at all."

"Good."

"Papa, I've been thinking about Jinx…"

"Not open for discussion."

"But if we got Black then why do we have to…you know…Soon we'll have more money than we could ever spend."

"Breezy, have you ever seen me play a game of poker?"

"No."

"Why is that?"

"Because you don't gamble. You strategize and conquer."

"Exactly. We're making calculated moves to ensure that our futures are secure. That means that nothing is guaranteed. We can't afford to let her go on the probability that Black will submit. We still have to pay bills."

"Well, what about Lisa?"

"What about her?"

"Why can't she go in Jinx's place?" I asked and almost thought that my father would knock the chess pieces off the board but he didn't. Instead he stared ahead and began twisting his goatee.

"She'll have her day."

"So, you've already thought of her?" I asked as my voice elevated from surprise.

"You're the only one who's not expendable. There are only two people in this world that are relevant: you and me. Where do you think she runs out of here to every day? She thinks I'm a fool. If I move on her now, I'll be the usual suspect. Sometimes, I think she's having an affair just to give me a tangible motive that would surely make me the prime suspect for the authorities."

I couldn't describe how relieved I was that my father didn't love Lisa. It always bothered me that my mother was killed trying to walk in Lisa's shoes.

"So, you've secured the policy?"

"For who? Jinx?"

"I guess…" I replied but I was talking about Lisa.

"Jinx's policy is secured as well as Lisa's. I've had Lisa's policy for eight years in the amount of five million dollars with the double indemnity clause. Her death has to come off without a hitch. My life will be riding on the proper execution. One false move and you'll be visiting me in Sing Sing."

I went up to my apartment and decided that I'd still work on my father in taking Jinx off the list. I jumped in a hot shower when my father knocked on my door with a huge bouquet of yellow roses.

"I bet these are from Black. They just arrived," he said and handed them to me. He gave me a sly wink before returning downstairs.

I tried to pretend that I wasn't excited as I opened up the card that read:

> *Breezy,*
> *This isn't working out. Sorry it had to end this way.*
> *BK*

My stomach dropped as a million questions popped in my mind. What did he know? What was this all about? I thought we were getting closer. Was there someone else? I wanted to burst downstairs and run to my father but I couldn't stand to see the disappointment in his eyes. Talk about being bamboozled. I never saw this coming. Was Nicoli behind this? But how could she be? She and Black were archenemies. He probably hated her now for dragging him into court. Was that it? Was he under such duress that he needed to be alone to deal with his baby momma drama? Maybe he thought that it was easier to let me go than to drag me through a court custody battle. I needed to speak to him. I raced to the phone. My fingers trembled as I dialed his number.

"At the subscriber's request, this number has been disconnected."

I felt sick. This didn't happen to women like me. I spoke five lan-guages fluently and went to finishing school. I was at the top of my class and would graduate with honors.

I needed to confront him. I needed him to see me and look me in my eyes and tell me that it's over.

In a panic, I drove to his apartment. I tried to sneak past security but was stopped as I tried to take flight into the elevator.

"Ma'am, may I help you?" the night clerk asked.

"I'm here to see Mr. King. He's expecting me."

"And your name. I have to call him."

Was it me or did he know that Black had ended our relationship that day? He had this look in his eyes that said he knew I was lying—or was I just being paranoid?

"Breezy Whitaker," I replied, wondering if that was the right thing to say.

"Sorry, ma'am. Mr. King isn't home at the moment. Do you want to leave a message?"

"No thank you."

I went back outside, got in my truck, parked in front of his building next to a fire hydrant and waited. I felt so very Jinx at the moment. To think I'd chastised her and boasted about not going through such desper-ate measures for a man, I turn right around and did the same.

I sat outside stalking Black's building for more than eight hours, peer-ing at every car that drove up and everyone who walked inside. A few times the doorman came out and glared at me. I was a little afraid that he would call the police but he didn't. Finally, I turned around and drove home.

58

No woman has ever been able to penetrate the concrete wall I've built up over these years but Jinx. I find myself thinking more about her. At first I had convinced myself that the feelings came from the role I was playing. That was a lie. It was her. I called Reggie and told him I was on my way over for a meeting. When I got there we went into his study, and I got right to the point.

"We gotta find someone else."

"What?"

"Jinx...we gotta find someone else. A different victim. I can't do it. She's a good girl, and she doesn't deserve this."

"None of the girls deserved it but those are the cards that were dealt to them. Do you think Breezy's mother deserved to get splattered across the Verrazano Bridge? Or that your mother deserved to get the life chocked out of her? But shit happens in life. Jinx met the wrong person at the wrong time, and she's gotta go. As long as I got a car note and mortgage, this bitch is next in line at the county morgue."

"But she's your daughter's best friend."

"Breezy doesn't have any friends but me and money. She doesn't give a fuck, and neither should you. We can't spare another day, second or moment debating whether Jinx gets it. She was dead the first day you met her."

"I can't do it."

"Yes you can. Because, to you, all women are hoes. Jinx is a ho too. Just listen to Breezy and she'll tell you all about it. Jinx is an insecure, clinging female who is so desperate for a man any man will do. She doesn't love you. She loves the idea of being in love. Don't let her penetrate you. Remember why we're in this and what we're going to get out of it. Now we're a year behind, and next week is Jinx's date of death, so whatever you have to do to get her out of your system, do it. You're too strong to come in here weak. Your mother was weak, and she got what she deserved. Your father was strong, and he's no longer here because of your mother. I don't know how you'll chose to carry out this murder but if it hurts, murder your mother. Replace Jinx's face with her and give yourself gratification. Kill her for killing your childhood and your happy life because she wanted to let some scumbag lick her pussy."

Reggie's words sparked the fuel that I needed. I was getting soft and I needed this pep talk. He was right. Jinx needed to go. She was just another slut bitch who'd open her legs to anyone with a dick. That's how women were—always ready to lay flat on their backs and have a man stick his dick to them no matter what the cost.

Jinx would be sorry for the day she'd crossed paths with Kaiser Jackson. All the while she's been thinking I'm the man of her dreams, I can't wait to see the shock on her face when she realizes I'm her worst nightmare.

59

Nicoli

I knew better than to call Black all weekend after I'd given him the mind-blowing news about my cousin. But I was a little leery about how she'd lie her way out of the situation. Black wasn't big on trusting me since I had deceived him in the past, so it would be easier for Breezy to manipulate him.

I prepared for bed and had to make a quick dash to the bathroom to throw up dinner. At that moment it dawned on me how often I've been sick since Black and I had made love. I decided to go to the drugstore and purchase an EPT pregnancy test to take in the morning before I went to church.

I almost couldn't sleep all night at the thought of having Black's second child. I didn't know if I was happy...I didn't want to raise two kids without their father being in the household. It was bad enough we had to keep shuttling BJ from house to house. BJ would also be subjected in the future to Black's women and my man—if I ever found one. I had been so caught up with battling Black that I didn't pay attention to how often I was leaning over the toilet throwing up my meals.

To my delight and dismay, I was pregnant. Somehow that news made me get right back in bed. I didn't feel like going to church. First thing the next morning I needed to contact my attorney and let her know that in about seven months I'd be needing support for two kids.

Black brought BJ home around dinnertime. I had ordered out from my favorite Chinese restaurant. When Black arrived I was in one of my moods. I had a major attitude at the prospect of going through my pregnancy alone. It brought back all the sadness that I suffered while carrying BJ. An abortion wasn't an option. I always knew that I didn't want BJ to grow up an only child. I didn't want him being selfish as I was, and I didn't want to have multiple fathers for my children. I decided that I had to tell Black, and I wasn't in the mood for his slick remarks. I could hear him: "You sure I'm the father?"

Let his ass say something slick and I would light his ass up.

I sat on the living room sofa eating my food as he lingered longer than necessary.

"What do you want?" I snapped.

"I don't want to fight anymore. Nic, I'm drained. I apologize for the way I've been treating you. I've behaved childishly and deserved everything I've gotten tossed my way thus far with the police and child support case."

I wondered if this was a ploy to get me to drop the case. Why was he being nice? My lawyer said he'd do this. I decided to stop the theatrics.

"I'm pregnant."

"What? When…our last time…?"

"Yes."

"Why don't you sound happy? You're going to keep the baby, right?"

"Yes, I'm not killing my baby. And no, I'm not happy."

"I know why…but I promise this time it'll be different. Nicoli, I'm ready to try if you are."

"Try what?"

Black walked over to me, got down on his knees and looked in my eyes.

"Nicoli, I love you. I never stopped loving you. That's why I tried to hurt you so badly because I was angry that we weren't together. There isn't anyone else out here for me. I keep trying to replace you and duplicate the things we've done together but it's just not the same. I need you in my life. I don't want to raise our kids in a broken home."

My eyes welled up with tears. Black took my face and kissed each tear as it dropped from my eyes.

"I want to marry you," he murmured through each kiss. "Say yes."

"Yes," I said as my lips began to tremble.

Black and I made love as we'd never made love before. As I lay on his chest, he decided he needed to confide in me about what he thought was his little secret.

"I need to talk to you about something."

"Okay. Go ahead."

"I was seeing someone, and it started to get serious."

"Do you love her?"

"No."

"Is she pregnant?" I asked fearfully.

"No, no. It wasn't like that. I...ummm...I didn't know and only just found out the other day that she's your cousin, Breezy."

"Black, please tell me it's a sick joke," I said, raising my voice.

"Nicoli, calm down."

"You calm down. I didn't fuck your cousin."

"I didn't know she was your cousin."

"She knew."

"You're right. That's why I let her go."

"Is that why you're in my bed? Out of guilt?"

"I'm in here because I can't fight how I feel about you any longer."

"Did you tell her yet?"

"Tell her what?"

"That the gig is up?" I said matter of factly.

"No. I haven't spoken to her. But she knows its over."

"Call that bitch right now and tell her."

"Nicoli, that's not necessary. Let's just move on with our lives. Besides, I've changed all my numbers on her."

I reached for my land line, which was private.

"Use this," I said, shoving the phone in his hands.

Reluctantly Black dialed her number. Her desperate ass picked up on the first ring. I could hear her through the phone.

"Hello," she eagerly replied, probably hoping it was Black.

"Breezy, this is Black—"

"Tell that bitch that she better not show her face around me because

I'll fuck her up. Tell that bitch that she better not dial you again because we're back together." I was screaming like a maniac, so Black couldn't even say what I made him call to say.

"Nicoli, let me do this," he said and held his hand up. "Breezy, you've lied to me from day one. I think it's best that you and I part. Nicoli and I are back together, and we're happy."

I heard her screaming through the phone losing her mind. She was calling me all types of sluts and hoes. I snatched the phone from Black and gave her a verbal assault. I told her how I was going to bust her ass all up and down Bed-Stuy. Black kept trying to take the phone from me but I wouldn't let him. Finally, I gave in and ended the call.

The next morning after we'd taken BJ to daycare, I made Black take me over to Breezy's house. The telephone conversation last night just wasn't enough. I wanted to confront her with my man by my side. I wanted to know how she thought she could get away with such deception. But most importantly I wanted her to know that no matter how she tried to upstage me, she'd always fall short.

60

Breezy

I'm *never* second to number one. Black wasn't ever supposed to treat me this way. How dare he hang up the telephone on me then bring Nicoli over here to embarrass me in front of my neighbors? The worst thing about this is that she got to tell her side of the story first. I breathed in then exhaled. My father taught me to never let a person see you lose control. It makes you look weak. Although I hate to admit it as much as I try to emulate my father the fact will always remain that I'm a woman first, soldier second.

Although I wished my father was there to help defend me, it was better that he wasn't. I realized that I would shame him if he knew that I was hiding behind a door. If Nicoli wanted a confrontation, I'd give her one. I flung open the door just as they retreated to their car. Black stared at me with angry eyes.

"Now what's all this you're talking?" I asked Nicoli.

"Yeah, bitch. You thought you were woman enough to take my man. Black told me all your lies."

"Okay, and what? It was good while it lasted. The dick was good and the money was great. No feelings were involved," I said, trying to pluck two birds at once.

"Breezy, who you think you're fooling? Your bum ass thought you'd hit the Lotto. It would have never lasted with your stale pussy."

"You should know. It's on your lips every time you kiss your man."

"I've never given you head," Black exploded, blatantly lying. Oh, I see how this is going down.

"Damn, you're really on her shit. You gonna sit up in here and lie like that. I can't wait until she disses you again. She'll fuck your man and your man's woman. If that's the type of woman you like then y'all can have each other. I'm done," I said.

"Done? You would have held on with bloody fingernails to get Black. You're a dirty bitch, living in a dirty neighborhood, sleeping on dirty furniture and wanted my man to give you a better life. You ain't never had a nigga do shit for you so you can front if you want to," she said, with grand theatrical gestures.

She took a step closer to me and Black pulled her back. That gesture caused her to behave wildly as if she was some sort of killer.

"You feeling frog jump bitch," I challenged.

In a wild rage, Nicoli broke away from Black and lunged towards me. We fell back into the front foyer and began tussling on the floor.

Before too much damage could take place, Black grabbed Nicoli off of me and practically had to drag her kicking and screaming out towards his car.

I slammed my front door.

A thunderous knock led me to believe that it was Black and Nicoli returning. I flung the door open, ready for battle, and there stood Joy.

"Joy, I'm not up for company right now. I'll have to get with you later," I said.

"How you gonna do that trifling shit to your cousin?"

"Excuse me?"

"Don't play stupid. I just saw Black and Nicoli leave here. He's the secret fling you've been talking about."

"So fucking what if he was. Stay out my business."

"How you gonna do that shit to your cousin? We don't get down like that in my crew."

I had no idea Joy knew Nicoli and I were cousins. At that point I didn't care.

"Joy, why are you tripping? This has nothing to do with you. I'll fuck who I want to."

"Black is all she has. She loves that man."

"And who are you? Cupid? You can't tell me who to love."

"Oh pah-lezzze, bitch. You don't love him. You love his money."

"As if Nicoli feels differently."

"I'm only going to tell you this once: Leave Black and Nicoli alone," she threatened.

"Bitch, you can't tell me what to do. You're fucking bugging. This is the same friend that you masterminded getting her face slashed into tiny pieces."

"I didn't have anything to do with that."

"Tell that shit to someone who believes you. Joy, get out. I don't have time for this."

"Breezy, don't make me have to choose sides," she said and moved farther into the foyer.

"You'd go against me for her?" I spat with disdain.

"You gotta let him go…," she pleaded.

"This isn't even about me. It's about you and the trifling thing you did. You want to clear your conscious at my expense! Some fucking friend you are," I declared. "As I said, 'get the fuck out.'"

BOOK TWO
Four Weeks Later...

61

Breezy

I sat up in my bed eating chocolate ice cream, vanilla wafer cookies and gummy bears. I couldn't believe my luck when my gynecologist said I was pregnant. I took three more tests with three other gynecologists because I still had my menstruation. I was eight weeks pregnant and put on bed rest per doctor's orders. Although this baby isn't a meal ticket as we'd planned on with the hopes of me marrying Black, it does warrant a healthy check per month for eighteen years. I haven't been able to tell Black about the baby because I haven't been able to get in touch with him. He's moved and so has Nicoli and her mother. I don't have any way of letting them know.

I know the baby is his; there wasn't anybody else while we were together. I'm just waiting until I safely deliver my baby before I go an obtain an attorney. I've seen on the news that Nicoli is pregnant too. I really wish that she could see me. Then we both would have high-risk pregnancies.

As I sat wallowing in misery, my father came up to tell me to turn on the news. His voice was stern as he barely gave me eye contact. Lately he's found it difficult to even look me in my eyes. His disappointment has affected me and I realize how I let him down.

"Turn to Entertainment Tonight," he demanded. "Hurry up before it goes off."

They showed a large white tent, a large array of flowers and an exclusive Mansion in the Hamptons. I turned the television up louder:

> *"Our sources have confirmed that a wedding will take place between Black King and his long-time girlfriend and son's mother Nicoli Jones. Ms. Jones is three months pregnant and met Mr. King in 2003. Mr. King's publicist was seen leaving the Vera Wang boutique and celebrity hair stylist, C. Homan was flown in from London to style the brides hair."*

I clicked off the television, put on a sweat suit and trotted to my jeep. My father called after me but I refused to be deterred. I was determined to interrupt this wedding and announce to the media that Nicoli isn't the only pregnant woman having Black's baby.

I sped down Atlantic Avenue heading east toward the Belt Parkway. Just as I was coming around the bend on the conduit a car came out of nowhere and lost control. The impact was swift. As the airbags dislodged and burst into my face, I felt my insides erupt. I blacked out momentarily. When I was brought to, I was being wheeled into an ambulance. My truck was totaled.

"My baby," I panicked.

"Your baby will be fine," the EMT said while he put oxygen over my mouth and told me to take deep breaths.

I arrived at the hospital at ten o'clock in the morning. By noon I was told that I had miscarried my baby. The fetus couldn't survive the trauma. I had nothing.

62

Kesha

I don't feel happy. I mean, no one wronged me but I had this heavy, dark cloud lingering over me, and I just couldn't shake the feeling. My husband came up with my breakfast. He was cheery as usual, and the happiness exuding from his body language irked my nerves. What the fuck was he so happy about? He was a grown man walking around in a sissy apron all day. Cooking, cleaning and carpooling seven days a week while his wife is fucking every masculine creature that stops to sniff her perfume long enough.

"I'm not hungry," I growled.

"Then I'll leave it by the bed," he said.

"Don't leave shit by the bed because I'm not going to eat it—now or five minutes from now. Take it back downstairs."

"Suit yourself," he said, and I detected attitude. "You can eat your fingers for all I care."

Did he just roll his eyes at me?

I showered, dressed and decided to head out to work a little early. Daniel stopped me just as I was about to walk out the front door.

"Kesha, we need to talk," he said in a serious tone. I noticed he was scratching his head, a nervous habit he'd picked up in college.

"Not now," I said and tried to open the front door to leave when he aggressively slammed it shut.

"Didn't I say I wanted to fucking talk," he blurted out without provocation. "I'm tired of you disrespecting me. I'm filing for a divorce, and I'm taking the kids. I want full custody."

My heart started palpitating. What did he know? Did he speak to Darren? Maybe Darren's wife found out about us and told Daniel? Did someone at the precinct snitch us out? Did he know about all the affairs?

"Daniel…baby…what are you talking about? We can't get a divorce. We have a family to raise," I said, trying to bid my time.

"Family? You haven't paid this family any attention in years. Your kids don't even know you. All you do is come in here smelling of some man's cum and crawl into bed. You don't care about me, and you don't care about those kids."

"Look, you're right. I haven't been much of a mother or a wife lately. We should sit down and talk about this," I pleaded.

"I said what I had to say," he said and gave a maniacal laugh. Tt snatched my breath.

"Which is…?"

"That I'm filing for divorce this coming Monday, and you better not contest it if you know what's good for you," he threatened. It hurt me to see the hate in my husband's eyes. I didn't have a clue that he even suspected that I was having affairs. I had hurt him.

"Daniel, there isn't anybody else. Please believe me. I know we haven't made love—"

He interrupted me with a hideous cackle.

"I wouldn't stick my dick in your polluted cunt if you were the last woman on earth," he spat.

"Watch your mouth," I threatened, suddenly getting agitated with his constant badgering.

"Or else what?" he said, trying to provoke me.

"Daniel, I know you're angry, but we could go to marriage counseling. I'm sure things will get better…go back to the way it was when we fell in love."

"I don't want to fall back in love. In fact, I never loved you. I just wanted someone to have my children. Now, I have that. You're nothing but a slut, whore-bitch," he smugly replied.

There were pangs of anger shooting from my temples to the pit of my stomach. Although I had looked at Daniel in the same way—someone to facilitate me with having children—it never dawned on me that he could have used me too.

I blinked a few times. My face showed no expression. He continued, "You may as well hear it from the horse's mouth. I'm leaving you for someone else. I'm in love with him—"

Those were the last words I heard. I took out my pistol and let it crash up against his head. The first impact dazed him. He reached up, and as he felt the blood ooze out he screamed out in pain. The second blow caught him in his temple. His knees buckled and he tumbled over. The third hit was an uppercut to his chin. His lips burst open and blood splattered on our China White antique paint.

"You sissy faggot," I yelled as he lay in the fetal position in our foyer. His hands were up above his head as he tried to shield himself from further blows. I must have landed one hundred blows before I realized that I needed to stop. I could barely recognize his face because he was saturated in blood.

"Go to your fucking lover but the kids stay here," I screamed out of hurt and pain and ran out of our house. I hopped in my squad car and headed over to the station. I was sweating profusely and needed to talk to Bosco.

I rushed straight to my unit only to find that Bosco hadn't come in yet. I called his cell phone. "Where the fuck are you?"

"Ma?" he joked.

"Not now, Bosco. I need to talk."

"I'll be there in two seconds. I'm turning the corner. Meet me outside," he said. Bosco was always there when I needed him. I was sure he'd understand my actions and make sense of my situation.

I jumped in the front seat of his black Jeep Cherokee and had to literally take deep breaths to calm my nerves. He watched my antics patiently and allowed me to regain my composure before he probed.

"Kesha, you're scaring me. What happened?"

I burst into tears. "He…he's…he's…a faggot…."

"Who?" he asked patiently.

Snot had begun to drip down my nose. I used the back of my hand

and wiped it away. I saw Bosco slightly cringe.

"He said he's leaving me...and taking my babies. He called me a slut, whore bitch!"

"Daniel?" he asked in bewilderment.

"Y-Y-Yes-s-s-s," I cried.

"Daniel's a faggot...?"

"Un-huh. And he wants a divorce," I said, trying to catch my breath.

Bosco burst out into laughter, which startled me. He was laughing so hard, holding his stomach that I joined in. We were both laughing hysterically until tears streamed down our faces.

"You stupid bitch," I managed to say, "what the hell is so funny?"

"You. Why are you crying over some fairy? Let him go and consider yourself lucky that you managed to get three kids out of the deal. Let him go and lick dick. Good riddance. You're not in love with him anyway."

"But I did love him."

"You're not in love with him. Kesha, I know you, and you like your freedom. You got married and settled down too young. Now, Kesha wants to play. Divorce him and share custody, but tell that fairy queen that he cannot have my godchildren around his lover doing sleepovers or else he'll have me to answer to."

63

I was drawn to her.

Her fierce eyes, sassy walk, and haughty personality captured my interest. She was a whore and it was my duty—no mission—to destroy her.

I sat watching the old, dilapidated building on Fulton Street in Brooklyn where she worked. Most businesses had closed for the afternoon and the streets were basically desolate. Traffic rumbled as cars sped down the cracked pavements. I licked my dry, cracked lips and clutched my goody bag of weapons.

I spit on the concrete next to a pile of dog shit and did a slow trot across the street. I inhaled a long breath and rapped on the door.

I heard movement inside and then a stifled giggle.

She flung the door open wildly and in a mock surrender tossed her hands in the air.

"Oh, I thought you were my boss spying on me. May I help—"

"Don't say a word and do as I say. You won't get hurt," I threatened.

"What the fuck—"

The impact was hard and swift. Her head snapped and her knees buckled underneath her as I hit her in the face with the butt of my gun. Her hands went up quickly to shield herself from further blows.

"What the fuck's going on?" she screamed, in a panicked tone.

"Let's try this again. Don't say a word and you won't get hurt," I said through gritted teeth. I grabbed her by her forearm and led her into the office where another stiff-looking, black woman was waiting for her. I could tell that they were in the middle of some sort of celebration. They had cracked open a bottle of Moët and had ordered pizza. I observed that the other woman was trying to sit as professionally as she could thinking that it was her friend's boss at the door. When we pushed through the door she had a large smile on her face. She began to open her mouth until I pointed my .44 in her face. Her smile faded and her eyes exuded fear. She looked at her friend imploring her for answers. I tossed my victim across the room where she toppled to the ground. She fell onto her back and groaned. Her girlfriend inched over to where my victim was hovering on the floor, and they both embraced each other.

For uncomfortable moments I just stared at her, directly in her eyes, never wavering my stare. After a few tense seconds, she cut her eyes and lowered her glare. When she looked back up, my penetrating eyes were still there. I tucked the gun in my waist and was unmovable.

"You look just like her…" I said, and managed a tight smile.

She was silent.

"Are you a whore just like her? Answer me!" I belted out, and they jumped from fear.

"N-N-No, sir. I'm not," she sniffed. Her eyes were wet as her lips trembled.

Our eyes met solidly.

"How old are you?" I questioned and inched closer. I pulled up a chair and sat directly in front of my victim and her unlucky friend. Next, I pulled my gun back out and placed it on my lap. I was taunting them. "Talk."

"I'm twenty-two."

"Do you have any kids, you slut-bitch?"

She shook her head.

"Good answer," I said and began to massage my penis, which grew hard instantly. The women began to cry louder.

"Are you married?" I asked.

Again, she shook her head.

"Good. Good…you just may make it. But listen to the question, and answer truthfully. I'll let your friend walk out of here right now depending on your answer.

"Are you a virgin?"

"No..."she said, and her friend burst out into tears and she chimed in.

"Y'all some silly bitches. What y'all crying for?" I asked in amazement suddenly changing my voice and lingo. "Oh, y'all think I want some ass? I ain't no pervert. I was just fucking with y'all. This is a straight robbery. I just want the cash and I'm out. I was just having a little fun."

Cautiously, the women began to relax. They both loosened their grips from each other and began to stifle their cries.

The level of anticipation was growing. I pressed, "What's your name?"

"F-F-Fertashia," the unlucky girl answered.

"Why are you here? You don't work for the insurance firm," I quizzed.

I had been watching my victim for weeks and she was always alone during closing hours.

"She called and asked me to come over to celebrate her new jobbbbb," she wailed. "She's been here for one month."

"Ain't that a bitch...some celebration," I exclaimed, sarcastically and slapped the table.

"Fertashia, any regrets in life?" I asked.

She gave a disappointed sigh and replied, "No."

"No? No regrets," I said, mocking her. "I think we got a little liar in our circle."

"I'll regret whatever you say I should," she pleaded.

"Wrong answer," I said. "You should regret being here!"

"Please, Jesus, I know I don't pray much but I don't deserve this," she whimpered, while her friend sat glumly.

"That's right, be a typical nigger. Only calling on God when ya ass is in trouble," I criticized. "Well you can stop being a hypocrite. Ain't shit happening to you. At least not today. Here, help me tape her up so that her boss won't think that she's involved," I said and then tossed duct tape toward Fertashia that I'd taken from out of my knapsack.

Hesitantly, Fertashia grabbed the tape and looked to my victim for answers.

"Just put the tape around her mouth and um...maybe around her wrists and legs. Yeah, that way her boss won't think that she's a double agent."

It took Fertashia a few minutes to do what she was told. I kept instructing her by saying, "Make it look good. If you do it right I may toss you girls a few hundred from the safe to buy you a pair of shoes. I know women love shoes."

As Fertashia rose from the ground after securely taping my victim up, sneakily I took a wire from out of my knapsack and quickly wrapped it around her neck and pulled. Her eyes popped opened and her hands were flailing in the air. My victim sat there wide-eyed and frozen. Even if she wanted to help she couldn't because she was incapacitated. My victim kept screaming, but her words muffled from the tape. I lifted Fertashia's small, five-foot frame off the ground, while she kicked for her life. As I choked the life out of her I was thoroughly enjoying the moment. My victim turned her head and sobbed heavily. Soon, you heard Fertashia's heavy weight hit the ground.

My boisterous voice leered, "Now that she's out the way we can finally be alone."

Vehemently she shook her head. She tried to crawl as far away from me as possible, but I grabbed a hold of her feet and pulled her back toward me.

"Where are you going? Huh? You're trying to go to that nigga, ain't ya? Which one are you slithering off to? The one who drives the white Escalade or maybe the one that picks you up in the BMW 645."

Her eyes conveyed fear.

"What are you thinking? You're wondering why I've been watching you," I said and pulled a knife from my bag. "I told you that you look just like her. My slut mother who ruined my life."

As I walked toward her with the knife she tried to kick her legs to fight back but Fertashia had taped them too tightly. I kneeled down with the knife and cut the tape from off her legs.

"No need to fight. You can't win," I said and glanced over to a coworker's desk. She had an edition of the *Daily News*. On the front page was the story about the Brooklyn Butcher. I tossed the paper down by her side, and she submitted. She gave up. She knew she was dead.

"Now it doesn't have to be like this. If you do as I say, you have my word that I won't hurt you. You'll live to tell your story, but if you disobey me in any way, or if you try to get away, I'll kill you slowly."

64

Kesha

The afternoon became unreasonably cold and dark. It looked as if it was night, and to top it off it just started to rain and thunderstorm.

"God is mad at someone down here," I commented to Bosco as we got into our undercover Chevy Impala. "This torrential rainfall is unexpected. The news said sunny skies, high nineties."

"You know those fucks get paid double what we pull in, and they can't even give us an accurate forecast," he sulked. I glanced over at him, and he seemed more disgusted than I was. But then I realized his aggravation had nothing to do with the weather. He was probably going through drama with his wife again. I didn't have to ask Bosco what was up. He'd tell me on his own time.

"So what's up for today?" I asked as I dialed my cousin Joy on her cellular phone. "Are we going to look for that piece of shit who failed to appear in court?"

"Yeah. I guess we would cruise down Halsey and see if he's stupid enough to show his face."

"Joy…this is the last time I'm going to call you, bitch. I know you must be getting dicked down but it's not that serious. Hit me when you get this message. Love you," I left on Joy's cell phone's answering machine before redirecting my attention to Bosco. "Sound's like a go."

As we crept down to the corner hangout on Halsey—a barbershop owned by a local drug dealer named Tru—I couldn't get Joy out of my mind. I was worried about her, and I had no idea why. We pulled in front of the barbershop, and it was packed because of the rain. Tru usually kept his shop open to the wee hours of the night. A lot of illegal shit went down in there regularly.

Before we got out I asked Bosco what the color of the day was. That's the color that an undercover officer will wear to signal his fellow brethren. I had missed roll call this morning dealing with my husband.

"A green wristband," he responded as he fidgeted with his nine-millimeter glock. "You ready to fuck with these dick heads?"

"No doubt."

As soon as we got out of the car all eyes were on us. They knew who we were, and they also knew they we didn't take no shit. Bosco led the way, and the crowd parted, giving us enough walking space to roll out a red carpet. We both spotted Tru sitting on a sofa in the back participating in a dice game. Bosco walked over and kicked the dice across the room.

"Tru, where's your brother?" Bosco said with his hand on his holster.

"I'm not my brother's keeper," he said, and the crowd erupted in laughter.

"Listen, wise ass. If he's in here I'm running you in for harboring a fugitive," Bosco spat, then continued, "Everyone take out your I.D.'s. Anyone that doesn't have an ID is going in."

"This is fucking harassment. I'm going to file a complaint with the Civilian Complaint Review Board," a voice warned.

Rapidly, I turned around.

"Nigga, you can't even spell Civilian Complaint Review Board, now take out your motherfucking ID," I challenged, getting up in his face. His name was Corey, and he wasn't more than seventeen years old. He was a block hugger for Tru pushing his crack and heroine.

While everyone was obliging to our threats I spotted One-fifty in the corner with a sour look on his face. I eased over and pushed up.

"What's up, One-fifty?" I said and licked my lips. Lately he'd been playing me distant. If only he'd act right I'd whip this pussy on him again and give him some fringe benefits of fucking with a detective.

He looked at me and rolled his eyes, then he thrust his license in my face and turned his head. I was insulted.

"Dayuuuummmm. What the fuck's the matter with you?"

"I'm not in the mood for your shit, Kesha. You're a pain in my right nut, and I'm tired of your lonely ass fucking with me. Get a man. Get a dick. Get a life, and stay the fuck outta mine," he screamed on me.

"I'm going to make you regret those words, you fucking pussy!" I screamed. I reached up and snuffed him in his face. Just as he was about to retaliate, I pulled out my .357 and backed him down. "Go ahead, nigga. Jump. Make my fucking day."

"You got that one…you got that," he said while shaking his head. "It ain't over."

"Nigga, I just put your fucking lights out. Good night," I bragged as Bosco gently nudged me out the front door. As I was backpedaling, never did a bitch put away her gun. When we were safely in the car, Bosco and I broke out into laughter as if we were two school kids.

"Did you see the look on his face?" Bosco asked as he pulled off.

"That nigga done lost his mind talking to me like that in front of everyone. I let him slide back at the barbecue, but I had to let him know shit ain't sweet."

"Yo, it was deadpan silence in there. All I remember is checking ID's when I heard, smack. I turned around and you got your piece all up in his face. You are one ballsy chick, Brown."

We giggled all the way back to the station to do some paperwork and decided to stay in for the rest of our shift. Nearly an hour later Levin, a fellow officer came into our section and said, "Jones, stay up here until I come back. We have about fifteen angry black men downstairs all wanting to fill out a report for the CCRB. The captain is going to flip. I'll be back shortly to tell you what's up."

"Damn, ain't this some shit? They really decided to go through with it," I said, almost to myself.

"Well they've just fucked up. Now they get fucking harassed on every corner. Bed-Stuy ain't big enough for all of us," Bosco said, trying to make me feel better but I knew shit was about to hit the fan.

65

"Strip," I commanded.

She didn't move. She looked over to Fertashia whose body was slumped on the ground. Her eyes were protruding open.

I'd removed the duct tape from her hands and legs but left it covering her mouth. She stood in front of a killer. Trembling. I'd pulled up a chair and sat in front of her. I put away my duct tape and knife but my grip was still tight on my chrome .44.

"Strip!" I demanded.

She shook her head frantically.

One swift motion and I cracked her upside her head with a drinking glass that was sitting on top of the desk. Splintered glass splattered everywhere and blood seeped from the deep gash in her head. Even through the duct tape you could hear a haunting wail.

"Strip, you whore bitch, before I strip you. And I don't mean your clothing. I will slice your skin off your bones if I have to tell you this again," I huffed.

She nodded, and then acquiesced.

As her clothes hit the floor, she stared at me with an undeterred conviction. Snot oozed from her small nose, and my guts twisted up. I felt nauseous from smelling a pungent, foul odor. I peered down at her panties and noticed she was on her menstruation. I was repulsed.

"Remove the tape from your mouth," I snorted.

Her hands trembled as they reached up to remove the tape.

"Do you have any regrets?"

She stood stoically and refused to answer my question. Perhaps because she knew that there wasn't a *right* answer. Any answer was wrong. The whole situation was wrong, for her.

The heavy impact from the slap knocked her off her feet, and she fell back against the wall.

"You stupid motherfucker," she screamed, as she staggered to her feet.

"Didn't you hear what I said? I asked 'do you have any regrets.'"

"I regret that bitch that birthed you," she sneered.

Clever. Clever bitch, I thought. *Clever, smart-mouthed, dead bitch!*

"You want to live you'll stop fucking around."

"My friend is dead. My head hurts, and you want me to believe your not gonna kill me."

"Look, I'm here for the five-finger discount. All I want is the money and to have a little fun before I go."

"And you'll let me live?" she asked, with a grateful tone.

I managed a sympathetic sigh and gave a noncommittal glance.

"Stick your finger in your pussy…and moan as if I'm fucking you. And you better act as if this is the best dick you've ever had, or I will splatter your brains all over your new desk," I warned.

Let the games begin….

66

Kesha

It took a little over an hour for each complainant to fill out there paperwork and a lot of uniforms to assist them. Finally my captain said that the CCRB would review the complaints, which could result in my suspension.

It was close to six o'clock in the evening and I still hadn't heard from Joy. I called her phone again, and this time I went straight to voice mail. I decided to call Breezy.

"Hello," she whispered as if she were in pain.

"What happened to you?"

"I miscarried my baby," she replied as if I knew she was pregnant.

"What? Why aren't you in the hospital?"

"Because I left," she snapped.

"Is Joy there helping you?"

"You know I'm not speaking to that bitch," she yelled.

"What? What happened?"

"She didn't tell you?"

"Nah…we've missed each other all day. What's up?"

"Kesha stop lying. This happened weeks ago and I know she told you."

"Told me what," I screamed, unable to hide my annoyance. I had too much shit going on to play games with Breezy at the moment.

"She had the nerve to come in my house and try to fight me over Black."

"Black? He's one of her sponsors? I know you ain't fighting over a nigga."

"Black ain't even her man. He's Nicoli's baby daddy."

"Her old friend Nicoli? The one who got her face slashed?"

"Yeah."

"Why is Joy tripping over that bitch?"

"Girl, I don't know. That chick was tripping. And to keep it real, Kesha, I'm not going to hang on this phone and chat with you. That's your cousin, and I know how you two stick together, but I'm telling you don't bring no bullshit to my front door because I'm not having it."

"What are you talking about?" I said. Why would I get involved over that childish shit?

"Let her tell you," she said and hung up the phone in my ear.

As I drove home I called Joy one last time to tell her about the conversation I had just had with Breezy then I cut my cell phone off. I was going home to hop in my bed and get some much-needed rest. I had to report back to work at 3:00 P.M. the next day.

When I got home my house phone was ringing off the hook. I missed the first call but as I was putting my key in the lock it started ringing again. I dropped everything and did a dash to the phone.

"Hello. Hello…" I said but soon I heard a dial tone. Again, I'd missed the call. As soon as I put the receiver down it rang again. I knew this was Joy.

"Bitch, where the fuck have you been?"

"Kesha …I…um…got some bad news. Are you sitting down?"

"Bosco?" I asked and switched ears. "Give it to me straight no chaser."

"The Night Strangler has struck again. This time there are two victims."

"Damn, this perverted bastard just doesn't stop."

"Kesha, she was found naked with her face bashed it," Bosco sobbed.

"Bosco, who the hell are you talking about?" I screamed but I really didn't want to hear the answer. Chills ran down my spine, and that prickly feeling rode the back of my neck.

"Joy…he strangled her with a wire…"

I dropped the phone, closed my eyes and collapsed.

67

Tonight was Jinx's date of death.

Reggie called her and told her to come over to help Breezy get over her depression from losing her baby. When she called to tell me that she was going to cheer up her best friend, I invited myself over. I told her that they were as close to family as she had in New York and that I wanted to meet them. She was ecstatic.

I needed to murder her over there because it was easier to dispose of the body. Reggie had a full basement that we'd soundproofed years ago. I had purchased a large, untraceable suitcase to transport her body in, and it was easy because Reggie's driveway extended to the back of the house.

We decided not to tell Breezy that we were going through with it today because although she seemed cool with it, we didn't want her to have second thoughts. Lately she was an emotional, unstable wreck. When I got there Jinx was already there talking with Reggie. Lisa had made a habit of being out of the house on Wednesdays, so that was always the day I did my dirty work. When I came in Jinx and Reggie were in the family room talking and drinking tea. He was encouraging her to go back to school. She smiled, walked over and kissed me on my cheek and whispered in my ear, "I have good news to share…"

I patted her gently on her back. When she turned back around to face Reggie, I pulled out my wire and wrapped it around her dainty neck. The tight pressure startled her, and her body jerked then stiffened before she reached up and began to try and loosen the wire from around her neck.

"Don't fight it, Jinx. It'll only make it worst for you," Reggie said and walked away to let me handle my business. I pulled tighter on the wire and had elevated Jinx's tiny body in the air when her legs touched the table. She kicked out with one last-ditch effort to save her life, and we both fell back onto the floor. I lost my grip and released her. She scrambled to get up, gasping for air.

"I'm pregnant…" she managed to spit out. "Don't do this…I'm having our baby."

She tried to crawl for the door but I was dead on her. I grabbed her by her feet, and she kicked me off. For a small, petite person she was strong. I guess she was truly fighting for her life. As we struggled on the floor she fought me with all the strength she could muster. She dug her nails deep in my face, and screamed, "Help!"

I back-slapped her silent.

During the commotion, Breezy came bursting in. She gave me a conspiratorial smile. Their eyes met. I could feel her body relax a little bit. She must have thought that Breezy was going to help her.

"Oh my gosh," Breezy said. "I didn't know you were doing this today."

I felt Jinx's body get aggressive again. She knew we were all a part of it. She struggled to talk. "Kelsey, please…don't…kill our baby…"

I wrapped my hands around her neck and tried to silence her. Breezy stood in the doorway unable to move. I was losing my focus. I needed to get this over with. I was torturing her more than I wanted to. I didn't plan to ever look her in her eyes. I was a coward. I wanted to strangle her from behind, but I wasn't applying the strength that I usually had with the other girls. I knew this was because I must have some type of feeling for her. I thought about the baby growing inside of her and got weak. I loosened my grasp, and she inhaled as much air as she could.

Breezy whom I didn't know was still standing there realized what was happening. I rolled over on my back and began to sob.

"I can't do it…" I whined. "I can't kill her."

Breezy ran to the kitchen with an undeterred conviction and just as Jinx was escaping out the front door, Breezy stopped her with a large gash to her back with a butcher's knife. Jinx fell to her knees. Breezy began pounding her with the butcher's knife over and over mercilessly.

"Hurry up and die," Breezy cried out. "I didn't want it to be like this. I didn't want to hurt you…please, just die."

Breezy pounded until Jinx stopped moving but her eyes were still open.

"Whyyyy," Jinx cried out. "Breezy don't do this…please…it hurts…it hurts Breezyyy…."

Finally, she closed her eyes, and murmured,"I'm dying…I'm dying…" Breezy collapsed on the floor covered in blood. Reggie came out and saw the first floor in disarray. Blood was covering from the family room to the front foyer where Jinx had crawled. Reggie panicked when he saw Breezy drenched in blood and me lying collapsed on the floor. He knew that it could have gone either way. I could see it in his eyes that he thought I'd hurt his little girl.

"Breezy, are you hurt?" he asked as he ran to her.

"I'm okay, Papa," she said and burst into tears.

I finally collected myself and stuffed Jinx's body into the suitcase that I'd purchased. I took all the money from her pockets, jewelry from off her person and placed some fake clues inside the suitcase. If the police decided to do an investigation they'd be on a goose chase.

I already had my jeep pulled around back, and I loaded her into. Meanwhile, I left Breezy and Reggie there to clean up all the blood. I told them they'd have two days to get a new floor. With blood even though it looks clean to the naked eye, a forensic scientist could come, spray Luminol and we'd all go to jail for life. I intended on dropping her body in a spot I had chosen in New Jersey off the turnpike. The area is rural, and I didn't expect anyone to stumble on her body for two to three days. That would give us enough time to lay down a new hardwood floor. I crept to the spot I had chosen and dragged out the suitcase. I tossed it then stood there for a moment. Was she telling the truth about being pregnant with my baby, or was that a last-ditch effort to save her life? I thought about being a father and possibly living a normal life. I let Reggie take that away from me. Did he feel that he deserved better than me? That he could have a daughter and a wife and I could have nothing. I pleaded with him to find someone else, not Jinx but he wouldn't hear of it. He was jealous. He'd always been jealous and always wanted to take away my happiness.

As I stood there, which was dangerous enough, I looked over at Jinx's body in that suitcase and knew she deserved better. I was supposed to give her better. In a split second I decided what needed to be done next. Reggie had to die.

68

Kesha

I sat in my kitchen in the dark after I'd heard the news about Joy. I was still numb when I heard someone pounding down my front door. In a trancelike state, I walked to the door and opened it.

"Kesha, we gotta make a run." He was breathing heavily and his face was beet red. Was this about Daniel?

"What's up?" I asked in a calm manner.

"Two park rangers over in New Jersey found a woman, half-dead. She's been stabbed nineteen times...Kesha, it's Jinx. She's asking for you."

My heart dropped.

"What?" I said, jumping up and running to Bosco's jeep. Did this have anything to do with Joy's murder?

"She's over at University Hospital in Newark, New Jersey. You've got to hurry up. I don't think she's going to make it."

Bosco and I jumped in his jeep and headed over to New Jersey. What the hell was Jinx doing in New Jersey found on a highway with nineteen stab wounds? Who would want to hurt her?

We dashed down the Belt Parkway until we hit the Verrazano Bridge. There we flew through the Gothels Bridge until we hit the New Jersey Turnpike. We made it to the hospital in under an hour. When we got there two uniform police officers were stationed outside of her room. We spoke with the detective in charge. He was waiting for me.

"I'm Detective Kesha Brown," I said.

"Kesha, I'm Detective Elliott Ross. I've been waiting for you."

"My God, what's happened? Any suspects?"

"She was found by two park rangers who noticed a suitcase dumped on the side of the road. There was fresh tire marks at the scene. She died twice in the EMS on her way over here. She's a strong girl. She's just come out of surgery where they gave her a blood transfusion. She won't give up."

"Who…why? Did she say anything?" I asked as I peered into her room. Jinx had all types of tubes running out of her arms, nose and throat.

Detective Ross started flipping through his notes.

"All she's said is that she knows who did this to her and that the only person she can trust is Detective Kesha Brown in the 88th Precinct in Brooklyn."

"That's it?"

"So far, yes."

"What if she'd died before I reached here without telling who hurt her?" I yelled. But it truly wasn't anything they could have done.

"We've done as much as we could. We're hoping you can take this to the next level," he replied calmly. He understood that I was under the stress of the situation.

I gently tapped on the door, and the nurse looked up at me and gave me a nod. I walked in.

Jinx lay there looking like a twelve-year-old school girl. I contemplated calling Breezy so she could reach here just in case Jinx didn't make it. She could at least say good-bye to her friend. Then I realized that I was in the middle of an investigation, and I needed to secure a statement first.

I leaned over and kissed her forehead. She struggled to open her eyes and focus on me. I could tell that she was in excruciating pain. My heart went out to her.

"Jinx, it's me, Kesha. You're safe now. I need you to tell me who did this to you so I can go and lock them up." As I said it tears streamed down my cheeks.

Jinx opened her mouth, moved her lips but nothing came out. She coughed a few times and crinkled up her face in pain. Although I needed to be patient I also needed the name of the person who tried to murder her before it was too late. The doctors didn't think she'd make it through the night.

I leaned down closer to hear her. Finally I could hear sounds but couldn't make out the words. Thinking quickly, I pulled out a pad and piece of paper and asked if she could write the name of the person. She nodded.

I placed the pen in her hand and placed the paper underneath. She started off slowly writing the letter B. Then the letter R. Then an E. Next the letter E. Last, the letter Z. She was too weak to finish.

Our eyes met.

"Jinx, are you telling me that Breezy stabbed you nineteen times?"

Tears streamed down her cheeks. She nodded.

"But why?" I asked incredulously.

She shrugged. She didn't have a clue. Bosco tugged on my arm and pulled me out of the room.

"At this point it doesn't matter why. We got an arrest to make," he announced.

We went back to the 3rd Precinct in Newark and called my precinct to set up the arrest warrant. Although I didn't believe that Breezy had stabbed Jinx, I didn't want any other officer arresting her. I needed to handle it. I knew that Breezy would never allow those silver bracelets to go on without a fight, and I didn't want any of the officers roughing her up.

It took hours before all the paperwork was processed and we had secured a warrant for Breezy's arrest. I said a quick prayer that Jinx was mistaken, that the Demerol the hospital gave her for her pain had some-how altered her judgment, but my gut told me that that wasn't the case. Jinx was lucid enough to give them my full name, title and precinct I worked at. That coupled with the fact that her hand never wavered as she wrote out B-R-E-E-Z had me in a state of confusion. I mean, I know us Brook-lyn chicks can play hard and rep hard but stabbing up your best friend, stashing her body in a suitcase and dropping her off in New Jersey was inconceivable. The cop in me had already made the connection in New Jersey to where Breezy's father had previously lived.

But if Breezy did harm Jinx…Why? Even Jinx couldn't answer that question.

69

Kesha

It was just past midnight when we all converged on Breezy's property. There was another car in the driveway, a black Tahoe, and the door was slightly ajar. I crept up the front stairs with my .357 drawn. I could hear slight movement coming from the foyer. Bosco was right on my heels as we inched in farther. There I saw a tall, muscular man strangling what appeared to be Breezy's father, Reggie.

"Police, don't move," I yelled. Nothing happened. The man was in deep concentration, and it didn't seem that he'd even heard my warning. Bosco ran over and hit the man on the side of his head with his billy club. The man released Reggie and fell to his knees. Reggie's lifeless body slumped to the ground. I ran over, put my index finger at the pulse of his neck and concluded that he was dead. As Bosco handcuffed the assailant I didn't have time to try to make sense out of what was going on. I crept upstairs to Breezy's apartment and slightly tapped.

"Breezy, open up. It's me...Kesha."

You could tell that she'd been asleep. She flung the door open and was completely naked. She jumped when she saw my gun drawn and aimed in her face.

"Girl, you scared the shit out of me," she said as she stepped back. "What are you doing here?"

As she asked me the question her eyes showed vulnerability and I knew Jinx was accurate. The fear in Breezy's eyes said she'd been up to mischievous things.

"Breezy, you're under the arrest for the attempted murder of Jinx Sin. You have the right to remain silent…"

"What? Kesha, this is me you're talking to. You can't arrest me. I'm your girl…we're cool."

"Breezy, hurry up and get dressed so I can take you down to the precinct. There are several officers in the foyer."

The room was ripe with fear….

"I didn't do anything," she wailed and took off running into her room. "I can't go to jail."

I was dead on her heels. Breezy ran to her bed where I knew she kept her nickel-plated .380 that her father had given her. As she lunged for it I gave her one final warning.

"Breezy, don't do it. Don't make me do it," I yelled and fired a warning shot up in the air. I could hear my fellow officers dashing up the steps. Breezy was unfazed. She still was determined to get her hands on the gun. I couldn't do it. I couldn't shoot my friend. Not my home girl. I thought about Club Reign, Roxy's, Envy…shopping in Bloomingdale's for Chanel shoes and Gucci boots. Why was she putting me in this position?

I yelled another warning, "Breezy, I'm stressed, I'm pressed and I will blow your motherfucking head off!"

Everything happened in slow motion. Breezy turned around with her .380 in her hands. I heard a loud noise. "Boom!" What the fuck— "Boom!" My body jerked, once, twice… "Boom!"

Breezy screamed.

"Boom!"

Breezy's body hit the wall, and she slid down in pain. She wasn't moving. Neither was I. I looked down. I'd been hit twice in the chest. I pulled my hand away, and it was covered in blood. My body was pierced with two holes that were leaking blood. I felt faint as I struggled to remain conscious.

"Kesha," I could hear Bosco. "Kesha, stay with me. Don't close your eyes, baby."

The pain.

"Kesha, help is on the way. I'm so, sorry," he cried. "Get a fucking ambulance!"

I'm gonna die....

"Kesha, hold on," Bosco yelled and squeezed my hand tightly. Soon I didn't feel anything at all.

Everything went dark....

70

Kesha

I awoke in the hospital two days later handcuffed to a hospital bed. It took me a moment to realize where I was and collect my thoughts on what had happened. Slowly the images came flooding back. Jinx being stabbed almost to death. Then going to arrest Breezy. Her father being murdered. And finally Breezy shooting me. But why was I in handcuffs?

As I came to Detective Snashall was at my bedside.

"Good morning, sleeping beauty," he said and planted a soft kiss on my forehead.

I struggled to get up.

"Just relax, Kesha. You took two slugs to your chest. You're lucky to be alive."

"Why am I in handcuffs?" I managed to ask. My throat was raspy. It felt like sandpaper.

Detective Snashall looked down at the ground when he spoke.

"They've arraigned you on a couple of charges. Internal Affairs has been snooping around for months investigating cops on the take. Bosco's name came up. I.A.D. had a sting operation going. The Gotti bust we did had several surveillance cameras set up. They have the both of you stealing drug money," he said.

"Undercover operation?"

"If it helps any Bosco tried to take the weight. He said he forced you to take the money and that it was all his idea."

I just shook my head in defeat. Tiny tears streamed down my cheeks. "Where's my husband...my kids..."

"Kesha, I don't know if you want to hear this but your husband hasn't been here to see you. He filed charges against you for attempted murder. You hurt him really bad. He was just released from the hospital this morning. You broke several of his bones...his nose...jaw...ribs..."

"My kids," I managed to blurt out.

"ACS had them until your husband was released this morning."

"Jinx?"

"She's still alive. That girl's a fighter," he said and wiped the tears from my eyes.

"Breezy?"

"She wasn't so fortunate. Bosco finished her off. She was dead on the scene."

I just shook my head. My life was over....

71

Jinx

Nana once told me that God had placed a veil over my face to shield me from any harm that would come my way. I used to think that was the words of a foolish, superstitious lady. How wrong was I? Fate would make me a believer. It wasn't enough that I was the sole survivor of a horrific plane crash. That only left me more confused. But now surviving this near-death experience as an adult, I do believe that God has placed me here for a reason. That veil has shielded me from leaving this earth sooner than God planned. The doctors said that Breezy missed every major artery in my body. There were stab wounds were she was off only by one-tenth of an inch. If only she'd moved more to the left or right, I wouldn't be here. I would have bled to death before I was even left for dead on the side of the road. At first I was hesitant to ask the nurse did my baby survive my trauma. I wasn't really sure that I'd want a baby whose father is a murderer. But when the doctor came to tell me that my baby was doing well, I can't describe the joy I felt. There wasn't any way I would have another abortion. I planned to love my baby enough for two parents.

For weeks I didn't have a clue as to why Kelsey whose real name is Kaiser Jackson, Mr. Whittaker and Breezy wanted me dead, but further investigation from the police and testimony from Breezy's stepmother Lisa revealed that there was an elaborate insurance scam going on for years. They killed innocent victims and collected hefty checks to help them maintain their lifestyles. When I think about the envy I'd feel every time Breezy received a material gift from her father it makes me want to vomit. I was jealous of a lifestyle that I thought she lived. A lifestyle that left blood on her hands.

In exchange for her testimony Lisa is going to testify against Kaiser who's facing the death penalty. She told authorities that not only was Kaiser the Brooklyn Butcher but the Night Strangler as well as the copycat Zodiac Killer. She's going to receive Life without the possibility of parole for her part in the murders. At first I wanted her to go to trial and face the death penalty as well, but without her testimony there wouldn't have even been any light shed on what was happening inside their household. It's true when people say all diamonds sparkle, but put them under the light for clarity...

Breezy was the brightest diamond I thought I'd ever know. And she had layers of dirt and was rough around the edges.

The doctor said that I'm going to make a full recovery. Right now I don't have any use of my right arm. It feels dead. But with physical therapy it'll be back to its normal use.

When I get out the hospital I'm going back down south to live with my father's side of the family. As much as I love the fast pace of Brooklyn, I think I've just about gotten it out of my system. I think the tranquility of the south will do me good. I've already spoken with my grandmother, and they're expecting me. She's a robust, seventy-six-year-old who's counting the days until I return.

I plan on starting my life over again. God has given me two chances to get it right, and I plan on doing just that. I don't want to jinx anything, no pun intended, but two times facing death is enough. I don't need a third lesson.

72

Nicoli

Black and I got married on the estate where we first met. It was owned by his friend Kevin in the Hamptons. It was a small, romantic ceremony with a huge ring. Black replicated my original engagement ring—a $1.5 million, emerald-cut pink diamond.

I wore white of course—a white Vera Wang hand beaded dress with a twenty-foot train. Black wore a tuxedo designed by Ralph Lauren. We got married on the beach by candlelight with only family giving us their blessings. We decided to honeymoon in the Hamptons because I didn't want to take BJ on a plane at such a young age.

My friend Stacy called me and said, "Turn on the news. Now!"

Black heard her through the phone and immediately clicked on Channel Nine news and what we saw had us both stunned.

> *"This is Gilt McGronner, WLTV, live at the home of commu-*
> *nity leader Reginald Whitaker. It's alleged that he, his daugh-*
> *ter Breezy Whitaker and his wife, Lisa Whitaker, were involved*
> *in a string of murders that spanned over ten years. Police*
> *say they sought out young, destitute victims, put huge insur-*
> *ance policies on them then murdered them. The latest attempt*
> *was Breezy Whitaker's best friend, Jinx Sin, who's in stable*

yet critical condition due to the injuries sustained. Authorities are still investigating this. We'll follow this case and keep you informed."

I was dumbstruck. I sat on the edge of the bed with my mouth gapping open.

"I can't believe this…" I whispered.

"Baby girl, it's a cruel world out here. Let's promise not to hurt each other again."

"I promise…I'll never hurt you," I said, sincerely.

My days of running wild on these Brooklyn streets were over. I had my man back, and we were happier than ever. And I wasn't *ever* letting him go.

Acknowledgments

"It was the best of time, it was the worst of times," Charles Dickens. That old adage is befitting of my life. First, I'd like to acknowledge **God** and Jesus Christ my savior for carrying me through this year. He's always consistent in my inconsistent world. My cousins: **Eirene "Wild Cherry,"** thank you for lacing my cover. The original version was too hot for the market...they wasn't ready for it...but this one is just as awesome. **Christine Renee** (who happens to be Eirene's baby sister) it's been an honor and pleasure working on the clothing line together. You're an amazing talent!!!!

Melodrama Publishing Fam: **Kiki Swinson**: first congrats on the baby! Second, I respect and admire your work ethics and your loyalty. We've come a long way together and can only continue to go up. **Amaleka McCall**: They slept on ATTOK just as the world slept on Reasonable Doubt (Jay-Z). I've said this many, many, times, "You are a great talent!" I'm a fan for life. I can't wait to see you at the top. **Endy**: You write so 'hood. It's an honor to have you under Melodrama. **Carl Patterson**: I was captivated and moved by your story. **Storm**: Your book was enlightening and what the book industry needs. **Jacki-da-ripper AKA Jacki Simmons**: the 18-year-old ingénue. Your pen game is tight! They ain't ready for you....

Divas: **Tracy Brown, KaShamba Williams, TN Baker, Danielle Santiago, Teri Woods, KaShan, Azarel**: Do the ladies run this mothefucker!!!.....You ladies are giving these dudes a run for their money.

My fav's (no particular order) **Michael Presley**: My Apple Martini cohort. Cheers to our friendship. **Mark Anthony**: You're an amazing individual and a motivator. **Rich Jeanty**: I've finally met someone who can talk just as much as ME! And you have a great sense of humor. And you're consistent with it. I don't think I've ever spoken to you and you weren't in an upbeat mood. You're uplifting and I like that about you. **Shannon Holmes**: From the first day that I met you I've included you in my acknowledgments. That's because you're always giving so much of yourself and not just to me but others as well. You have a BIG, kind, sharing heart. **Al-Saadiq Banks**: Slow downnnnnn! Geez, how can I be down with the 'drop a book e'vry six month' movement? **Erick Gray**: Rumor has it…(I'm only joking). I'm still waiting for that book to drop…remember in Queens you told me the concept…FIRE!!! **K'Wan**: I've always liked you as a writer but fast forward and I LOVE your pen game. **Mu (JM Benjamin)**, "Lace what's good?" I always smile when you say that. It's all good, Mu…all good! **Relentless Aaron:** You're relentless!!! Nothing else needs to be said. **To my PUNK:** Sometimes you amaze me with how your mind stretches. You're more than clever. You're more than intelligent. You're more than I've known in a long time. I'm motivated and inspired and work toward being a viable person. Now my sentences start off with, "PUNK said…" You were the first to say that if I'm the smartest person in my circle—get a bigger circle. You're never condescending. Never calculating. Never cocky. Never arrogant. Never judgmental. You've never asked or taken anything from me and have only given in return. I think I told you once before but I'll say it again, 'you remind me of my Gucci shoes.' LOL. Stay humble and embracing God. He shines through you!

Book Clubs: **OOSA, Coast 2 Coast, AALBC, Mosiac, and Rawsistaz.com.** I thank you for supporting me and Melodrama. **Lori H. and Norma**, thanks much for holding me down. If I've left you out please know that you're in my heart!

EAST NEW YORK STAND UP!!!
FLATBUSH STAND UP!!!
PINK HOUSES STAND UP!!!
B.K. STAND UP!!!

Christine Renee

BIO:

Christine Renee has always had a flair for fashion. When she was a young girl she began designing outfits by cutting up old clothing and sewing them on her great-grandmother's machine—a machine she still owns. So it wasn't a stretch when she enrolled in Katherine Gibbs and earned her associate degree in fashion design. She went on to intern with the best: Sean John and Anne Klein. She's currently working at Daron Fashion Group and plans to launch her own clothing line, Christine Renee in the very near future. "Coming from a mixed heritage has helped me understand that the world is not just black and white. There are a lot of in betweens, like me. My designs are colorful reflections of what and how I see my world."

Christine Renee recently hooked up with her first cousin, Crystal Lacey Winslow and collaborated on a new line of high end jeans for Melodramatic Brat's clothing line. She's busy at work and has a host of innovative new designs for the upcoming fall season.

Check out her at www.myspace/christinereneee.com

SPOILED by MELODRAMATIC BRAT
Designed by Christine Renee

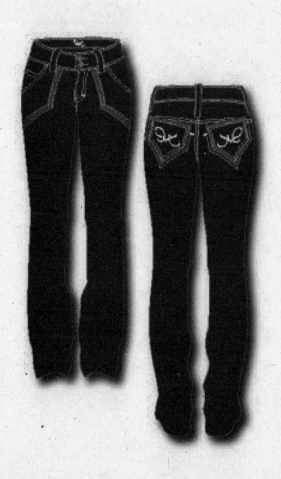

NOVEMBER 2006
STRIPPED
FROM THE DESK OF JACKI SIMMONS

NOVEMBER 2006
IN MY 'HOOD
by ENDY

SEPTEMBER 2006
CROSS ROADS
CARL PATTERSON

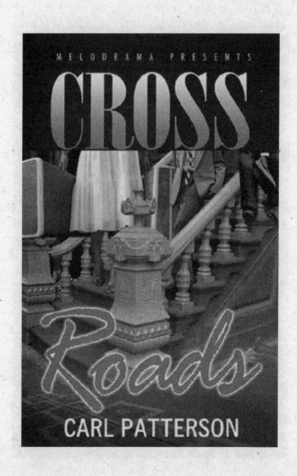

**JANUARY 2007
EVA FIRST LADY OF SIN
by STORM**

WIFEY
by KIKI SWINSON

#1 ESSENCE MAGAZINE BESTSELLER

I'M STILL WIFEY
by KIKI SWINSON
ESSENCE AND BLACKBOARD MAGAZINE
BESTSELLER

COMING SOON!!!
LIFE AFTER WIFEY (PART 3 OF TRILOGY)

THE CANDY SHOP
FEBRUARY 14, 2007
KIKI SWINSON

A TWISTED TALE OF KARMA
by AMALEKA G. McCALL

MENACE II SOCIETY
by Al-Saadiq Banks, Mark Anthony, Crystal Lacey Winslow
Isadore Johnson, and JM Benjamin

Other books by
author
Crystal Lacey Winslow

Life, Love & Loneliness

The Criss Cross

Up Close & Personal

Four Degrees of Heat

Kiss the Year Goodbye

Menace II Society

ORDER FORM
(PHOTO COPY)
MELODRAMA PUBLISHING
P. O. BOX 522
BELLPORT, NY 11713-0522
(646) 879-6315
www.melodramapublishing.com
melodramapub@aol.com

Please send me the following book(s):
THE CRISS CROSS ISBN: 0-9717021-2-8
WIFEY ISBN: 0-9717021-3-6
I'M STILL WIFEY ISBN: 0-9717021-5-2
A TWISTED TALE OF KARMA ISBN: 0-9717021-4-4
MENACE II SOCIETY ISBN: 0-9717021-7-9
SEX, SIN & BROOKLYN ISBN: 0-9717021-6-0
CROSS ROADS ISBN: 0-9717021-8-7
IN MY HOOD ISBN: 0-9717021-9-5
STRIPPED ISBN: 1-934157-00-7
EVA FIRST LADY OF SIN ISBN: 1-934157-01-5
THE CANDY SHOP ISBN: 1-934157-02-3
ALL ABOVE BOOKS ARE PRICED AT **$15.00**

UP CLOSE AND PERSONAL ISBN: 0-9717021-1-X
THE POETRY BOOK IS PRICED AT $9.95

@ 15.00 (U.S.) = _____

QUANTITY

Shipping/Handling*   = _____

Total Enclosed   = _____

PLEASE ATTACH, NAME, ADDRESS, TELEPHONE NUMBER(for emergencies)

***Please enclose $3.95 to cover shipping/handling ($6.00 if total more than $30.00 AND under $50.00)**

FOR BULK ORDERS PLEASE CALL THE PUBLISHER.
To pay by check or money order, please make it payable to <u>Melodrama Publishing</u>.

Send your payment with the order form to the above address, or order on the web.
Prices subject to change without notice. Please allow 2-3 weeks for delivery.

WWW.MELODRAMAPUBLISHING.COM